T0193302

From Black Ops veteran Leo J. Maloney comes a nonstop thrill ride straight into the secret world of covert agents . . .

Rogue Commander

Four-star general James Collins has been accused of stealing a cache of Tomahawk missiles—and reaches out to his friend, CIA veteran Dan Morgan, for help. But Morgan is playing with fire. The Zeta Division, chasing down a black-market middleman, discovers a connection to a North Korean military officer—and one of his team winds up a prisoner in Pyongyang. As Morgan takes a series of escalating risks, it becomes clear that a global plot is already in motion—and if they can't stop it, an unimaginable number of innocent civilians will be slaughtered . . .

Visit us at www.kensingtonbooks.com

Highest Praise for Leo J. Maloney and his thrillers

Arch Enemy
"Utterly compelling! This novel will grab you from the beginning and simply not let go. And Dan Morgan is one of the best heroes to come along in ages."
—Jeffery Deaver

Twelve Hours
"Fine writing and real insider knowledge make this a must."
—Lee Child

Black Skies
"Smart, savvy, and told with the pace and nuance that only a former spook could bring to the page, *Black Skies* is a tour de force novel of twenty-first-century espionage and a great geopolitical thriller. Maloney is the new master of the modern spy game, and this is first-rate storytelling."
—Mark Sullivan

"*Black Skies* is rough, tough, and entertaining. Leo J. Maloney has written a ripping story."
—Meg Gardiner

Silent Assassin
"Leo Maloney has done it again. Real life often overshadows fiction and *Silent Assassin* is both: a terrifyingly thrilling story of a man on a clandestine mission to save us all from a madman hell bent on murder, written by a man who knows that world all too well."
—Michele McPhee

"From the bloody, ripped-from-the-headlines opening sequence, *Silent Assassin* grabs you and doesn't let go. *Silent Assassin* has everything a thriller reader wants—nasty villains, twists and turns, and a hero—Cobra—who just plain kicks ass."
—Ben Coes

"Dan Morgan, a former black ops agent, is called out of retirement and back into a secretive world of politics and deceit to stop a madman."
—The Stoneham Independent

Termination Orders
"Leo J. Maloney is the new voice to be reckoned with. *Termination Orders* rings with the authenticity that can only come from an insider. This is one outstanding thriller!"
—John Gilstrap

"Taut, tense, and terrifying! You'll cross your fingers it's fiction—in this high-powered, action-packed thriller, Leo Maloney proves he clearly knows his stuff."
—Hank Phillippi Ryan

"A new must-read action thriller that features a double-crossing CIA and Congress, vengeful foreign agents, a corporate drug ring, the Taliban, and narco-terrorists...a you-are-there account of torture, assassination, and double-agents, where 'nothing is as it seems.' "
—Jon Renaud

"Leo J. Maloney is a real-life Jason Bourne."
—Josh Zwylen, *Wicked Local Stoneham*

"A masterly blend of Black Ops intrigue, cleverly interwoven with imaginative sequences of fiction. The reader must guess which accounts are real and which are merely storytelling."
—Chris Treece, *The Chris Treece Show*

"A deep-ops story presented in an epic style that takes fact mixed with a bit of fiction to create a spy thriller that takes the reader deep into secret spy missions."
—Cy Hilterman, *Best Sellers World*

"For fans of spy thrillers seeking a bit of realism mixed into their novels, *Termination Orders* will prove to be an excellent and recommended pick."
—*Midwest Book Reviews*

Books by Leo J. Maloney

The Dan Morgan Thriller Series
Termination Orders
Silent Assassin
Black Skies
Twelve Hours
Arch Enemy
For Duty and Honor

Published by Kensington Publishing Corporation

Rogue Commander

The Dan Morgan Thriller Series

Leo J. Maloney

LYRICAL PRESS
Kensington Publishing Corp.
www.kensingtonbooks.com

Lyrical Press books are published by
Kensington Publishing Corp. 119 West 40th Street New York, NY 10018

All Kensington titles, imprints, and distributed lines are available at special quantity discounts for bulk purchases for sales promotion, premiums, fundraising, and educational or institutional use.

To the extent that the image or images on the cover of this book depict a person or persons, such person or persons are merely models, and are not intended to portray any character or characters featured in the book.

Special book excerpts or customized printings can also be created to fit specific needs. For details, write or phone the office of the Kensington Special Sales Manager:
Kensington Publishing Corp.
119 West 40th Street
New York, NY 10018
Attn. Special Sales Department. Phone: 1-800-221-2647.

First electronic edition: October 2017
ISBN-13: 978-1-61650-979-8
ISBN-10: 1-61650-979-1

First print edition: October 2017
ISBN-13: 978-1-61650-980-4
ISBN-10: 1-61650-980-5

Printed in the United States of America

*This book is dedicated to my family
and my dearest friends
who are in my circle of 10.*

Chapter One

Dan Morgan stood against the stone back wall of the Church of Our Lady Before Týn, a lit cigarette dangling between his fingers.

He didn't smoke—couldn't stand the smell, really—but nothing gave him better cover to stand around in the street, out of the way of most people. So he let the reeking thing burn, pretending to puff every few seconds to avert suspicion, and shielding the ember from the wind. It was early October, and the sun was low in the sky even though it was 10: 30 A.M., so none of its rays made it to the level of Prague's narrow streets.

He was in a tiny area reserved for parking, which held the sort of places that grow like weeds on the periphery of big tourist sites. They didn't catch torrents of tourists, just the runoff—selling cheap souvenirs and small necessities like water and smokes.

"Morgan, report in." It was Diana Bloch's voice coming over the wireless transmitter in his right ear. As always, she was terse and all business. Everything about Bloch, the head of Zeta Division, carried authority. She may have been a pain in his ass, but even Morgan, who could also be a pain in the ass, acknowledged it was mostly in a good way.

"Nothing yet."

A group of four American college kids stopped as one of them took a picture of the back of the church. One of the couples stood close to each other, with a sort of awkwardness that told Morgan theirs was a new relationship. The other couple had been together long enough to be more interested in other things but shared a kiss before they moved along.

They didn't give him a second glance. Good. Being invisible had its perks in the business.

Morgan buzzed with energy, like he always did at the start of a mission. He felt the reassuring weight of his black Walther PPK in its shoulder holster, well hidden under his black trench coat. It wasn't a popular concealed weapon anymore—too heavy and not as much firepower as the polymer nine-millimeter pieces that many favored. But he was a man with classic tastes, and he had a soft spot for the gun. It felt solid in his hand, nicely balanced, with light recoil. That, and he could hit a fly at ten paces with it.

Morgan leaned back against the stone of the centuries-old Gothic church and feigned drawing in smoke from the Marlboro when he caught movement in his peripheral vision. Across the small parking lot, a man emerged from the front door of the Ventana Hotel. He had a coarse face, a receding head of blond hair, and a strong nose, but a weak chin that he hid, poorly, with a goatee.

"It's Pulnik," said Morgan. "Moving west from the hotel."

"Keep your distance," said Bloch over the comm. "Team, get moving. Stick to the plan. Morgan, do I have to remind you—"

"You don't. It's my damn plan. I'm sticking to it." Morgan tossed the half-burned cigarette and ground it against the pavement, then set off after the man.

Their quarry was Havel Pulnik, a sleazy small-time underworld businessman who happened to be the second cousin of Enver Lukacs, the evasive big fish they were really after. With no leads to Lukacs, Zeta Division had had Pulnik under surveillance for months while he had begged his family to have Lukacs contact him. His persistence, and theirs, had finally paid off when one of Lukacs's people set a meeting with him in Prague.

"We're on the move." That was Bishop, the leader of the Zeta Tactical Team, somewhere within a two-block radius.

Morgan walked thirty feet behind Pulnik. The streets were teeming with tourists from all nations—he could tell the people from warm climates, who were bundled up as if they were in the Himalayas in the dead of winter. As he passed a souvenir shop, Morgan caught sight of Spartan. She had a good four inches on him, her close-cropped blond hair hidden by a dark gray beanie. She was looking through postcards on a rack, positioned so she could catch glances of their quarry.

Morgan then caught sight of Bishop, walking a ways ahead of Pulnik. Spartan set off a few seconds after Morgan had passed, walking on pace with a group of Germans who seemed to be going out for a stroll rather than gaping at the sights.

"Looks like he's moving toward the plaza," Spartan said. "Good call."

Morgan walked on the cobblestones, worn smooth over the years. Prague had old-world elegance, with a picturesque hodgepodge of architectural styles—but all, unlike the utilitarian bent of American engineering, with an eye for beauty. The condition of the buildings, however, betrayed its Soviet past. They did not have the polish, the fresh paint, or the recent renovations found in England or Germany.

Morgan liked it, though. The city had character. A gloomy, character, sure. Nothing more appropriate for the city of Franz Kafka. But anywhere he went, at least in the old city, there was no mistaking that, yes, he was in Prague, all right.

It was a short walk before Morgan followed Pulnik into the historic Old Town Square. The perimeter of the sprawling tourist attraction was lined with restaurants with outside tables, where tourists braved the cold with hot drinks. Many others sat right on the ground. One girl was drawing the Old Town Hall—its gothic spires reaching toward the sky. Most were standing around, listening to guides, studying their smartphones, or just milling about, taking pictures of the old buildings that marked the square's edges. A band was setting up, a standing bass, a clarinet, a banjo and a washboard, with a half-dozen people already sitting in a semicircle, waiting for them to begin. A handful of protesters were there too, demonstrating about refugees from the Middle East. The younger and more diverse crowd was for, the older and local against. They kept a tense peace, but Morgan had a feeling things could break out in violence quickly.

Pulnik was making his way toward the green bronze statue of Czech philosopher Jan Hus at the center of the square.

"Fan out," Morgan said. "I want people on all sides. We need to see Lukacs coming."

"Moving in, northwest corner." The voice belonged to Peter Conley, code name Cougar—Morgan's old partner from his CIA days. There was no one Morgan would sooner trust with his life.

Morgan walked to the middle of the east side of the square and watched as the others got into position. He surveyed the tourists, who were oblivious to the importance of this moment. The wheels of their world turned, and they were none the wiser. They didn't know anything about the silent machinery hidden deep in the bowels of their world. All they saw was the surface.

Morgan was here today to stop one of these cogs from turning. Enver Lukacs was the name of this particular cog—a shadowy underworld player with a finger in every poison pie. His currency was contacts, linking people who were selling black-market items and services with those who wanted them. Weapons, drugs, mercenaries, slaves—Lukacs had it all. If they got him to turn over even a fraction of what he knew, they could bring down dozens of illegal operations. But that depended on today.

"Hello! American!" It was a slight young man with a local accent. His baby face was draped with scraggly hair, and he had on a dirty red coat over a stained T-shirt.

Shit. This was all he needed. "I don't have any money."

He smiled with mock offense. "No! Come on, American friend! I just want to have a conversation!"

"I don't have any of that either. Good-bye."

He went off to bother someone else. Morgan looked at Pulnik, standing by the statue with his hands in his pockets, looking around at the crowd for the man he was there to meet.

It was Conley who spoke first. "I have eyes on the target. Approaching from my corner."

"Keep your distance," said Bloch. "I want confirmation before we do anything."

Morgan leaned against a lamppost and looked at the man now crossing the plaza. He looked more like a fashion designer than anything, with a svelte silver-fox thing going on and a stylish designer suit.

"Positive ID," Morgan said. "That's Lukacs."

"Get in position," Bloch instructed. "Diesel, on alert. You need to arrive with the van just as they reach the street with Lukacs. Lily will provide a distraction." Lily referred to Lily Randall—young, green-eyed, eminently distracting to any heterosexual male with a pulse.

Morgan caught sight of her coming in from the far side, her auburn hair glistening in the morning sun. "We need to attract as little attention as possible," he muttered.

The band incongruously broke out into a Dixieland rendition of "When the Saints Go Marching In." The singer had a voice that suggested he'd been a heavy smoker since age five. The effect wasn't exactly beautiful, but, hell, if it didn't work.

A small semicircle of tourists formed, but some went about their business without a glance at the musicians. That nagged at the corner of Morgan's mind.

"Hold positions," he said. "Lukacs's got company."

"Where?" Bishop asked.

"Tall, bearded guy by the church. Short and stocky next to the tour group on the north side. Red hair by the lamppost, near the southwest corner. And another likely suspect sitting on the far side of the statue."

"The bastard brought a security detail."

"Bishop. Conley." It was Bloch. "Scan the windows for snipers. If he brought this much backup, it's doubtful he'll be stopping there."

Morgan joined the scan, looking at the rows of windows that surrounded the plaza. Two churches, two hotels, a museum, and a government building. All old and elegant.

"Got one," Bishop said. "White building, north side, fourth floor. Third window from the left."

"That's bad news," Lily said.

Morgan shifted his gaze to the band as they launched into a rollicking rendition of "Mack the Knife." "The sniper's in a hotel," he said and called on one of Zeta Division's resident computer geniuses. "Shepard, can you get me room access?"

"Already working on it," came the man's clipped, assured, even cocky, voice.

"Cougar—"

"On my way." Peter Conley moved toward the hotel entrance. One good thing about working together so many years was that they had a connection that seemed, at times, nearly psychic.

"I don't like this." It was Bishop. "This is getting hairier by the second. I suggest a reassess."

"You're running point on this, Morgan," Bloch snapped. "Your call."

Morgan squinted into the cloudless blue sky. Then he looked at Lukacs, who was talking closely with Pulnik.

"Stay in position," Morgan ordered. "Move in as soon as Lukacs breaks away from Pulnik."

"And Lukacs's people?" Bishop demanded.

"Fan out with the team. I want one of us on every guard. Cuff and drop them. Lily, you go ahead with the diversion on my mark. We're going to need perfect timing on this."

"And Lukacs?" Bishop asked.

"I'll take care of Lukacs," Morgan said. "Extraction van ready?"

"I'll move out on your mark," Diesel answered. "Pick you up on the southeast corner."

Morgan watched as the team moved through the crowd as naturally as any tourist, betraying no sign of their purpose.

"I'm in position at the sniper's door," Conley said. "Shepard, how close are you to getting access?"

Shepard scoffed. "I'm in, big guy."

"Morgan, awaiting your signal," Bloch said.

"Hold. Not yet." Morgan kept his eyes on Lukacs and Pulnik, who were still having their conversation. But then Lukacs pulled him close.

Morgan watched, silently swearing, as Pulnik's mouth popped open, his eyes widened, and he grabbed at his own belly.

Morgan couldn't see the stabbing clearly, but he did see blood as Pulnik bent double. Lukacs casually eased him down to sit against the low ledge around the statue.

"Damn," Bishop seethed. "Morgan, call it off."

"The mission doesn't change." Morgan was not going to let Lukacs get away. "Target's moving out. Lily, that's your cue."

On the far side of the plaza, Lily pulled a megaphone from her pack and turned it on with an earsplitting whine.

"Wake up, sheeple!" she screeched, her voice amplified and flattened by the megaphone. "The Illuminati run your lives!" Lily was really selling the insanity, and people took notice. "The reptilians have invaded the highest level of government!" Tourists moved toward her or rubbernecked to get a look at the crazy girl. "They want us for our blood!"

That was the Zeta team's cue. They moved in on Lukacs's security. Lukacs had left Pulnik on the ground and was moving back from the direction he had come from. As he turned, Lukacs' eyes met Morgan's, and they held his stare long enough for the message to come across as clear as a New York glass of water.

"Goddamn it!" Bishop exploded. "I told you this was a bad idea. Didn't I goddamn tell you?"

"Too late now," Morgan snapped. "Move!"

They had lost the element of surprise, but Pulnik was losing his life. Morgan heard the sound of Conley kicking the sniper's hotel door in as Lukacs's security drew their guns. Morgan couldn't spare the attention to see what was going on. He heard gunfire, then screaming, as he ran straight for Lukacs.

There was just one problem. Two guards were converging on him, fast, from the left and right. Morgan turned his run evasive, reaching for his Walther.

Lily, having cast off her megaphone, came dashing from the left and tripped one of the men, sending him reeling to the ground. This gave Morgan the opening he needed to fire at the other guard. Three bullets perfectly placed in the man's chest, and he was down. Although there was the risk of him having a bulletproof vest, Morgan couldn't chance a head shot causing collateral damage on any innocent bystander.

He took the man's gun and tossed it to Lily, who had come weaponless.

"I owe you!" she said and ran off to help out Spartan, who was struggling to fight off two of Lukacs's security guards. Then Morgan took off running again toward Lukacs, who was by now at the edge of the square.

Morgan charged as hard and fast as he could. Someone crashed into him, sending his Walther flying. Morgan rolled to his feet to face his new attacker. It was the young man in the red coat. But instead of flashing an annoying smile, he was pointing a Beretta M9 directly between Morgan's eyes.

"I always give my enemy a moment to think," he said, "of their last words."

Morgan darted his gaze all around the smugly grinning killer. His team was scattered. None of them could help. The man was too close for him to run, but too far for him to attack and survive.

"Think of any?" the man in the red coat sneered.

Morgan turned his hand and raised his middle finger.

"Eloquent," the man chuckled and shrugged, tightening his finger on the Beretta's trigger.

Then the sound of a gunshot filled Morgan's ears.

Chapter Two

Dan Morgan knew he wasn't dead. The dead never hear the sound of the gun that shoots them.

His daughter, Alexandria "Alex" Morgan, however, grimaced at the sharp smell of gunpowder. Body still humming from the Heckler and Koch MSG90 sniper rifle recoil, she watched through the scope as the man in the red coat fell to the ground. The blood from his chest wound mingled with the color of his outerwear and started spreading onto the cobblestones.

"Hell of a shot, Alex," she heard her father saying in her ear.

"Compliments later, Dad," she murmured. "We got to spot Lukacs."

As people drained from the square, Alex scanned the space, looking for their target or his other men, but the survivors had disappeared from sight. She'd taken out two others before nailing Red-Coat, as Morgan and his team were discovering.

Morgan sniffed in appreciation of his daughter's burgeoning skill and his superior's previous doubts. Bloch had been concerned about putting Alexon on this mission. She had hedged her bets by ordering Alex to nest in the hotel room overlooking the square, where Bloch did not expect the younger, female Morgan to see any action.

Both father and daughter would have enjoyed seeing Bloch eat crow... if the rest of the assignment hadn't become such a hash.

"Anyone got eyes on him?" Morgan asked.

A chorus of negatives came over the radio. Alex made one last survey of the square. "I'm no good up here anymore. I'm moving out."

"You stay where you are," her father said.

"Make me." She set the rifle on the hotel room carpet and wiped her fingerprints from it—not expecting any retort from her father and not getting it. After stowing her 9mm Taurus compact automatic in its holster and a stun gun in one of her pockets, she pulled on her coat, pulled up the lapels to obscure her face, and left the room, the hall, the stairway, and the hotel—all the while remembering his advice.

"Insubordination is one thing," he had told her quietly one day in private. "Insubordination in front of the team is another. That's like germs. One sneeze, and everybody catches a cold."

Her old man might have a good point. It certainly might explain Bishop's behavior. She'd have to give it more thought, but she had bigger fish to fry at the moment.

Alex pushed against the flow of people seeking refuge inside the hotel, then squeezed her way out into the chill air. She couldn't pick out Lukacs or his men, but every panicked face in the crowd could conceal an enemy.

"Eyes on Lukacs," she heard in her ear. It was Peter Conley. "He's moving past the astronomical clock."

Alex ran toward the square's old timepiece. As far as she could tell, she was ahead of everyone else. A fantasy flashed before her eyes—Lukacs, in handcuffs, and her, Alex Morgan, bringing him in.

"We have police incoming," Shepard said. His words went in one ear, the sound of approaching sirens entering the other.

"This mission is already a shit show!" came Bishop's continued whining. "I'm telling you we need to call it off."

"This isn't a democracy," Bloch snapped as Alex plunged on, regardless of the infighting.

"If we don't get him now, we might never," her father said with remarkable restraint. "Move!"

"Just spotted a secondary security team coming in from the southeast," Spartan said. "I can keep them busy, but I'll need some help."

"On my way," Lily said.

Alex heard gunshots behind her as she ran out of the Old Town Square alongside the town hall. The clock was chiming eleven as she passed. Alex spared a glance at it, just in time to see the mechanical figurine of death coming out of the clockwork door.

Her head snapped forward, catching sight of Lukacs getting into the back seat of a black Mercedes C-Class. She noted the license plate as she ran toward it, elbowing past people as the car pulled out.

But despite her youth and fleetness of foot, it was too far away. She knew she'd never make it. But just as she thought about slowing, she heard the familiar sound of a "rice bike" motorcycle starting to her right. With a glance she was pleased to see that she had nailed the make, a Honda, and model, the CB500F, just by the rev noise. Seemingly as if she intended to go there all along, she grabbed the rider's leather jacket and stuck her 9mm in his face.

"Need the bike," she said. "Sorry."

The surprised man raised his hands and backed quickly away, leaving the Honda motorcycle to topple over. Alex caught it, hopped on, and took off, keeping her thumb tight on the horn to get the frenzied crowd to part.

There was a reason the 500F was nicknamed "Naked." The sleek little Honda was light, slim, maneuverable, and fast—perfect for street weaving.

"Target in a Mercedes C-Class," she reported to the team, giving them the license plate as well. "In pursuit on a borrowed Honda cycle." Alex maneuvered around the people until she cleared the crowd enough to gain some momentum, the bike jolting on the uneven ground.

"Spartan!" Morgan barked. "Cover her!"

Alex heard gunfire over the comm, deciding she wouldn't hold her breath for back-up. It sounded as if the rest of the team's hands were full as it was. As she concentrated on their quarry, she saw that the Mercedes was widening the distance between them. That would not do. She leaned down and opened the throttle full.

The Honda shot forward as if she had harpooned the trunk of Lukacs's car. But just as she was getting close another C-Class appeared from her left, nearly making confetti of her front tire. She just barely managed to stay upright, quickly breaking, but not stopping.

"He's got a decoy!" she said, straining to see the numbers and letters on the second license plate as she weaved through traffic. "Lukacs is in the front car!"

The right back window of the second car rolled down, and a man lifted himself out so that his torso was free in the air. His right hand held onto the hood of the car. In his hand was a Glock semiautomatic.

She banked left hard as he fired, the bullet shattering a store window behind her, and had to make a tight right to avoid a post on the edge of the sidewalk. She zigzagged as he tried to aim. He fired another shot, which she felt skin her left earlobe. If she didn't do something fast, the next one would nail her.

She didn't have to. At that moment, the Zeta tactical van roared out of a side street and rammed the decoy car, which spun out and crashed into the storefront of a butcher shop.

Alex drifted right, just missing the van. She lost speed with the maneuver, but she began to pick up again once she was clear of the crash.

"Diesel," she called through clenched teeth. "You okay?"

"In one piece," Diesel replied. "Go get Lukacs!"

Alex heard the insistent blare of a car horn coming from behind her, getting louder. A maroon Toyota Camry came speeding down the road, weaving through people and traffic to catch up to her.

That would be her father.

"Alex, clear the way!"

"You clear the way!"

"Got a free hand; need a clear shot. Do as I say!"

Bless the man, she thought. Rather than engage in a familial pissing contest, he gave her a good reason. "I'm faster and closer," she reminded him. "As soon as you're clear, I will be too."

She pushed harder, and pedestrians leapt out of the way. Traffic was light, so Lukacs managed to move fast even in the narrow streets of Prague. Alex followed suit, the old pastel-colored buildings that lined the street blurring from the speed. Her father's experience came in good stead as he managed to stay close behind her.

They all saw police cars turning into the street three hundred yards down. The Mercedes took a squealing, tire-smoking right onto a pedestrian-only boardwalk, sending passersby scrambling. Alex made the turn, yanking the bike up so the front tire wouldn't collide with the curb. Recovering, she picked up speed, covering a short distance to a stone archway under a tower.

The Mercedes screeched out onto the Charles Bridge, which had crossed the Vltava River since the late Middle Ages. Alex was right behind him, and somehow, her father was still behind her. Pedestrians parted like the Red Sea to hug the stone guard walls that bordered the bridge edge.

"Out of the way!" Morgan barked over the communicator. "Now!"

He had his hand out the car window, the trademark Walther in his grip. Almost as if they had practiced it, Alex banked right, just as he rapid-fired four times at Lukacs's car.

The countless hours spent on shooting ranges and obstacle courses paid off. The Mercedes's back left tire burst. The car swerved left, then right, and plowed straight into the side of the bridge. The heavy stone held firm, crumpling the frame of the Mercedes like it was wrapping paper.

Dan Morgan brought his car to a screeching halt. Alex Morgan drove past Lukacs's car and swerved to a stop on the far side. Her father took cover behind the door of his sedan, Walther in hand. They had their quarry surrounded.

The two front doors opened, and a security guard emerged from each one, in black suits and ties, Glocks in hand. They opened fire—at her father. They obviously thought that the young woman on the motorbike was just some thrill seeker—not a well-trained sniper.

Alex was about to prove them wrong when Lukacs stumbled out of the car on the other side—her side.

She let him come a short distance away from it, just so he couldn't disappear back inside. Then she stood up and drew her Taurus automatic.

"Freeze," she said calmly.

He looked at her, first in shock, then with amusement. He straightened, looking at the Taurus like it was a water pistol.

Alex motioned with it to put his hands up. The bastard just smirked and stepped in her direction. "It is not like TV or the movies," he said reasonably in lightly accented English. "The bad guy does not stop just because you have a pea shooter."

He must have heard that term in one of those movies. Okay, I'll play along.

"Don't test me," she told him, letting her voice shake. She discovered her hands were trembling as well. And he kept walking toward her. "Stop, or I swear I'll shoot."

"Will you now? Your people could have killed me from a window, but you went through all this trouble to catch me alive. So no, I don't think you will."

Alex glanced at her father. He had taken down one of Lukacs's men but was pinned by the other. Alex had a clear shot to the remaining bodyguard, but she didn't think she could nail him with all the crumpled metal in the way, and she was even less protected than he was.

"So? What's it going to be?" Lukacs said. "Are you going to shoot me now?"

Movement in her peripheral vision attracted her attention: the Zeta tactical van was barreling down the bridge, its front bumper in splinters from the crash. She shifted her eyes to look fearfully at Lukacs, who was smugly smiling and placing his fingers on the 9mm barrel.

"Now just give me the gun," he said, pulling lightly, " and everything will be just..."

He stopped when Alex gave him a big, assured, knowing smile—at the same second she pushed the stun gun just under his sternum and thumbed the trigger.

More than fifty thousand volts clawed into Lukacs's body. The unctuous a-hole danced like a marionette having a convulsion and then cannoned onto the cobblestones like a tree felled by lightning.

The Zeta tactical van came to a skidding halt alongside her, sliding the door open before they fully stopped. Spartan took care of Lukacs's final security guard with a salvo of bullets from her MP5 while Alex and Bishop unceremoniously launched Lukacs inside.

Spartan hopped in, pulling the door shut as Diesel peeled off toward the far end of the bridge.

"Team?" Bloch asked. "Report, please."

"Bishop here, with Diesel, Spartan, and Morgan Jr. safe and in possession of the package. We're on our way to switch cars."

"Morgan safe," Dan started and added, in a tone mixing appreciation and realization, "Morgan Senior." Alex smiled at the acknowledgment. "Nice work," he told her.

"They keep underestimating me," she said quietly. "So they keep losing."

"Conley," they heard Bloch inquire.

"Here," they heard the man code-named Cougar reply. "In one piece."

But before they could all relax, there was still one team member left to check.

"Lily," said Bloch.

No answer.

"Lily, come in," Bloch repeated.

Silence.

Chapter Three

Lily Randall woke up to the rocking of a vehicle, her left cheekbone aching from the hard floor of the van. It wasn't long before she felt a hard tug on her hair, which pulled her up to a seated position. She tried to fight the person off but found that her arms had been tied behind her back.

She flailed, trying to wrest herself free, and found herself staring down the barrel of a gun.

"No," the man holding it said. "Chill out."

She complied, resting against the side of the van as well as she could, given the circumstances.

The back of the van was windowless, and she was sharing it with three men. The one opposite her, who had threatened her with a gun, looked to be, like her, nearing his thirties. He was wearing a plaid beret covering his shaved head, and when he grinned, she saw that one of his top front incisors looked to be made of gold.

They spoke in what she supposed was Czech. She had the distinct impression that they were debating whether to kill her.

Her eyes darted, straining to see the men sitting in front, looking for Lukacs among the occupants of the van. He wasn't among them. Did the others succeed in capturing him? If so, that gave her a chance to survive this.

She ventured to speak. "You want your boss back."

The man with the gold tooth sneered. "Not boss. No boss."

"Still, Lukacs didn't pay everything up front, did he?"

The men looked at each other, and she knew she was right.

"So you want him back. Maybe we can help each other out."

Gold Tooth leaned in toward her. "What are you going to do, all tied up?"

"Call my people. We'll make an exchange."

The men exchanged some words. One of them raised his voice in anger. Gold Tooth snapped at him, then turned back to Lily. "Number."

The man said something and held out his hand, and one of the others handed him a cell phone.

"Let me make the call," she said.

"No," the man said. "We call."

She gave him the number—the emergency local number they had each committed to memory for the mission.

The man dialed and waited, until Lily heard the faint response—not enough for her to make out who was talking or what was said.

"Who is this?" the man demanded. Then, after the response, "We have your agent. The sexy woman with the green eyes." Lily shuddered with revulsion at his description. He continued. "We want Lukacs back."

Lily held her breath. She wasn't sure whether they would make the exchange. She wasn't even sure whether she *wanted* them to make the exchange. She wanted to be saved, but they had worked long and hard to catch Lukacs—a man responsible for dozens, probably hundreds, of deaths. To give her up to hold on to him—she might take it if the roles were reversed.

But they must not have made the choice, because the merc responded with, "Good. Stromovka Park, at the pond, south side, at midnight. We will exchange the prisoners then."

He listened as the person on the line spoke. Then he brought the phone to Lily's ear, holding it there.

"She wants to talk to you."

"This—" she stammered. "This is Agent Randall."

"Randall." It was Bloch. "Are you hurt?"

"I don't think so."

"Keep talking to me as long as you can, understand?"

"Yes," Lily replied and continued. "Yes, you want to do exactly as they say. I think they took me as leverage only, in case something like this happened. The impression I get is that they're men just trying to do a job they were hired for, nothing else."

She could practically see Bloch doing one of her death's head smiles at how Lily was following her orders as well as subtly instructing the men holding her captive. "Do you know where you are? Any identifying elements you can tell me?"

She couldn't see anything outside. "No. There's nothing...nothing seems done to me while I was unconscious. These men seem intent on their job, that's all. No reason to contact any local authorities."

"Very good, Randall," Bloch reassured her. "Tell me anything more."

Lily thought furiously of some way to pass on details without alerting her abductors. "It was five," she said. "Five o'clock your time when they took me. I don't know how many more minutes since then..."

The man with the gun yanked the phone away from Lily's ear.

"Stromovka Park," he repeated for Bloch. "Midnight." Then he hung up.

The blow came too quickly for her to dodge, hard on her right temple. She felt dizzy and retched from the pain.

"I did not let you talk to give information to your people. Do not play with me."

The man removed the battery from the phone. *Damn.* There was no way Zeta could track it now.

* * * *

"I lost the signal," Shepard said over the video connection.

Morgan walked restlessly around the living room, which held his daughter and Peter Conley. They were in a city apartment a few blocks from the historic downtown. It had belonged to an old widower who'd died heirless a few weeks before. Zeta had arranged their occupation by pulling a string of favors, which gave them a near-ideal base of operations with no paper trail.

"Of course," Alex said sarcastically. "Don't you always?"

"Find it again," Morgan said.

"It's no use," Shepard said. "It's gone."

"Then do something else! Track the vehicle!"

"Spoken like a field agent," Shepard sighed. "It's not that simple. We don't know which vehicle it was. Tracking the phone gives us a radius, that's all. It was on the highway. Too many cars, too many ways to go."

"Just get it done, Shepard."

"If you really need me to, I can prove to you mathematically that we can't," Karen O'Neal broke in. "Too many variables. Too little data."

Morgan felt like he was going to explode at any second. Lily had been captured, and he couldn't stand doing nothing.

"So what do we do?" Alex asked.

"We go get her," said Morgan. "Of course we go get her. We make the goddamn exchange and get our agent back."

"Actually, that question is not settled yet." The speaker was Paul Kirby, who was back at Zeta headquarters in Boston with Bloch, Shepard, and Karen O'Neal.

"We expended significant resources and manpower to find Enver Lukacs. If he disappears now, we may not get a second chance."

Morgan was seeing red. Kirby ought to have been glad that he was on another continent. "You can't be serious."

"Let me remind you that this is a man who moves top of the line Russian arms to US enemies in active war zones, who puts high explosives in the hands of Colombian militias, who provided chemical weapons to ISIS. Let's not forget who we are dealing with here, and what the price would be if we were to lose him again."

"Bloch," said Morgan. "Tell me you're not going to leave Lily in the hands of these—"

"We will make a decision and let you know."

"There's nothing to think about. We don't leave an agent behind."

"Your position on the issue is noted, Morgan. I need to discuss this with my superiors. I will let you know."

"You tell that dickless Smith that if he doesn't—"

Bloch cut the connection. Morgan pounded the wall with his fist. Paintings and a cuckoo clock rattled from the force.

"Dad..." Alex said softly.

It didn't work. He was filled with bile and darkness.

He looked at the door to the guest bedroom, where they were keeping Lukacs. "I'm going to get that bastard," he growled.

"Morgan," Conley said, holding his hand up to calm him down.

"Get out of my way," Morgan said, pushing past his friend. He opened the door and found Lukacs tied to a heavy wooden chair, a sack stuffed over his head.

"Wake up, you piece of shit."

Morgan pulled the sack off. Lukacs squinted in the light, blinking as he adjusted.

Morgan punched him in the face.

"Ouch," Lukacs deadpanned. Blood trickled down from his nose.

"You're going to tell me where I can find the bastards who work for you."

Lukacs licked the blood from his lips. "They took your agent, did they?" He laughed, showing his red-stained teeth. "My men?" Morgan stared at him, eyes slits from rage. "The door is not so thick, you know."

Morgan smacked him with an open palm. "Tell me where they are!"

"You hit like a girl."

Morgan grabbed him by the collar of his shirt. "I can do a lot worse if you'd like."

"Break some bones, pull teeth, I don't care," Lukacs said, laughing. "You need me alive, and you need to give me back today. That means I don't have to tell you shit."

"You'd better hope they decide to make the exchange," Morgan said. "Or else it's you and me until the day you die."

"Or until the day they set me free, after I tell them what I have to give them."

Morgan drew his knife from its sheath and held it two inches from Lukacs's eye. "I think you'll still be able to talk even if you can't see. Don't you?"

Lukacs's eyes flitted to something behind him, at the door to the room. Morgan turned to look behind him. Alex was watching him from the door.

His rage seeped from him, and he lowered the knife. No. He couldn't torture a man in front of his daughter.

Morgan sheathed the knife and put his foot on Lukacs's chest, shoving the chair half a foot up against the wall with the force that the arms dealer knocked his head. "This isn't over, Lukacs."

Alex stepped back as he walked out of the room and slammed the door. Conley approached him. "Got it out of your system, buddy?"

"No." Morgan sank into a musty armchair. "There's a lot more where that came from."

"Keep your cool. This isn't over yet. Shepard might catch a break—"

"He won't," Morgan said. "Have you ever seen that cocky bastard underestimate his own ability?"

"Well, maybe something else will come up," Alex said. "Maybe Lily will manage to get away somehow."

"Maybe," said Conley. "But I don't like her odds."

The ticking of the cuckoo filled the room. Dust mites, accumulated over the years, danced in the afternoon light filtering in through the window.

"I'm going," Morgan said. "No matter what Bloch says. We're not leaving Lily behind."

"If it comes to that, I'll go with you," Conley said.

"Me too," Alex said.

"Not you. Don't argue."

It took all of Alex's willpower not to roll her eyes.

"I'll go," Conley broke in to stem an argument. "But Lukacs stays. That's my price."

Morgan gritted his teeth. Conley laying conditions like this grated on him, but truth be told Morgan didn't know whether he'd bring Lukacs to the exchange either. It made his skin crawl to agree with Kirby, but the bastard was right about what it would mean for Lukacs to go free.

Morgan did not have to make up his mind because they were hailed on the screen by Bloch.

"I spoke to Smith," said Bloch. "We've come to a decision."

Morgan's fingers tightened on the chair's armrests.

"We are going to make the exchange. We're going to get Lily back. Get in touch with Tactical and plan this operation. We are not losing anyone today."

Chapter Four

Dan Morgan moved forward, tense, alert like prey in predator country. Lukacs, with a bag over his head, was walking alongside him, hands in cuffs. Morgan led him by the arm.

Stromovka Park was dark, all the lights having been turned off because it was hours after closing time. The ground was carpeted in yellow and orange leaves, fallen off the trees. They crunched underfoot as the team advanced, well spaced out.

"You're coming up on the rendezvous, dead ahead," Shepard said through their comms. "I got five of them total. Only one with the build to be Lily, in the center."

"Time to break off," Morgan said. "Take positions and keep out of sight."

The team, wielding rifles and night vision, disappeared into the darkness to surround Lukacs's mercs. Morgan, who was taking the lead, couldn't afford the clunkiness of the goggles, so he had to see by the scant light of the moon.

His eyes had adjusted enough that he could make out the shape of things. They were approaching a broad open space—a pond whose shore was dotted with low-hanging willow trees, its limp branches swaying in the chill wind.

He saw the figures in the darkness, moving as he approached. Five of them in all. He spotted Lily in the middle, where Shepard said she'd be, in a heavy jacket that didn't belong to her. The lower part of her face, from nostrils to chin, was tightly wrapped with industrial tape.

A merc with a golden tooth, glinting even in the moonlight, stepped forward. "She is a screamer," he said, motioning to Lily. Then he looked at Morgan's prisoner, head hidden under a bag. "Show me Lukacs."

Morgan pulled the bag off Lukacs's head. He squinted as the merc shone the flashlight in his face.

"Good. You have your own men, watching us, of course."

"Of course," Morgan said. "I want my agent back. Now."

"Fair exchange is fair," the merc said. "Nobody wants violence here. Give us Lukacs, we give you the girl, and we each go on our way."

"Fine," said Morgan. "I say go, and both begin walking."

Lily's eyebrows were doing a dance like they were straining to meet in the middle. She was trying to tell him something. She looked down pointedly, then looking back at him in expectation.

Damn. Anything could be under that coat with her. He was going to have to play it by ear. "All right," he said. "Let's go. Nice and easy."

Morgan nudged Lukacs, who started walking, as Lily did the same.

Tension filled the air as the two prisoners walked. Lukacs's men had their hands on their guns, holstered, and Morgan was ready to draw.

"Eyes on the prize," Morgan said, through the communicator. "Anyone seeming to go for a detonator should be dropped."

Lily passed Lukacs halfway between Morgan and the merc with the gold teeth. Their footsteps crunching on dry leaves were deafening in the silence.

She crossed the distance to Morgan. When she reached him, she looked down at the tape around her mouth and moved her jaw around. But instead of trying to tear the swath off, Morgan grabbed her coat and tore it open.

"They strapped her with explosives!" Morgan barked, sending the team into immediate action—including Shepard, whose fingers were flying over his keyboards half a world away.

As Lukacs's team drew their guns. Morgan moved to reach for his, but he didn't have to. Conley, Bishop, and Spartan were flanking him within a fraction of a second.

"If we die, we take you with us," the gold-toothed merc said and added, for effect, "Boom."

"Then defuse her," said Morgan. "Then we all leave here with everything we want."

The man grinned, tooth glinting in the scarce light. "I do not think so. Good luck. You have about forty-five seconds."

They walked backward, guns drawn, deeper into the darkness, taking Lukacs with them. Bishop and his team had them in their sights, but a slaughter was the last thing they needed right then.

"Stand down," Morgan said, turning his attention to Lily and the two packets of C4 duct-taped around her torso. "You, too, Shepard. No signal to block. It's a classic time bomb." He quickly pulled out a pocket flashlight and spotlighted the device.

"Forty," Bishop said, already counting down.

"They've run wires twice around her waist," Conley noted, looking for any booby traps as he started unwrapping Lily's mouth. Her breathing was heavy, and her green eyes were wet with fear.

"It's a hasty job," Morgan said. "Amateurish." Even so, his hands remained careful.

"Piece of cake, then?" Spartan said flatly, trying to keep even a hint of hope out of her voice.

"Didn't say that."

"Thirty-five," Bishop said.

The C4, detonator, and blasting caps were all encased in a thick envelope of duct tape. Morgan pulled out his pocket knife and probed at it. "At least it looks like there's no shrapnel," he said.

"Hooray," Spartan deadpanned.

"Let's do it," he said as much for his own benefit as hers. Then he barked to the others, "Take cover. There's nothing you can do here."

Conley snorted. "Yeah, right," he drawled. "And leave you two exposed to snipers?"

"Thirty," Bishop said.

Conley tore a hole in the tape gag, finally freeing Lily's parched lips. "You all go," she gasped. "I'll dive into the lake."

Morgan's lips curled into a mirthless smile. "I'm not abandoning you here, English. It's either both of us or neither of us."

"Twenty-five," Bishop continued quietly.

Morgan brought the blade against the tape and started cutting. It was so thick and jumbled with wires he could only cut half an inch at a time. It didn't help that every slice might reduce the two of them to mincemeat.

"Twenty," said Bishop.

"Hurry up." The words seemed torn from Lily's teeth.

"This is not the time to be rushing me!"

"Then when is?"

He finished slicing through. The wires and tape were a tangled mess, but it was enough for Lily to wriggle free in record time. But one thing remained holding the bomb vest in place: the wires winding around Lily's torso.

"Fifteen."

Morgan was certain he couldn't cut through them—breaking the circuit would most likely set off the bomb, if the mercs were half-competent, which from the looks of the circuits they were.

"Oh yeah," Conley said. "The old which-wire-to-cut conundrum."

Morgan felt his lips pull back from his teeth in a wolf's grin. *Yeah*, he thought, chastising himself. *For this I gave up a loving family and peaceful life.* He used the knife to strip the wires, trying to move as fast and steady as he could. A false move would have him cut them clear through, which would be bad.

Cut. Pull. And two sets of copper wires gleamed in the moonlight.

"Ten," Bishop said.

He twisted the exposed wires together.

"Lily?"

"Yeah?"

"If there's a time for this to kill us, it's now. Just a heads-up."

"Oh. Okay. Good to know."

"Five," Bishop said, his tight tone communicating that this might not be the best time for small talk.

Morgan cut the wire and survived to see the next moment.

Lily exhaled in relief.

"We're not done yet!" He pulled the vest over her head, holding the wires where he had twisted them together.

Once the vest had cleared her head, he yelled, "Run!"

They all took off. Morgan swung the vest around like a discus and hurled it as hard as he could. The vest sailed in the air toward the lake.

Morgan turned around and ran after Lily, feet pounding grass.

"Get down!"

Morgan jumped onto the ground and covered his head.

The explosion rocked the ground and sent a burst of water thirty feet into the air.

Morgan turned over onto his back and watched as water rained down and the waves resulting from the burst lapped at the shore.

"Zero," Bishop said drily.

"Fellas," Shepard said over the comm, "get moving. Someone's going to come check this out. Pickup spot, sixty seconds."

Morgan and Lily ran side by side in the darkness, the others close behind. She was safe. But Lukacs was gone...again.

Chapter Five

Alex Morgan forced a yawn to clear her ears from the pressure buildup in the cabin of the Dassault Falcon 2000.

Flying in a private jet was one of countless new experiences that had become commonplace after she'd joined Zeta—along with handling deadly weapons and being in frequent danger. Her father was as secretive as anyone about the organization itself, but some things were becoming clear. The first was maybe that her father was secretive because he knew little more than she did.

The internal structure was easy enough. Diana Bloch, implacable and professional to a fault, was their chief executive director. Her right-hand man was Paul Kirby, director of operations. He always had an expression on his face like he smelled something unpleasant, and she sometimes endured long rants from her father about what a spineless weasel he was. For a professional special ops agent, Dad was surprisingly invested in his rants.

Zeta also had their brain trust. Lincoln Shepard was their IT guy—the now somewhat standard kind of child genius who had gotten into hot water by hacking into classified intelligence databases like it was some sort of video game. Bloch got him out in exchange for his service.

Karen O'Neal, their numbers analyst, was the same deal, except with her it was some kind of insider trading thing. Though Karen was probably Alex's closest friend in Zeta after her father, she'd never been too forthcoming about those details. Alex didn't blame her, press her, or really even want to know.

Karen and Shepard were dating, kind of. They thought they were being sneaky, but it'd been going on for more than a year now, so it was fairly inevitable that everyone would catch on. But no one said anything. Alex figured everyone enjoyed the sneaking around part—Zeta being a nest of spies and all.

The tactical team was the muscle, whenever it was needed. They were physically quick—in and out, whenever they needed to move in with overwhelming force. They were also an insular group, so Alex didn't know them all that well, despite nominally being a part of them.

Once they spread out into the Dassault, the team had gone into decompression mode. Bishop, their nominal leader—a tall black man with a shaved head and bulging muscles under his white T-shirt—had raided the minibar and was in one of the chairs toward the back. He was alongside Diesel, their resident sniper, laughing about something they'd probably be all too eager to tell her about if she asked.

Alex had a special admiration for Spartan, the only woman in tactical. Short blond hair, muscled, and tattooed, she wasn't the kind of woman her father might consider beautiful, but he still lived in the Stone Age. Spartan, who Alex thought was magnificent, was lying back in a seat next to Bishop, downing a beer.

That left "the operatives," like her. Well, not like her—she was as green as they came. But that was her role.

She liked to think that the operatives were the versatile ones. They did what needed to get done. Sometimes it was spying, sometimes extraction, sometimes infiltration, sometimes who knows what. They needed to be flexible, independent, smart, quick on their feet, and constantly develop new skills. Alex realized that the operatives were like interns, only the business they served specialized in killing.

She'd gotten good experience in training. They taught deception from both sides—giving and getting, in other words, how to lie so she would be believed and how to discern lying from truth when someone tried it on her. She also was given stunt driving courses, Krav Maga training from actual Mossad teachers, seminars in explosives, and constant target practice in both shooting ranges and obstacle courses with every kind of handgun, automatic weapon, and sniper rifle.

But the prime lesson she learned was that training and practice were very different from actual field work.

It was a good thing she was working with pros. Lily Randall was formerly MI-5, and, like Alex, a relatively recent addition. Lily was curled up in a corner seat with a book in one hand and a flute of champagne in the other. Peter Conley was her father's old partner in the CIA. He was now in the cockpit, conferring with the pilots. Her father had said that Conley could fly anything, so his presence on any flight was reassuring.

Speaking of her father, Dan Morgan was hunched over the table, working on his own hobby, building a model Duesenberg SJ Special. The pungent smell of the model glue tickled her nostrils. He had been a spy for the CIA before she was born—sort of a private contractor, the kind who gave the Agency maximum plausible deniability. He'd left after some disagreement he didn't talk about and was recruited into Zeta a few years back.

That was also around the time Alex found out who he really was—at the tender age of sixteen. Happy birthday to her. Those had been a rough couple of months, but once she had made the decision to shoot a man who had been sent to kill her, her mother, and her father, the transition had gone smoother—at least for her. Her father, already filled with guilt for lying to his family for years—they'd thought he was a classic car dealer—was still not sure he should have brought Alex to Take Your Daughter to Work Day. But once there, there was no turning back.

Above Diana Bloch was Smith, the man with no title and no other name other than perhaps "Mister." Both Dan and his daughter had initially thought he was merely a recruiter—like a baseball scout for assassins and spies—but it turned out he actually represented the mysterious Project Aegis, the shadowy power behind Zeta. Alex had read up on it. Aegis was the shield of the Greek Gods—Zeus, Poseidon, Hera, and those guys. Zeta was the sixth letter of the Greek alphabet or the sixth star in a constellation.

As far as Alex could tell, their Aegis was not, strictly speaking, a government agency. It was more like they had some bigwigs in government—military and intelligence top brass—plus, she guessed, major financial backers in the private sector. Who they were was kept very close to the chest, though. And she was not about to rattle any cages by prying into it.

"Alex." Her father had set down his model and was looking at her with that expression he always had when he wanted to say something but couldn't find the words. He wasn't the most communicative person—and a lot of things between them ended up going unsaid because of it. "Back there, with Lukacs. In the apartment."

To see her father like that had both scared her and pissed her off. It was one thing to see him hurt and kill people in the heat of combat. It was another to see him go so uselessly off the rails. Do that at the wrong time, and everyone's life would be at risk. But she knew this was the sort of thing he was anxious about—her knowing who he really was, warts and all.

"It's fine, Dad. Your macho man took over. You felt protective of Lily's virtue."

Relief and consternation seemed to mix on his face, but, as usual, he wound up hearing what he wanted to. "People like Lukacs—there's no other language they understand. And I'll stop at nothing to help the people I care about. That's true for Lily and Peter, but it goes double for you and your mother."

Alex took his words at their face value. It was certainly a language her father understood. "I know how far you're willing to go," she assured him with affection. "I've seen it before."

"So you understand?"

"Yes," she said, breaking into a warm, knowing smile. "I do, Dad." Maybe more than he did.

He sat back and took a deep breath. "You know, you did well out there. Quick on your feet, remembering your training, working as a team..."

They were interrupted by an alert from the laptop computer which was open at an empty table—an incoming video call from Zeta. Morgan accepted the call, and Diana Bloch's face appeared—brown hair in a professional short trim, muted, sober makeup, and a face that rarely cracked a smile. Beside her was Lincoln Shepard, his messy black hair sticking in every direction, wearing a Japanese anime T-shirt.

"I trust everyone is having a good flight," Bloch said. "And I respect your need to rest. But we need to talk about what's next."

Peter Conley walked back from the cockpit and asked them, "Any word on Lukacs's whereabouts?"

"I've cast a wide net," Shepard said. "Not surprisingly, he's careful. Despite our best efforts, I'm concerned that little worm may wriggle away again."

"So I want to see Lukacs's belongings," Bloch continued. "There might be something useful there."

Morgan reached into his carry-on, pulled out a bag, and set it on the table. He placed a wallet, a few coins, and a phone on the table.

"The phone's a burner," Morgan explained.

"I might be able to get something off of it anyway," Shepard said. "Let's see what's in that wallet."

Morgan opened it and carefully spilled its contents on the table: an ID, presumably fake, some money, and credit cards.

Something caught Alex's eye. "Hold on." She reached out and took something from the wallet—a golden rectangle about the size of a business card. She held it up, and it gleamed in the light of the airplane cabin.

"That's real gold leaf." That was Lily, looking up from her book. "I know gold when I see it."

"Looks like there's something on it. It's really hard to see, hold on." Alex ran her fingers over the surface and tilted it to catch the angle of the light just right. "Looks like some kind of symbol."

"Let me see," Lily said, reaching out for it. She examined it, tilting it against the light as Alex had done. "Yes, there's definitely something there. I need paper," she said. "A notepad, anything."

Alex looked around and settled for the nearest thing—a barf bag in the pocket next to her seat. She handed it to Lily, who made a quick sketch and held up the paper. "Anyone recognize this?"

"You're not very good at drawing," Alex said. "Hold on."

Using the card as a reference, she made a closer approximation of the design on the card—a broken circle, with a sort of pinched triangle in the middle. "Is this a bit closer?"

"Yes, looks more like it," Lily said. "But I don't recognize it."

"Hold it up to the camera," Shepard said. Alex held up the card and the design. "Nothing I know of, but I'll see what I can find."

"The circle reminds me a bit of the Ouroboros," Peter Conley said. "The snake that eats its own tail."

"Morgan." It was Bloch. "I need to talk to you privately."

Bishop, in the back, snickered like Morgan was a schoolkid being called to the principal's office.

Morgan took the computer and brought it into one of the tiny cabins near the cockpit. "I'm sorry, but saving Lily was the right call," he said. "We'll get Lukacs soon enough—"

"That's not what this is about, Morgan. We can get into the details in the full debrief, and we'll go into the specifics of that decision. But it was our decision, ultimately, and I take responsibility for it. But that's not what this is about. I'm pulling you off Lukacs."

"What? Why? We were close, Bloch. Closest than anyone's been in a long time."

"I know. But I have another mission for you—one that only you can perform."

"What—" Half the screen was occupied by a familiar face, one he did not expect.

"General James Collins," Bloch said. "I understand you knew him back in your days at the CIA."

"I worked under him," said Morgan. "I did several black ops under his command in Africa."

"What can you tell me about him?" she asked.

"Currently under investigation by a Senate committee for misconduct in Iraq. It's bullshit. He's a good man. Real American. Best boss I ever had."

"Maybe not so good," said Bloch. "A cache of Tomahawk missiles went missing from a silo last week. Disappeared into thin air. And eleven soldiers dead, killed by whoever took them. The Pentagon's covering, calling it a training accident." She held up both hands and made air quotes. "But DIA says it had to have been an inside job."

"And they're trying to pin it on him?"

"His codes were used to access the base and deactivate the security systems. He had access to blueprints and schematics of the base, as well as details of its contents. The evidence doesn't look good."

"What does he say?" Morgan asked.

"That he had nothing to do with it. That he doesn't know how his codes came to be in the possession of whoever orchestrated the heist."

"And you want me to see if that's true?"

"That's the gist of it, yes," Bloch said.

"What makes you think he'll open up to me? We haven't seen each other in years."

"You received a voice mail today." A recorded voice played over the speakers.

"Dan, it's Jim Collins. Something's happening. I need your help. There's no one else I can trust."

"You're listening to my voice mails now?"

"Of course," Bloch responded without a hint of humor. "But we're monitoring Collins. We couldn't be coy about this. It's too urgent. We need to find those missiles, Morgan."

"I get the picture."

"We need you to get him to talk," she said. "You know how this goes. Use your relationship with him."

"And then stab him in the back?"

"If he's a traitor, yes. If not, get him to help you find the missiles. The truth is what we want."

Morgan was again amazed by the cold-blooded practicality of the woman. He also realized that was maybe what he liked about her the most. "That hasn't always been my experience," he reminded her. "Sometimes, what you higher-ups want is a fall guy."

Bloch sat back, and her lips got very thin and straight indeed. "This is Zeta, Agent Morgan," she said carefully. "*I* am Zeta. If you think that is true, or even possibly true of me, I'm sure the classic car dealerships of the world would welcome a salesman of your caliber back into the fold. Don't put your personal relationships ahead of your objectivity or the nation's security. You're a better agent than that."

"When the chips are down, I hope that's more than just talk, Bloch."

"If you have to hope, then you don't know Zeta at all." She restored the placid authority to her expression. "You in, or can you give me a solid lead on a Porsche 916?"

Morgan almost grinned. "Yeah, I get it. You need me to save the day. Must be Tuesday."

Chapter Six

Lily gave her name at the lobby of the San Francisco St. Regis. Bright sunlight streamed in from Third Street through the floor-to-ceiling glass wall and fell on the interior's mild modern decor.

"Everything looks good with your reservation. Your car is also ready."

"Car?"

"Let me see here. Yes, that's right. We have a car for you. Courtesy of a Mr. Renard."

That would be Scott Renard. Young multimillionaire, Silicon Valley prodigy—as so many were— and Lily's boyfriend. She thrilled at being left this little surprise.

The man at reception handed her the keycard snugly inserted into a heavy stock envelope. "You're all set. Are you going up to your room now, ma'am?"

"No. Can you have the car brought around?"

The valet drove it into the drop-off area at the hotel door. It was a silver Alfa Romeo 4C Coupe, all sleek curves and low to the ground. She was a sucker for European sports cars, and Scott knew it.

She got in, settling and arranging the seat and mirrors—which always felt like a ritual in a new car—getting to know its layout and particularities. She ran her hands over the interior, feeling the plump smoothness of the leather. Then she twisted the key and pulled off into the street, delighting in the responsiveness of the accelerator and the easy, fluid way in which it drove.

She couldn't wait to get that baby on the highway. But for now, she just played on the hilly San Francisco streets, as much as she could get away with and not attract the attention of the police. Once the sheen started wearing off, she activated the hands-free communication panel and called Scott.

"Hello, stud. Guess where I am?"

"I think you're looking for something more specific than Frisco."

"Very specific. My present company is sexy, curvy, European and *very* powerful."

"If you're trying to make me jealous, it's not going to work." He chuckled. "Do you like it?"

"I think you know the answer to that question. You *do* know how to please a girl."

"In more ways than one. Speaking of which, I'm at work. Come pick me up."

"Don't you have big executive things to do? Hire people, fire people, look at fiscal reports?"

"I got all that done. I have a very important board meeting in five minutes, during which we are going to see if anyone can beat my high score on the office video game, but I can skip out early...if you sweeten the deal."

Her smile widened at the suggestion. "Suppose I just leave you there playing games with the boys?"

"Okay. You win. I miss you desperately. Come now, or I'll wallow forever in sorrow."

She grinned. "Be there in twenty."

"That's the best you can do with my little present?" he asked incredulously.

"Be there in ten."

A short time with an exaggerated proportion of driving violations later, she found him at the curb outside the building that housed SR Holdings, his electronic security start-up.

"Hey, baby," she said. "Looking for trouble?"

"Looks like I found it," he said, flashing his gap-toothed smile. He made his way around the coupe and into the passenger seat.

"I wish you'd stay with me," he said. "There's no need for you to stay at the hotel."

"What's the glamour in that? I prefer expensive cars, five-star hotels, and nights out on the town."

"You would," he said. "Not that we can't have all that. You've been to my place, Lily. A five-star hotel isn't an improvement."

She let it hang. Eventually Scott took the hint and changed the subject. "You said you needed help with something? Or was that only a ploy to see me?"

"I did want to see you. But I really do need a favor." Eyes on the road, she reached into her bag and pulled out the golden card.

Scott examined it.

"Fancy," he said, turning it around. "Looks like real gold leaf. Got a chip embedded there too. Any idea what it is?"

"None at all. Lifted it from an arms dealer. We're hoping it'll give us some idea of where he's going next. Think you can help us?"

"I might. I've got a friend who has this software, like face recognition but for anything. Searches through millions of online pictures for any object, any image really. I've seen it find a particular house from a picture of one corner of a window. I'll have him run it through the algorithm, see what turns up. Meanwhile, I can run my own analysis, see what I can get from the chip. I'm going to need to go home and get some equipment."

"We can afford to take a little break," she said. "I was hoping we could take this baby down to the track." She turned the full intensity of her jade eyes and rosy smile on him. "I could give you a few lessons."

His eyebrows rose. "Well, as much as I'd love to take that offer," he replied, "I had something else in mind," he said. "Something a little more exciting."

"Exciting is good."

"You're going to need a special outfit, though."

She raised her eyebrows to meet his. "Is that so?"

* * * *

"Let me see," Scott coaxed.

"I look ridiculous," she said.

"You look in-freaking-credible."

Lily was wearing a full wingsuit, which resembled a jumpsuit with webbing between the legs and arms so that, with limbs extended, she looked more than a little like a flying squirrel. A ram-air parachute container nestled at the back of the suit against her spine. They were on a rocky promontory overlooking a cliff miles outside the city, the sun low in the sky over the Pacific Ocean. A brisk wind was blowing from inland, and wisps of her crimson hair sticking out of her helmet beat against her face.

She inched toward the edge of the cliff and looked down. The sheer height made her stomach jump.

"Chicken?" Scott said, a teasing smile playing on his face.

Not about to let that stand, Lily pulled her goggles over her eyes and jumped off.

She fell through nothingness. She screamed in fear and glee as the wind rushed her face and through her hair, in the exhilaration of the free fall.

As instructed, she opened her arms, and the flaps caught the wind. And then she was flying.

They glided together, down, under the California sun.

* * * *

"I'll admit you arrange the best dates." She was speeding down the highway in the little Alfa Romeo, squinting against the sun setting over the ocean. "I'm wired," she said. "That was such a rush."

"I can think of a way to work off that energy." He laid his hand on her thigh, pulling her dress just a few inches up with his fingers.

Lily unthinkingly stepped harder on the accelerator—her unconscious mind's way, she supposed, of saying, *oh, yes please*.

She bit her lip and moderated the speed. She turned on the car stereo, and the Turtles' "Happy Together" came on.

"Is this the radio?" Scott asked.

"No, that's my phone hooked up to the sound system."

"You're kidding me?" He looked like he was holding back laughter.

"What's wrong with it?"

"This is the sappiest, cheeriest song in the whole world. It's, like, for the closing credits of cheesiest rom-coms."

"Is there a problem with that?"

"It's just that you're this badass international spy. I figured you'd like music with a little more edge to it, that's all." He chuckled and sang along. "So happy togetherrrrr."

"Shut up! Tosser."

He ran his fingers through her hair, pulling it back, and stopped. "What's that on your temple?"

Crap. She hadn't concealed it with makeup as well as she had hoped. "Nothing."

"Was it from the base jumping? Did you hit something when you landed?"

"You know I didn't. I had it already. Minor work injury." She turned her high beams on him. "I'm a badass international spy, remember?"

"That looks pretty nasty. What happened?"

"Scott, you know the deal. Don't ask, don't tell. That's the only way this is going to work."

"Well, I hate the deal. The deal sucks. I can't believe I let you go off into danger on your own—"

"Let me? What, now you're going to pull out the apron and housecoat?" she teased. "Is Scott Renard going to go toe to toe with a bunch of hardened mercenaries to protect his lady's honor?"

"You could stand to say that in a slightly less emasculating way," he mockingly pouted.

"If you weren't being so 'masculated,' I wouldn't have to emasculate you now, would I?"

The multimillionaire turned to look out of the windshield. Lily could see that behind the slick veneer and cocky self-assurance wealth and success brought was still an insecure nerd. It made her like him even more.

"Let's not dabble in shop talk, all right?" she suggested with a grin. "I came here to see you to get away from all that."

He chuckled with appreciation and relief. "Fine. Let's get back to my place. We'll see what we can turn up on your golden ticket."

Chapter Seven

Morgan arrived at his house, a two-story ranch in the Boston suburb of Andover, Massachusetts.

Alex had her own apartment now that she was drawing a paycheck. It felt strange not having her around anymore, but it was also great that he and Jenny had the house to themselves. No matter how often his work took him away from home, he always craved being back in Jenny's arms. With Alex off doing her thing, he wouldn't have to wait.

Morgan opened the front door and walked right into the middle of a ladies' book club. Eleven pairs of eyes turned to face him.

"Dan!" said Jenny, standing. "I didn't know you were coming!" She hugged him tight. Her warmth was cruel, mocking his desire. He felt the urge to order everyone to leave.

"We were just discussing *When the Horses Wild Ran.* Keri was just about to talk about the symbolism in—"

"I'm going to go take a shower," he interrupted. Then, with the best smile he could muster, he said, "Please make yourselves at home."

He wasn't lying—at least about half of it. He took a quick shower, pulled on a pair of jeans, buttoned up a shirt, and went back downstairs. The club, thankfully, was on a break. He wasn't sure how much *Horse* symbolism he could take. Jenny was having an involved conversation with two other guests, one of whom he knew to be their next-door neighbor, Cynthia. So he went to the kitchen to raid the refrigerator instead.

He heard the clicking of heels, and a woman he didn't know came in after him. Her skin was tanning-bed orange—looking like a warning poster for melanoma. Her lips were plumped with Botox, and he wondered whether she didn't also walk around with a perpetual pout on top of that.

Her hair was calculatedly messy—blond highlights clashing against reddish-brown straw.

She flitted her fake eyelashes as she shot him an "Oh, hello there." She had a glass of sangria in her hand. "Would you like a drink? Oh, look at me, offering you a drink in your own home!"

"No, thanks."

"Well, you must be Dan." She pronounced his name with two syllables more than it could carry. "I've heard so much about you. I'm Steffani. That's two *f*'s and an *i*. *Enchantée*." She held out her hand. He knew she meant for him to kiss, but he shook it instead.

"So where did you run off to?"

"Traveling," he said, "For work."

"Oh yes? What business are you in?" He held back the urge to laugh at how transparent her feigned interest was.

"Cars. Classic. Vintage. Especially American muscle cars from the fifties and sixties."

She reached out her hand and put it on his shoulder. "I like American muscle...cars." She emitted a high-pitched laugh, like she had said something hilarious.

"I can send you a catalog," he said. "Excuse me. I need to go find Jenny."

Leaving Steffani-with-two-*f*'s-and-an-*i* behind, he cut into Jenny's conversation. "Pardon me, ladies. Could I borrow my wife for one second?"

Jenny looked from him to the ladies. "Excuse me, girls."

As soon as he got her two steps away, he said, "I need your help with something. Upstairs."

"Of course," she said casually, following him up the stairs and into the bedroom. As soon as she had shut the door, he pounced and kissed her, pushing her against the wall. She ran her hands through his hair and his back, feeling his flexing muscles.

"I didn't know you were having the Real Housewives over," he whispered between kisses.

"Oh, hush, you," she said and did it for him with her lips.

"So how was your mission?" she said huskily. "Get a lot of bad guys?"

"I don't want to talk about them. I'm more interested in this one bad girl." He ran his hands under her shirt.

"Dan," she complained through an irrepressible grin. "My guests. They'll—"

He kissed her neck, and she moaned softly, grabbing his shirt to pull it up over his head.

* * * *

That night found Morgan in Brookline, in a neighborhood that was pure old money, filled with colonial houses with broad yards. It was some of the most expensive suburban square footage in the country.

The afternoon with Jenny—especially her awkward return to the party, adjusting her clothes and pretending they hadn't been doing what they were just doing—was now a glowing, but regretfully fading, memory.

He drove his Shelby Cobra down Heath Street, where Collins lived. Some two hundred feet from Collins's gate was a car parked on the street. He made out two men sitting inside as he passed.

He knew a stakeout when he saw one. Morgan drove on.

"We have company," he said. "Collins's house is being watched."

"To be expected," Bloch said in his ear. "Find your own way in."

"Gonna have to be the backyard. Shepard, a little help?"

"Take your next right," the IT wiz instructed. "Park three hundred and fifty feet along—there's a dark spot there with no security camera coverage. You're going to have to run through the yard of another house, then jump the fence to Collins's place."

Morgan parked where Shepard suggested and approached the house. This wasn't exactly a high-crime area. The area was surrounded by a low brick wall. Morgan braced against a sycamore tree and hoisted himself, straddled the top of the wall, then pushed off, and landed on the other side.

He ran along the yard and took cover behind the tool shed. "How am I doing?"

"So far, so good," Shepard said. "But you're not there yet."

Morgan looked around the corner of the shed, estimating how far he had to go. The backyard had more open space and was in full view of the back windows of the house.

That's when he heard it—the muted pounding of paws on the ground, approaching him fast from the direction of the house.

Dog. A Doberman pinscher, to be precise. Sleek black coat, ninety pounds of lean muscle, and a bite made to pulverize bone. His bones, to be precise.

Morgan took off running, moving as fast as he could. He was halfway there when he heard the thump of dog's paws behind him, getting closer and closer.

Morgan held his breath. He was going to have to time this to the millisecond. He listened for the steps, and then the final one—when the dog launched into the air—before taking a running leap.

Morgan dodged faster than the dog was expecting, and the Doberman caught only air. He stumbled as he fell, causing him to tumble and hit a tree trunk with a whimper.

That gave Morgan the opening to cover the rest of the distance to the fence. As he pulled himself up, he felt a tug at his foot—the dog's jaw was clamped on his heel. It was growling, pulling. Morgan kicked down, wrenching his foot free, and pulled himself over the fence.

He took a moment's rest and then, panting, crossed Collins's backyard to the door.

Collins was divorced, never had any kids. He'd inherited the house, an old redbrick colonial, from his family. *Too large for one man to live in alone*, Morgan thought. He examined the windows, but they were solid wood, and all were locked. So he went to the back door and picked the deadbolt. He stepped inside and shut the door behind him.

"I'm in," he murmured.

He made his way through the house, stepping lightly, trying not to make a sound. It was a real old-fashioned, old-money New Englander—with old wallpaper dotted with paintings of ships and harbors in ornate frames. He moved up creaky stairs, making a vague guess about where Collins's bedroom was. He hoped he wouldn't startle the old guy too much, then fully realized where he was, who he was sneaking up on, and acknowledged what would happen if Collins had tried the same thing at Morgan's house.

Sure enough, when he pushed open the one upstairs door that was closed, Morgan found himself facing down the barrel of a .357 Colt Python snub-nose revolver, held by General James Collins, in a ratty white T-shirt and boxer shorts.

"Crap on a cracker," the old warhorse rumbled. "Is that Dan Morgan or the tooth fairy?"

"Hello, Jim."

He didn't lower the gun. "Are you here to try killing me?"

"Jesus, Jim, of course not. I'm here to talk. "

"Last thing I heard you weren't in the talking business."

Morgan shrugged. "I'm not in the breaking-into-houses-in-the-middle-of-the-night business either. You're being watched."

"Yeah," Collins replied. "I noticed." He let the gun droop and took a step back. "I've also been noticing you since you met my neighbor's dog."

Morgan grimaced. "Any idea who it is? The watchers, not the dog."

"Who knows?" Collins shrugged, heading back to sit on the edge of his big wooden bed. "NSA, DoD, FBI? Go ahead. Put together any three letters, and there's a possibility that's them." He emitted a hollow laugh.

Morgan took a look around. The place was messy, with clothes, books, and papers piled on the nightstands, the dresser, and the floor. "You becoming a hoarder in your old age?"

"That's General Hoarder to you, plebe," Collins retorted wearily. "What do you want, Dan? Pretty certain it's not whether I wear boxers or briefs to bed."

"No," Morgan said. "Is there any chance we might be able to sit down somewhere?"

"What, the mattress isn't good enough for you?" Collins didn't expect an answer. Instead, he seemed to have a little conversation inside his own mind and grunted, "All right. Come on."

Collins grabbed a frayed tartan robe and led Morgan down to the living room without turning on a single light. They sat on dusty couches opposite each other, a fireplace with a marble mantelpiece and brass pokers between them. Collins still held his .357 in his hand.

"Take a wild guess what I'm here about," Morgan said.

"Those goddamn Tomahawks. They're gonna be the death of me. Are you wearing a wire?"

"Ear comm."

"Turn it off," said Collins. Without hesitation, Morgan popped the tiny transceiver from his ear and clicked it off, setting it on the coffee table between them. He could just imagine Bloch's face. He was certain it would give a lemon a run for its pucker.

"All right," Collins said. "What do you know?"

"I know the missiles are gone, on your watch, using your access codes."

"So they say."

"You're telling me that's not the way it went down?"

"It's a sham," Collins said. "A frame. I don't know how. I don't know who has my access codes or how they got 'em. But they sure have got me by the short hairs."

Morgan had gotten a few lines on his face and gray hairs in the intervening years. But Collins had gotten old. He looked withered.

"Do you think this has to do with the investigation or Iraq?"

"Not *or*," Collins contended. "*And*. It has everything to do with it, although maybe not in the way you imagine. They're both part of a campaign against me. But I have information, a way to clear my name."

"Why don't you bring it to the investigation committee?"

"Because it'll take investigating, and I can't trust them to do it. As you probably know, there's a lot of ugly politics in the armed forces. You heard of General Sheldon Margolis?"

"The name is familiar, but I don't know anything about him."

"You'll know soon enough. He has big ideas. Major player, lots of friends in high places. He's angling to make a presidential run. But I have dirt on him, which means he needs to get me out of the way. And the bastard might do it, too, if I don't get some goddamn help." His flint-hard eyes locked onto Morgan's. "You gonna be some goddamn help, Morgan?"

"I don't know what I could do for you."

"Please," Collins scoffed. "Yeah, I know we haven't seen each other in years, and I have no call to demand anything of you. But while they're putting the screws on me, the people who are really behind this are out there. And whatever they mean to do with those missiles, it's bad."

"How do I know you're not the one who means to do something bad with those missiles?" Morgan asked pointedly.

Collins looked at the operative as if he had lost his mind. He leaned back on the sofa and spread his arms. "Because I'm right goddamn here in front of you, man, with some big-time badass special-ops wonk doing a dance with my next-door neighbor's Doberman before breaking and entering into my goddamn house, that's how!"

Morgan couldn't argue the point. And to be truthful, he didn't want to. "Can't you go to the Department of Defense? You must know people."

"Yeah, and Margolis knows those people too," Collins said. "He's isolated me from my allies." Collins frowned. "They might be in on it; they might not be in on it with him. But they wouldn't have to be. His word would be enough. Even if the truth got out, by the time things are sorted, it'll be too late...for me and whoever those missiles are launched at."

Morgan formed his hand into a fist. "Okay," he said. "I'm going to be some help. Tell me what I can do."

"You can't trust the government. You can't trust your people. You can't trust anyone. Except..."

"Except who?"

"There is one person. Navy Commander Alicia Schmitt. An old friend, the only one I trust. A good, patriotic American who'd never put herself ahead of her country. I'd put my life in her hands any day. She knows what's going on. She'll be able to tell you what to do."

"Morgan." It was Shepard, through the comm. That surprised him. Until then Morgan was unaware that the comm link could be restarted from HQ. Shepard's voice was tinny and distant, like his conscience, but the message was important. "The police are coming. Time to go."

"What is it?" Collins asked, his older ears unable to pick up the reedy words.

"It's my people. They say the cops are coming."

"I was expecting this. Morgan, find Alicia. She'll know what to do. If she doesn't believe you, ask her about Virginia. Tell her I told you to say that."

"I will," Morgan promised, standing. "Trust me. I'll make this right. I'll find the missiles and clear your name. And we'll put Margolis in prison where he belongs."

Collins stood opposite him. "Well," he said, "put him someplace he belongs—that's for sure."

Police lights flashed against the curtains, lighting the dark rooms of the house. Morgan was going to have to go out the back, through the neighbor's house, and get past the dog.

"Jim," he said, "you wouldn't happen to have a steak I could borrow, would you?"

Chapter Eight

The night was still pitch black when Morgan turned his Shelby Cobra into the property that housed the Zeta Division's new headquarters. It was in an old warehouse a couple of miles south of Boston. The property was registered under a front corporation, and it was always packed with boxes that were changed from time to time, although Morgan never knew what was in them—if anything.

It had been five months since they'd officially moved, and after strings of technical issues, things were only now falling into place.

Morgan scanned his keycard, and the automatic gate opened. He knew that hidden sensors had also scanned his car for weapons and explosives.

He pulled his Shelby into an indoor garage via a ramp that led underground. He parked and walked to a reinforced steel door, where his fingerprints and retinas were scanned. Only then did he input his personal password on a keypad. He had also passed at least two dozen hidden cameras to get this far. This sort of security was annoying but absolutely necessary. Zeta had made a lot of enemies since its inception and had endured its share of attacks.

An elevator took him even deeper underground. After another set of heavy security doors, which opened electronically from the inside, he emerged into what they called the foyer—which was a small concrete room with a blast door.

The first person he saw was weasel-faced Paul Kirby, who held out a stiff hand in greeting. "We're in the War Room, Morgan. Please join us."

Kirby led the way down a short corridor that was laid out radially from the nerve center of the operation.

The War Room was the largest area in the place, where they gathered for group mission debriefs. The layout was circular, with a large, round wooden table in the middle. A screen followed the curvature of the wall for half of the circle. Far above, a skylight opened onto a bright blue sky— fake, of course, as it was night outside. But it was the best fake sky money could buy, and it seemed surprisingly close to the real thing.

They'd adopted it based on research by Karen O'Neal that said it made people more alert and productive. For a short time, they'd put pictures of eyes on the walls under the theory that it made people more honest, but Morgan had torn them down—to everyone else's gratitude.

Diana Bloch emerged from her office right on cue. Her skirt and dress shirt were still wrinkle-free, as was her makeup, even though she had been at work for at least eighteen hours. But Morgan knew how to look and saw the signs of fatigue—slightly sagging posture, a bit of swelling under her eyes, and movements just a little slower than usual.

Bloch turned on the recorder and spoke. "This is a debrief for operation number 1198M-9. Subject is Daniel Morgan, code name Cobra, internal designation AZ27-F. Speaking is Diana Bloch, AZ04-D, with Paul Kirby, AZ43-I. Gentlemen, please confirm your presence."

"Paul Kirby. Confirmed."

"Dan Morgan. Confirmed."

"Thank you. Agent Morgan, please relate your interaction with General James Collins on the night of October ninth."

Morgan rattled off the details with little emotion. "When I arrived at his bedroom, he was already alert to my presence and trained a handgun on me. He did not know it was me until I identified myself. He was paranoid. Jumpy. He was being watched."

"By whom?" Kirby asked.

"Unknown. He, and I, assumed the government. Nothing more specific than that."

"It was at this point that you removed your communicator. Is that right?"

"Yes."

"Why did you do that?"

"He asked me to," Morgan said.

"But you told him about it."

"That's right."

"Why did you do that?" Kirby demanded. "If you'd left it in and on, he'd never have been the wiser."

"It's called trust," Morgan said simply before turning his head to look directly into Kirby's intent gaze. "It's the reason I was sent to talk to him and not you."

"Maintain focus," Bloch said in warning. "Morgan, what exactly did Collins say when the communicator was off?"

"He maintained his innocence and that he was being framed by another army general: Sheldon Margolis."

They tried to hide it, but Morgan caught their twitching reflex to look at one another. That name meant something to them.

"Did he say anything else about General Margolis?" Bloch asked flatly.

"That he's powerful and getting rid of his rivals in order to consolidate power. And Collins is the last obstacle in his path."

"That all?" Kirby asked. "No details?"

"Nothing," Morgan said about as flatly as Bloch had spoken. "He asked for help."

"Did he say how you might help?" Bloch asked.

"He asked me to investigate Margolis and clear his name. That was it." Morgan didn't mention Alicia Schmitt.

"Thank you, Morgan," said Bloch. "That will be all for now."

"That's it? What are we going to do about this?"

"*You* are not going to do anything," Kirby said.

"But I know him. I'm the one who's best positioned to help him."

"Our mission is not to help General Collins."

"What the hell do you mean? That *is* the goddamn mission."

"Your mission," she stressed, "was to contact Collins and find out whatever possible. You did that, and you're done. We will call you as soon as we have a new assignment."

"This isn't right, Diana. You know it isn't."

"Finding those missing missiles are not our prerogative. We do what we are told. Nothing more."

Morgan's next words were quick but strong. He wanted to get them on the record. "The feds aren't going to do jackshit about finding them. Not while they have the wrong damn guy, especially not if someone in the government is in on it. They're wasting their time on him while—"

"Your trust in Collins is misplaced and misguided," Paul Kirby interjected. "We used your familiarity with Collins to attempt extracting useful information from him. We have exhausted that approach. You're too close to this. We cannot rely on you to keep your objectivity."

Before Morgan could retort, Bloch cut in. "I have to agree with Kirby on this," she said evenly. "You have strong personal feelings invested in this. You are dismissed." With a short stab of her finger, she switched off the recorder.

Chapter Nine

Lincoln Shepard was not a field operative, so when someone grabbed his T-shirt and yanked him into a maintenance closet as he was hurrying to the War Room, he expected the worst. To his shame, his hands went up, and he opened his mouth to shriek, only to have fingers clamp his lips shut—fingers that were firm but also soft and smooth.

He stared into the blue eyes of Karen O'Neal, gleaming in the small enclosure's darkness.

"Shhh, shh, shh," she urged with a conspiratorial grin.

To his credit, Shepard got over his surprise almost immediately. "Well, hello there."

But O'Neal had no time for niceties. Her hands were already on his pants' zipper. "We have ten minutes until Bloch gets out of her meeting, and I intend to make them count!"

At first Shepard thought the beeping he heard was his heart, but when Karen's fingers stopped dancing he realized it was someone hailing him on his vid-trans—a car-key-sized device in his pocket. He grinned apologetically. "I gotta get that." He dug into his pocket as O'Neal stepped back, folding her arms grumpily.

"It better be important."

It was Lily. "This better be important," he said to her.

"It is," the redhead announced. "Scott has it. He found the origin of the card!"

Shepard alerted Bloch, joined her and Karen in the War Room, and threw Lily's image up on the big screen as if by digital magic.

"The card comes from an exclusive nightclub and casino in Seoul, South Korea," Lily reported. "Probably VIP access. It's for a specific date, too—tomorrow night."

"Lukacs isn't exactly the club type," Shepard surmised. "He's probably going for a meet."

"And this kind of access is expensive," Lily added. "Whoever it is, if this is worth the cost, he's meeting a big fish—a very big fish."

"But wouldn't he change the date and place of the meet if he suspects we have the card?" Shepard wondered.

"Maybe not," Lily answered. "Scott...Mr. Renard says that no one would have been able to decipher the card except him."

"Not even Zeta?" Shepard retorted doubtfully.

"Not even Zeta," Lily maintained. "Sorry, Linc."

"If there's a prize bigger than Lukacs," Bloch interrupted, "it's worth the risk. Lily, you take this one."

Lily's words caught in her throat, just before she said, "I was afraid you'd say that." She had been truly enjoying her vacation.

"We'll have a flight arranged by morning," Bloch briskly continued. "We'll send details shortly."

She cut off the call and stood up, mind already on the next piece of business. "O'Neal, I want to go over your models of world arms sales in my office."

Shepard grimaced, but Karen just shrugged and made the I'll-call-you gesture behind Bloch's back

Lincoln Shepard collected his things and sulked his way out of Zeta headquarters—driving home along the empty night streets. He arrived at his apartment and turned on the lights to find someone sitting in his living room.

"Sweet mother of Sam, Morgan, don't do that!"

"Sorry. I need your help."

"Those are, literally, my least favorite words." Shepard threw his coat on the couch. "You couldn't have called?"

"I didn't want anyone to know I was here."

"Oh, that makes me feel better." He pulled a bowl from a cupboard. "Lucky Charms?"

"No thanks," Morgan said. "Shepard, listen—"

"Should I bother to tell you to find me during office hours? That whatever I can do for you should be done through official Zeta channels rather than—"

"This can't go through Zeta," he said.

Shepard poured the milk into the cereal. "Of course it can't."

"I'm serious, Shepard. Can you keep this quiet?"

"I can't promise without knowing what it is."

"I can't tell you what it is until you promise."

"Well, that's a real conundrum, isn't it?" He spoke through a mouthful of sickly sweet cereal.

"It's not a big deal. I promise. It won't take long."

Shepard looked at his associate with an expression that said "Does it look like I was born yesterday?" "Yes," he clucked. "I'm sure that any favor that's no big deal requires breaking and entering."

Shepard put down his spoon. He couldn't say no to Morgan. He had never been able to in all the time they worked together. He felt sure that if it was important enough for Morgan to ambush him this way, it was important enough for him to try accomplishing. It wasn't as fun as Karen's ambush, but still...

"What's the nature of this favor?" he asked.

"I need to find someone," Morgan said.

"Who?"

"I'll tell you when you promise."

"Damn it, Morgan, I don't know. This is going to get me in deep shit with Bloch."

"Nobody should know. Least of all Bloch."

"Would she agree with that assessment, you think?"

"No, because she wouldn't find out about it."

The computer whiz couldn't argue with that, and his quizzical expression encouraged Morgan to press his advantage.

"Shepard. This is important. You know I wouldn't be asking if it wasn't."

"Yeah. That's what I'm afraid of." Shepard put the now-empty bowl in the sink. He wouldn't even consider the request were it coming from anyone else. But Morgan was not just anyone. Shepard didn't know anyone whose loyalties had been tested more harshly and had maintained his principles throughout. "Fine. I promise I won't tell anyone, and if I can help you, I will." He crossed the small living room to pick up one of his many laptops. "So who is it that I am looking for?"

"Alicia Schmitt. She's a navy commander. Number and address are unlisted. I need to find her."

"Is this about Collins?"

"Do you really want to know?"

"Good point."

"I promise, this will all be explained eventually. Even to Bloch. And you'll understand why I had to keep it a secret. But right now, I just need you to trust me."

"Already do," Shepard reported absently since his fingers were already flying over the keyboard and track pad. The search was a little more difficult than Shepard had anticipated, which is to say that it took longer than a minute. "Here. Is this her?"

"You got it?"

Shepard scoffed. "Do I got it? Who do you think you're talking to here?" Shepard had something to prove. Lily's comment that her boy toy was better than him still smarted. He sent the document to the printer. "This is her home address in D.C. Family connections, known friends and associates, stats, and details on her training." He picked up the packet from the tray and held it out for Morgan. "Will that do?" he inquired innocently.

"That will be just fine." Morgan stuffed the documents into his messenger bag. "And remember—"

"Not a word. Don't worry. It's my ass as much as yours now."

Chapter Ten

Alex pulled her black Kawasaki Ninja motorcycle into her parents' driveway. It was little wonder she had been so good on the Honda back in Prague. She had taken to motorcycles ever since the seat of her jeans had touched the leather of motorbikes' seats years ago. It was early morning, so birds were singing, and the suburban cul-de-sac was all but deserted. Everyone was either at work or indoors, hiding away from the slowly intensifying cold.

She was hoping to catch her father still at home. Something was up. She could tell from his voice when she'd talked to him the day before. They grew up with great love, but now that they were in the fire of espionage together as well, he let his guard down with her. But, for whatever reason, she had a kind of sixth sense when it came to him.

She opened the front door and did catch him—red-handed at that—with a travel bag in his hand. It was the one he kept packed, in his office, ready to go at any time. The one he took when he was going on a mission, which he wasn't, or she'd know. At least not an official one.

"Where are you going?"

"Don't ask me. You never saw me. You were never here. *Capisce*?"

"Sorry," Alex replied, standing her ground. "You can't talk to me like that anymore. In case you hadn't noticed I'm not just your child. Now I'm Zeta's child too."

Morgan appreciated the meaning in her message. But the love they had for each other went both ways. "Well, I'm still your father. That doesn't change no matter how old you are or what job you have."

Alex nodded, allowing him to score the point. "But that doesn't mean you can boss me around," she reminded him. But as he was opening his mouth for a quick reply, she put up her hands in a surrendering position.

"Oh, let's just cut to the chase, shall we? You're going to help Collins, right?" He didn't respond, but his determined expression was all she needed. "Okay. Why go alone?"

Morgan exhaled sharply. "Zeta's not letting me follow where this is leading. Someone's playing them—someone behind the scenes. And while they go after the wrong guy, the missiles are going to slip right through their fingers. I'm not going to let that happen."

"Then let me go with you."

"No. You'll..." She saw him struggling to find the right words. "You'll get in the way."

Anger burned on her cheeks. "I won't accept that. How many times have I saved you already? I'm an operative now, Dad. Just like you."

"Just like me?" Morgan echoed, leaning in. "Do you have twenty years' experience in the field? You're barely twenty years old! Tell me, Alex. How many times have you had to stare death in the face?"

"Plenty."

"Not enough. Not by a long shot. This is not going to be a careful operation with backup and surveillance. This is going to be me, solo, off the grid, with the US government on my ass."

Alex couldn't argue with that, so she retreated to her original position. "It doesn't have to be solo. Let me help you!"

"You can't. Not this time. Stay here and do what Bloch tells you. Nothing good will come of you getting involved in this."

"Dad, I've proved myself—again and again. Whenever I got caught up in one of your missions, I went beyond all expectations. And now I'm holding my own with seasoned pros. Honestly, don't you even see me? Do you really give me that little credit?"

"Goddamn it!" Morgan seethed, nearly dropping his bag. "Don't you get it? When I'm with the others, my full attention is on the mission. No distractions, no fears. But when you're there...when you're there..."

His expression softened, seeing that tears were playing on the corner of his daughter's eyes. "You really are a remarkable young woman. I don't think I tell you that enough."

"I am, Dad," Alex replied yet finally with a full understanding of his situation. "But as much as you want to think of me as your little girl, as much as I know you want to protect me, you have to let me grow up. You have to let me make my own mistakes."

"But in this business," he answered quietly, "mistakes can get you killed."

She shrugged. They both knew that risk was part of the job they had chosen. "You have to see me as I am," she said simply.

"I do, Alex. Sometimes I forget how much you've grown."

She crossed the distance to him and hugged him, squeezing him tight. She released, looking up into his eyes.

"I love you, honey," he said.

Click.

She felt a tightness on her right wrist as her father moved away from her.

"Dad?" She tried to raise her right hand, but something jerked it back.

"I'm sorry, honey." Her right wrist was in handcuffs, which were affixed to a wrought-iron bar from the heavy side table. "I can't have you coming with me. Not this time."

"Dad? You can't leave me like this." She yanked at the cuffs, trying to twist herself loose. "Dad!"

"Careful. You'll hurt yourself."

Tears streamed down her face. She was rubbing her wrists raw by tugging against the cuffs, but she didn't care. "You can't do this!"

"I'm sorry, sweetheart. You left me no choice. This is going to be too dangerous for you. If I have to worry about you, I'm going to put both of us at risk."

"Dad, let me go."

He drew the keys from his pocket and tossed them into the kitchen. "Your mother will free you when she gets home."

"Let me go!" Alex screeched.

"Stay safe. I love you." He turned around. "Neika, come on!" He walked out, shutting the front door behind him.

"Dad!" she hollered. "Don't do this, Dad!"

But he didn't respond.

Alex pulled at the side table, trying to drag it across the floor toward the kitchen. But it was too heavy. It hardly budged.

"Dad! Come back!" As she screamed at him, she heard the sound of his car engine as he drove away.

Chapter Eleven

Lily woke in Scott's arms. Early-morning light peeked through the floor-to-ceiling window overlooking the bay. Scott didn't care about decoration—it was like he hardly even noticed the spaces around him since his mind was always on some abstract problem—so his bedroom had been put together by a second-rate decorator who'd probably charged him a fortune to sprinkle his living spaces with ugly modern art. The exception was his bed—a California king with the most perfectly balanced mattress she'd ever slept on.

She left her sleeping boyfriend to shower, letting the warm water clear away everything from the day before, the good and bad. It was something approaching a ritual, preparing her to leave for her new mission.

She returned to the bedroom, wrapped in a fluffy white towel, to find him sitting up on the bed, looking despondent. She didn't feel like dealing with him, so she just said, "Good morning," as she wiped her exposed skin with a facecloth.

"I wish you could stay," he said.

"Me too." Her heart wasn't into it, though. Not that it wasn't true. It was just that her mind was already on the mission, and the danger to come.

"I wish—" he continued. "I wish you could come live with me."

"Scott..."

"Well, why not? I'm crazy about you, and I think you like me too—"

"I do, but—"

"Then what's the problem?"

She squirmed in her towel. "Headquarters is in Boston."

"Maybe they can transfer you over here. Or I can afford to send you to Boston whenever you'd like. Business class, private jet, you name it."

"Scott ..."

"I mean, do you even need it? This job, I mean."

"Are you asking me if I need a job? Christ, do rich people know anything about real life?"

"I wasn't born rich, Lily. In fact, I've been rich for only twenty percent of my life. I know what it means to want money. What I'm saying is that you don't have to do *this* job."

"And what is it that you think I should be doing?"

"Someone as smart and competent as you—I could get you a job that pays twice what Zeta's paying you, guaranteed. Hell, I bet you've never worked an office job in your life, but smart and ruthless as you are, I already know you'd make a killer executive."

"Well, technically—"

"I'm serious, Lily. Even with gaps in your business experience, any company in the Valley would be lucky to have you. Hell, worse comes to worse, I'd hire you myself. We'd have plenty of uses for you. And it's not like you'd need the money anyway if you were with me. I already have more than I'd know what to do with for several lifetimes."

That struck a nerve with Lily. "Have you considered that I wouldn't want to be your lapdog? Or that I don't want to work in an office where I have to talk about quarterly earnings and marketing strategies and profit margins?"

"Is that really so much worse than risking your life?"

"What, wasting my life on something I'd hate? Yes. I mean has it crossed your blinkered male mind that I do what I want because I want to do it?" Fuming, she stood up, the towel falling to the floor. "And has it occurred to you that you fell in love with me because this is who I am and that changing everything about that would make me another one of the many women you're bored to death of?"

"I could never be bored of you."

"Oh yeah? Just wait until I'm two years into a high-powered corporate job. Damn it, Scott, you can barely stand to talk about that stuff. Imagine if that's what you had to come home to as well?"

He stared at her naked shape, having a hard time maintaining his concentration. "It'd still be you."

"It doesn't matter," she said, "because I don't want it. I'm not a damsel in distress waiting for someone to save me. I'm already exactly where I want to be." She picked up the towel and wrapped it around her remarkable body.

Scott took his time to reply and did not make eye contact with her. "Sorry, I guess."

"Don't sulk. It really isn't a good look for you." She got into a pair of tight black denim pants from the night before. "Anyway, I'll be back in a couple of days."

"Unless something happens to you, which isn't all that unlikely, right?"

"Nothing's going to happen to me."

"You can't promise that."

"Tell you what," she said, clasping her bra. "What I can promise you is that, next time I'm in town, I'm staying right here with you. Okay? No more hotels for me." She pulled on a wrinkled emerald-green top.

"Yeah, fine," he said without much enthusiasm. "That'd be good."

"Whatever," she said, now fully dressed. She planted a perfunctory kiss on his lips, knowing that he was going to resent the dry farewell. "I'll call you."

"If you survive."

She shut the bedroom door behind her, swearing under her breath as she made her way out of his labyrinthine house.

Chapter Twelve

Jenny Morgan came home to find Alex's motorcycle in the driveway.

Her daughter at home was a nice surprise, but oh, how she hated that bike. It was everything she hated about Alex's and Dan's lifestyle: risky and reckless and too damn fast.

She knew that loving a dangerous man would mean a lifetime of worrying, and she loved him enough to live with that.

Jenny went inside and set her purse and keys on the kitchen counter. "Alex?"

Her daughter's voice came from the living room. "Mom?"

"Alex? Where are you?"

"In here."

"What are you doing—oh my Lord, are you okay?"

She was sitting on the floor, holding her hand up close to her head—and only then did Jenny see the handcuffs.

"Yeah, I'm fine," Alex said.

"You sound awfully calm for someone cuffed to the furniture. What happened? Who did this to you? Was it burglars? Are we in danger?"

"No, Mom, it's fine. It was Dad."

"What?"

"Mom, it's really no big deal."

"No big deal?"

"Could you let me out? The key's somewhere in the kitchen. On the floor, I think. I'll explain everything."

Jenny was annoyed by Alex's attitude, as if she had no call to be worried at finding her daughter locked to a table, as if finding that her husband had left her there made any kind of difference.

She just let out a weary groan and went to grab the key, which she found in the corner, hidden under the edge of a kitchen cupboard. She came back to Alex and knelt to unlock the cuffs.

"I don't suppose you'll do me the courtesy of explaining to me why my husband left our one and only daughter chained up like an animal."

"It's classified," Alex said, getting up and rubbing her wrist where the cuffs held it.

"Young lady, you will tell me what is happening."

"I can't—"

"Do *not*," Jenny said. "I am your mother, and we are talking about your father. I have had it with being kept in the dark. I have had it with you two disappearing on me. Tell me what's going on."

"Oh, all right. We had a bit of a disagreement about an assignment. I mean 'we, ' including our bosses at Zeta. I wanted to stop him from doing something stupid, and he went ahead and did it anyway. You know Dad."

"I certainly do." Something struck Jenny all of a sudden. A curious absence. "Where's Neika?"

"Dad took her with him. I have no idea why."

Jenny's heart sank. "I think I can imagine, and it doesn't make me happy."

"What?"

"Neika was trained as a bomb-sniffing military dog. Your father worked with her on a mission, and I guess he grew attached. That's where we got her."

"Yeah," she said. "That makes sense."

Alex's nonchalance was infuriating. "Sense?" she exclaimed. "As in, it's no surprise that my husband would need a bomb-sniffing dog?"

"Mom, really. I found out Dad wasn't a classic-car dealer at about the same time as you, remember?"

Jenny controlled herself. "All right, all right, I get it."

Alex rubbed her wrist. "Good. Thanks. I need to go. I need to take care of this. Are you okay?"

"Yes, I'll be fine," Jenny said unconvincingly, hoping her daughter would take the emotional bait.

But instead, Alex just said, "Great. Love you!" Then she disappeared out the door, leaving Jenny there, steaming.

Mrs. Morgan was tired of being shunted aside whenever they went off on their little adventures. She was tired of being kept out of the loop until it was all over, hoping it would work out but being blocked from any information or involvement—as every single day all she dreamed about was, first, standing at her husband's funeral, and then, maybe even worse, standing at her daughter's grave.

Standing in the foyer of her house, Jenny made a decision. She didn't know how. But she knew what she was going to do.

Chapter Thirteen

Morgan parked his car in sight of Alicia Schmitt's house in Arlington, Virginia, half an hour before dawn—which was scheduled that day for 5:22 A.M.

She was military, which meant she wouldn't go one day without exercise. And if she was military, it was going to be obscenely early. He knew the type, and from what Shepard had been able to dig up on her, she was *definitely* the type.

A precocious talent, the decorated veteran had shot up through the ranks of the navy. She'd made commander the year before and was now the youngest woman of her rank. She wasn't assigned to a ship but served as an executive officer. Whatever work she did was highly classified, and even Shepard couldn't get to it—at least not fast enough to be useful to Morgan.

He needed to talk to her away from prying eyes. Ringing her doorbell was a bad idea, approaching her at work was out of the question, and it wasn't unlikely that she was being watched, which meant he was going to have to force a chance encounter.

Right on cue, Schmitt emerged from her house at dawn in sneakers and a green track suit. She took off at a brisk jog as soon as her feet hit the sidewalk. He needed to keep up without attracting attention to himself. He was already dressed as a jogger in muted grays. He let her gain a little distance and then got out of his car.

His bad knee complained for the first hundred yards or so, but after a little bit of warm-up he had no trouble keeping up with her—maintaining the distance while putting cars and trees between them as much as possible.

Within a few minutes they arrived at a park with a sign that read Alcova Heights. Instead of following her outright, Morgan took a parallel path, rounding the tennis courts. She greeted an early guard who was keeping watch. She headed for a wooded area, out of sight of any of the public.

Morgan made his move, cutting across the woods to intercept her. He slowed to a walk, keeping cover behind a thicket as he neared the path. She was approaching, her jogging keeping a steady rhythm on the crunchy leaves, growing louder as she approached. He was going to have to be careful not to spook her. In his mind, he rehearsed what he was going to say, playing out her possible reactions and how he might convince her of his good faith.

Turned out it was unnecessary. When she was on the other side of the thicket, the running stopped. He emerged from behind it, in full view of her, to find her holding a gun aimed at him. It was a Smith and Wesson Model 60 Lady. Matte stainless finish, wood grip, 2.125-inch barrel. .357 Magnum, capacity five rounds, which was four more than necessary to make corned beef hash out of his brains.

"You're a little big to think you can sneak up on me."

Schmitt had the face of a woman who was years past taking any shit from men, like she'd hit her quota of leering jokes, drunken passes, and underestimation somewhere around her first tour of duty and decided she was having none of it from anyone.

But even she was surprised when he laughed with honest, self-deprecating, mirth, and said, "Like teacher, like student."

She instantly recognized he wasn't being disingenuous or smarmy. "What's the game?" she asked. "What teacher, what student?" He shifted, and her aimed moved to his crotch. "Just so I can decide where to shoot you if you take another step toward me."

He put up his hands and tried to look as honest as possible. "Student, you. Teacher, General James Collins.

Hearing the name took her aback. He could see it in her eyes that her mind was processing, reassessing assumptions about the encounter, and trying to figure out what it meant. She opened her mouth to speak but didn't seem to know what to say until she settled on, "Who are you?"

"Dan Morgan."

"That means nothing to me."

"Jim asked for my help."

"Funny way to make an introduction," she said, but he could see she was stalling.

Morgan frowned. "You don't know."

"Know what?"

"He was taken into police custody last night."

"No shit." She seemed, somehow, not surprised.

"Did you know he was in trouble?"

Instead of answering, she said, "Why you? Why me?"

"He sent me. He told me that Margolis is setting him up, and planning to have you take the fall with him. If we don't stop him."

"What do you mean 'we'?"

"Okay," he said. "If you won't help, I'll do it anyway." He pinioned her with a stare. "But that's not the way Jim wanted it."

"Excuse me if I don't believe you. Who really sent you?"

Morgan finally got it. He finally understood why Schmitt was being so furtive. "You weren't really worried about burglars in the park, were you?" he asked. "Who's after you?"

"You don't get to ask," she maintained, the gun rising to his heart level.

"Hey," he complained, "I approached you unarmed."

"Maybe you wanted information," she said.

"I definitely want information. General Collins told me you had enough of to clear him."

Her eyes began to waver. He saw she was waging some sort of internal battle. The stress on her, maybe since just hearing of Collins's arrest, must have been enormous and was building.

"I don't know you from Adam," she finally said. "My trust is not so easily earned, not even by mentioning the general."

"He told me to ask you about Virginia."

Her countenance changed. Surprise. Anger. "What did you say?"

"You heard me," Morgan said. He had succeeded in bringing her up short, which was a good thing when someone was threatening you with a gun. It was a step up from her wanting to kill him.

"What else did he say?"

"Exact words: 'If she doesn't believe you, ask her about Virginia. Tell her I told you to say that.' That's it. He said you'd know what it meant. He suggested you'd trust me if I said it."

She holstered her gun.

"He was wrong. Today, that buys your life. Don't try a second time. And if you follow me now, I will shoot you down."

He watched as she jogged away, disappearing around a bend in the path.

Chapter Fourteen

"He's gone dark."

Lincoln Shepard was working two of his laptops, side by side, his gray eyes flicking from comm apps to trackers as his fingers flew like a mad pianist's. The War Room tabletop was greasy with half-eaten pizzas and sloshed-over Styrofoam cups, and the fake blue sky above streamed shafts of sunlight onto the gleaming wood through wisps of phony clouds.

"What do you mean 'dark'?" Paul Kirby was incredulous, his flabby lips turned down more than usual.

"I mean like in nighttime, black, silent, impenetrable," Shepard said as his fingertips stabbed at the keys. "You know, like you can't see shit."

Diana Bloch paced behind her command chair. She was wearing a gray pantsuit, pink blouse, and a string of modest pearls. She rarely paced over anything or anyone, but they'd been trying to raise Morgan since the start of business, which at Zeta headquarters meant 0700, sharp. She slapped a manicured hand on the leather.

"I told him to stand down. You all heard it."

"Yes, we heard it, Diana." Kirby dropped his heavy glasses on the table, where they bounced once and clattered. "And we recorded the debriefing." He rubbed his wispy eyebrows. "Mr. Smith may not be pleased," he concluded.

Bloch stopped pacing, looking at her subordinate as if he had invoked Bigfoot or the Yeti. "Excuse me?"

Kirby glanced at her sideways. "He already knows. I had to tell him. You know I did." When Bloch said nothing, simply stared at him as if trying to see where his brain stem met his spine, Kirby continued, seemingly trying not to babble. "Standard operating procedure, Diana. You made those regulations yourself. If an agent fails to respond for more than two hours, he's either dead or something else."

"Something else such as what?" Her voice sounded like a scalpel cutting flesh.

"Gone rogue." Kirby leaned back and puffed up his chest.

"Nonsense." She flicked her wrist and a bracelet jangled.

"Really? We've been trying to raise him since breakfast."

Bloch looked at him, rolled her chair aside, pressed her hips to the table edge, and leaned on her palms. "Yes, AZ43-I, I made the regulations concerning agents missing for more than a hundred twenty minutes. But I know of no standard operating procedure where the chain of is superseded to report concerns to the head of recruitment..."

Kirby knew he was in trouble. Bloch only used official internal designations when she was one step from decapitation. "You know he's more than..."

"The...head...of...recruitment," Bloch repeated in a tone so far beyond stern that even Kirby snapped his jaw shut.

Bloch's eyes blazed, but then she turned sharply away and started barking orders. Within minutes, the faces remaining from Lukacs's extraction team were looking down from the wide, curving screen that encircled half the table. It was Conley, Bishop, Spartan, and Diesel—each in a different location—reporting in as ordered. Both Dan and Alex Morgan were notable by their absence.

"Good afternoon, people." Bloch sat down in her chair. "Cobra has been AWOL for half a day."

"We're working on that," Kirby interjected. "I'm thinking that perhaps he's..."

Bloch cut him off like a hangnail. "The situation requires actualities, not suppositions," she snapped before twisting her head toward Shepard. "Well?"

Shepard's cheeks flushed crimson. "Um, I've tried everything I could. Apparently he's done something with his earpiece and stripped the battery out of his cell."

"What about his car?" Kirby prodded Shepard.

"That's why he drives that old muscle car," Shepard said. "Anything with a computer chip I can crack, but that thing's about as trackable as a bicycle."

Bloch leaned forward. She already knew about the untraceability of the muscle car. "People, this behavior is clearly indicative of something other than Cobra wishing for a bit of respite while he engages in a morning tryst. If you recall, we are in the midst of a critical operation. The bodies of US servicemen and women are arriving at Dover this very afternoon, and I believe we still have an issue of missing ordnance of the most troubling type. Now, none of us apparently knows what Cobra is up to. However, should he interfere with the other strains of your operational activities, there will be hell to pay. Do I make myself clear?"

"Crystal clear, ma'am," Conley answered for the team.

"Good. Now, I, with significant urging"—she nodded at Kirby— "am placing Zeta on full alert." She swung her steely gaze on the team. "Gentlemen, madam?"

"Yes?" Spartan replied to the latter designation.

"Reel in our snake," Bloch ordered. "At your earliest convenience." Her meaning was not lost on any of them. Their only assignment for the foreseeable future was to find, and bring in, Dan Morgan, with all the help of Zeta's considerable reach.

With a flick of a switchblade-like fingernail, Bloch punched the button that rendered the screen blank. Shepard exhaled a slow hiss of relief from his lungs. Bloch noted that Kirby was barely concealing a satisfied smirk, yet she controlled her steam.

"Paul, make the rounds to all the departments, brief them, and get them up on Alert Status Alpha."

Kirby frowned. "I can do that from my office on intercom."

"Do it on foot, as of now."

He pushed himself up from his chair, made a show of finishing up a cup of cold coffee, and went out. Bloch turned to Shepard.

"Where's Alex?"

He leaned into a laptop and punched up the operative schedules. "Day off."

"Cancel it and bring her in."

"Will do."

Bloch picked up her leather briefcase and her cell phone and made for the door. Then she turned. "And Shepard, the utility and storage closets are meant for just that. If you and Ms. O'Neal desperately need some private time, ask me, and I'll send you to lunch. Whether you eat or not is up to you."

She walked out as Shepard's blush returned full force. He'd forgotten somehow that the whole place was wired and that Bloch could listen into to any Zeta conversation, or whatever else, anywhere, anytime. But what made him shake his head and feel really idiotic was that he'd designed that whole bug job himself.

Mentally kicking himself, Shepard set about finding, and calling in, Alex. But as he did it, he couldn't help wondering what was that all about. If he didn't know better, he'd guess that there was some sort of trouble in paradise.

Although the computer whiz was used to Dan Morgan ignoring protocol to do what he thought best, he had never witnessed such a near confrontation like that in the War Room before. Even so, experience told him it was best not to get involved. Biting his lip, he looked at the door Bloch had just left from.

"Weasel bites *you*; then you bite *me*. Just like corporate."

* * * *

Diana walked into her office, tossed her briefcase on the desk, took off her suit jacket, and slumped in her chair. She rolled her pearls in her fingers and thought about Dan Morgan. He'd gone rogue all right, disobeying orders and trying to clear General Collins despite his instructions to stand down.

Morgan was a top-notch operative, but he was also like some rebellious elementary schoolkid she always had to keep her eye on. Tell him not to play with matches, then leave him alone, and the next thing you know the house is on fire.

She sat back, and slowly, a smile grew on her lips.
Perfect.

Chapter Fifteen

Jenny Morgan drove her crimson Toyota Camry in a fit of frustration, running a few stop signs as she gunned it through Andover.

She didn't exactly know where she was going, but she had to get out of the damn house and go *somewhere*. Dan was gone again, leaving her for probably the five hundredth time, tight-lipped and secretive and sharing nothing. It was always like that and had been forever. She was the stay-at-home mom waiting and worrying, and then he'd show up and charm her and ravage her, and she'd forget all about how painful it was until that damn cell of his buzzed and he'd do it all over again.

Honk!

She slammed on the brakes at the middle school intersection. A blue pickup full of rakes and leaf blowers crossed right to left, the baseball-capped driver shaking his fist out the window. She stuck out her tongue and shot him the bird, something she never, ever, did on the streets—too many road-rage crazies out there. He laughed and shot her the finger right back. It felt good, but she rolled forward again, more carefully.

And now it was all so much worse, she reminded herself. Alex, who'd grown up despising her father's secrecy and emotional distance, had gone right ahead and joined him in his "national security" misadventures. That was the last thing on earth she'd seen coming, and now all her fears about someday losing Dan were doubled.

Oh God, she fumed inwardly as the tears glistened at the corners of her eyes. *I could wind up at both of their graves, side-by-side, while some government asshole gives me two folded flags instead of just one!*

She tried to focus on driving again and coasted up carefully to a stop light. The Camry went quiet and just idled with barely a whine. She fumed some more. Dan roared around in his hotshot Shelby, Alex rode her stupid motorcycle like some *Mad Max* movie stunt girl, and she was stuck with the prissy hybrid. Typical.

She took a right and drove south on Main Street, past the majestic old Memorial Library and the rows of quaint and cozy stores—thinking about how all her fellow New Englanders bustled happily along without a clue or a care about what was really going on in the world. She made a quick, illegal U-turn in front of the post office, parked in front of Kabloom, got out, and slammed the door.

She looked down and frowned as she realized she was dressed to please Dan: pointy pumps, tight jeans, that cowboy belt he'd bought her somewhere, and a frothy cream sweater. She knew she looked good and still turned heads for a woman her age, but she wished she'd dressed in an ugly frock.

As she headed into Starbucks, a good-looking young blond man coming the other way smiled at her.

"Miss, could you tell me what time it is?"

"Yeah," Jenny snapped. "Time for you to get a watch."

He jerked his head back and gave her a wide berth.

The place was packed as usual, with college kids and young execs hunched over the tables and pecking away at their laptops. She should have gone over to Dunkin' Donuts; nobody was ever in there. The girl behind the counter smiled when she ordered an Americano and asked, "Grande?"

"Just small, thank you," Jenny mumbled and paid.

She found a seat at a table the size of a bathroom scale, sipped the bitter brew, and stared out the front window. *I'm changing this arrangement. I'm not going to be the third wheel in my own darned house!*

"You mind, hon?"

Jenny looked up. A woman was standing in front of her, one hand on the facing free chair. She looked sort of like that country-western singer, Reba what's-her-name, with glossy red hair and smiling green eyes. And she had that accent.

"Sure," Jenny said, although the last thing she needed was company. The woman smiled and sat. She was wearing an open-necked green blouse and a dungaree jacket with some shiny studs. She took a sip of her latte.

"Thanks. Sorta crazy 'round here today."

"Always is," Jenny said, "which I never understand because the coffee's so bad."

"I know!" The woman chuckled. "Not my cup of tea either, so to speak."

Jenny smiled. "You're not from around here."

"Atlanta. Came up to visit my sister. My husband's gone half the time so I gotta keep myself busy."

"Oh?" Jenny sat back in her chair. Her shoulders were tight, and she rubbed the back of her neck.

"Yep. Army man." The woman rolled her eyes. "Shoulda known better."

"Boy, do I get that." Jenny sighed. "Mine's a government guy."

The woman put her elbows on the table and leaned in. "Are we gals stupid, or what?"

Jenny laughed. "I guess you don't see it coming when you're young."

"Don't see it comin', and it hits you like an eighteen-wheeler, right? Everything's a gosh-darn crisis. Everything's a big top secret. And if you ever put up a fuss and want some attention, you're a regular communist traitor or something!"

Jenny slapped the table with her fingers. "That's *exactly* how I feel, all the time."

"I know it, Hon." The woman opened a purse, took out a lipstick and touched up using the screen of her cell phone. "We girls oughta start some government widows' revenge club. Next time Jim's comin' back from wherever, I'm gonna leave him a blowup doll in our bed, a wilted rose, and a 'see y'all' note."

Jenny laughed again. Just by chance, this encounter was exactly what she'd needed today.

The woman looked around, leaned in again, and whispered.

"Know what I finally did?"

Jenny leaned in too.

"No. What?"

"I *snooped*." The woman nodded. "That's right. I figured his business is my business. Not playin' that game anymore. Now, whenever he goes, I know where to find his orders, where he's goin', what he's doin'. First time I did that he Skyped me and I said to him, 'James, you sure as heck better be in Kabul!' Thought he was gonna have a bird, but he knows not to mess with me now."

"Wow," Jenny said. "You're something else." She stuck out her hand. "I'm Jenny."

"Melissa." They shook.

"So, how'd you do it, Melissa?"

"Oh, come on, girl!" Melissa flicked her fingers in the air. "They're men! They can't find the milk in the fridge when it's starin' them right in the face. Think they can *actually* hide something?"

Jenny sighed. "My husband doesn't tell me a thing."

"That's a dang male power trip, hon. Gotta take back the power. Girl power!" She looked at her watch and downed the rest of her coffee. "I better scoot. Sis is picking me up, and we're gonna spend some of Jim's money." She reached out and squeezed Jenny's wrist. "Now you show Mr. Secrets who's boss."

Jenny grinned. "I think I will, Melissa. And thanks."

"You betcha." Melissa got up, turned to go, then stopped beside her chair, and twisted around. She was wearing tight jeans like Jenny's, and she pointed one pink fingernail at her cheek.

"See this?" she said. "*This* is the power!" and she grinned and was gone.

Jenny sat there for a while, stunned by this strange woman's wisdom that seemed to have dropped out of heaven. But she was totally right. Why should she let Dan play his silly secret games while he kept her in the dark all the time and let her worry herself gray? She remembered some old army phrase he loved using whenever he felt like his superiors were screwing with him. "Yeah, treat me like a friggin' mushroom. Keep me in the dark and feed me bullshit." Well, she was no longer going to be *his* mushroom. If he wanted her to be his partner at home and in bed, then he'd have to accept her as his partner *everywhere*.

She got up, tossed the empty cup in the wastebasket, went to her car, and burned rubber, heading for home.

* * * *

Down the block, tucked back into Post Office Street, Melissa sat in her silver Lexus and watched Jenny's crimson Toyota flash by. She smiled, reached up, took off the red wig, and scratched her itchy scalp.

Jenny was now in play, and with Alex already a major worry for Morgan, adding his wife to the mix would keep him from doing anything too wild and crazy. The woman who had made herself "Melissa" opened the back of her cell, slipped the battery back in, powered it up, and called an unlisted number.

Lincoln Shepard answered.

"This is Bloch," Diana said. "Tell me you've got something on Cobra."

"Negative, ma'am. And I've been trying to reach you about something else."

"I was having a manicure. A girl's still a girl. Be back in half an hour."

She hung up, put the Lexus in gear, and headed for Boston.

Chapter Sixteen

Jenny stood in the kitchen, arms folded, leaning back on the central butcher-block island and nursing a large mojito.

The house felt so empty with everyone gone, silent as a graveyard, except for the raindrops starting to patter the tree leaves outside. She'd cruised around Andover for a while after her Starbucks epiphany, but then she'd rushed home, thinking she had to walk Neika. Halfway there, she remembered that their beloved shepherd had been snatched away by the family alpha dog, Dan. Evening was coming on now, the sounds of the wind making branches click on the window panes like spooky fingernails.

Fingernails. She saw the glossy pink ones again of that woman, Melissa. *This is the power.* It had sounded good, but by the time she'd gotten home her enthusiasm had run out of gas. In twenty years of marriage, she'd only beaten Dan twice at checkers, and both times she suspected he'd thrown the game. What made her think she could capture his kings now? He was just so much better at all that stuff. Heck, he'd been born for it, and she'd been born as a hanger-on, his fangirl, sitting home and twirling her hair while her superhero saved Gotham.

Snoop! Melissa's urging rang in her head, but it seemed so slimy to do it. Her marriage with Dan had always been based on trust. But was it really? She trusted him to always do the right thing, for their family, God, and country. In turn, he trusted her with nothing. She downed the rest of her drink and jammed the glass on the counter.

All right, I'm doing it. Not going to find anything anyway. And if I do, that doesn't mean I have to do anything about it. But it'll still feel good.

She headed for the stairs and took them two at a time, her wedding ring clanging on the banister. She walked down the carpeted hallway to the end and into Dan's office. He never kept the door locked, which probably meant there was nothing in there to find. She flicked on the light, stood there with her hands on her hips, and looked around.

Mostly everything in there was about classic cars, which was why she'd never paid much attention to any of it. Rally posters on the walls, a bunch of the models he'd built displayed in Plexiglas boxes, a couple of trophies he'd won with the Shelby.

His big mahogany desk was pretty neat, for a man: just his computer and the requisite pictures of her and Alex. His low bookshelf was off to the side, packed mostly with car catalogues and a few war history books. Dan never read novels.

On top of that were a few framed pictures of him in his army days, and one of him and Peter Conley, both much younger, wearing nondescript uniforms and parachute gear. In all his years with the CIA, if he'd gotten any presidential citations or medals you'd never know it. Behind the desk was the evidence of Dan's only other "collector vice," his hundreds of DVDs.

She looked at the room's single closet. She knew that in there at the bottom was a digital gun safe. That was no secret. He'd given her the combination long ago, just in case she ever had to use it. It would have been nice if he'd taught her to shoot, but she knew that was her own fault because she'd always resisted.

She opened the closet, swept his dress shirts and suits aside, and squatted. Then she punched in the code, and the small door hissed open. Nothing. It was totally empty. She slammed it closed and stood.

"Damn it, Dan," she spat. He'd left her defenseless on top of everything else! She spun around, looked at his desk, and charged it, pulling his drawers open and fighting the urge to just spill everything all over the floor. Then she stopped dead still.

He'd told her once that if everything went south, he had a special place where he kept all his "real" stuff, as he put it. There, he had said, she'd find his last will and testament and some other insurance policies besides the one they kept at home. What the heck did that mean? and wherever that special place was, she knew it wouldn't be here in the house.

What else had he said? All those weird, off-hand remarks and "spy advice." *Think*.

"If you want to really hide something, you leave it out in the open."

She spun around again and looked at every inch of wall space, but nothing jumped out. Maybe a key taped behind a poster frame? No, too obvious—he'd never do that. Then her eyes came to rest on his DVD collection. They were mostly action and war movies, a few classics, pretty much nothing of interest to her. Maybe that was the point? She'd never snoop here because their movie tastes were polar opposites. But she still ran her finger slowly across every row, scanning the titles for some sort of hint.

She stopped. *Hide in Plain Sight*. What the heck was that? She pulled it out, some old mystery movie from the 1980s. She opened it up, but there was nothing in there but the disc. She popped it way from its holder; nothing behind it. And then she turned it over and looked at the silver, glossy back. Carefully written with a black felt pen was one word: *warm*.

Her heart started pounding and her eyes went wide. She tossed the case and disc on Dan's desk and started madly staring at the movies nearest to the empty black slot. *Guns of Navarone?* She snapped it open and found nothing and tossed it on the floor. *Heat?* That made no sense, but she tried it anyway; nothing. *Help?* Maybe that was it! Dan was a die-hard Beatles fan! Fingers shaking, she popped that one open and came up empty.

She scanned the row below and the one above, looking for place names now. She pulled *Casablanca*, getting the same results, threw it onto the growing pile on the floor and mumbled, "Idiot. He's not hiding his stuff in friggin' Morocco."

Calm down. Think.

She leaned back on the desk and took a long breath. Then she glanced down at the first case and picked it up. *Hide in Plain Sight*, starring James Caan. Tapping her fingernails on it, she looked at the DVD rows again. *Warm. That means close, right?*

To the left of where she'd found that first one, was something called *Gardens of Stone*. She reached out and slipped it from its slot and looked at the cover. Starring. . . James Caan.

She snapped it open and pulled out the disc and looked at the back. Another word in carefully scripted black letters: "Toasty."

"Oh my God," she yelped, and she dropped the disc and charged right for the stairs.

She hit bottom and ran through the kitchen, then skidded to a stop, and ran back. Between the fridge and the wall as an antique wooden ammunition crate that Dan had picked up at a yard sale. She popped it open, snatched up a flashlight, and bolted for the backyard door. When she pulled it open the rain was sheeting off the upper sill like Niagara Falls, and it was already pitch dark outside. She snatched a blue slicker from a hook, thrust herself into it, and charged into the backyard.

The tall elms were whipping in the wind, and thunder boomed nearby as she marched across the sodden lawn. *Gardens of Stone*. Well, they only had one garden like that. Dan had once come back from some trip to Japan and announced how much he admired their Zen gardens, which turned out to be bare of greenery, floored in manicured sand, and decorated with rocks, whose positions were supposed to mean something spiritual.

She'd gone along with his plan, mostly because it was rare that they had the time to enjoy some project together. It had turned out nicely—a small raised plateau of white sand with beautiful stones poking up like the thick dorsals of whales. It sat there on a small rise at the edge of their back fence, between a pair of lush, normal gardens.

She clicked on the flashlight and scanned the stone garden. Her hair was already soaking wet so there was no point in pulling the hood up. The stones were arranged in no overtly specific pattern, but she counted them anyway. Thirteen. That didn't mean anything. A bolt of lightning split from the sky a few houses away and she jumped. *This is sooo stupid, Dan*, she fumed. *You're going to get me electrocuted on a dumb-ass treasure hunt!*

She stopped herself again and calmed her pounding pulse. *Treasure. Where do you find the treasure, like if you're a pirate? On a treasure map. What's on a treasure map? An X! X marks the spot!*

She looked around and found it, a broken stick from one of the trees above. She picked it up, fell to her knees in the soaked earth, and leaned over the garden, drawing a thick line in the sand from the top above to between her knees below and then left to right in as perfect a symmetrical design as she could. Then she tossed the stick away, lay the flashlight on one of the rocks, crawled to the middle of the garden, and jammed her wet fingers straight down in the middle of the *X*.

Nothing. Just soaking-wet sand crawling through her fingernails. Her other hand joined the first, and she dug, tossing gobs of wet sand between her legs, just as Neika always did when she was digging up one of her bony treasures. She went deeper and deeper, thinking that this was the stupidest wild-goose chase she'd ever been on. Except it was real, and he'd left her the clues for a reason, and, heck, if it wasn't somehow exciting to be out here in the dark in the rain with the thunder and lighting and...

She hit something. It was probably just another rock. No, it felt smooth and flat on top. She leaned down and dug some more, the water dripping off her chin and her lungs panting steam in the air. She got her fingernails and around whatever it was, leaned back hard, and pulled. It popped from the ground. She stared at it. A small, rectangular black metal box.

She snatched up the flashlight, sprinted back for the house, and slammed the door behind her as she puddled the kitchen floor. She put the box on the island and whipped off her slicker. She took a breath and turned the box over, carefully. There didn't seem to be any way to open it: no latch or lock—in fact, no top. Then she gripped it with one wet hand and smeared the bottom with her thumb. Something clicked. She pushed harder. It slid open.

A key. It was brass and about two inches long. She plucked it out, and there underneath was a small green tab of waterproof paper, like from one of those Rite in the Rain pads that Dan used whenever they'd all gone camping. Typed on the tab were two words: Uncle Bob.

Who the heck was Uncle Bob? Did anyone in the family even have an Uncle Bob? No, there was nobody like that. Wait, maybe it was a restaurant or something. Jenny looked around and spotted her iPhone where she'd left it next to the sink. She snatched it up and pressed the home key.

"Siri, who is Uncle Bob?"

"I don't see Uncle Bob in your contacts."

Jesus. "Siri, show me Uncle *Bobs* in Massachusetts!"

"Okay, here's what I found."

Jenny looked at the list. At the top was "Uncle Bob's Storage, North Andover."

She grabbed the slicker, her car fob, her phone, and the key. She was out the door in five seconds.

* * * *

It was a huge, three-story tan corrugated metal building at the end of a road at the edge of a forest. The sides gleamed with drenching rain under the pale wash of floodlights. A few moving trucks were parked in the lot but no other regular cars. Jenny hurried into the office entrance, where a college girl with big glasses sat behind a high octagonal counter surrounded by plastic plants.

"Hi." Jenny swept her soaked slicker hood back and smiled. "I need to get something out of our locker, but I forgot the number."

"Do you have the key?"

Jenny fished in her pocket and pulled it out. "Right here."

The girl took it from her, turned it over and showed her the back of the thumb grip. "It's right here, three twenty-six." Her expression said, "Poor old folks."

"Oh, of course! Thanks!"

"You bet. It's down the first hall all the way to the end, then turn right."

But there were no lockers in the building, per se. They were all big, corrugated, garage-like doors, one after the other. She found 326, the last one at the end of a hallway of smooth concrete floors. A huge padlock hung from its hasp. She held her breath as she slipped the key inside, turned it, and the lock popped open. She bent down and hauled the door up.

A light flicked on, automatically. The space was huge, and it was filled with...junk. There were boxes and old chairs, a wooden table turned up on its side, old lamps, rubber tires, steel wheels, and hubcaps, and they were all piled up and impassable. Right in front was a tall French closet. Jenny stepped inside the space, pulled the garage door back down, and then perused the mess with a shake of her head. *How am I supposed to find anything in here?*

She reached over and pulled the closet doors open. Nothing but a tightly packed row of old clothes, like Salvation Army finds. Maybe Dan's big secret was that he watched *Hoarders* too much. She pushed some of the clothing aside, just out of curiosity, and saw nothing behind but the back wall of the closet. Just for the hell of it, she pushed it...and it opened. She gasped as another light clicked on, deeper.

She scrambled her way through the closet and the clothes, and then she was standing inside some sort of container, like one of those "pods" people used for storage or moving. It was totally pristine, with shiny aluminum walls, standing filing cabinets, a small metal desk in the center, and behind that, a tall and wide heavy green safe of some sort. It had a digital lock. Her fingers trembled as she punched in the same code she'd just used for the one in Dan's office. The door hissed open.

Guns. Of all kinds. There were automatic pistols arranged on steel pegs on both side walls, and in the back stood racks of longer guns, mostly black and scary-looking—some of them in cases. At the top was a shelf of ammunition boxes in all sorts of colors, with numbers and names like Remington. A small leather satchel hung from one peg, right in the middle. Jenny unslung it and opened it.

Inside was Dan's CIA diary. At one point he mentioned that Zeta thought they had found it, but then he'd just smiled. This one was nothing more than a small black leather notebook, but he'd also mentioned before that it was something he'd kept throughout the years, a habit that was strictly forbidden as an intelligence operative. But Dan had a mind of his own, as she knew only too well. *This* was his "insurance policy."

She flipped it open and scanned through some pages. His writing was careful and legible, but none of it meant anything to her. The pages had dates at the top, but the rest of it was just code words and numbers and phrases she couldn't possibly decipher. She flipped through the yellowed pages, looking for the latest entry. And then she found it.

Yesterday's date, and below that, two words: *Collins* and *Tomahawks*. Neither one meant anything. But wait...Collins. That was someone, a person Dan knew. And Tomahawks? She'd have to ask Siri. Below those words was a weird sort of message.

"Need to find me? Call the Civil War president."

And below that was something that looked like a phone number, no dashes. She took out her iPhone and tapped the number into her Notes. She thought about taking Dan's diary with her, but somehow that seemed like going too far. She put it back in the satchel, hung it back up, got ready to go, then stopped, and looked at the gun rack.

That one there. The ugly-looking one with the wide black tube and wooden grip underneath—like the one on her gardening trowel. That was a shotgun, the kind Dan always said was a "showstopper." She pulled it out of the rack, holding it like it was a hissing cobra, and stuffed it nose first into one of the empty black canvas cases, zipped it shut, and looked up at the shelf. She took a box that said "12 Gauge Shot," stuffed it into her slicker pocket, crawled back through the closet, closed the secret door, and reordered the clothes. She went out, pulled the big metal door down with a clang, and locked it up.

The shotgun case was heavy and menacing, and just holding it made her feel like a bank robber. She held it alongside her leg as she passed through the office again, hoping the girl wouldn't ask any questions. But the kid was head-down in her phone and only mumbled, "Good night."

"Thanks. See ya."

The rain was still pounding. Jenny looked around and opened the truck of the Camry. She stuffed the shotgun and the shells deep into the small shelf at the back and then pushed some of her canvas shopping bags in front to conceal it. Then she closed the trunk quietly, got in the car, pushed the starter button, belted in, and took off—heading back down that long, slick road toward town.

She was smiling like a schoolgirl who'd just been asked out by her dreamy crush. For once in her life, she felt what it was like to be a *spy*.

She didn't even notice the black Audi with its headlights off that pulled out from a grove of trees and followed her.

Chapter Seventeen

Lily was no stranger to the club scene in Seoul.

She'd been to the city before, once as a student, and twice on jobs. The first time, as a freshly liberated university grad, she'd explored the exotic foods throughout the Itaewon district, a place designed mostly to separate spoiled foreigners from their cash, and she'd wound up thrashing the night away at a wild disco called Octagon.

The second two times had been quick in-and-outs, albeit not the sexy kind. The first was a simple package recovery—spotting a chalk mark on a lamppost and finding a dead drop, the old-fashioned way. The third time was supporting a hit on, ironically, a hit man, and it had nearly cost her life.

She had a crawling feeling in her stomach that tracking down Lukacs was going to wind up more like the third type.

"What's your twenty, Lily?" Shepard's tinny voice crackled in her ear piece.

"Just got out of the cab."

"Okay, walk north along Quan Jo."

"Is that the opposite of south?"

"That's a little snarky," he complained. "Even for you."

"Sorry, mate. I'm a bit cranky. Karen booked me on a whirlwind tour."

"Well, airline seats are tough to get on short notice, you know."

"I know, but Ho Chi Minh City, really? And then she put me on Aeroflot. I thought the bloody rivets were going to pop out."

Shepard laughed. "Well, you made it."

"Barely. The room at the Hilton's all right, but I hardly had time to bathe, pretty up, and put on the black wig. It's almost midnight."

"From what I've heard, that's when things just get going in Seoul. How do you look?"

"Smashing," she said. "Absolutely smashing."

Shepard almost giggled. "I'm sure."

Her black stiletto heels clicked on the sidewalk, which was gleaming and slick from an earlier drizzle. The city was chilly, but she'd forgone her wrap because the flights were exhausting and the cold would kick-start her bloodstream. A snug black sequined dress, very short and with a plunging neckline, squeezed her shapely form.

An emerald choker girded her throat, and, during the Aeroflot flight, she'd had plenty of time to apply and paint a set of cinnamon nails. Her long red hair was pinned up under the wig, which was now cascading onto her shoulders, and a pair of Versace shades hid her eyes, which she'd painted up into a Eurasian slant.

The pissy thing about operative travel was that you could never just bang around with a carry-on and jump from flight to flight. There were "things" to be carried that had to be stowed underneath to avoid the scans, so she'd suffered lots of foot-tapping and waiting at baggage claims. But now she was all kitted up.

High up inside her right thigh was a slim Fairbairn–Sykes blade scabbarded to a snap garter, and she was wearing one of those newly fashionable, small leather backpacks which subbed for a purse. Nothing could be found in there but her iPhone, makeup clutch, cash, the gold access card to the club, and a silk bag of female "unmentionables."

However, all those items rested on a false bottom, below which nestled her Walther P22 and spare magazine. The underside of the pack had a Velcro tear-away cover, so with a simple finger snatch, she'd be well armed.

Shepard's voice popped in her ear again. "You should be nearing a subway stop."

"I see one, coming up."

"What does it say?"

Lily laughed. "I don't believe it, Linc. It says Hak-Dong. A bit of castration, shall we?"

Shepard grinned through the comm. "I thought that might cheer you up. I routed you past it on purpose. Take a right."

"You're a card."

She waded through a trio of obviously American troops on leave, whose eyes scanned her lustfully, and then she heard them whistle from behind.

"Think you picked up any tails?" Shepard asked.

"No, only the random piglet. They've only got eyes for my legs, and no one seems to mind that I'm talking to myself."

"It's the norm now."

"Indeed."

Lily smiled, remembering the stories Dan Morgan had told her about the advent of cell phones and the very first Bluetooth devices. All of a sudden, in Boston, he'd said, everyone seemed to be having neurotic conversations with themselves. But she and her peers had grown up with that, and the habit was a boon for spies.

"You should be seeing it by now," Shepard said. "It's three stories, flat granite entrance with big black doors and probably some heavies out front."

"Got it, fifty meters. But there's no lettering anywhere that says the Pentagon."

"Above the doors, just an engraved pentagon."

"Yes, I see it. Strange name for a club."

"They don't think so in Arlington."

Lily snickered. "All right, mute your end for a bit. I'm going in."

"Good luck."

She took a breath, emphasizing the jut of her breasts, and she added a bit more sway to her hips as she strode up to the entrance. There were no velvet ropes because no one waited in line for access at the Pentagon; you were either invited or not.

Two large men in black suits who looked like San-Do practitioners glared down at her without a hint of interest in her body. She wondered if they were eunuchs. One of them stuck out a ham-sized hand.

"No pubbrick," he growled in a heavy accent. She assumed he meant "public."

She smiled, unslung her backpack, reached inside, and showed him her gleaming gold access card. Then both men bowed their cinder-block heads and pulled on a pair of shiny brass handles.

She stepped into a large "submarine chamber" as the doors closed behind her. Another Sumo type stood behind a high black podium with a computer on top and a reader that looked like a Baccarat shoe. He took her card, and the reader swallowed it up.

Game time, she thought as her calves tensed. *If alarms are going to go off, it shall be now.* She wondered if she'd even be able to bolt past the gorillas out front.

"List," the man said.

She stared at him for a nanosecond before realizing what he had said. She held out her wrist, and he snapped a slim black bracelet around it—cinching it with a device that resembled a notary's seal.

She hoped she was home free, but he pointed at her backpack. She shrugged it off her shoulders and opened the top for him. He rummaged through it perfunctorily and waved her on through the next set of doors.

Yesss, she triumphed in her mind.

The music hit her like a mortar barrage. It was German techno thumping in blast waves—making the floor vibrate as if a squad of giant blacksmiths were pounding their hammers. She'd been in plenty of nightclubs, casinos, and discos in scores of cities around the world, but this place made her stop and gape.

The Pentagon's three stories comprised one enormous space, with a circumference of angled silver tubing arching skyward to a domed ceiling of somehow floating stars. Halfway up the tubes, nests of razor wire held disco spotlights that swung on gimbals, flashing neon like machine guns—an epileptic's nightmare.

In the center of the space was a raised pentagonal stage, with a DJ team of Amazon-size girls in black spandex working six turntables of vinyl disks. Bracing the stage were four faux-stone towers with turrets atop, each sporting the huge head of an animatronic dragon. It was like a mix of time-travel décor—a prehistoric altar inside a space station.

There was no discernible dance floor as the packed bodies swayed and twitched everywhere. Two curved aluminum liquor bars with neon ledges flanked the space against the walls, and between the spinning revelers she saw round tables with red leather banquettes filled with drinking guests. She watched as a team of male "selectors," bare-chested with leather vests and black bow ties, pushed through the crowd, pounced on a buxom, German-looking blonde, and carried her up to the stage.

She was clearly half in the bag, and they cooed and wooed her as she surrendered and danced solo. The crowd swarmed closer to the stage, hands thrust up and clapping to the pounding techno rhythms, and at last she pulled her tube top off. Her breasts bounced out, and the crowd roared its approval while the dragons spit gouts of flame.

This is going to be quite a challenge, Lily thought as she perused the crowd. Finding Lukacs in this mess would take some doing, but she had to make sure he wouldn't spot her first.

She rose on her toes and twisted her head until she spotted it—a mermaid bust protruding above a recessed door.

She worked her way along the wall to the Ladies', where a gaggle of Korean girls spilled out, laughing as they wiped powder rings from their nostrils. They were dressed to the nines and looked terribly easy. She figured that to get into the Pentagon, you had to be a very wealthy man, his squeeze, or a high-priced hooker.

Inside the restroom, Lily passed three girls at the sink, adjusting their push-up bras and makeup. She sidled up to the mirror to make sure her disguise still held up. She looked good: somewhat Eurasian but nondescript. She could play it both ways.

She looked around. For a fleeting moment, she was alone in the restroom. She tapped her right ear. "Linc, you can say anything you like to me now. No one'll hear a bloody thing in this mêlée."

He laughed. "Is it a wild joint?"

"It would curl your hair, luv."

She marched out and right away absorbed the pounding techno beats into her body. She swayed her hips from side to side, clenched her fists out in front of her chest, and pumped them back and forth. She started to dance, taking a planned strategic search pattern. She'd circle the outer perimeter first and then tighten that circle, around and around, until she spotted her quarry.

She picked a sweating young Asian executive first, his open shirt displaying a gleaming, hairless chest. She gripped his shirt with her left hand, bumped her left hip into his crotch, then turned, and gave him her right one as he grinned and gripped her waist. Then she spun him, twisting across the floor in dirty-dancing pirouettes, her fingers gripping his belt buckle as her eyes took in three hundred sixty degrees behind him. Nothing yet, so she kissed his cheek, pushed him off, and rocked on to her next buoy in the sea of gleaming, bouncing bodies.

Next she chose a girl, a punky type with fire tattoos, bobbed black hair, and ample breasts. Lily gripped her muscled arms and grinned, letting the tips of her chest rub over the girl's, and again she covered more of the floor as her green eyes flicked over faces and forms, searching for Lukacs's silver-blond hair and angular face.

After that she backed up into a surprised, middle-aged European—a banker type— and she smeared his fat fingers to her belly and let him hump her from behind as she covered another swath of floor. She passed close to the stage, where this time a lithe, buxom redhead was cooed into flipping up her microskirt. The dragons spat flame, and the crowd roared.

She spotted him. Twenty meters from stage left, a group of men were hunched over one of the large round tables. Apparently the club was also a roving casino, without set games or playing installations. Instead, the croupiers were roving ladies dressed like German bar girls—in black leather lederhosen and bouncing cleavage.

They carried playing trays, dangling from straps around their necks, and gamblers could summon them over for a round of five-card stud or blackjack. Lukacs sat among a quintet of Asian men—a pile of chips and cards and cash between them. A couple of his ugly bodyguards stood back from the table and watched. She quickly abandoned her hopeful paramour and danced to somewhere else.

"Acquired," she said as she smiled and pranced, barely moving her lips.

"Say again?" Shepard prodded.

Lily put her fingers to her throat and pressed. That sometimes helped with the audio.

"Got him."

"Outstanding! Who's he with?"

"Unknown. Hang around for video."

"I'm glued to my chair, lady!"

This next part was going to be dicey. First, she ran a check on the emergency exits, spotting one to the right near the Ladies, and another directly opposite, near the Men's. There was likely another somewhere behind the stage, but getting back there would be a last-ditch thing.

Now she needed some cover, at least one "mark," or two would be better. She had to get near Lukacs with her cell, shoot some images, and send them to Linc.

Ahh, there you are, gents. She smiled as she spotted a pair of European-looking men in their thirties, sitting at a small round table about twenty meters from Lukacs's position. They were fashionably dressed in gleaming black, with chest curls poking from the tops of silk shirts. One was blondish, and the other one had darker ringlets, probably French or maybe Corsican.

She strode right over to their table, pulled out a chair and plopped herself down. She leaned back, blew out a breath that flicked her bangs, and said, "Whew!" as she fanned herself with a hand. The two men looked a bit startled, but then they scanned her body and grinned. She took a stab at her instincts.

"*Bon soir, mes amis.*" She nearly had to shout it above the techno fray. Then she leaned forward, displaying her cleavage, and stuck out a hand to the blond one. "Amanda Flay."

He smiled and took her hand and kissed her knuckles. "Pierre," he said.

The other one took it and squeezed it. "Antoine."

"A pleasure." Lily leaned forward, one elbow on the table as she cupped her chin, perused their chest curls and smiled.

"Do you speak French?" Pierre asked in a heavy accent.

"No, but I know *how* to French. And I've always dreamed about a ménage-a-trois."

The men jerked their heads back and leered at each other. Lily fingered her emerald choker.

"I'm *terribly* thirsty," she said. "Escort a lady to the bar?"

"We shall lose our table," said Antoine.

Lily got up and motioned for her newfound friends to do likewise. She gripped the top spars of their chairs and tilted them both across the table. Then she reached for Antoine's belt buckle as his eyes went wide, whipped the belt from his trousers, and girded the two chairs together.

"There," she said. "Now no one would dare!" She unslung her backpack, took out her cell, draped the pack over one shoulder again, and took their elbows. "Onward!"

She guided them through the thumping crowd, pulling them close, letting her hips rub theirs as she felt them stealing glances at her bouncing breasts. They passed fairly close behind Lukacs's table, where she took a quick glance at the back of his head. Across from him sat a stocky Korean with a flat-top haircut, a forehead scar, cruel black eyes, and a boxer's nose. That one had to be Lukacs's contact; the rest looked like hangers-on.

The trio pushed their way to the neon bar on the left. The bartender was a girl with spiked blue hair. Pierre and Antoine ordered martinis. "Amanda?" Pierre inquired.

"Vodka, if you please," she said.

"With?"

"With vodka." She smiled and turned her back to the bar, leaning her elbows on the neon tubing as she gripped her cell casually. Lukacs's table was about seven meters away, appearing, and then blocked again, at intervals, as the crowd ebbed and waved by. She pressed the button and recorded in bursts.

"Okay, I'm getting it," Linc said in her ear. "Try to hold it steady."

She did, as Antoine leaned down from her left.

"So, mademoiselle, where are you from?" he asked.

"Your dreams." She smiled up at him as she dug her nails in his ribs.

"That's a good one," said Linc. "You're from everyone's dreams. Give me one more burst, and I think I've got this."

She did, but then some instinct caused Lukacs's Korean contact to swing his head around. His black eyes met hers for a split second before she turned back to the bar. Pierre, to her left, had their drinks and was slapping some cash on the counter. She squeezed his ass cheek and looked up at him.

"Kiss me," she said. His eyes widened, but he did. He was fairly slimy, but it was not the worst she'd ever suffered.

The three of them pushed back toward their table, and she made sure not to glance at Lukacs again. Antoine recovered his belt as Lily tucked her cell phone away. They sat and drank while she boldly hinted about her most sensitive spots and favorite positions while Pierre and Antoine squeezed their thighs together. It seemed to be taking Linc forever, but at last his voice murmured in her ear.

"Okay," he said. "The dude across from Lukacs is Colonel Shin Kwan Hyo, *North* Korean, which means he's got a big set of balls showing up in Seoul. The other dudes don't register, except for three of Lukacs's thugs, who I just matched from Prague. If you're copying this, give me a cough."

Lily took a swig of her vodka and ice, coughed once, and played with Pierre's fingers.

"Received," Linc said. "You also got a shot under their table. Hyo and Lukacs both have identical briefcases beside their legs. They're gonna pull a switch. You did good. Now you better hightail it. Copy?"

Lily coughed one more time and finished her drink. She smiled at Pierre and Antoine as she sketched a crimson nail along her cleavage. "Gentlemen, I would love to see your hotel room. Is it far?"

They downed their martinis as quickly as possible. But Lily glanced to the right and froze.

Two of Lukacs's goons were moving toward her through the dancing patrons, one of them taking a wide berth to the left while the other came straight on. The crowd seemed to have gotten even larger, the music louder, but, as some dancers push together and parted, she glimpsed Lukacs and Hyo staring her way. She turned back and touched her throat.

"Blown," she muttered.

"Pardon?" Pierre said.

"Get the hell out," Linc said in her ear.

But it was too late. The first heavy was already beside her chair, staring down at her. She looked up. He was shaved bald and brick-faced with slitted gray eyes, and he was wearing one of those safari vests. *Armed.*

"My employer would like to have a word with you." His accent was thick and Slavic.

"So sorry. My dance card's full."

He leaned down and gripped the back of her chair, and his face turned stony. "Now," he growled.

"Later," she sneered up at him. "I'm with friends." She slipped her feet out of her heels.

He slapped the top of her head, ripping off her wig, and her red mane came tumbling out. But his look of triumph lasted only a millisecond as her left hand slammed up under his crotch. She crushed his scrotum and pulled. He screamed and folded in half. She bolted up as her chair crashed back, and she brought her right elbow down on his neck, smashing his face to the table.

She caught only a glimpse of Pierre and Antoine, recoiling from her in horror because dead on to the left, Lukacs's second goon was roaring and pulling a handgun. But she was quicker, her right hand already under her skirt, and her commando blade spun through the air.

It pierced his throat like a laser. His head snapped back, and his trigger finger clenched. His gunshot banged and flashed as he slammed on his back, and, for an instant, the dancers around them froze as if they were playing a party game.

"ISIS!" Lily screamed as she reached behind her back, tore the bottom of her pack open, and pulled out her Walther.

The crowd panicked, yelling and running and diving. She crouched and spun to the right, where Lukacs's third goon was already charging, a black handgun looming from his fist. She jumped up, gripped the Walther two-handed and double-tapped him with two quick shots to the face. He spun and fell as his handgun clattered away.

She saw patrons diving to the floor, the DJ girls on the stage running for cover, and Lukacs's table flipped up on its side as cards and casino chips flew into a cloud. Another gunshot boomed, much louder than hers, and she slammed facedown on the floor behind her table where Pierre and Antoine were curled up like babies, mouths open and bug eyes staring at her in terror.

"*Je suis tellement désolé!*" she shouted. "Another time!"

She jumped up and sprinted for the left side exit, firing her Walther once more at the ceiling as the patrons in front of her split like sheep being charged by a frothing wolf. They were falling all over each other and streaming out toward the main entrance, as she leapt barefoot over squirming bodies. She slammed her shoulder into the exit door and tumbled out into a narrow side street.

Even then there was no time to catch her breath. She turned right and ran flat out down the sidewalk, as she unslung her pack, stuffed the Walther inside and pulled out a thick wad of Korean *Won*. She slowed at the corner and waved the cash at an orange taxi with "Haechi Seoul" and a cartoon polar bear stamped on its flank. It screeched to a stop. She dove in the back and stayed low. She was breathing and sweating like a marathon runner.

"Where you go?" the driver asked.

"The Hilton, and *fast*," she panted. "Big tip!"

He took off. She peeked up over the back seat. Nothing. Then she straightened up and smoothed her dress and just breathed. She looked at the bottoms of her feet. Her stockings were shredded, and her right foot was bleeding. She licked her fingers and rubbed it.

"Lily, come in, for God's sake." It was Linc in her ear.

"Here."

"Jesus! Didn't you hear me begging for a sitrep?"

"I was a tad busy."

"Are you all right?"

"Right as Korean rain." She smiled. "Just another day at the office."

He sounded relieved. "Okay, check in when you're safe and sound."

"I'm already safe," she said as calmly as she could. "I'll never be sound."

Linc laughed and clicked off. She sat back in her seat and watched the nightlife lights and neon signs flash by. And she realized that since landing in Seoul, and right up until now, she hadn't thought about Scott Renard.

Not once.

Chapter Eighteen

Dan Morgan wasn't so smart, Alex thought—half between a realization and an accusation.

He thought he was, especially when he was making all those stupid rules around the house and lecturing everyone else because he had oh-so-much experience. Sure, he could MacGyver stuff together and think fast on his feet, but so could a plumber and a boxer. Half the time he acted like he was some Einstein genius, but in fact he just fell back on all his dumb secrets, which made him think he never had to explain a damn thing.

Whenever Alex challenged him on something he insisted she do, even after she'd started working for Zeta, he'd get that smug I-know-better look on his face and utter that expression she'd come to hate: "Nike." In other words, "Just do it." Disgusting.

For most of her childhood she'd adored him. Then, when she found out he'd been lying her entire life, she hated his guts—for awhile. That had turned around as he'd started to accept her being an adult and, begrudgingly, a skilled operative. But right now the dislike was flooding back full force.

Handcuff me to a pipe in my own house? Man, you're gonna pay big time for that.

She drove the Kawasaki Ninja down I-95, just south of Baltimore, with the night coming on. That made her glad she'd worn her full leathers. Her father surely figured she'd just give up on this Collins thing and skulk back to the office with her tail between her legs. Wasn't going to happen. If he didn't want her around, then he should never have let her join Zeta.

I'm your pissed-off partner now, big shot, like it or not.

She smiled inside her helmet and glanced down at her console, where her iPhone was gripped in a rubber mount. The navigator app was on, showing her the route to Arlington. But it wasn't live; it was a replay of

the route her dad had taken two days before. She'd figured out long ago
that she couldn't really trust him, at least in terms of "sharing." So, she'd
gotten a hold of Bobby Zaks, that genius nerd from school, told him what
she wanted, and paid him good money.

Bobby got a burner phone, stripped everything off it, and loaded up
an app he'd hacked from Uber. It was the back end of the software that
tracked their drivers and could replay anyone's route. Then he added a
pirated mirror-image app and linked the burner to Alex's cell.

Late one night, when her dad and mom were snoring, she'd sneaked down
to the garage and climbed into his Cobra—gluing the burner and a power
pack right under the passenger seat. She knew the batteries wouldn't last
forever, but she figured she'd check on it and repeat the exercise whenever
necessary. Stroke of luck, it was humming along like a glee club tonight.

"You're not so smart," she said aloud in her helmet, and she
added, "*Daddy.*"

It took another hour to weave her way down to Arlington. Traffic around
the D.C. area was always a bear, but eventually she was cruising through
clusters of quaint brick homes—many of them sporting American flags,
Marine Corps pennants, or black MIA/POW banners.

The neighborhood was something of a military reservation, from which
people went off to serve, spent scant time in their ordered homes, then
returned to retire, and, eventually, die. The gardens were so manicured
they stood at attention and the mailboxes were freshly painted while brass
door knockers and house numbers were polished to a gleam in the night.

Alex looked at her navigator, then coasted down a street called Zumwalt,
which vaguely rang a bell: some navy admiral or something. The long
lane was dark and quiet, with light-pole lamps glowing yellow at distant
intervals, and cars, many with government license plates, parked at the
curbs or tucked into driveways.

The target house was halfway down on the right. When she got closer,
she killed the engine and toed the bike up to the mailbox. The house was
chunky and all brick, with white windows, blinds pulled, and a single lamp
glowing over the slate stairs. She looked at the number on the box, took off
her gloves, and punched up a Zeta app on her phone that reverse-checked
addresses and phone numbers. She typed in "206 Zumwalt Street, Arlington,
VA," and after a moment got a pop-up: "Schmitt, Alicia, Commander USN."

Alex's brow furrowed. A female naval officer. Somehow she'd expected
to find General Collins at this address.

Dad, you better not be having an affair with some navy bimbo half your age, 'cause if I find you doing the horizontal tango in there, I'll shoot you both.

Alex got off the bike, leaned it on the kickstand, took off her helmet, and shook out her smooth, short russet hair. She left her helmet on the seat, opened a saddlebag, and pulled out a large UPS envelope. As she stepped to the sidewalk and turned for Schmitt's door, she glanced down the street. Among other vehicles, there was a dark blue Econoline van, light off, parked and dark. Her dad had taught her to never trust vans.

She trotted up the stairs and rang the bell. The door opened a crack, with a chain lock holding it. One blue eye and some blonde hair appeared in the narrow opening. The eye blinked.

"Yes?"

"Hi there," Alex said brightly. "I have a package for Alicia Schmitt."

"What's the package?"

Alex dropped her voice. "I'm the package, Commander. May I come in, please?"

The eye blinked once more; then the door closed and the chain rattled. It opened again, so Alex stepped inside and palmed it shut with her left hand.

Alicia Schmitt had retreated ten feet into her living room. She had neck-length blond hair that Alex imagined was usually wrapped up tight in a bun, a small nose, no lipstick, and her blue eyes looked shadowed and fatigued. She was slim and athletic, but she was wearing a Navy peacoat, all buttoned up. Alongside her right thigh she held a brushed steel automatic. Alex looked down at it. "That's a Lady Smith," she said. "I like it, but it's single stack. Not enough ammo for my taste."

Schmitt stared at her face. "What are you carrying?"

"Shrouded hammer thirty-eight, right-ankle holster under my boot. Same problem, only five rounds, but I use three fifty-seven hollow. Want it?"

"No," Schmitt said. "If that's what you're here for, you would've used it by now." She cocked her head at a navy-blue couch. "Have a seat, but sit on your hands."

"Thanks." Alex walked over to the couch, her leathers creaking. She dropped the UPS envelope on the cushion and sat on her upturned palms.

"Who are you?" Schmitt asked as she sidestepped over to the door, replaced the chain, and checked the lock.

"Alex Morgan." She glanced over the living room. It was very orderly and somewhat prim, with throwback brocade chairs and doily-covered end tables—as if Schmitt had inherited the place from her grandmother.

A few framed pictures of Schmitt in dress uniform stood on a closed, upright piano, along with a one of her hunting with an older man. There was also a bronze statue of a runner with what looked like a marathon ribbon and medal dangling from its bony shoulders.

"All right, Alex Morgan," Schmitt said as the Lady Smith twitched in her grip. "I'm a little wrapped tight these days, so let's get to the point."

"My father was here a couple of days ago."

Schmitt dipped her brow. "Your father."

"Yes. Mind if I unzip my jacket? It's kinda warm in here."

"Go ahead. Slowly."

Alex smiled, unzipped, and stuck her palm back under her thigh.

"My father and I work for the same organization."

"Which would be?"

"The name's not important. It's an NGO."

Schmitt sneered. "Nongovernmental organizations are, in the end, all governmental."

"Not this one," said Alex. "But it doesn't matter. Dad told me about the Collins thing."

With that, Alicia Schmitt pulled her chin in and cocked it slightly, her blue eyes boring into Alex. Then she touched a wall switch, which killed the overhead chandelier and left only a standing lamp next to Alex glowing. She touched the blinds on the front bay window, peered out, and looked at Alex again.

"Collins," she said. "Means nothing to me."

"General Collins," Alex said. "And yes it does, unless you meant that in a personal way."

Schmitt's pale lips curled up. "Clever girl. What's a kid like you doing working for spooks?"

"I'm a college dropout, but I can shoot like Carlos Hathcock."

With that, Schmitt laughed. "You're no dummy. You know your history all the way back to Vietnam."

"Dad." Alex grinned.

"Right." Schmitt seemed to relax a little. She pulled a wooden chair over, turned it around, and mounted it backward, but she gripped the automatic draped down over the top spar, still ready. Alex saw she was wearing black running spandex and pro running shoes. "Your dad, so you say."

"Dark brown hair, touch of gray, chestnut eyes, boxer's nose, broad shoulders, and an arrogant attitude."

Schmitt nodded. "Sounds like him." She looked at her watch. "Now listen up, Alex. I was just about to get out of here, and you're holding me up." She gestured to a spot near the piano, where Alex saw a heavy black duffel and a navy camouflage backpack. "So, stop screwing around and tell me why you're here."

"My father's gone rogue from the organization. He's disobeyed orders to stand down, but this Collins guy was his friend, and he's determined to clear his name, although I have no idea why it needs clearing. But he's my dad, and I'm going to help him, even though he bugs the crap outta me half the time. He mentioned that you're the key to this whole thing, Commander. But a key's no good unless it turns."

"Your dad must be very proud of you."

"Ha," Alex snorted. "You'd be surprised how he doesn't show it."

"No I wouldn't," Schmitt retorted before glancing at the hunting picture on the piano. "My dad was proud of me too. Didn't show it until he was on his deathbed."

"I'm sorry. I'm hoping mine won't wait that long."

A car engine came to life somewhere outside. Schmitt stiffened, looked at the front windows and listened. Then she turned back.

"What's in the envelope?" she asked.

"Blank paper."

Schmitt nodded in recognition of the gambit. The envelope wasn't for her. It was for anyone watching from the street. "Okay, Alex. I have no idea if you are who you say you are. But you're good—I'll give you that much. Your dad, if that's who he is, seemed to know about the general and his mentor relationship to me, but the people who are trying to take him down would know that too. They'd also already know what I'm going to tell you, so it won't matter much."

Alex leaned forward on the couch. She felt that Schmitt was trusting her somewhat now, so she pulled her sweaty palms from under her thighs and wiped them on her knees. "Do I need a pen and paper?"

"No," said Schmitt. "You just need to tell your father that Virginia isn't a place. It's a corporation."

"That's it? Virginia is a corporation? A business entity?"

"Correct. That'll give him plenty to chew on." Schmitt looked at her watch again. "Okay, your session's over. I'm catching a..." She stopped herself before revealing more.

"Okay, Commander. Thanks. I appreciate the trust." Alex rose carefully from the couch, making sure her right hand went nowhere near her boot. The navy officer was clearly jumpy, exhausted, and seriously spooked. "Hey, mind if I use your bathroom before I go? It was a long ride down here, and it'll be the same going back."

Schmitt waved the pistol to the left toward a hallway. "It's down there, on the left."

Alex walked through a slim arched alcove. She saw a door at the back with paned windows and a curtain and the bathroom door to the left.

"And, Alex," Schmitt called to her. Alex turned and looked back at her. "If you come out with anything in your hands other than a tissue, I'll drop you right there. Are we clear?"

"Extremely."

She slipped into the small bathroom and blew out a long breath. *Wow*, she thought, *that poor woman's nervous as a kitten on a hot plate.* She unzipped her jacket, wriggled her leathers over her hips, and sat to pee. *Virginia. A corporation, not a place.*

She smiled, thinking about her father off on some wild-goose chase, trying to figure out what to look for somewhere here in Virginia, when, in fact, the real target could be a warehouse in Guatemala. It was going to be so much fun to break the news to him, but she'd make him work for it. Maybe she'd handcuff him to his stupid Cobra first.

She finished her business, buckled back up, zipped up tight, and flushed. Then she froze. She heard a sound from the living room. Someone outside was pounding on the front door, but it sounded less like a fist and more like something metallic. *Jesus!* It sounded like a SWAT team battering ram. She jerked the door open and stuck her head out.

Schmitt was nowhere in sight, maybe off to the left or the right, but because of the hallway, all Alex saw was a tunnel and the white front door across the living room floor. It trembled with a thunderous slam. There was a pause, followed by the whole thing exploding. Alex dropped to one knee, her pulse pounding up into her neck. She yanked her .357 from her boot just as two figures in SWAT gear, helmets, and shotguns burst through the door.

The truth announced itself to Alex like a proud child. *Those aren't cops. Cops would have surrounded the house first and called Schmitt out with a bull horn.*

A gunshot banged from somewhere to the left, the room flashed white, and the first guy collapsed as his knee cap exploded. The second one leapt over the first as his shotgun barrel thundered with smoke and yellow flame. He pumped it for a second shot, but Alex heard Alicia Schmitt scream something, and a double-tap from her Lady Smith sent him flying back out the door.

Alex jumped up to charge down the hallway, just as two more of the killers clambered inside. She took the first one down with two quick shots to his Kevlar, center mass, and his shotgun went off and shattered the chandelier. The second one ducked, ignoring her, and fired a handgun.

Alex heard Schmitt scream as she nailed the shotgunner with a bullet to the collarbone. He jerked around and bounced off the wall as if he had been thrown there.

Alex spun around to run at the back door. She yanked it open, dove over a concrete stoop, somersaulted across the grass, and popped up, spewing hot breath. She sprinted full tilt around the right side of the house and leapt over a bush, as her boots hit the front yard.

Sure enough, that damn Econoline was parked in the front, doors flung open, and another phony cop was pounding up the sidewalk toward the splintered front door. He spun and saw her heading for her bike. Each took a wild shot at the other as she ran and he dove to the grass.

Alex leapt on the seat while flinging the bike away from the curb. The kickstand snapped up as a gunshot shattered the mailbox. Alex revved it on, gunned it, and fishtailed to the left as she heard the van door behind her slam. She ducked low as the bike speared forward and another bullet zipped past her left ear.

In three short seconds she was doing seventy, her .357 still gripped in her sweat-soaked right hand. She thought she had one round left in the chamber, but she wasn't sure. She'd lost her gloves, but her helmet was still there between her thighs. Her hair whipped back from her face, and her eyes burned with the wind and her unwanted tears.

I could have saved her, she told herself.

No, you couldn't, she heard her mind reply. *Commander Alicia Schmitt is dead.*

Chapter Nineteen

Dan Morgan sat on a pile of gold and maroon embroidered pillows, his back against a cream plaster wall.

To his left, on another array of cushions sat Lieutenant Colonel Kadir Fastia, late of Libyan Army Intelligence. They were ensconced on the top floor of Fastia's brownstone in Columbia Heights, the northern environs of Washington, D.C. Many such quaint architectural structures flanked the tree-lined lane of Georgia Avenue Northwest, which were usually split up into apartments, but Fastia had bought the whole building.

His continuing work as a "security consultant" was lucrative and was enhanced by the many friends he'd made along the way. In a business rife with distrust at best and betrayals at worst, even Dan Morgan, who could make enemies the way other people make coffee, could repeatedly attest to Fastia's remarkable ability to satisfy even the most devious client. Thankfully Morgan wasn't one of them. He was honored to call Kadir a friend and a valued *rajul hakim*—wise man.

"Are you sure you do not wish to partake, Cobra?" Fastia asked as he offered Morgan a saliva-slick mouthpiece at the end of a long curling tube. Between them on the Persian carpet sat a round silver tray holding a large Middle Eastern waterpipe, commonly called a *nargila*. There was also a brass *finjon* and two ceramic cups steaming with black Turkish coffee. Morgan waved his hand.

"*Shukran*," he said. "Between your cigars and that thing, I'm going to need a new lung."

Fastia chuckled. "As you wish." He drew on the tube. The water in the *nargila* bubbled, the coals at the top glowed red, and twin columns of blue smoke streamed from his wide nostrils. He was wearing a long-sleeved white chemise, no collar, over a pair of gray trousers and house sandals.

With his trim white beard against his olive skin, he always looked like he'd just walked out of the desert.

Morgan reached for one of the ceramic cups, sipped the muddy brew, and sat back again, rubbing his knee. "One of these days you're going to live in an elevator building, Kadir," he said.

"Never," Fastia said. "All these stairs discourage unwanted guests."

In the past they'd always conferred in Fastia's office a floor below, but whenever the soft-spoken Libyan wanted absolute privacy, this traditionally decorated space was his bastion. It was Levantine Bedouin, with not a stick of furniture; only pillows arranged along the walls. Fastia adored his wife and daughter, but this was off-limits even to them.

The *rajul hakim* leaned back with a knowing smile as his eyes grew serious and piercing. "So," he said. "You are at a dead-end, yes?"

"Yes," Morgan admitted.

"As am I, Cobra," Fastia said. He always called Morgan by his CIA code name, as he had since meeting him in the Libyan desert many years before. Together with Peter Conley they had come within a hair's breadth of assassinating Muammar Gaddafi, but the hit had been called off by Morgan's handlers at the last second.

Gaddafi's beasts had murdered Fastia's first wife and family, causing him to turn against the dictator, and the mission's failure had sat like a stone on his heart for many years. Now, with Gaddafi dead and gone, he slept very well at night.

"Virginia is simply too broad a clue and much too large an area," he added. Then he raised a finger. "Perhaps it is a woman rather than a place?"

"I thought of that, Kadir," said Morgan. "But I think Collins would have somehow hinted at that, and this Commander Schmitt didn't give any indication of that either."

"Why must people always be so obtuse?" Fastia wondered.

"Folks love secrets," said Morgan. "They feel like it gives them power."

"At this point in my life, they only give me a headache." Fastia returned to his pipe. It seemed to help him think. "And this thing about the missiles, Cobra. As I recall, the Tomahawk is nothing like the American Stinger or the Russian Strela, correct? It is not a shoulder-fired weapon."

"Not unless you're a fairytale giant. It's about eighteen feet long and weighs about three thousand pounds. Usually ship-or submarine-launched, but there are a few vehicle-mounted versions."

"*Ya-Allah*," Fastia intoned. "So then, perhaps that is a help to us. One couldn't hope to hide something like that in an urban center. Therefore, we should think open areas, perhaps farm country."

"Unless that's what they want us to think."

Fastia waved a finger. "You are always playing checkers in your mind."

"I know." Morgan grinned. "Keeps me suspicious— and alive. So, think you could put the word out to your network?"

"I already did, from my office while you were relieving yourself. I asked for any information connecting 'Virginia' and heavy ordnance, though I did not mention Tomahawks per se." He looked down at the smartphone sitting beside him, where text messages were popping up in Arabic. "Everyone seems to think that I am referring to Langley and shoulder-fired missiles. I keep having to reply 'la.'"

The word meant "no." Morgan nodded, understanding Fastia's contacts' confusion. "I guess it's a valid assumption since Benghazi."

Fastia looked at Morgan as he rubbed his white beard and smoothed his neat mustache. "You are out on a limb again, aren't you, Cobra?"

"Way out."

"You were like that with the CIA, and it appears you are still like that with your new organization." Fastia tapped his nose. "What was that old James Dean movie? *Rebel Without a Cause?*"

"Oh, I've got a cause all right." Morgan grinned. "I'm just a stubborn pain in the ass."

"It is what I always liked about you. You are relentless—but sometimes foolish as well, I think."

Morgan shrugged. "Well, it's tough to teach an old dog new tricks."

As if on cue, a low canine whine came from the landing below. Fastia had broken with Muslim tradition and allowed Neika into the house but not all the way up here to his most sacred spot. His wife and daughter served meals to him and guests here; no dog would cross the threshold. Morgan sat forward on his pillows and listened.

"She's trained to only do that when she means it," he said.

Fastia lifted up his billowy tunic, pulled out a Browning Hi-Power and rested it on his lap. "I shall assume she is simply hungry," he said before pinioning Morgan with a sharp gaze, "while you check."

Morgan got up, reached into his shoulder holster for his PPK, walked to the arched doorway, and pushed the door open. He looked down the long narrow staircase to where he'd left Neika leashed to a radiator on the next landing. She was sitting up facing a tall bay window, emitting urgent moans from her throat as her thick tail flicked on the floor. But the window was curtained, and she couldn't see anything outside.

Morgan reached the landing and ruffled her head. "What's out there, girl?"

He leaned to the side of the window, pushed the curtain open just a slit, then peered out and down. He could see the Shelby parked across the street where he'd left it, and just behind that, a black Kawasaki Ninja motorcycle....

"Jesus," he growled and called up to Fastia. "Kadir, it's my daughter. I'll be right back."

"Your what?" Fastia asked, but Morgan was already pounding down the stairs.

He tucked the Walther away as he reached the front entrance, yanked the door open, and quick-marched across the small front yard, instinctively glancing around for any signs of an ambush—his beloved family had been used as bait before. Then he hurried across the street, where Alex was leaning against the trunk of his car, her helmet off, her arms folded, her head hanging down, and her pageboy haircut obscuring her face.

"Alex, what the hell?" he snapped as he stamped up to her. But then she lifted her face and looked at him, and his breath hitched in his chest. Her eyes were glassy, her flushed cheeks shiny with tear tracks, and she was shaking. He reached out and gripped her shoulders and turned her as a spear of panic rushed up to his throat. "Are you all right? Whatever it is, tell me now. Is it Mom?"

She looked at her boots, seeming unable to speak.

"Look at me, Alex," Morgan said. She looked up. "What are you doing here? How did you find me?"

"I...I was pissed," she stammered, and then more disjointed phrases tumbled out. "You treat me like some stupid teenager, cuffing me like a perp...I'm on your team, supposed to be your partner, but you won't let me so I put a tracker on your car." Her voice warbled.

Morgan glanced at the Shelby and then back at her tear-filled eyes. "I'm sorry." He bent his knees a bit so their faces were even and he smiled. "And, I'm impressed. Now tell me what happened."

"Oh God." She hugged him with such strength that it took Morgan's breath away, her face buried in his neck. "I went to Alicia Schmitt in Arlington. She let me inside, and we talked. She was really jumpy and packed up to go somewhere. . . But she was cool, and it was all good, and she told me some stuff, and I was going when they showed up."

"*Who* showed up, Alex?" Morgan glanced over the top of her head at a passing young couple staring at him and his daughter. He smiled reassuringly, so they kept walking.

"A hit team." She shuddered. "They were in tactical getup and looked like cops, but they weren't...I was in the bathroom when they hit the front door. I got a couple of them but I couldn't stop them. She fought back too, but..." She took a long breath, and then she settled. She stopped quaking, and she whispered, "They killed her, Dad."

He pushed her away gently and gripped her shoulders again. He looked her over, head to boots. "Are you hit? Are you okay?"

She shook her head. "I'm okay."

Morgan's gaze went steely again. Whoever was running this operation, setting General Collins up for a fall, killing American troops and hijacking Tomahawks, they'd just taken it up a notch. They'd just murdered an American naval officer.

"What did she tell you, Alex?"

Alex saw that her father was back to business. His sympathy was fleeting, and now he was treating her like an operative again. Somehow, that made her feel good.

"Virginia isn't a place, Dad. It's a company, a business entity."

He took her face in his calloused hands. "You did good. You got more out of her than I did, God rest her soul." Then he took her elbow and walked her back over to Fastia's front door.

She took off her gloves and wiped her face with her hands. "Where are we?"

"Friend of mine."

"I'm surprised you still have any left."

He smiled at that. She was all right.

They went inside, Morgan bolted the door behind them, and they headed up the stairs. As they reached the third landing Alex could hear Neika's urgent whines and her nails clicking on the floor. Then the shepherd saw Alex, and Alex ran to her and hugged her and ruffled her all over. Neika gave her face a tongue bath, and Alex saw she was leashed to the radiator.

"At least I'm not the only one around here who gets locked up," she muttered.

Morgan ignored that as Fastia came down the stairs from above. Alex stood up and scanned his face and his garb.

"Welcome, young lady." He smiled. "I am Kadir Fastia."

"Alex," she said, but she didn't extend her hand. Instead, she touched her fingers to her chest and dipped her head. Fastia did the same, looking impressed.

"You are culturally sensitive, Alex."

She smirked. "That's about all they teach us in college these days."

Fastia laughed. "Yes, so I have heard." He waved a hand toward a hallway. "Please, let's go into my office."

Morgan and Alex followed him into his study. He skirted his large desk, pulled his HiPower from his waistband, laid it carefully on the polished wood, and sat in his large leather chair. He gestured at two plush chairs on the other side. "Please."

Morgan remained standing. Alex looked at him and followed his cue.

"Kadir, I don't think we have much time," Morgan said. "Alex has some fresh intel." He looked at her. "You can say anything in front of Mr. Fastia. He already knows the issues."

Alex looked over the friendly face framed in a trim white beard. She had no idea who this man was, but if her father trusted him then she could too. "Virginia is some sort of company," she said.

"Ahh, so we have one more piece of the puzzle!" His brown eyes gleamed, and he opened up a silver laptop and started to peck. "I think we shall need the darker net."

"You know how to do that?" Alex marveled.

"I have studied the ways of the young."

"You should teach my dad. He still can't figure out how to work Netflix."

Morgan punched her shoulder, but he was smiling. She looked up at him and grinned back. Something different passed between them, an acceptance that was new, and it sent a flood of warmth through Alex's heart.

"I am entering parameters," Fastia said as he squinted at his monitor. "Assuming a radius of one hundred miles, with Richmond at the epicenter... just in the event that this clue is meant twice, should we be so lucky. And now..." He pecked some more. "We shall see if certain other qualities bear fruit, such as the ordnance details, pertinent warehouse facilities." He tapped the Enter key with a flourish and sat back.

The door to Fastia's office opened. And his wife peeked in. She was considerably younger than Fastia, wore a blue silk scarf over her head of glossy black hair, and had large merry eyes. Fastia smiled as if always pleased to see her.

"Yes, my dear Nadia?"

"Would you be wanting anything, husband?" she asked.

"Tea, if you please, for our guests."

She smiled again and closed the door.

Alex looked at her watch. "Dad, they've been trying to call me back up to..." She stopped herself from saying Zeta. "Headquarters. I had the day off, and they canceled it and called me back in, but I ignored the messages. They're probably freaking by now."

"You're gonna have to go and take care of that," said Morgan. "Tell them you were down here visiting a friend and you shut down your cell. She'll be pissed," he added, meaning Diana Bloch. "But youth trumps good sense, no offense."

"None taken." She put her hands on her hips.

"Just don't tell them you saw me."

"Why don't I just tell them you handcuffed me to the house? *That* they'll believe."

Morgan's cheeks flushed, but Fastia interrupted before the exchange could turn sour.

"Ah yes, some results." His finger moved down his monitor. "No, not this one...nor this. Here!" He tapped the screen with his nail. "The Virginia Cigar Company, with a substantial warehouse, approximately forty-five miles west of Richmond. Nothing else fits. I shall message the address to your cell, Morgan."

"No, Kadir." Morgan stopped him. "Write it down."

"You are trusting no one, are you?"

"Only her." Morgan touched. "And you."

Fastia penned the location on a pad, tore the page off, and handed it to Morgan, who turned to Alex. "Stay here for a while. Keep an eye on Fastia."

Alex glanced at the pistol on the desk. "He doesn't look like he needs any protection."

"I don't." Fastia grinned. "But you shall have something to eat, young lady. Then you can go."

Morgan looked at her and held her eyes. "I'm taking Neika. Hold here for about an hour, then head back North. And be careful on that damn bike."

"You be careful," she said.

"Where'd you put that tracker?"

"Under your passenger seat."

"I'll leave it there for now."

Wow, Alex thought. *He's really trusting me. It's a brand-new day.*

Morgan kissed her forehead and squeezed her shoulder. He headed for the door, opened it, and turned back. "Virginia Cigar, huh?" He smirked at Fastia. "Just what I needed. More smoke."

And then he was gone.

Chapter Twenty

Morgan lay in a thicket of tall wet grass, not moving, just breathing and watching.

Beside him, Neika snuggled close, her soft, steady panting warming his ear. The dawn was just starting to break, the early sun shimmering off the sides of the warehouse half a mile away. It sat in an unmowed clearing, surrounded by dense, lush, forests, with a brick-colored, slanted roof, and a big stencil on its flank that had once said "Virginia Tobacco." But with the years and the weather the sign now said only "Virgin Toba."

They had driven through the night, turned west at Richmond, and cruised for another hour along Route 13, which Morgan thought might not be lucky. He'd gassed up the car at a Wawa and gotten himself a greasy burger, more dog food and water for Neika, and they'd cruised on past Hideaway Lake, reaching Tobaccoville before turning north.

Two miles short of the target, he'd driven the Shelby off the slim dirt road and into some trees, wincing as he heard branches scraping the paint. That would mean a day in the garage at some point, but he actually, kind of, looked forward to that. At least it would mean he was still alive.

Then they'd walked, slowly, through the woods in the night, as occasionally Morgan stopped, listened, and went on. Neika mirrored his every move, and he didn't have to worry about her making noise or barking. She'd done this many times before, in Afghanistan. She was a retired military working dog, and Morgan knew those instincts and that that training would never fade.

He'd chosen a spot at the edge of the woods where the tall trees and thickets gave way to a clearing, and they'd hunkered down and waited for the light. Now he reached into his field jacket pocket for a pair of mini-binoculars, pushed up the edge of his black woolen watch cap, and slowly scanned the warehouse, left to right.

He saw no evidence of recent activity: no vehicles, shipping containers, or overflowing dumpsters waiting for pickup. Granted it was early, but a big facility like that would still have a light or two glowing, and some sort of guard service protecting its wares. Nothing. Just a flock of crows pecking at the gutters.

"What d'ya think, girl?" Morgan murmured.

Neika, her large paws stretched out in the grass, looked at him, whined softly, and licked his face. He wiped her spit off with a glove.

"Okay, let's take a walk."

The grass was gleaming, heavy with dew, which soaked the bottoms of his black jeans as they walked. Neika trotted beside him, her eyes bright and her pink tongue lolling. As the side of the warehouse loomed large, Morgan stopped to examine two thick lanes of crushed grass: double tire tracks—something heavy like an eighteen-wheeler— and fresh.

Then he turned as he continued to walk, scanning a full three hundred sixty degrees like the tail-end Charlie in a combat squad. But he saw and heard nothing other than the morning birds in the trees. The warehouse, three stories tall and maybe three hundred feet from stem to stern, had a glassed-in office area at the left-hand corner. That entrance might be alarmed, so he chose a side door at the center of the building's flank.

It had a standard steel knob with a keyhole. He took out his lock-pick set and then noticed a slit in the jamb exposing the catch. He skipped over the keyhole, opened a flat metal probe, slipped it inside, and tripped the catch. Carefully, he pulled the door open.

No alarms went off. He didn't know if that was a good or a bad sign. *Only one way to find out*, he figured and stepped inside.

The space inside was enormous— and empty. There was no machinery, assembly tables, packing crates, or conveyer belts leading to the right-hand wall, where a pair of huge garage doors were pulled down and locked. Slat windows two stories up lined the flanks. Through them early sunlight streamed in shafts, but the vast concrete floor looked broom clean. Barely a wisp of dust curled through the golden haze.

"Jesus," he muttered. "You could put the friggin' space shuttle in here."

Neika sat next to him, her tail flicking.

"I don't see anything that looks like tobacco leaf racks, do you?"

She looked up at him silently.

"That's right. No cigar."

If Virginia Tobacco had ever made smokes, they'd lost their shirts to the no-smoking culture a long time ago and turned to some other line of business. Maybe the place had been "acquired" and used as cover—hell, he'd done that himself with a myriad of business fronts—but cover for what?

Whatever it was, General Collins knew, but he wasn't at liberty to say. Tomahawks were big-time bullets, some of them nuclear, so they had to be stored in hardened facilities. But the supporting vehicles, radar, and fire-control modules...maybe. He turned and walked across the floor toward the office enclave on the left.

He spotted some oil stains on the concrete, bent down, took off a glove, and ran a finger across the shallow pool. Not congealed. Fresh.

He trotted up three cement stairs, pulled a door open, and entered the office. Neika clambered inside, and Morgan shut the door. But this was no tobacco factory shipping and accounting center; it was a sophisticated security and control room. Three large flat screens were mounted above a semicircular steel desk, with DVR sets, UHF radios, intercom mikes, and shotgun racks—empty. He touched a pair of padded office chairs, dented but cold. He looked at the floor; there were recent caster runnels in the dust.

Morgan reached into one of his pockets and took out a small baggie with his earpiece and miniature battery inside. He fired it up and tucked it deep in his ear. It crackled.

"Cobra?" It was Lincoln Shepard's voice, echoing inside some large space. "Is that you?"

"It's me, Shep. How copy?"

"Five by five, and it's about friggin' time."

"Missed me, huh? What's your twenty?"

"I'm at Faneuil Hall, picking up some gourmet brew."

"Good," Morgan said. "Who's on this comm?"

"You, me, and God," Shepard said.

"For some strange reason, I believe you," Morgan said. He heard Shepard's footsteps, pacing, and a vendor in the market calling out something about cheese.

"Listen, Cobra," Shepard whispered. "You're way, way out in the cold. The boss put the firm on alert about you."

"The boss with the bra? Or the one she answers to?"

"The latter, so that means both. They'd shoot me for telling you this, but they've got air tactical, so you'd better get the hell out of there."

Morgan's eyes narrowed a little. He reached down and ruffled Neika's head. "How do they know where I am?"

"ISR," said Shepard.

That meant Intelligence, Surveillance, and Reconnaissance; in short, a drone.

"They've got a drone on me? I'm flattered."

"Well, get yourself a white Subaru. That Shelby sticks out like a turd in a punchbowl."

Morgan laughed. "You're getting pretty gnarly for a geek. Got your laptop?"

"Of course. But don't ask me, Cobra. I gotta get back to the office..."

"Open it up. I need some help here."

"Shit."

Morgan heard Shepard cursing under his breath as he found some sort of flat surface and flipped his laptop open.

"All right," Shepard said. "Now what?"

"I'm looking at a security rig, three flat screens, modules, probably some sort of digital recording mechanism. I need all the tapes, probably seventy-two hours."

"That's all?" Shepard was no doubt rolling his eyes. "Okay, where's the server?"

"Big thing under the desk here."

"Tell me it's got a USB port."

"It does."

"And tell me you've got a charging cord for your cell phone."

"Course I do," said Morgan. "I'm an aging millennial."

"Turn on your cell and plug it into the server," Shepard instructed. "But the minute you do, you're gonna be naked, just sayin'."

"I've been working out. I look pretty good."

"No offense, Cobra, but there's something seriously wrong with you."

Morgan powered up his cell and plugged it in. All three flat screens flickered and came on. Surveillance videos showing different angles of the warehouse and its exterior appeared, first at normal speeds and then they started to flash by in streams as Shepard controlled the replay.

Most of what Morgan strained to see showed no activity other than deer walking by in the grass outside and a couple of squirrels on the warehouse floor. But then he caught the fleeting image of a large trailer truck, which was instantly gone as Shepard downloaded everything and the monitors went blank.

Morgan looked up at the office ceiling, where a fluorescent light fixture was vibrating. Then he heard that familiar sound: helicopter rotors.

"Got all that?" he asked Shepard.

"Yes. May I go now?"

"Yeah, and when you get back to the office run through it for me. Think license plates."

"Jesus, Cobra. If they catch me I'm toast!"

"Yeah? Well, they'll burn me. You know I'm not asking for my health."

There was just a moment's hesitation. "Understood," said Shep. "Stay low."

Morgan pulled the earpiece out, dropped it in his pocket, and did the same with his cell and the cord. There was no mistaking the sound now as the windows rattled and the grass outside flattened like waves in a typhoon.

Neika looked up at him, emitting agitated whimpers and trembling. He looked down at her and smiled. "It's all right, girl. They're friends." Friends with guns—which were loaded, with any luck, with either sedative darts or rubber bullets.

The rotor sounds settled to a steady *thwop*. Morgan opened the office door, stepped down to the warehouse floor, and stopped. Neika sat beside his left leg, a low growl buzzing from her throat.

Bishop, Spartan, and Diesel were standing in the center of the space, Spartan taking point, with Bishop and Diesel flanking. They were all wearing tactical vests—Kevlar, Morgan assumed. They carried no long guns, only pistols in thigh holsters. Spartan's arms were bare, displaying her angry tattoos. They didn't look pleased.

"Time to come home, Cobra," Spartan called out, her low voice echoing off the walls.

"Thanks for asking," Morgan said. "But I'm still on sabbatical."

"It's not a request." Bishop stepped forward. "Like *now*, buddy." His large bald head gleamed in the shafts of light.

Diesel took a step to his left, opening up the triangle. His black hair looked a little wild and crazy from the rotor wash. "Boss put the place on alert 'cause of you. So just chill and get on the chopper."

"Can't do that," Morgan said. "I left my car with the valet, and he looked kinda slimy."

"You gonna make this hard, Morgan?" Spartan puffed herself up, and Morgan saw her fists ball.

"Ahh, so it's a Mexican standoff." Morgan smirked. "But it looks like I'm short of amigos." They'd clearly been told not to use their weapons; otherwise, they'd have drawn them right off the bat. He kept his hands away from his holstered Walther. "Been awhile since we sparred in the gym. Who's first?"

"We're not playing games, smart-ass," said Spartan. "We're bringing you back." She started moving forward, then Bishop and Diesel joined her.

Morgan reached down, took a good, strong grip on Neika's leather collar, and said, "Guard." She instantly jumped to her feet, straining forward and baring her icepick canines, growling and slathering drool. The trio stopped in their tracks and stared at her.

"Y'know," said Morgan. "Everybody thinks these bomb dogs are passive. Truth is when they train MWDs at Lackland, the first thing they do is teach them to rip flesh."

"Calm her down," Spartan snarled.

"Oh, she's calm," Morgan assured them. "She's just hungry, and she doesn't like you." He crouched down and spoke to Neika as she shuddered and made unholy sounds in her throat. He pointed at Spartan. "Don't go for that one. She's got no balls." Then he pointed at Bishop and Diesel. "But those two, girl, they've got nice big scrotums. You can rip 'em right off."

Bishop and Spartan's eyes went wide and their fingers twitched toward their guns.

"By the way, boys and girls," Morgan warned, "she's gonna hurt you. But if you hurt *her*, I'll kill you, and slow."

"Screw you, Morgan," Spartan raged. "You're coming with us!" and then she charged, which was exactly what Morgan knew she'd do.

He commanded, "Hold!" in Neika's ear, twisted her collar to the left, and released her. She exploded from his grip in a blur of muscle and fur, charging right past Spartan for Bishop. He tried to spin and run, but the hundred-pound dog launched off the floor and hit him like a sledgehammer, sinking her teeth in his triceps as he screamed and went down.

Spartan slammed into Morgan just as hard, but he'd already squatted and jammed his open right hand up into her pubis, gripped her spiky blond hair with his left, straightened, and flipped her over his head. He was already spinning back for Diesel as he heard Spartan slam to the floor. Her head bounced once on the concrete.

Diesel came on in a Krav Maga stance, fists beside his head, legs slightly parted and pigeon-toed. Morgan feinted to the right, took Diesel's swing, blocked it with his left and kneed him hard in the gut.

Diesel hissed out a groan and bent over as Morgan slammed the back of his neck with his left elbow, looped his right arm around his neck and fell flat back on the floor, slinging both legs around Diesel's trunk and squeezing with everything he had.

Morgan gripped his right wrist with his left as Diesel writhed and kicked and wind-milled his arms, trying to reach Morgan's head. But Morgan kept his face tucked down tight as he increased the crush on Diesel's carotid and watched Neika dragging Bishop across the floor as she tore his clothes and his skin, and he cursed and screamed, "Get her off me!"

Morgan grunted in Diesel's ear. "Go to sleep, bro."

"Fuuuck yooou," Diesel wheezed as the blood drained from his brain.

"Maybe later, though you're not my type. Just tap out." But he kept on squeezing until Diesel went limp. Morgan flipped his head back upside down to check on Spartan. She was just coming to, moaning and holding her skull.

He squirmed out from underneath Diesel and got up. Neika was still working Bishop over, and he was curled up in a ball. Morgan walked over, his bad knee aching and his lungs heaving, but he grinned as he bent to Bishop's fetal form, pulled his comrade's handgun from his thigh holster, dropped the magazine, ejected the round, and slid them both across the floor. Better not to get a bullet in the back—some folks got riled up by dogs.

He gripped Neika's collar and said, "Out." She released her bite on Bishop as if a switch had been thrown and sat, grinning and panting and looking up at Morgan for approval. He ruffled her head and said, "Good girl!" He patted his left thigh, and she followed him as he made for the side door.

"My goddamn arm, Morgan," Bishop groaned behind Morgan's back.

"Well, don't pull that three-to-one shit on me," Morgan said as he stepped outside with Neika and slammed the door.

The Lakota helo was sitting on the rippling grass about a hundred feet away in the clearing, its black rotors spinning as it idled. Morgan took out his Walther and aimed it at the gleaming cockpit and the form of the pilot sitting behind it. The pilot raised his hands, and then Morgan saw his wide grin. It was Peter Conley. Morgan grinned back and put up the pistol. Cougar gave him a snappy salute as he and Neika trotted by.

Morgan looked down at the shepherd and smiled as she kept pace with his strides, her long tongue lolling. "Girl, I owe you a bone."

She smiled back and barked as they ran for the car.

Chapter Twenty-One

She was a lithe blonde with hazel eyes, her tow-colored tresses roped in a perfect braid to her midback and her tortoise-shell glasses offering an air of proud intellect.

Her gray suit was modestly cut, the double-breasted jacket revealing only the top of a buttoned-up tangerine blouse, the skirt hem exposing just half her knees. Her stockings were plain, her shoes flat black and made for walking, and her fingers that gripped the brown Marks & Spencer briefcase showed no rings. She wore no jewelry, except for a brushed-steel Tag Heuer watch, and she carried no purse.

With a glance at her purposeful gait, it would be hard to tell if she were gay, or straight, or neither at all.

Inside her breast pocket, her British passport announced her as Rosalind Stone, as did a pack of glossy business cards in a silver case. They stated her employer as Thales, a military communications company, of which she was an assistant vice president of sales. But her given name was Lily, and she was approaching Zijin Cheng, the Forbidden City in the heart of Beijing, the People's Republic of China.

"I see you're on the move," Lincoln Shepard said deep in her ear. "So it's showtime."

"Mm-hmm."

"You're not gonna talk to me much today, are you?"

"Uh-uh."

"Fair enough. I like quiet girls," Shepard said. "So, listen up. Bloss wants you to get eyes on Hyo and see if you can find out what he's up to, but she says keep it low risk and then just exfil. Copy?"

Instead of answering, Lily muttered "Bloss?"

"You like it?" Shepard replied. "I made it up. Combines Bloch and Boss. Nice, huh?" He could practically hear Lily's eyes rolling and then remembered that the operative was not on vacation. "FYI: it's a shit storm back here. Cobra's rogue, working some other angle. At least that's what we think, and the Wizard's duly pissed. Got any questions before you're down the rabbit hole?"

"Uh-uh," Lily grunted again.

Shepard waited. "Whenever you get like this, I can tell you're a little tight."

Lily coughed in her hand and whispered, "and a bit wet."

Shepard laughed. "You're so twisted, just like everybody else around here. I'll keep the comm open till you're clear, okay?"

"Mm-hmm."

She walked along now in the hazy morning sunlight, the Meridian Gate looming before her at the end of a vast plaza of flat gray stones. The term *gate* was deceptive, as the southern entrance to the Forbidden City was composed of an enormous red building, with high-walled wings on either side—angled outboard and topped with double cupolas. With its arched opening in the center, the whole thing looked like an angry Chinese lion just waiting to swallow her up.

For a moment, she wished she were a tourist, and could spend the day exploring the hundred square acres of 980 ancient buildings, its museums of treasures from the Zing and Qing dynasties, and its walls and ramparts and moats. But she wasn't here for the view. She was here to track down Colonel Shin Kwan Hyo.

CIDEX, the China International Defense Electronics Exhibition, was being held in the capital at the Exhibition Center, where hundreds of manufacturers from the around the world had come to pitch their wares to Beijing. Of course, given that the show was run by the Peoples Liberation Army, China's purpose in throwing the party was to get their hands on all the latest drones, tactical communications packages and missile command and control.

The PLA's tactic was to charm and smile and purchase, for double the asking price, any new toy they thought worthy of reverse engineering. The people who attended knew this, but they all went home happy with bulging wallets. After all, the Chinese had invented piracy on the high seas a millennium ago. Why should they stop on the low ground?

Lily, as Rosalind the sales rep for Thales, had arranged to meet with a PLA general named Deng Tao Kung, who she'd e-seduced into taking an interest in Thales' most sensitive encrypted radio packages. Some careful research by Zeta had revealed that General Kung was a missile regiment commander and that Colonel Hyo was in the same game, so the odds were good that they'd be sharing tea.

None of the serious business meetings were held at the convention center; too many prying eyes and ears. General Kung had chosen to hold court this morning in the Forbidden City and had invited "Rosalind Stone" for a brief, friendly chat. She was hoping that was all she'd need.

Lily entered the entrance archway and headed straight for the Gate of Supreme Harmony. Then she walked left along a marble-lined moat for the Hall of Military Eminence, which was a modest red building with wooden-screened windows and a sloping orange roof. It had once housed thousands of ancient historical strategy books, which had all been burned in a conqueror's fire. It was now simply an empty hall, perfect for quiet conferences. Unlike the other opulent structures, it held little attraction for tourists.

Her heart rate picked up a little as she saw a small gathering on the slate walkway before the central door of the hall. They were mostly military officers—predominantly men, but there were a few women. nd they were all Asian. Among them stood a few Westerners in business attire who she assumed were sales people like herself, or rather, like she was pretending to be. A pair of uniformed PLA military police stood between her and the throng, observing anyone who approached with their steely gazes.

Nothing fancy now, lass, she told herself. *All we want is a handshake with Hyo and to pique his interest in another meeting. Then we're out.*

She had to remind herself that she wasn't doing her usual "honey trap" thing today. She had to be absolutely sexless, which was a challenge for her.

One of the MPs pushed out a palm and looked her over. "Yes, miss?"

"I am here to meet General Deng Tao Kung. My name is Rosalind Stone."

The first MP nodded and pointed at her briefcase while the other one stepped in and extended his arms, palms up. Lily placed her briefcase on his palms and thumbed the catches. The first MP opened it, poked through the contents with a finger, closed it, and waved toward the doorway. She wasn't surprised that they didn't frisk her because that was a cultural no-no here. But it wouldn't have mattered anyway because there was nothing under her suit but modest lingerie. Sometimes you just had to go weaponless, and pray.

"Thanks," she said.

The MPs nodded jerky head bows; she excused her way through the small crowd and stepped inside. It took a few moments for her eyes to adjust. The Hall of Military Eminence was a large rectangular space with a polished floor of teakwood planks lit only by the stream of diffused sunlight slanting in through the screen windows. The floor space had been carefully arranged with red brocade divans, thick wooden armchairs, and low tea tables.

Military officers and business people occupied the sitting spaces, heads bent close, discussing catalogues and technical specs as translators hovered nearby. A small flock of young Chinese women in blue silk wraps moved around the floor carrying trays of teapots, cups, and small finger snacks.

Looking around the room, Lily spotted General Kung by matching his face to the image she'd memorized. He was sitting on a divan against the far wall, sipping tea and chatting with a younger Chinese officer. A pair of bodyguards hovered nearby. He wore a sage-green dress uniform nearly identical to the older American "Class-A," with brass buttons, five rows of ribbons over the left breast pocket, a light green dress shirt, and an olive tie.

On his lap rested his officer's "wheel hat," with red piping and a large red star on the peak. His gray hair was cropped close, and his face appeared almost kindly, with smooth skin, half-smiling lips, and gentle eyebrows.

She walked toward him as, to her left, she noticed a group of North Korean officers. They were easy to spot in their subdued, badly tailored, brown dress uniforms—with big red epaulets and huge hats the size of apple pies. She didn't look at them again as she approached Kung's low table. He looked up from his conversation, rose, and bowed.

"Ah, Miss Stone."

"Yes, General." Lily bowed slightly and offered him her business card, presenting it with both hands in the Japanese fashion. Although Sino-Japanese relations had always been, in the dry, pragmatic terms of the Communist Party, "interesting," the Nippon ritual of two-handed, bowing, business card exchange was now the preferred norm throughout Asia.

Kung took it and motioned to the empty chair beside the divan. They sat.

"Tea?" He asked, but he didn't wait for her answer and said something in Chinese to one of the passing tea ladies. The woman placed a steaming cup in front of Lily, and she nodded her thanks and sipped. "So, Miss Stone. I was intrigued by some of your offerings." He had very fine English and a soft, reedy voice.

"I rather hoped you might be interested," she said, using her native, lightly lilting accent to her advantage. She placed her briefcase on the table, smoothly opened it as if exacting a choreographed ritual, and presented Kung with a brochure. He flipped through it quickly, then closed it, and smiled.

"I am actually more interested in the items that are not in your catalog. The items that are, shall we say, in special limited editions."

Lily released her first smile, although she kept it tight, without teeth. She knew the man would not use words like *restricted*, *embargoed*, or *prohibited*.

That was not the East Asian way. But *limited edition* was particularly deft. She only hoped she could be as adroit.

"At Thales," she said softly, "we are pleased to discuss anything. We are, after all, an ecumenical corporation."

Kung laughed, but only with his belly. His eyes, however, narrowed, his eyebrows taking on a position that could be seen as shrewd. "I like that word, *ecumenical*," he said, although she interpreted his use of the word *like* as meaning anything but. "Does it mean you have no rules?"

"Or that all rules are flexible," she countered. She glanced up to find the North Korean contingent turned their way, but she ignored them—focusing only on the general. "We have some new guidance systems, both GPS and laser, that we have recently reclassified as, to borrow your most insightful term, strictly limited editions...in both number and availability."

Kung's head rose and then slowly lowered. "Then, I gather, that means time is of the essence." The general sat back, sipped some more tea and gazed at the ceiling. "I recall this anecdote about Winston Churchill...It was something about morality and commerce."

"Yes," Lily said slowly. I think I know the one you refer to." When Kung did not reply, "Miss Stone" cautiously continued. "Churchill was at a soiree, was he not, where he encountered a pretty woman and asked if she would sleep with him for a million pounds sterling. When she quickly agreed, he then asked if she would do it for a single pound. She asked if he thought her a whore, to which he replied, 'We've already established that, madam. We're simply negotiating the price'."

Kung's smile widened, and at first, Lily thought he was having an adverse reaction to the tea. But she realized he was silently laughing—quaking.

Lily resisted internally exulting herself, even though she felt certain she had him where she wanted him. But it was at that moment that she dared look away—to see Colonel Shin Kwan Hyo looking down at her.

She hadn't seen him up close in Seoul. His short black hair was so dense that she couldn't discern its roots. He had thick arching eyebrows, black eyes, a flat nose, and to the left of his thin lips a white scar that curled up like one end of a handlebar moustache. He looked like a crouching tiger packed in a uniform. His officer's cap was tucked under his right arm, his thick fingers tapping the brim.

Lily dipped her head politely. Hyo did the same and pulled his gaze from her eyes. Instead, he looked at General Kung and said something in Chinese. The general gestured at the colonel and spoke to Lily in English.

"Miss Stone, this is Colonel Hyo of the Korean People's Army. Colonel, this is Rosalind Stone."

"A pleasure," said Lily.

"*Bingo*," she heard Shepard whisper in her ear.

"You are from?" Hyo asked in a tone that sounded like he regularly chewed glass.

"Thales Group, sir." She plucked out a business card and offered it up, again with both hands. He looked at it as if it were a particularly interesting fire ant and then retrieved it.

"Yes. You make Starstreak."

"Yes, sir. From the Belfast office."

"Starstreak?" General Kung inquired.

Lily turned to him. "It's an HVM, General, a high-velocity missile used in the air defense role. It has multiple variants, such as man-portable, attack helicopter, vehicle, and so forth."

Kung looked very pleased, as if his own granddaughter had just passed her graduate exams. Colonel Hyo interrupted the exchange.

"I would meet with you," he said to Lily.

She smiled. "At your convenience, Colonel."

He turned away, and strode back to his coterie of younger officers, who looked over his shoulder at her as he spoke to them. She saw him examining her business card and then take out his cell phone.

Lily's pulse started throbbing in her neck. *He's running a check on me. Bloody suspicious bastard's smart.*

"He's calling the main number," Shepard whispered in her ear. "No biggie. I've got ambient office noise running and Charlotte's handling the pickup." Charlotte was another Brit working in Zeta's back office.

Lily turned her focus back to General Kung as she tried to control her adrenaline surge. "He seems...pleasant, General," she said, lying with a smile.

...Kung snorted a short laugh. "The colonel is many things, Miss Stone, but pleasant is not one of them. However, he treats my guests well because *I* control his budget."

"Yes, I rather assumed so," she said as she heard the drama at Zeta HQ playing out in her ear—the recorded sounds of office chatter, keyboards clicking, and Charlotte picking up a line.

"Thales Group, London. How may I be of service?" There was a pause, and then, "Oh, I'm afraid Ms. Stone is overseas, Sir, at CIDEX in Beijing. I can put you through to her extension if you'd care to leave a message." Another pause. "Yes, perhaps in a week. Thank you, sir."

The conversation ended, and Lily glanced at Hyo again. He was tucking his cell phone away, but a chill rippled up her spine as one of his officer's blatantly snapped a photo of her with his own cell. Then Hyo turned around and came back, followed by two of his uniformed men. He stopped and loomed above the tea table.

"When are you free?" he asked.

"Well, I..." Lily looked at General Kung. "The general and I were going to discuss some potential acquisitions..."

Hyo looked at his watch. "Today is good."

"Yes, of course." Lily touched the bridge of her glasses and adjusted them on her nose. A trickle of sweat crawled down her armpit. The young officer who'd taken her photo was staring at his cell, and then he whispered something in Hyo's ear. The colonel nodded, and his face turned to granite.

"The Pentagon has very good surveillance cameras," he hissed.

General Kung laughed. "Well, of course it does, Colonel."

"Not that one, General," Hyo said to him. "A different Pentagon." And then he reached out, pulled Lily's glasses from her face, and handed them to his officer.

General Kung jutted his head back, and Lily felt her bowels clenching. Hyo turned to Kung and spoke in clipped, angry Chinese, and Lily felt her palms going hot and slick.

"*Damn,*" Shepard croaked in her ear. "Get the hell *out.*"

But she couldn't. There was nowhere to go, and she was surrounded by a storm of uniforms from every country but her own. General Kung was already recoiling from her, his face going crimson.

Hyo leaned down across the table and stared into her eyes. "Facial recognition is so good these days. And, how do you say...speedy?"

"I'm afraid I don't know what you mean." Her voice trembled.

His smile was like ice. He reached out with his right hand and touched her left temple. And then he cocked his left hand back and slapped the other side of her face so hard that the crack turned the heads of everyone else in the room. She saw a burst of white light as her head snapped around, and then Hyo was looking at his right palm, where her green contact lens sat there like a screaming little mouth.

General Kung jumped up from his seat and snapped his fingers at his bodyguards.

"Arrest this woman!" he snapped to his men. "She is a spy—and an *assassin.*"

Chapter Twenty-Two

Dan Morgan's gleaming Shelby Cobra roared down a long, straight highway—its snarling mouth eating up ribbons of tarmac and spitting them out from its rumbling tailpipes. He was coming up to his thirteenth hour of driving and felt it. His butt was sore, his trick knee was throbbing, and his eyes were starting to feel like he'd rubbed them with sand.

But none of that mattered. It was all about the mission. He'd been tired before.

Route 64 had started out interesting, winding its way northwest through the scenic lush mountains of West Virginia, where the high forests and looping turns kept him alert and feeling alive—the kind of driving he liked. But then it had straightened out, like a long pull of gray taffy, with barely a wave through the flats of Ohio—the kind of driving that he wasn't as thrilled with.

Still, the weather had been sunny and warm, and Neika was the perfect road trip companion. With the windows rolled down, she sat there on the passenger seat, pink tongue lolling, toothy smile wide, eyes squinted in pleasure, and the wind pinning her ears back. Even as the day faded, she never asked, "How much longer?"

"You on comms, Cobra?"

Shepard's voice startled him. He turned down the western drawl of Kenny Chesney singing "Save It for a Rainy Day" on the radio. The song had made him brood about Jenny, so he was glad for the interruption.

"Here," he said. "You home from Wonderland for the night?"

"Yeah," Shepard answered. "You're my dinner date."

"Then work your magic and beam me up some grub. I've been living on sour coffee and stale donuts."

"Can't do that," Shepard scoffed. "At least not yet."

"So, what's the big rig's twenty?"

"Approaching Lexington, Kentucky from the east on Sixty."

Morgan glanced at his navigator. "We're about half an hour out."

"What are you going to do when you see him, Cobra? Run an eighteen-wheeler off the road with a muscle car?"

"Maybe," said Morgan. "Appreciate the track on this, Shep. Not sure why you're still in the game, but thanks."

"I'm your biggest fan—actually, your *only* fan at the moment."

Morgan reached over and ruffled Neika's head. "Hey, my dog still likes me."

"Okay, so that's two."

By the time Morgan and Neika had reached the Shelby in the woods outside Virginia Tobacco, Shepard had already still-framed the video of the truck from the surveillance tapes, enlarged the image, and extracted the license plate. Then he'd tracked the truck down as a lease from a freight hauler in Colorado.

Some sort of front company had leased the truck, so he couldn't find any shipping manifests or delivery schedules. However, all the big trucking companies were using GPS trackers on their rigs to keep eyes on their drivers, so he'd simply hacked into the main company's net and pinned the truck as a glowing blue dot on his laptop's nav app.

Unfortunately, the truck was already moving from west to east through southern Kentucky, so he had no point of origin. Finding that out would be up to Morgan, but Shepard had no doubt that he'd do it...somehow.

"Heads-up," Shepard said. "Got some news. That rig just pulled up somewhere. Might be a truck stop, on One Twenty-Seven just west of Lexington, right after the river."

Morgan squinted through the windshield at the fading sun. "Well, talk about timing. It's obviously chow time. I think I'll go spoil his dinner."

"Okay," Shep said. "Don't let him spoil yours."

Morgan concentrated on the dinnertime traffic, which was nothing like the snarls back east. Within the half hour he was on the other side of Lexington, gunning the Cobra down a double ribbon of highway. The night had fallen fast, and the roadside lamps threw shimmering glows on the tarmac like hovering flying saucers.

He spotted a "Flying J" sign pinned to a tower above a twenty-four-hour eatery. To the left was a large gas-up area with extra-high roofing so big rigs could fit, and to the right was the truck parking area, with eighteen-wheelers snuggled flank to flank like beached whales. In one quick scan, he counted no less than thirty. He pulled the Cobra around to a smaller parking lot meant only for cars, where he tucked it behind somebody's U-Haul before cutting the throbbing engine.

"Shep, you there?"

"Yeah," Shepard said. "Just making popcorn."

"Whatcha gonna watch?"

"*Road Trip.*"

"Funny. Listen, there's about thirty rigs parked in this lot. Which one is it?"

"Can't help you there, Cobra. I've got the truck pinned to a nav, but it's not deep detail or satellite overhead. Just the general location."

"Okay, I'll recon it. What's the plate number?"

"Z two six ATR."

"Got it."

Morgan got out, stretched his back, and shook out his knee. Then he zipped up his field jacket, pulled his watch cap on, closed his door, and came around for Neika. She squatted right there on the blacktop, peed a long river, and then looked up at him as if to say, "Okay, good to go."

He leashed her, and they strolled over to the truck park side, where almost all the cabs were dark. The drivers either slept in their tucked-away bunks or were inside the restaurant shoveling food. It didn't take long to cruise past the tails of all the trucks, where he checked every plate against the letters and numbers in his head. But he came up empty, so he walked the walk again, as if he were holding a lottery ticket and one of those plates just had to be the winner.

But none of them were Z26 ATR. He walked Neika into a small picnic area under the trees. "Shep, you copy?"

"Five by five."

"No match here. Bet they switched license plates."

"Shit," Shepard spat. "I know the damn truck's there somewhere. Now what?"

Morgan merely smiled, looked down at Nieka, and scratched her thick scalp. "No worries," he assured his eyes-and-ears-in-the-sky guy. "The nose knows."

"Huh?"

"Never mind," Morgan said. "Hang tight." He bent down and took Neika's big head in his hands. "We're going to do a little search, girl." The moment she heard *search*, her tail flicked. "You do this right, and I'll buy you a pig's ear."

Military working dogs don't stay with the same human handlers throughout their careers. When a handler finishes his or her tour, the K9 gets passed to someone else, which is why all the training and signals are uniform. Morgan knew this, and he'd worked with enough MWDs in the past, so he also knew how to run Neika through a sniff track.

If the Tomahawks were on any of the trucks, or had been so recently, she'd pick up the scents of high-explosive warheads. But even if the warheads were, God forbid, nuclear, she'd still hit on the solid-fuel rocket boosters.

He walked back into the truck park and looked around. A tired driver was jumping down from his cab. He glanced at Morgan, just another guy with a dog, before trotting away toward the eatery.

Morgan began with Neika at the tail of the first truck, holding her leash loosely with his left hand as he whispered, "Neika, *search*."

They started cruising along the flank. She dropped her head and sniffed the big wheels and the well while Morgan ran a finger along the ledge of the long box. She trotted beside him, occasionally rising up on her hind legs. She poked her nose into the metal gutters, snorted at rivets, and stuck her face in the front wheel well. She sensed nothing and moved on, Morgan close behind.

They started at the nose of the next truck, then the tail of the next, and, by the time they'd sniffed out six trucks, Morgan was getting edgy. Whichever one it was, the driver could show up any minute and just take off. But at the tail end of the seventh truck, Neika acted differently, with shivers rippling through her and the hair standing up on her spine. She tucked her gleaming black nose up under the floorboards, snorted deeply a few times, then backed out, looked up at Morgan, and sat.

Morgan's smile crinkled his eyes. Bomb dogs never barked or whined; they just sat. But just to be sure, he pulled her away from the rear of the truck, made a small circle, and had her go at it again. Sure enough, she sniffed, shivered, and sat, looking up at him with an expression that said, "What do you want? An engraved invitation?"

He bent down, ruffled her furry head madly and crooned in her ear, "Good girl, Neika. Good girl!" He walked her quickly back to the Shelby and locked her inside with a couple of large Milk-Bones. Then he quick-marched back to the truck. "Shep, I've got a hit."

"Seriously?"

"Don't I sound serious?"

"As a heart attack."

"I'm at the cab now. Looks like nobody's home."

"Wait," Shepard said while he hammered at his laptop. "What's the model?"

"Kenworth."

"Take out your cell and hold it up to the lock, back side against the door metal."

Morgan placed his foot on the runner, gripped the side handle of the cab, hauled himself up, and did what he was told. The locking mechanism clicked, and the lock button popped up.

"You're friggin' amazing," he said.

"Kreskin is amazing." Shepard grinned. "I'm incredible. But kiss me later. You got quick work to do."

Morgan climbed into the cab and slid over to the passenger seat. He looked around but could see nothing more than the darkened slumber bunk. There was no way to see from there into the big container behind the cab.

He then examined the dashboard, noting a grip for a cell phone, and spotted something unusual: a small surveillance monitor, probably attached to a camera in the cargo box. If you were only hauling something harmless—like chickens—you didn't need to check if they were happy or not. He locked the doors, crawled between the seats into the back, and waited.

Ten minutes later, the driver hauled himself up into the cab and shut the door. Morgan stood on no ceremony. He jammed the barrel of his PPK behind the guy's ear.

"Both hands on the wheel," he said. "And let me see your knuckles go white."

The driver hunched and did as he was told, but slowly. Morgan could practically hear the guy's brain whirring and teeth grinding as he looked at the driver's hands in the dim light. He had heavily calloused knuckles, so he was a martial-artist type...or just liked punching bricks. Morgan kept the gun barrel bruising the guy's skull flesh as he worked his way into the passenger seat.

The driver turned only his eyes and stared at him. He was Asian, in his thirties, with thick black hair banded in a "samurai" bun on top. His eyes were like a shark's: dark, shiny, and dead. His coiled muscles bulged under a lightweight black jacket.

"What you want?" the driver snarled in a heavy accent Morgan recognized. Not Japanese, not Chinese. Korean. Kadir had taken pains carefully explaining to him the difference one day. He now knew they were far from the same, no matter how similar the skin color and eye shape. "No got money," the truck driver now said.

"Don't need any," Morgan said. "I'm rich. Where's your phone and the keys?"

The driver glanced down at his right side. "Pocket."

"Don't even breathe fast. I'm cranky." Morgan reached into the driver's jacket, yanked out the things, and eased himself back on the seat, keeping the PPK trained on the driver's face. He pocketed the cell and tossed the keys in the guy's lap.

"Right hand only. Turn it on, but just the electrics. And then hands back on the wheel."

The driver inserted the key and turned. The dashboard glowed, and the surveillance monitor flickered—showing the length of the cargo box in black and white. It was empty. He gripped the wheel again, his fingers white.

"Where are they?" Morgan growled.

"Where what?" The driver turned and looked at Morgan fully now, his nostrils flaring.

"Your cargo."

"What cargo? You crazy, man?"

"The Tomahawks," Morgan said, catching a reflexive flicker in the driver's eyes. "Tell me right now where you dropped them, and I won't blow your kneecap off."

Then the driver smiled like a panther. "You gonna shoot me? Big bang right here?"

Morgan smiled back. "You're right." He reached inside his jacket, took out a black, five-inch, snap-on Gemtech suppressor, and popped it onto the end of his barrel. "I prefer the threaded versions, but these are usually okay for a couple of shots."

The driver's neck veins bulged, his eyes blazing. "Screw you! I tell you nothing, *dickhead.*"

"All right, which knee's your favorite?"

The driver made his move. He yelled like a Tae Kwon Do black belt; his right hand released the wheel and bladed hard as he swung it in a lightning arc at Morgan's silencer. But Morgan simply dropped flat on his back and flicked the barrel down. The driver's stiff hand smashed into the passenger headrest and broke it right off the mount. Then the driver launched himself out of his seat, and Morgan saw his left hand snap up from his boot, gripping a very long serrated blade. Morgan raised his gun barrel and shot him in the heart.

The cab flashed white, but there was barely a sound, other than the driver's skull bouncing off the steering wheel as he toppled over to the left.

Morgan looked at the corpse. "I was hoping you'd do something like that, *dickhead.*"

Chapter Twenty-Three

It was 3 a.m. when Morgan found himself lying in the grass once again, staring through his binoculars at a cluster of buildings across a wide clearing. But this time it was dark, cold, and wet, and his black jeans were soaked through from a recent rain. His knees trembled from the chill and adrenaline.

The Shelby was nestled behind him in a hedgerow of high bulrushes, with Neika curled up in the back seat. His instincts told him this might get ugly and he wasn't going to risk her taking a bullet. Shepard had a fix on the Shelby, so he could send someone out to rescue Neika if Morgan didn't come back. At the very least, she'd make it to his funeral. Before he could prevent it, he saw a flash of Jenny and Alex wearing black on either side of a gravesite. He swept that image from his mind, choosing to review how he'd gotten here instead.

Using the dead driver's cell phone, Shepard had hacked into its apps, reversed the navigation history, and pinpointed the location where the driver had probably delivered the Tomahawks. How the hell the missiles had been hijacked, remained undetected and were then smuggled out here, Morgan had no clue, but he'd run down that tidbit later.

At the moment he was way southeast in backwoods, hayseed Kentucky, looking at a ramshackle white farmhouse, a few smaller outbuildings, and a towering grain silo with a peeling black cupola. The missiles were definitely there somewhere because he could see small, dark figures patrolling the grounds—bulky in tactical gear, weapons gleaming in the dim starlight. With those assault rifles, they sure as hell weren't guarding sheep.

He swept his binos to the left and focused on a line of three black Suburban tac vehicles. Between where he lay and the farm, those trucks would be his only cover.

I hate low combat crawls, he muttered in his head. But there was no other way to do it.

Beside him in the grass lay his Smith & Wesson M&P15 tactical rifle, which he'd pulled from the trunk when he parked the car. It had a double magazine rig in the well and an Aimpoint red-dot sight mounted on the top rail, but no night-vision scope—he was old school and didn't care for the grainy green.

He put the binos away, slipped the rifle to the ends of his upturned palms, and started elbowing forward, one slow inch at a time.

It took about an hour. But then he was there, soaked and breathless, behind the rear bumper of the first Suburban. He'd powered-down his ear piece so nothing would break his concentration, and for a while he just lay there and worked on his heart rate and lungs until the pulse stopped pounding in his ears so he could hear again.

Slow footsteps crunched from somewhere in front of the cars. He quietly laid his rifle down, slipped the silenced PPK from his jacket, pulled himself up into a squat at the right rear of the truck, and peeked around its trunk with one eye.

Another Asian dude. Morgan's brow creased as he saw him in side silhouette—spiky black hair, muscular neck, a tactical vest thickened with ceramic plates, and an MP5 "Kurtz"—the short-barreled German subgun.

What the hell's this? Some sorta Kkangpae drug-gang rocket-smuggling thing? But it didn't matter. *American soldiers are dead, and so shall you be.*

He tucked back in, ducked-walked from the rear of that Suburban, and over behind the next one to the left. He took a long breath and emitted a low-pitched mourning-dove whistle. The boots stopped and then crunched as they turned.

Morgan did it once more. He now heard the boots moving between the two vehicles, coming his way, and he waited until they were almost on him.

He stepped out and shot the sentry point-blank in the throat. The sentry's head snapped back, and he stiffened as if electrocuted. As he toppled forward Morgan caught the MP5 and stepped back, letting him fall. But the guy twisted to his right as he collapsed, and a large carabiner clipped to the back of his vest banged off the hide of the truck.

Damnit!

"*Dong Pil?*" Someone was calling the guy's name. "*Eodi Keysayo?*"

Morgan recognized the words: *Where are you?* Definitely Korean.

He slung the MP5 strap over his back, holstered the PPK, slithered back to the first truck, and retrieved his rifle. More boots were tramping from the direction of the farmhouse, the pace picking up to a trot.

"Dong Pil!"

Shit, Morgan cursed in his head. *So much for a sneak attack.* If he let them get to the trucks they'd surround and take him. He snap-rolled quickly to the right and saw two more Koreans sprinting in full tactical. Center-mass shots would only dent their "chicken plates" and piss them off, so he opened up on their hips.

He had a flash suppressor on the end of his barrel, but the explosions still blazed like yellow lightning, and the reports banged off the buildings like sledgehammers on an anvil. The Koreans went down screaming.

He heard more slamming boots and shouts. He glanced to the left at the trucks, hearing the voice of his old combat-tactics instructor from "the Farm" in his head: *"Whatever makes the most sense, don't do it."* In other words, don't take cover behind the trucks. But he had to make the next crew *think* that's what he was doing.

He got up and hustled over between the first two Suburbans, took a knee in a pool of the first sentry's blood, and fired one shot in the air, so they'd see the flash. Then he sprinted straight back into the field, skidded flat like he was hitting home plate after a triple play, and quick-crawled twenty feet to the right.

He hunkered down behind an old iron farm pump. Sure enough, two more Koreans appeared from the left side of the farmhouse, subguns blazing at their own trucks—the tires hissing out like gut-punched fat men, and the windshields splintering like glass spiderwebs in a gale.

Morgan edged up, braced his rifle on the curved head of the pump handle and took aim at a range of fifty meters. Two quick doubletaps exploded the skull of the closer Korean, and as the second one spun toward Morgan and let fly on full auto, Morgan shot him in the face.

Then the pump shaft thwanged as a bullet struck the iron right in front of his chest. Needles of flying lead stung his face, and he launched himself backward onto the ground—gasping as his spine met the slung MP5. Another bullet whip-cracked just above his nose as he spun himself around on his back like a crab and took two quick rolls to the left.

This one was nuts, coming straight at him from the right corner of the house, screaming something as he unloaded his MP5 in long bursts. But, blinded by his own muzzle flashes and rage, he was still chewing up the water pump. Morgan just lay there and waited until he heard the blessed sound of the subgun's bolt locking back on an empty chamber; then he jumped up. He saw the guy madly trying to load a fresh mag, just before he stitched him with lead from his crotch to his throat.

Silence—except for the ringing in his ears and the groans of the first two guys whose legs he'd shattered. He waited for a full two minutes, letting his breathing calm to something like normal. He wasn't sure how many rounds he'd fired, so he switched magazines and chambered a round. Then the front door of the farmhouse opened. Another guy came out, wearing his tactical gear like the rest, but Morgan could see no weapon, and his hands were held high over his head.

"I surrender!" the last sentry yelled in a heavy accent as he stepped off the stoop. "No more!"

Morgan looked around to check his perimeter, then rose to his feet, keeping his red dot trained on a spot just above the Korean's chest plate. *A prisoner might be useful,* he thought. *But odds are, he won't talk.* The guy was wearing black gloves at the ends of his bare arms.

"Stop right there," Morgan called as he advanced. But the guy kept coming as if he didn't understand. Between him and Morgan, the two wounded sentries were writhing on the ground.

"I give up!" the Korean yelled out again.

"Stop *right* there," Morgan shouted this time, and then he saw the guy was clutching something in his up-thrust right hand. Morgan pulled the trigger, and his bullet smacked into the Korean's chest plate, lifting the bastard off his feet, but he also heard the familiar *pop* of a hand grenade firing pin. Its spoon went twirling up in the air as he slammed himself down face-first. Then the damn thing exploded with a heavy crump and a blinding flash.

Nobody was screaming anymore. The last guy had killed himself, along with his two wounded buddies. Morgan got up on his knees and sat back on his haunches.

What is this? Guadalcanal? Or, maybe more accurately, *Inchon?*

He spent fifteen minutes checking over the corpses—gathering up their guns and tossing them out in the high grass, just to make sure. He was surprised and pleased to find the old water pump still working, and he sucked down half a gallon before splashing it over his stinging face and his neck.

Following that, he walked over to the towering white silo. The door wasn't locked, so he took a breath, opened it up, stepped inside, found a light switch, and flicked it on. He took out his cell and tapped some numbers.

"Collins," a sleepy growl answered.

"Guess who?" Morgan said.

"Sounds like a hissing Cobra."

"That's right." Morgan looked up at three enormous Tomahawk missiles, racked on mobile gantries and with their vicious noses pointing at the silo cap. "And I'm looking at three big red dildos." He heard General Collins sitting up in bed.

"Out-freaking-standing," Collins said.

"As I remember, sir, that's your highest compliment."

"That is correct, Mister Morgan. Fine job. Where are you?"

"Ass end of Kentucky. I'll text you the coordinates so you can send in the cavalry and be a national hero again. But you'd better make it a spook team, 'cause I made a little mess here."

Of all the things Morgan thought, or hoped, his ex-commander would say, he never imagined the man's next three words.

"No can do."

"No what do?" Morgan blurted.

Collins's voice remained even, in control. "We need one more thing."

"We do?" Morgan frowned at the phone.

"*I* do. Without the tracking logs, there's nothing to prove I wasn't involved in this."

Morgan regained his equilibrium as fast as he'd lost it. "Okay. What do they look like and where do I find them? Some sort of maintenance hatch on the birds?"

"They're not with the birds. The logs are all digital, on a chip."

Morgan resisted the urge to roll his eyes. "All right, let me have it. Where do they keep these chips?"

"Utah. A place called Coldcastle Mountain. Technically, it doesn't exist."

"You know what, Jim?" Morgan growled. "If I didn't owe you some debt of honor, I'd tell you to go screw."

"After this one, Dan, I'm the one who'll owe *you.*"

"Small comfort. All right, so you text me those cords instead, and I'll let you know when I'm close."

"Roger," Collins said, and he clicked off.

Morgan turned off the light, left the silo and closed the door. The air still smelled like gunfire residue and blood. He started trudging his way back to the Shelby.

"Blast it," he muttered, well aware of the choice of words. "I'm so sick of driving."

At least Neika was happy to see him.

Chapter Twenty-Four

The engraved bronze plaque on the door to Paul Kirby's office was etched with the bold capital letters *D.O.*

The initials stood for "Director of Operations," but Alex couldn't help but smirk as she knocked softly on the door. Some tactical team members always made fun of Kirby's sign, claiming that he actually didn't "DO" anything except kiss Mr. Smith's ass and try to undermine Diana Bloch. Others wanted to add another *o* and another *doo*—separated by a dash.

"Come," said the imperious voice from the other side of the door.

Alex pushed it open and walked in. Kirby was seated at his large L-shaped Staples office desk, which Alex figured he'd selected to prove he was "low-budget." The desk had a phony veneer, sort of like Kirby's face. He was leaning back in his chair, reading an open manila file that had a dark red stripe on its border. Alex stood there at attention until he looked up over his thick glasses.

"This isn't the army, Morgan," he said, "which you haven't been through anyway. Sit."

Kirby's guest chairs were a pair of metal folding types, probably chosen because he never wanted people to feel too comfortable. She pulled one over and sat. She'd motorcycled all night from D.C. to Boston, grabbed a short stack at a Pancake House, and cruised right over to headquarters. She was physically wiped, but her mind was still sharp. She was definitely Dan Morgan's daughter. Her leathers creaked on the chair.

Kirby dropped the file and stared at her, with that weasel-like expression—as if he was poking his nose from a burrow. "Where have you been, Morgan?"

Alex shrugged and gave him her college girl smirk. "It was my day off."

"You were recalled."

"Yeah, I came as soon as I got the word. But I was down in D.C."

Kirby picked up a pencil and let the eraser drum on the desk in triplets. "And what were you doing in our nation's capital?"

"I was in Arlington," she said, which was partially true. She didn't know if Kirby might have had her tracked, so she hung her hat on one of her dad's spook wisdoms: *If you have to lie, take the truth and just twist it.* "Tomb of the Unknown Soldier," she added.

"You don't say."

"Uh-huh. One of my uncles is buried there." That was true too.

"Very touching," Kirby snapped, then dropped the pencil, put his elbows on the desk, steepled his fingers, and propped them under his bony nose. "You don't really understand this organization, do you, Ms. Morgan?"

Alex resisted the temptation to snap back, "Maybe better than you," and chose to say instead, "Well, I'm new, but I'm learning..."

"This is not like a job at Target. We don't call in sick; we don't show up late or crave the ends of our shifts. We don't commiserate with our fellow employees about the stressful conditions or paltry benefits. And we never, *ever* have a genuine day off."

"Okay, I know." Alex lifted her palms in partial surrender. "I just thought, you know, the regulations manual talks about stand-down intervals and rest..."

Kirby smacked the desk with his palm, and Alex purposely flinched. If Kirby wanted to put on a show of dressing her down, who was she to deny him?

"This is a tactical intelligence and special operations organization!" he barked. "We follow orders here, daytime, nighttime, anytime. And we are *never* off comms, even if we're banging our boyfriends!"

Alex jerked her head back. Did he mean *her* boyfriend, which she didn't actually have, or his?

"Are we clear, Ms. Morgan?"

"Uh-huh."

"Uh-huh?" His wispy eyebrows flared up.

"I mean, yes sir, we're clear."

He wagged a bony finger at her. "You have a strain of genetic malfeasance, Ms. Morgan."

"Excuse me?"

"Your errant father. He didn't want you involved here, and frankly, neither did I. This isn't some mafia crime family where all the progeny must make their bones. However, Ms. Bloch overrode our objections, apparently seeing some raw potential." Kirby laced his fingers together and loomed closer. "All *I* see is a renegade cobra's slithering snakelet."

With that, Alex's cheeks flushed rosy pink, and she fumed. *You're about to cross the line, a-hole.* Her brown eyes slitted.

"Let's leave my dad out of this, *sir.*"

Kirby's thin mouth twisted up. "Yes. You're a big girl. In a few years, you'll be able to order a drink. But for now, you're going to stay right here at HQ and busy yourself with some admin work until I task you otherwise." He flicked a hand, picked up the file again, and opened it. "Dismissed."

Alex got up, her fingers clenching her sweaty palms. She moved toward the door and turned back. "I don't really have any admin work."

Kirby rolled his eyes. "Then go clean your sniper rifle."

"It's spotless."

"Then go clean someone else's!" he snarled. "Out!"

Alex was still steaming inside as she walked past a row of open cubicles reserved for the wizards and worker bees. Paul Kirby was no different than any other corporate slob, throwing his weight around and making himself feel bigger by stomping on his underlings.

You're right, Kirby, she thought bitterly. *This isn't like Target. It's worse. We don't actually make or sell anything. And there's tons of bureaucratic bullshit.*

She saw Lincoln Shepard glancing at her over the top of one of his monitors. He looked paler than usual.

"Hey there, hotshot," he muttered.

"Hi, Linc." She flicked a weak wave. She liked Shepard, more than most of the people at Zeta.

"You're not looking too chipper today," he observed.

"I'm as happy as a kitten in a dog kennel," Alex grumbled. "You look a little burned out yourself."

"Brain fried," Shepard said. He would have liked to commiserate with Alex about the horror of Lily's capture, but different mission threads were strictly compartmentalized.

"Hey, do you know where Cobra is?" Alex asked.

Shepard glanced around and dropped his voice. "Nobody knows."

"Figures," Alex huffed. "Just like home."

She walked down a hallway and pushed through the door to the Team Room. It was mostly the purview of Tactical—a large space with a long table in the middle for preparing gear braced by wooden benches. Then there were rows of wide, tall, steel-gray personal lockers on either side.

The lockers were intended mostly for Tac operators' gear, clothing, and weapons, but a few were reserved for the "lesser" operatives such as herself.

Nobody was around, so she sat down on a bench and brooded. She sure as hell wasn't going to clean her rifle, *again*, or anyone else's for that matter. "You shoot it, you preen it." That was the rule. Another rule was "Never stop thinking."

So she did. Where the hell was her dad? He'd left Kadir Fastia's with that spring in his step of ridiculous boundless energy, off to tear up the world like some pit bull. That stuff had annoyed her all the time as a kid, but now she knew she'd inherited that strain. Sitting around made her nuts.

He was running down this thing for his old pal, General Collins, determined to clear his name. But after he'd left, Fastia had shared with her that the cause of Collin's career crash was a much bigger fish, namely, one Lieutenant General Sheldon Margolis. So, who was going after *him*? Nobody? It sure seemed that way, though she couldn't exactly ask. *Then go clean your sniper rifle.* Bullshit!

She was hunched on the bench, picking bug residue off her leathers, when she looked at her locker across the room. Then she slapped her knees, got up, left the Team room, and cruised back down the hallway. Shepard was gone, probably off to lunch, and most of the other cubes were empty as well. She spotted Karen in the back, sitting alone. She adopted a phony brightness.

"Hi, Karen!"

"Well hi there, Alex." Karen smiled. "You seem chipper today."

Alex grinned and rolled her eyes. "Actually, I'm fried. But it's cool 'cause Mr. Kirby told me to just do some admin stuff today."

"Admin stuff?" Karen cocked her head. "Like what?"

"Oh, just some file clearing and maintenance. Works for me, though. I just need a machine."

Karen gestured at an empty cubicle off to her right. "You can use that one there. I'm going to grab a bite outside. Want something?"

"Thanks, but I'll do that later. Don't want him to think I'm disobeying his orders."

"God forbid." Karen winked, picked up her backpack, and left.

Alex slipped into a chair at a lone computer, took out her Zeta CAC card, and swiped it in the access strip. The monitor brightened up with its weird wavering Z, which resembled the logo from that movie, *Zorro*.

She opened the Internet, did some Googling on Lieutenant General Sheldon Margolis, then picked up a white telephone headset from the desk and pushed the mike close to her lips. By then she had accessed the

Department of Defense telephone listings and dialed a certain number. A woman answered.

"Pentagon, Public Affairs."

"Morning, ma'am," Alex said brightly. "My name is Alex Steenbeck. I'm a journalist with *The Mandible*."

"*The Mandible?*" The woman held her snicker. "You mean, as in jawbone?"

"Well, yes. It's a college newspaper, Ohio State."

"Oh, I see. And what can we do for you, Alex?"

"So, I'm doing this story about the Eighteen X-Ray program. You know, the one where Army Special Forces takes guys straight out of college?"

"Yes. And?"

"Well, I was hoping to get some quotes from General Margolis. He was head of US Army Special Operations when they started Eighteen X-Ray."

"That's true," the woman said, apparently impressed. "Hold on a sec, please."

Alex waited, shifting in her chair and trying not to glance up at all the "Big Brother" cameras poking down from every corner of Zeta. The woman came back on the line.

"Alex, I'm afraid General Margolis is out of town."

"Oh, that's too bad. I've got a deadline, of course, and a grade goes with it."

"Well, he's apparently down at CENTCOM for the Special Operations Expo. He should be back in a few days."

"Okay," Alex said. "That's in Tampa, right?"

"Yes it is. Seems you know your subject."

Alex grinned into the mike. "I read a lot of Clancy."

The woman laughed. "Good for you. Call us back on Monday, and I'll see what I can do. I'm Gail."

"Thanks, Gail."

"You bet."

Alex took off the headset, shut off the computer, and strolled back over to the Team Room. She went to her locker, worked the combination, pulled out her black gear duffle, and set it on the linoleum floor. Then she swept through her hanging rack of "costumes," selected a bunch of stuff that seemed schoolgirl-reporter appropriate, and folded them into the duffle. She shut the locker, hefted the duffle, left the Team Room, and turned right.

She pushed through the exit door, took the elevator up and popped out into the underground garage. But she walked right past her Ninja and trotted up the ramp and out into the bright daylight. She hailed a Boston Cab and piled into the back.

"Logan Airport, please."

The driver took off. Alex pulled out her wallet and chose her own Visa card, rather than the Amex one linked to the Zeta accounts. She tapped her cell phone and smiled as she found Travelocity.

"Dad's gonna *love* this," she mused.

Chapter Twenty-Five

SOFIC, the Special Operations Forces Industry Conference, is held every year at the Tampa Convention Center. It is an enormous undertaking, composed of hundreds of private companies hawking their military wares in a space that seems about a square mile in size. The convention is an endless labyrinth of booths, from the smallest ones displaying items such as the latest field dressings, tactical flashlights, and combat knives to the stalls the size of small-town playgrounds offering everything from armored assault vehicles to Little Bird helicopters.

Over the course of three days, special operators from fifty nations roam the aisles in search of the latest implements of warfare. Some are in uniform, some not, and for the most part, they're men. So, a comely young female striding through this "mall of death" always draws winks and smiles.

Alex had no idea exactly how she was going to track down General Margolis, but she was determined to walk the convention until her feet were blistered and the lights were turned off. She'd caught a late flight to Tampa, discovered that every decent hotel room in town was booked, and slept in a fleabag out near Busch Gardens.

In the morning she'd dressed in her college reporter outfit—a tartan skirt, low black heels, a cream-colored chemise, and a black cotton-cashmere cardigan—bought a thick notebook at the nearest stationery store, and cabbed it down to the convention.

Admission was by invitation only, so she'd gone to the Press Office, presented her phony Ohio State ID and lied about *The Mandible* having applied months ago, as well as that she'd flown down on her own dime. When her eyes welled up and she looked on the verge of hysteria, they'd given her a patronizing smile and a press pass.

As it turned out, she'd arrived at the last day of the conference, which made her grimace. Margolis might have already finished up all his business and left. But fretting over that wouldn't do any good, so she started an alphabetical grid pattern, beginning with Aimpoint gun sights. By the time she got to Columbia Helicopters her calves were already aching.

The place was packed with handsome, buff men, and if she'd been looking for a boyfriend that would've been great, but she only had eyes for a middle-aged, three-star general. It was like looking for one particular goldfish in the Boston Aquarium.

With her feet on fire, and having already been offered six invitations to lunch, she arrived at the Defense Logistics Agency booth. There was no equipment on display, just a bunch of American army officers discussing the trials and tribulations of quartermasters. She tugged on the sleeve of a tall blond captain, who turned, looked down at her, and smiled.

"Good morning, ma'am," he said. It was the first time she'd ever been called that. "You interested in parachute rigging hangars? They're on sale for half a mil."

Alex glanced at his nameplate and smiled back. "Sorry, Captain Ross, don't think so. Actually, I'm looking for a friend of my dad's."

"And who'd that be?"

"Sheldon Margolis. General Sheldon Margolis. Ever heard of him?"

The captain laughed. " 'Give-em-hell Shel'? Sure. He's probably chewed out everyone here at some point or another. Friend of your father? Wow. Good to know he actually has a friend." Ross took another look at Alex's wide-eyed expression and coed outfit and pointed off to the farthest corner of the convention hall. "Last I saw him, he was over at Northrup Grumman, probably buying some killer drones."

"Great!" Alex said brightly. "Thanks!"

"Hey, want some coffee before you go over there? Long walk."

"Can I swing back afterward?"

"You bet." The captain grinned as Alex waved and took off. The last thing she wanted was a date with some army guy. She was probably a much better shot.

She quick-marched all the way over to Northrup, praying that the general hadn't already moved on. On the way over, she shrugged off her clingy cardigan and slung it over one arm. Then she spotted the display, a sprawling presentation of aircraft models spread out over a carpet of fake grass. In the middle, a small cluster of officers from various branches were listening to a larger man holding court. He had steel-gray hair, a Roman nose, and a turned-down mouth. His ink-blue dress uniform gleamed with "fruit salad" and jump wings, and his black nameplate said "Margolis."

Alex waited until the group of officers moved on to another display, leaving Margolis alone with a navy lieutenant dressed in light khakis and short sleeves. She took a breath and, hugging her notebook to her chest, made her approach.

"Excuse me. General Margolis?"

He turned from the navy lieutenant and looked down at her. "Yes, miss?"

"Hi," she said, extending her hand. "I'm Alex Steenbeck, Ohio State." She slipped the notebook away from her chest, exposing her dangling press pass.

"Good for you, Miss Steenbeck," Margolis said without any warmth or further invitation, but he shook her hand.

"You're press," the navy lieutenant observed with all the pleasure of spotting a cockroach in his soup.

"Yes, sir," said Alex.

Margolis cocked his head to the left. "Lieutenant Honesdale is our PAO down here."

Alex nodded at him as well. "Yes, well, I spoke to the Pentagon public affairs officer, Gail, and she told me where to find you."

"Oh she did, did she?" Margolis frowned. "I'll have to have a word with her."

Before Alex could rush to the woman's defense, the lieutenant cut in. "What's the issue?" he asked, as if every reporter was a problem, which, in his world, was usually the case.

"Well, as I explained to Gail, I'm a reporter for the college newspaper, *The Mandible*. We're doing a story on the Eighteen X-Ray program." Alex turned back to Margolis. "As I understand, General, you were integral in the start-up of that at Fort Bragg."

Margolis's reaction told Alex that her opening gambit was a winner. He clearly felt proud of it, and wanted to let the collegiate world know.

"I was indeed," he told her, his stern expression softening an almost infinitesimal bit.

"*The Mandible*," the lieutenant mused. "Funny name for a publication."

"Go get some coffee, Honesdale," Margolis said. "I think I can handle this one."

"Roger, sir." The lieutenant moved off, but Alex caught a glimpse of him taking out his cell. She hadn't had the time to set up any backup for her cover, so she might not have much of a safety window. She opened her notebook and clicked a pen.

"Sir, so just a few questions, if you don't mind?"

He smiled at her old-fashioned reporting tools, apparently pleased he wouldn't have to speak into the butt end of a smartphone. "Shoot." He backed up onto a high metal bar stool in front of a glass display case and sat, but he was still looking down at her.

"Okay, so, this is for our college seniors. Is the program still in effect? I mean are Special Forces still looking for young men with no prior military service?"

"I don't run that program anymore, Ms. Steenbeck. But my understanding is yes. However, the quality of grads is on the downside for the last few years. It's hard to lure them out of their 'safe spaces'."

Alex looked up at him. No smile or irony in his eyes. He wasn't joking. "Is it all right if I quote you on that?"

"It's the unvarnished truth, so why not?"

Alex glanced sideways, spotting Honesdale over by a refreshment stand. He was mixing his coffee with one hand and talking on his cell with the other. She scribbled head-down in her notebook.

"So, Sir. The program's fallen off, you'd say."

"It was hot and heavy in the few years after 9/11. Then some of those college kids started coming back in body bags, which happens to be the nature of warfare. But a lot of universities started bad-mouthing the idea. They're mostly run now by leftist professors babysitting millennial brats."

"Yes, I see," said Alex as she continued writing, and then she took her shot. "I was talking to General Collins about some of this..."

"Say again?"

She looked up. Margolis's thick gray eyebrows were turned down at the middle.

"General James Collins," she said innocently. "I heard you know him."

"I know him," said Margolis, and he rose from the stool and stood up. "I know him very well. And he had nothing to do with Eighteen X-Ray, or anything else you should be interested in for a college newspaper." He stared at her with a pair of lizard green eyes for a long moment. "What are you here for, Ms. Steenbeck?"

"Well, what I said, Sir. General Collins's name came up in connection with yours, so I just figured I'd reach out to him too."

Margolis's expression turned dark as a thundercloud, and he reached out and gripped Alex's arm. "*What* are you here for, young lady?"

She looked as his fingers and back at his scowling lips. "Just for a quote. It's still a free press, isn't it, sir?"

Lieutenant Honesdale appeared to her right, holding his coffee cup and snarling down at her. "You don't work for *The Mandible*, miss—which would be impossible anyway, since the last issue was published a year ago."

"Honesdale," Margolis snapped. "Go get security."

Shit. Alex's mind raced through her options, which were few. She saw Honesdale nodding, and she felt Margolis's grip tightening, so she reached out and slapped the bottom of Honesdale's cup. It sent a shower of steaming black coffee all over his crotch.

"Goddamn it!" he yelled and jumped back.

Alex jerked her arm from Margolis and took off. She sprinted down the closest display aisle as heads snapped around, and she heard a shout from behind. Then she took a hard right.

Thankfully, she hadn't forgotten to note where all the emergency exits were, and she pounded her way through a craft services area and a slew of round tables with men wolfing hot dogs. Using them as cover, she charged toward the restrooms but took a hard left away from them—exploding through a barred exit door as an alarm went off.

She didn't stop running for three blocks, even in the low heels, until she spotted a Tampa cab, jumped in, and panted to the driver, "Get me out of here! Some homeless dude's been chasing me, and I'm scared!"

"Where to?" The driver hit the gas and took off.

"Busch Gardens. Hotel Nine." She scoured the area out every window in the taxi, and waited for a full block before she slumped down in the back seat and cursed herself.

Dumbass. What the hell had she expected to get out of Margolis? Some babbling confession from a hard-ass combat leader? "Oh, yes, I'm trying to blackball that hero James Collins and ruin his life!" Now she couldn't even go to the airport. She'd have to grab her stuff, take a bus somewhere else, and then fly back from there. She was nothing but a total freaking amateur.

She looked around at the back of the taxi, both sides of the leather seat. Her cardigan. She'd lost it somewhere. Her phony student ID was in one of the pockets, with a really nice picture of her face on it. She smacked herself on the forehead.

The cab filled with flashing red lights, the driver muttered, "Sorry, lady," and pulled to the curb. Alex heard doors slam, and a pair of cops appeared on both sides, hands on their pistols. Then a big black Suburban zoomed past the taxi and screeched to a halt right in front. The passenger door opened and General Margolis got out. Alex rolled her eyes.

"Dad's gonna *hate* this," she moaned.

Chapter Twenty-Six

"I hate having to call you like this, Scott."

Scott Renard stood in the gleaming kitchen of his labyrinthine house. Early-morning sunlight glinted off the brushed-steel appliances, and the coffee mug he'd been raising to his lips was now frozen in mid-gesture. His cell phone was docked, and everything was wired for Bluetooth, so the disembodied voice of Lincoln Shepard echoed in the room like a call from Olympus.

"It's about Lily, isn't it?" Renard's stomach muscles tightened, and he saw the creamy surface of his latte trembling. "Just tell me."

"She's missing."

Renard put the cup down on the granite counter and then sat heavily on a stool—his blond head hanging as he sucked in a long breath. It was the call he'd begun to fear, and the reason he'd tried so hard to get her to give up this deadly game.

But then the tech genius part of his brain took over, as if his id had flicked a switch.

"Missing where, how and when? Just give it to me, Linc. All of it."

Shepard realized why Renard had gone from being a college kid to a billionaire in less than a year. When he spoke, Linc felt compelled to reply. "She was on a mission in Beijing," said Shepard. "It was supposed to be a simple reconnaissance thing, but her cover got blown, and they arrested her."

"Jesus, Linc." Renard shut his eyes and rubbed his thumb over the deep crease between his eyebrows. He was half-dressed for work, wearing skinny black jeans, running shoes, and an "SR7" T-shirt. The initials were his, along with his lucky number. "Couldn't care less about the details of the mission. Couldn't care more about the details of the arrest. Let's have them."

Once more, Shepard was impressed by the man's concentration and thinking process. Automatically trying to regain his mental balance, he blurted out, "Aren't you going to ask if we're in negotiation with the Chinese?"

"You wouldn't call me to report a special girlfriend news bulletin," Renard snapped but not unkindly. "If you're calling me, it's for some IT beyond the call of your duty and ability, right? and by the way, this line's secure."

Renard gave Shepard time to blink and gape on the other end of the automatically secured line. He was used to that by now. It was just a hint of his company's superior capabilities.

"R-right," Shepard admitted, gulping. "This is extra-governmental, Scott. And it's worse than that. They've destroyed her ear comm but not her cell. My guess is she won't give them access, so I've been able to track that till now. She's moving fast. I think on a flight to Pyongyang."

Renard rose from the stool and gripped the counter, his fingers pale. "Are you kidding me? North Korea?"

"That's our assumption. We're fairly sure her cover was blown by a North Korean."

Renard banged a fist on the counter. "North...Korea. Hold on, hold on, let me get my brain around this. North...Korea. . . Wait a minute. You said she was on a plane? Now?"

Shepard was taken aback. "What? What do you mean?"

"Is she still on the plane, or is she in the bowels of some North Korean prison?"

"On the plane. She's still in transit..."

Renard was moving as fast as his namesake—it was French for *fox*—in both mind and body. As he raced toward his study, his fingers were already twitching in remarkable patterns. "I need the aircraft details, as many as you can give me..."

Renard heard Shepard giggle—a weird sound of excitement and self-acknowledgment. "I knew it was right to call you! Already transferring all I know about it. Hack that aircraft, Scott." Shepard's voice had turned from apoplectic to a plea. "Stop it from reaching North Korea. We can't handle it, but maybe you can. Once she's there, she's gone."

"Forget you people," Renard snarled. "And I mean that in the broadest possible terms."

"Got you, Scott. Really sorry."

Renard sped into his study, which looked like a combination of the *Dr. Strangelove* war room, an Apple Store, and FAO Schwarz. "No apologies wanted, Linc—just send me a live link to your nav system, and make sure her cell's blinking at me like a lighthouse. Think you can handle that?"

"Yes!"

"Good. I'll do what I can do and maybe call you back later."

"Thanks, Scott."

"Don't thank me. We can't save Lily from here, but maybe we can help her save herself."

Renard snapped his fingers, the programmed audio signal for his smart-home to accept a new task.

"How can I help you?" a woman asked.

"Call the office."

"Calling office."

A young woman answered. "SR Holdings, how can I help you?"

"Hi, Jackie, it's Scott."

"Hey there!" Things were very informal out at SR.

"Listen, I won't be coming in today, at least not till much later. But I need some help. Send me our two craziest gamers." He could "hear" her blink and gape, too.

"Chilly and Hot Shot?"

"Yup. And Jackie, don't use Uber. I need them here fast, so use the car service and tell them we'll pay double if they step on it. Got it?"

"You bet!"

Scott disconnected the call, and then Renard's cell phone dinged. He picked it up, tapped in his code, and a link popped up in a text message from Lincoln Shephard. Tapping on that, Renard's screen filled with an overhead satellite image of unfamiliar greenery, mountains, and a weaving, blinking yellow orb moving quickly from left to right as the background scenery swept underneath. And when that screen filled, the study became that image. Renard was standing in the middle of it.

"She's right there," he whispered. "If I could just reach out and grab her..."

For the next twenty minutes he studied every millimeter of the terrain like a caged leopard. *I can do this*, he promised himself, knowing that whatever he did could well make it worse. *And if I can, maybe she'll realize that this is no life and that her real life is right here, with me.*

The front doorbell rang, and he opened the door remotely, his security equipment informing his visitors in the kindest voice that the master of the house was in his study. Within seconds, Chilly and Hot Shot were in the doorway. Chilly had a crop of bright red hair gelled straight up, and Hot Shot looked like a Tom Cruise stand-in circa *Top Gun*.

They both wore torn jeans, ratty high-tops, and sweatshirts. Before coming to SR, Chilly had made a living hacking for anyone who'd pay. Hot Shot had served in the air force as a UAV pilot, or a "drone jockey" and then turned his skills to advanced software development.

"Mornin', bossman," Chilly said with a wide grin.

"What's up, sir?" Hot Shot still had the air force in his blood.

"Morning, boys," Renard said. He managed a gap-toothed smile, but he pointed his first and middle fingers at their chests. "Here's the deal. We're going to do something terrible, dangerous, and illegal, and which may even cause World War Three. If you talk about it to anyone, I'll fire you, sue you, and make sure that you never work in this town again. But that really won't matter, because I'll also have you killed. Clear?"

Chilly's red eyebrows shot up. "You had me at *illegal*."

"Shut up, Chilly." Hot Shot elbowed him in the ribs and nodded at Renard. "Clear."

"Okay," said Renard. "Let's go."

Chilly looked around in confusion as Renard walked to the far wall. "Go where?"

"Never told you this, Hot Shot," Scott said with his back to them. They couldn't see what his hands were doing, but they were moving fast. "But I secretly wanted to be a fighter jock. That's why I'm always asking you about UAVs."

"Didn't know that, sir," Hot Shot said. "Why didn't you do it?"

"Low pay and too many rules."

"That's for sure." Hot Shot laughed. "And long stretches of boredom between trigger times."

But then the bookcase Renard was standing in front of hissed and popped out from the wall. It then rolled to the left on quiet Teflon-coated casters, revealing a gray steel door with a digital keypad.

"Too cool, dude!" Chilly said with glee.

Renard pressed the keypad and let a laser read his palm print and retinas before he pulled the door open and waved a hand inside the sill. A light glowed on.

Inside was a room the size of half a shipping container, with black lacquer walls that curved to an apex of dim blue lights. The far end was occupied by racks of servers on heavy steel shelving, before which two forty-inch monitors were angled downward at a pair of thick leather seats, side by side. A pair of heavy-duty Motorola headsets snuggled the headrests, and each chair featured a right-handed joystick with multifinger controls. At the foot of each chair were sets of aircraft brake rudder pedals. Renard flicked a switch on the wall and the servers began to blink and wine.

"Jesus," Hot Shot whispered. "This looks just like that friggin' box I sat in for three years at Wright Patterson. How come you got the whole double rig?"

"When I had the house built," Renard explained, "I was dating a former navy pilot. Thought she'd like it for recreation, but it turned out she preferred this room over the bedroom."

Chilly snickered. Hot Shot murmured, "Yeah, pilots have egos. Zipper-suited sun gods."

"Right," Renard said. "She was tight and not in a good way. Gentleman, take your seats."

Hot Shot slipped into the right seat, Chilly into the left, and Renard leaned over the backs between them. He handed Chilly his cell phone.

"Okay, turn on that left-hand computer; then transfer the nav on my cell over to the system. The registry's stamped on that metal plate on the keyboard."

"Got it," Chilly said.

Ten seconds later he had Lincoln Shepard's tracker up on the big monitor. The blinking yellow dot was just crossing above a wide swath of green and entering a vast area of blue.

"Shit," Renard said.

"Where are we?" Hot Shot asked as he leaned to the left and watched.

"That western section is mainland China, with Beijing off to the left. That aircraft is headed due east to Pyongyang."

Hot Shot turned and stared at Renard. "As in North Korea?"

"As in the Hermit Kingdom," Renard confirmed.

"What's on that plane?" Chilly asked.

"A precious jewel. Can you tell us what kind of aircraft that is, Chilly?"

"Only if I hack into the FAA, but even that might not do it 'cause it's international. Might have to break into Geospatial." Chilly turned and looked at Renard with the biggest shit-eating grin he ever had. "Illegal, nothing, bossman. This is forbidden, prohibited, and criminal, supreme!"

"Chilly," Renard said. "Remember how much your bonus was last year?"

"Shit, yeah."

"Double it."

"Double it?" Chilly scoffed. "Hell, man, I'd pay you for this!" Then he started hammering away at the keyboard.

In the meantime, Renard instructed Hot Shot to bring up his flight simulator. It was one of the best in the business. It was called Proflight, but SR Research and Development had already improved it. Hot Shot's monitor glowed with the beta version, with maps and landscapes and aircraft in drop-down menus.

"Nice," Hot Shot exclaimed. "We used one for training sometimes, but nothing like this."

"Got it," Chilly interrupted. His monitor had switched over to a different navigation system, which was much more advanced than Shepard's. It had latitude and longitudinal lines, three-dimensional features and ground altitude markers. The blinking yellow dot had changed to red, beside which a box showed the flight number, altitude, and airspeed.

"Nice." Renard squeezed his shoulder. "Now give me the remaining distance to Pyongyang, an ETA at the current flight speed, and any air strips between the current location and the target."

Chilly tapped some more. "It's five hundred thirty miles, four hundred thirty-seven nautical. Looks to me like they're a third of the way there. The only airport I've got between current and target is that, like, finger of China poking down into the ocean. It's got a strip called Dalian."

"Okay, now tell me what kind of equipment that is."

"Equipment?" Chilly scrunched up his face.

"He means what kind of airplane, dumbass," Hot Shot said.

"Oh." Chilly moved his mouse and clicked on the transponder signal. "It's a Gulfstream G550."

Renard jabbed a finger at Hot Shot's monitor. "Call up that model and give me cockpit view."

The image of a business jet cockpit filled Hot Shot's monitor. The instruments were "all glass," meaning state-of-the-art digital. "You can fly that, right?" Renard asked Hot Shot.

"Piece of cake."

"Okay, boys," Renard said. "Here's the hard part. Chilly, can you hack into that Gulfstream's computer via the transponder?"

"Not from here. Maybe if I backdoor Space ."

"Fine. Do it."

Chilly blew out a breath. "Okay, but it'll take a while."

"What's the time on target to Dalian?"

"Looks about twenty-five minutes," said Hot Shot.

"Chilly, you've got five minutes to turn over the controls of that aircraft to Hot Shot. I'm going to run downstairs and get us some coffee."

"I don't do coffee," Chilly complained. "You got any Red Bull?"

"Will you *please* just shut up and hack?" Hot Shot sputtered.

Renard had already exited the play room. Hot Shot called out to him.

"Sir? What do you want me to do once I have the controls?"

"Bring it down at Dalian, but don't crash it," Renard called back.

Chilly beamed at Hot Shot, his eyes as big as golf balls. "Boy, oh boy, bossman's gone cray-cray. That's multiple federal offenses, I don't know how many international infractions, and maybe a side of manslaughter..."—he raised his eyebrows at his now-literal partner in crime—"that is, if you screw the pooch on landing."

Hot Shot snorted as he aimed all his concentration on the controls. "Screw the pooch, nothing. This baby's gonna have beautiful puppies. I don't know what's on that bird, but we're getting it on the ground in one piece, *capisce?*"

"Cap Peach." Chilly leaned deep over his keyboard and started to play it like Mozart at his most possessed. "Get ready to fly, a-hole, and fasten your seat belt."

Chapter Twenty-Seven

Lily sat in a buttercream-colored, plush leather aircraft seat inside the spacious cavern of an opulent jet. The Gulfstream's interior was arrayed for fifteen passengers, its fuselage carpeted and polished to a gleam, with drop-down mahogany tables, a full galley up forward, and a water closet with bidet in the back. There was an onyx wet bar, and even a small couch; it was an airborne suite fit for a queen. But Lily's appearance failed to match the décor.

Her prim gray suit was torn at the shoulders, the buttons all gone, and her tangerine blouse was stained with her sweat. Her dyed-blond hair was unwashed, greasy, and bound in the back with a thick rubber band.

Her wrists lay on her lap, aching and raw from a pair of black handcuffs, and her ankles were bound with thin rope. A Chinese guard at the temporary detention facility in Beijing, who'd attempted to explore her panties, had discovered the power of her legs.

"You realize, Miss Stone, or whatever your name is, that soon you are going to talk."

Colonel Hyo sat in another chair facing Lily, his back to the galley and the cockpit. His large officer's cap sat on the table between them, next to a repast of Chinese delights, which he chopsticked languidly while Lily's stomach growled with hunger and thirst. She looked at his cruel face with her gleaming bloodshot eyes and said nothing.

"Who you work for exactly, is not of interest." Colonel Hyo raised a glass of white wine, taking his time. "The Americans, the British, or some other corrupt Western entity. Your objective is all that I want, and you will tell me."

"Not in this lifetime," Lily croaked.

Hyo smiled. He had a gold-capped tooth just behind one incisor. "Perhaps not in mine, but certainly in yours, which, if you fail to cooperate, is going to be tragically short."

Lily turned her face away and looked across the fuselage to a large oval window. It was late at night, though she had no idea what time, and the twinkling lights of land far below had disappeared. They were either above unpopulated tracts or over the sea.

She'd had some hope when General Kung had ordered her detained because relations between the Chinese and the United Kingdom, of which "Rosalind Stone" was a citizen, were generally positive, and delicate. So, she'd waited it out in a dank cell somewhere in Beijing, insisting she was an innocent sales rep and that the whole thing was some sort of horrible mix-up. She'd cried and whined and fussed in character, hoping that Zeta would drum up some indignant British "ambassador" to come pounding on Chinese government doors.

But apparently Kung's kindly face belied a wily tactician. He knew the Chinese couldn't hold her for long without suffering some sort of official British visit, and certainly torturing the truth from her would result in very bad press. However, the North Koreans were another animal altogether. Nothing decent was ever expected of them, so he'd turned her over to Hyo.

Lily heard laughter from the rear of the plane. Six of Colonel Hyo's officers were relaxing back there, enjoying their luxury—something they rarely experienced—as their own military aircraft were bare bones. Two of them were playing Baduk, the Korean version of Japanese Go. She heard the black and white oval game pieces clicking on the board, then a curse, and another laugh. She closed her eyes as a tremor of terror rolled up her aching spine.

How the bloody hell am I going to get out of this? She hadn't slept for two days, and the exhaustion was opening a flood of despair. *Does Shepard even know where I am?*

She was certain that Hyo still had her cell phone in his possession because he clearly wanted its contents, and she'd refused to give him the code. If he hadn't pulled the battery, then Linc might still be able to track her.

But then what? Bloch couldn't send Tactical on a mission to North Korea. She'd be in a cold, dark prison for years. Her eyes welled up as she thought about hearing those maddening clicks as her guards played Baduk, over and over while her body withered to sagging flesh and bones.

Her buttocks clenched, and her eyes popped open as she felt Hyo's fingers gripping her jaw. He snapped her face around as he leaned across the table, his black eyes squinting at hers.

"You are not paying attention, Miss Stone." He sat back down in his chair. "You should think about what will soon happen." He looked at his watch, a simple plastic G-Shock. "In approximately one hour, you will be in Pyongyang. It will be your last full view of civilization, as you know it. And then"—he picked up a chopstick and flicked it against his wine glass, where it made a sharp *ding*—"you will be gone forever."

Lily cleared her sand-dry throat. "You think my government will just let your dear leader do as he pleases?"

Hyo laughed. "Your government, whoever that is, barely protests his nuclear ambitions. So why would they care about you?"

"I am an innocent civilian. You've made a ghastly mistake."

"We shall see." Hyo tapped the ivory stick on the face of his watch. "It should not take long to discover. I think we shall start with freezing cold, then unbearable heat, and then some electrics in sensitive places. If you still resist, we shall move on to serious measures, things that will leave you unpleasant to look at." His lips turned up in a smile, and, as they did, his curving scar turned white.

The airplane shuddered. At first it seemed like a hard shiver of turbulence, but then a strange noise came from the right rear outside, somewhat like a car engine in overdrive. Then came a sharp bang and a declining whine, and the Gulfstream dipped hard to the right.

Lily slid to the right in her chair and her head bounced against the fuselage. She heard the Koreans in the back cursing and the sounds of ceramic play pieces scattering over the floor.

Then the airplane corrected, and she heard urgent voices from the cockpit up forward.

Colonel Hyo pushed himself from his seat and stormed up front. There was no door to the cockpit, and he gripped the open sills on either side, spread his stance for balance, and thrust his head inside. The two Chinese pilots were hunched forward in their seats, chattering in staccato grunts as they flicked switches while stall warning bells went off.

"*Zheshizen me huishi?*"—What's going on?—he demanded in Mandarin.

"*Wo men buzhidao!*"—We don't know!—the right-seat copilot said without turning around. "We have lost the right engine, and when we took it off autopilot, we still have no control!"

With that, the pilot in the left seat took his hands from where they were gripping the yoke and raised them up in the air. Both yokes, his and the copilot's, continued to jerk and twist on their own, as if the aircraft were haunted by some ungodly ghost.

"Will it still fly?" Hyo demanded.

"It is flying now," said the pilot. "But *I* am not flying it!"

Hyo snapped his head around to the rear and yelled in Korean, "Seat belts!"

Lily had no idea what was going on, but she heard the men behind her hissing in whispers. She looked down at her cuffed hands and tried to twist around to grab her seatbelt, but she couldn't reach it. The galley's orderly, a young Chinese man in a white chef's coat, burst from up forward and threw himself into the empty seat to her left. He belted in, gripped the armrests, and prayed—most likely to Buddha.

Hyo turned back and snapped at the pilots. "Where is the nearest airport?

"It's Dalian," the chief pilot said. "I have already called them and asked for crash trucks."

"Can you make it to there?"

"I have no choice!" the pilot nearly squealed. "The aircraft is heading there by itself!"

With that, the Gulfstream nosed over hard to the right. Hyo lost his grip on the left-hand sill, and he slammed back into the bulkhead. He slithered along it back toward the cabin, then staggered over to Lily, whipped her belt from its holder, and snapped her in. Then he crashed back into his seat and did the same for himself, as he stared at her face in fury. She raised her cuffed wrists and sneered back.

"Do you think I did this from here?"

"I think someone is doing it *for* you, but you are the one who will pay."

The Gulfstream descended in a sickening spiral. Lily closed her eyes, praying to a God she didn't really believe in. For a moment she thought about Scott and how he'd begged her to quit and take up a "normal" life in San Francisco with him. If she'd done that right there and then, she wouldn't be here.

Well, everyone's entitled to cocked-up choices.

Then the airplane straightened out, but it was still in a nose-down dive. The Koreans behind her were absolutely silent, but the Chinese pilots up front were cursing. She kept her eyes tightly shut; Colonel Hyo's face wasn't going to be the very last vision she ever saw.

She felt the aircraft's nose slowly rising again, and the engine off to the left was no longer screaming. She opened her left eye, and saw a blur of bright lights streaming past the window. She heard the undercarriage whining open, and then the tires screeched and bounced on the tarmac.

She opened both eyes and her pounding heart felt like it was up in her throat as off to the front right she saw the spinning red beacons of fire trucks, very close; the left engine reversed in a howl as the Gulfstream skidded to the left, and the right-hand winglet was sheared right off by a fire truck ladder.

The brakes squealed, and the nose dipped hard and the airplane jolted to a stop. One of the pilots threw off his headset, got up, staggered to the forward toilet, and charged head-down inside. Lily heard him retching.

Hyo wrenched himself up from his seat, stomped to the passenger door, and cranked the emergency handle. It hissed outside on its hinges, and the airplane filled with the scream of emergency sirens. A Chinese soldier scrambled up a stairway and popped his stunned face inside. He was wearing an olive fatigue cap with an embroidered red star.

"I am here as the guest of General Deng Tao Kung," Colonel Hyo snapped in Chinese. "Get me a truck."

The Chinese soldier saluted and disappeared. Hyo turned around and walked to Lily. He bent down, gripped her armrests, and nearly touched her nose with his.

"You must think that you have a reprieve," he snarled. "But now, Miss Stone, we shall be going to the Dalian Jinlon Forest. It has a lovely, ancient, and very remote temple." His lips turned up in a sneer. "You will need every opportunity to pray."

Chapter Twenty-Eight

If Dan Morgan had been on a nice long vacation with Jenny, he would have loved The Oaks Eatery in Ogden Canyon, Utah.

The place was the oldest establishment around—a small wooden structure with a peaked roof, just off the winding Route 39 state highway. It didn't look like much from the front, where all the hiking aficionados parked their Jeeps and RVs, but inside was a comfy old place with slat wooden banquettes, red tablecloths, cloth napkins and porcelain dishware, with towering windows providing a vista of the tumbling river out back, braced by lush pines. Folks drove many miles for The Oak's juicy burgers, fat fries with BBQ sauce, and handmade ice cream, and Morgan was certainly enjoying the first decent meal he'd had since Virginia.

However, he wasn't on vacation, with Jenny or anyone else. Besides, he wasn't even Dan Morgan on this fine cool evening, where the sun was just going blood orange behind a magnificent granite peak. He was Air Force Master Sergeant Daniel Martin, and he was on the hunt.

At least he'd been smart enough not to try driving another thousand miles. Instead, he'd headed due south from Kentucky to Nashville, found a local kennel with five-star reviews, and parked Neika there with a promise to be back in a couple of days. Then he'd headed for the airport, long-termed the Shelby, spruced himself up with a close shave in the restroom, and boarded a flight to Salt Lake City, where he'd rented a two-door black Wrangler.

It wasn't far from there to Hill Air Force Base, where Morgan presented his retired army ID at the gate and headed right over to Military Clothing Sales. He picked up a set of air force ACUs, a sage T-shirt, and boots that were much nicer than the army "rough-outs." Finally, he plucked master sergeant ranks off the rack and went over to the express tailoring and name tape counter, where a nice blue-haired lady with half-frame glasses on a beaded lanyard looked up at him.

"Morning, ma'am," Morgan said with a wry grin as he dropped his pile on the counter. "Can't believe I'm doin' this again."

"Doing what, son?"

"Six-month stint, in *blue* no less."

"Well, we're all blue around here."

"Yep, it'll all be new to me." Morgan flashed her his army ID. "I was green for almost twenty."

The elderly woman patted his hand. "Air force food's much better. So, what can I do for you?"

"Well, if you've got a spare slot, I need these ranks sewed on and some name tapes."

"We could do that. Take about an hour."

"Outstanding! Could use a cup of joe anyway."

She glanced at his ID. "Morgan for the name, Air Force on the other side, right?"

"Roger that," Morgan said. "And if you don't mind, I promised my buddy I'd pick him up a set too. His name's Martin, just like it sounds."

"All right, young man. Come back in an hour."

Morgan strolled around the base exchange for a while and bought himself a five-inch Gerber folding blade and a coil of 550 parachute cord. He'd flown out "naked" from Nashville, leaving his firearms locked in the Shelby's trunk, so all he had were his cell phone, his ear comm, and his lock-pick set. Coldcastle Mountain was a Department of Defense facility, nestled in the crags of Ogden Canyon and managed by air force personnel. No matter what happened, he wasn't going to kill anyone there, but a knife and some rope might come in handy.

Sixty minutes later, he picked up his uniform, paid for the service with cash, kept everything in the shopping bag, and headed north on Route 15 in the Wrangler. An hour after that, he was in a gas station restroom in Ogden proper, where he pulled the new "tiger stripe" ACU trousers right over his jeans and switched out his running shoes for the boots.

He kept his black T-shirt on, pulled the sage green one over that, and zipped on the air force tunic. Only then did he pull off the Velcro name tape that said "MORGAN" and switch it to the one that read "MARTIN." When he adjusted his cap and put on his sunglasses, he looked like a typical "short-timer" master sergeant that nobody'd want to mess with.

From there, he'd turned east on Route 39 and wound his way into the peaks and pines. Using the coordinates that Collins had passed to his cell, he crossed over the Goodale River and started searching for the telltale signs of an access road to Coldcastle Mountain. Sure enough, off to the left, he spotted a break in the brush that revealed a dirt road with a small sign that read "US Government Property—Restricted Access."

Ain't restricted to me, Morgan mused, but he drove on for a couple of miles, looking for the one spot to which all the Coldcastle troops would gravitate. It was the same with every secure base; no matter how good the chow might be inside, you'd get sick to death of it soon enough and start foraging for tastier grub. It turned out that The Oaks was the only such place around. So now he sat there in the eatery, taking his time. He was already fairly stuffed, but if he had to order another full meal and just nurse it, he would.

The night fell fast and hard in the mountains, and stars outside the rear picture window were starting to pop. His ear comm was tucked in his auditory canal, but he'd switched it off and had no intention of using it unless things got desperate. He trusted Shepard, but the kid had masters at Zeta, and if they decided on making their renegade bad-boy Cobra disappear, then breaking into an Alpha-3-level federal facility would present an unassailable opportunity.

He wondered what Jenny was doing. One of these days his beautiful wife was going to get wise and dump him for a lawyer—maybe the same one she'd wind up using for their divorce. From that discomfiting thought, his mind wandered to Alex, and a surge of guilt for getting her into this game. And while he was brooding about all that, losing his appetite, his prey walked in.

They were a pair of young airmen, both second class, and, as they strode in through the front door, Morgan could see their frog-nosed LMTV truck parked out front. They doffed their hats and nearly bounced on the balls of their boots as they stared up at the menu poster above the order counter. A blond and a carrot-top, they both had normal haircuts rather than "high and tight," and neither carried a sidearm. They weren't Security Forces guys, probably desk-jockeys.

Morgan slowed down with his apple pie and sipped his coffee. He glanced around and saw that most of the other tables were full, so when the two airmen got their food baskets and searched for a spot, he caught their eyes and pointed at his own table. The airmen grinned and sauntered over.

"You can have this one, boys," Morgan said. "I'm done here."

"Thanks, Master Sar'nt," the blond said as they slid into the bench facing him.

Morgan squinted at the kid's name tape and smirked. "You're ex-army, Perry. Don't try to hide it."

The kid laughed. "How'd you know?"

"Used to be green myself. Army guys say 'Sarn't. ' Air force guys say 'Sarge-ant, ' like friggin' Gomer Pyle."

"Who's that?" the redhead asked.

"Just some old dinosaur, like me." Morgan looked at his watch and finished his coffee while the kids dug into their burgers.

"Where you headed, Chief?" the blond airman asked between bites.

"Hill," said Morgan. "Spent the day out at the lake. Tomorrow I start my sentence."

The redhead's eyebrows went up. "You do something wrong?"

"Nah. Just bein' funny," Morgan said. "I'm doing a six-month tour in these lizard pajamas, just to round out my retirement points. You guys headed down there too?"

"Nope." The blond sipped his Coke and offered nothing more. Morgan nodded.

"I get it. You guys work in the castle."

They glanced at each other, and the redhead muttered, "Can't confirm or deny."

Morgan grinned. "You just did."

The two airmen laughed. Then he finished his coffee, picked up his basket, and slid out from the bench. "Well, gonna grab a smoke and head down to Happy land. See ya, boys. Watch your sixes."

"Roger that," the blond said as Morgan mashed his cap on his head, dumped his trash, and headed out the front door.

Outside in the parking strip, he didn't bother to make sure the airmen weren't watching him because he'd set them up with their backs to the entrance. His Wrangler rental was parked at the end of the row of vehicles, locked up tight, so he strode down the flank of the air force LMTV, turned right behind its rump, and stood there for fifteen seconds—waiting for a passing car to cruise by. Then he popped one corner of the canvas cover, hauled himself up, slithered into the cargo bed, and reset the canvas from inside. It was dark as a coffin, but he wasn't going to risk using the light from his cell. Instead, he felt his way around a pile of file boxes and curled up in a spot just behind the cab.

Half an hour later the air force kids came out, jumped in the cab, and the LMTV started to roll. Now Morgan prayed that the Coldcastle sentries at the Entry Control Point didn't search every vehicle coming inside or, worse, use dogs. Neika would have picked up his scent in a heartbeat, especially since he stank like burgers and fries.

His prayers were answered. The truck cruised down the two-lane highway, then turned off along a winding gravel road for about twenty minutes. When it stopped at the ECP, he heard Airman Perry joking with the sentries as he handed them a bag of fries. Then came the sound of powerful pneumatics moving heavy doors on rollers, and the truck's wheels were rolling forward on a surface smooth as glass.

The way the engine sound echoed tightly, he could tell they were in some sort of long tunnel, and then the sound expanded as if the space had opened wide. The airmen parked the truck, got out, slammed the doors, and disappeared. For a full minute, Morgan listened intently for the sounds of other boot steps or voices nearby. Hearing nothing, he slipped out the back of the truck, jumped down, and reached back inside for one of the file boxes.

A hardened facility like Coldcastle would have surveillance cameras bristling all over like porcupine spines, so if someone spotted him on camera, he'd look like a noncom with a task rather than a stowaway. He took care to move only his eyes, not his head, as he started walking. It was an enormous motor pool the size of a small-town armory, with battleship flooring, ten parked LMTVs, six Humvees, floodlights, and a high arched ceiling of power-chiseled granite. He headed straight for the high black maw of the entrance, then out into the access tunnel.

It was about a quarter mile long, with a treaded steel floor, fluorescent lights, and slimy, gleaming brown walls gnawed from the rock. It sloped up fifteen degrees to a distant pair of heavy steel doors—the ones he'd heard hissing open. Off to the left and right were two long hallways with gray steel walls, interspaced office doors, and more hallways splitting off from the mains.

Camera snouts poked down from everywhere. He couldn't be seen to hesitate, so he chose left and walked. Collins had told him what to look for, vaguely. "It'll be a cyber-lock door with a swipe pad and a window. Probably with a 'Level Two Clearance' sign."

Great, Morgan thought. *They all look like that.*

But actually, they didn't. He spotted it, off to the left just ten feet onward. A red slab on the door said "Level Two Only." And coming straight at him down the hallway was a young lieutenant. Morgan switched the box to under his left arm and started fishing in all of his pockets with his right.

"Damn it," he muttered.

The lieutenant cruised up and stopped. "What's up, Master Sergeant?"

"I'm a dumb ass, LT," said Morgan as he fumbled through his Velcro pockets. "Must have left my CAC card in my locker."

"Yeah? Haven't seen you in the hole before. You new?"

"I'm old as dirt." Morgan smirked. "Just here for one last TDY; then I'm going fishing for life."

The lieutenant laughed. "This one's on me." He pulled out his own CAC card and swiped it through the lock. The door buzzed, and he pulled it open.

"Much appreciated, sir." Morgan grinned. "Saved these old legs from another marathon."

"You bet."

Once inside the level two area, none of the doors in the next hallway had keypads, but they all had steel doorknobs with keyholes and were locked from the inside. Following Collins's coaching, he strolled along until he found the one with a blue nameplate and letters stamped in white: Sequences & Logs. He knocked on the door and it buzzed.

Morgan walked in with his box. A female technical sergeant sat facing the door behind a large steel desk with a barrier countertop for signing in and out. Behind her, the large room was lined on three sides with tall steel filing cabinets, with each vertical row of drawer handles speared from bottom to top by what looked like iron railroad pikes—each of those locked at the top with silver tubular key locks.

No combinations. Thank you, God. Morgan dropped the box on the countertop and glanced at the tech sergeant's name tape just before she looked up.

"What's up, Master Sergeant?" she asked. She had short black hair and green eyes, and was wearing a thigh holster with an M9—Security Forces type.

"Are you Tech Sergeant Stepfield?" Morgan asked.

She smirked and glanced down at her name tape. "Last I looked."

Morgan tossed a thumb over his shoulder. "Some wet-behind-the ears second louie told me to send you over to Medical Squadron."

"Me?" She touched her chest. "I just had my dental last week. I'm Class Two, good to go."

Morgan shrugged. "Don't ask me. I'm just a noncom boot like you."

The young woman got up. She had a huge jangle of keys dangling from her belt. She gestured at the box.

"Whatcha got there?"

"Property logs. You're supposed to sign off, individually."

"Okay," she said. "Stay right here. I'll shoot over there and be right back."

"Roger." Morgan gave her a thumbs-up.

"And don't touch anything," she said as she headed out the door.

"Wouldn't dare."

As soon as she was gone, Morgan blew out a sigh of relief. If she hadn't taken the bait, he would've had to take her down and tie her up. But now he'd have to move fast because he had no idea where Medical was or how long it would take her to come back. Thankfully, just like with most such facilities, the security cameras were only out in the corridors.

He took out his lock picks and started quickly scanning the standing files, looking for that one label Collins had relayed. And there it was, middle of the fifth high cabinet on the left: Sierra 626. He worked the tube tumbler with a long pick and a tension wrench until it popped, then hauled the pike out of the top, and pulled the drawer open.

Inside was a double row of small standing files, greeting-card size with alphabetical tabs, and inside each folder was an air force chain-of-title card with a plastic sleeve containing a black square chip resembling a digital camera flash card. As instructed by Collins, Morgan plucked up the card from the *M* file and then took land *N* as well, just in case Stepfield was dyslexic.

He stuffed them into his chest pocket, closed the drawer, slid the pike back down from the top, and locked it all up. He was just pocketing his lock pick set and scooting back around the desk when the door lock cranked. He leaned back on the wall with his arms folded, looking half asleep.

Tech Sergeant Stepfield walked in and faced him with her knuckles on her hips. She didn't look pleased.

"You screwin' with me, Master Sergeant?" she accused. "Medical says my file's fine."

Morgan raised his palms in surrender. "Hey, just tryin' to help. Don't shoot the messenger."

Stepfield looked around her office and then eyed him again. "I haven't seen you before. You got orders?"

"Sure." Morgan came away from the wall, thinking, *Shit, so close.* He looked down, pulled open his right-hand breast pocket, then balled his fist, and coldcocked her right in the chin. Her head snapped back, and she went down like a sack of potatoes—lights out.

He bent over and looked at her, shaking his head. *Damn it, kid. Why'd you have to be so smart?* He didn't see any blood. She'd have a wicked headache, but she'd be all right.

He walked out, pushed his way back through the Level Two door, took a right, quick-marched back to the vehicle tunnel, and then into the motor pool bay, his ears feeling pinned back like Neika's as he waited for the first shouts and alarms.

Even so, he couldn't look rushed or panicked for those eyes in the ceiling, so he slid casually into a Humvee, cranked it up, and drove out of the bay and up the long tunnel, holding his breath.

Please tell me you don't need a code to get out. But sure enough, right before the pneumatic sliding doors was a metal stanchion with a keypad box at the top. *Damn it!* But there was also a big red button. He pushed it, and a disembodied voice echoed from a speaker above the truck.

"Gate, here. Whatcha need?"

"A Big Mac, large fries, and a Coke," Morgan said.

"Funny. Hit the keypad."

"Gimme a break," Morgan pleaded. "I'm new, TDY, and nobody gave me a friggin' code yet."

"It's three two eight two."

"Thanks, brother."

"Don't thank me. Memorize it."

"Will do."

Morgan punched the numbers, and the doors whined open. He drove through, wound the Humvee slowly through the big red labyrinth barriers at the Entry Control Point, waved to the Security Forces Squadron guys at the booth, and gunned it.

Just before reaching Route 39, he swung the wheel hard to the left and took the Humvee down into a thick grove of brush. He jumped from the truck, stripped out of the uniform tunic, trousers, and sage-green tee—leaving himself wearing his black tee and jeans. He pulled the jeans cuffs down over the tops of his boots and then made sure to strip everything from the uniform and its pockets and stuff them into his jeans—especially the name tapes, chips, and his car keys. He kept the knife, ditched the 550 cord, and took off.

Twenty minutes later, he popped out of the woods across from The Oaks, crossed the highway, climbed into the Wrangler, and burned some rubber—heading back west toward Ogden. As he passed the cutoff for Coldcastle Mountain, he heard sirens and saw a wink of blue lights. Tech Sergeant Stepfield had apparently woken up, pissed.

He stepped on it hard, racing back toward Route 15. But he knew he couldn't go anywhere near Hill Air Force Base again, and certainly not Salt Lake City airport. If those air force cops were halfway decent, they'd flash his description to Homeland Security. He'd have to turn north, drive his ass off to somewhere else, and take a train.

His knee was throbbing, and he felt bad about slugging the girl.

"You're getting too old for this shit, Cobra," he muttered. But then he smiled. "Hell, but she'll have a great story to tell her grandkids."

Chapter Twenty-Nine

Cold.

Bone-splintering, lung-sucking cold.

Lily had never felt anything like it. Not in Berlin in January, that safe house in Islamabad with no heat, or even in the Alps where she'd once lost her way on a climb. This was something else: the unmoving ice-brittle air of an empty Buddhist temple in the mountain forests of Dalian Jinlon—a structure constructed centuries ago before the concept of steam and one with no regard for a hearth. It was a place for monks to go dizzy with suffering and meld with their deity in delirium.

But she wasn't a monk. Even so, she stopped shivering. She had nothing left. She was done.

She sat on a hard wooden chair in the middle of a conical space the size of an ancient Greek Orthodox apse. The floor was made up of polished, interlocked, stones, and the curving walls had been hewn from nearly black teak. A hundred small stone Buddhas sat in pocketed recesses in the walls, their lifeless fingers caressing unlit candles in their laps. From high above her head, where a convex ceiling braced the bottom of the temple's cap, beads of ice water fell to the floor in a constant, maddening rhythm. Except for the grinding of Lily's teeth, it was the only sound in the room.

Her gray suit jacket was gone, and her bloody spittle had turned to sleet on the front of her sleeveless tangerine blouse. Her bare arms were cranked behind the chair's rattan back, her wrists locked in cuffs, and her ankles were roped to the bottoms of the chair's pole legs. She was barefoot, her skirt was pushed up, and her blouse torn open. She no longer cared.

Ten feet in front of her sat a squat wooden table, arrayed with everything Hyo's men had found—her Thales brochures, wallet, money, false passport, phony driving credentials, and ear comm. In the middle of the table sat the prize which, thanks to her stubborn resolve, still eluded Hyo's desire: her cell phone.

She still hadn't given him her access code, which was why she was due shortly for much more suffering. Next to that was a boilerplate confession—a single page typed in Korean.

"In exchange for your signature and four numbers," Hyo had said, "you will have your life, Miss Stone."

He'd said that only once, six hours before. Or maybe it was ten; she couldn't be sure. Then he'd taken off his uniform coat, rolled up his sleeves, and begun with slaps until her nose and lips dripped blood and her ears rang like a rectory bell.

Then he'd summoned two of his men, who'd ripped open her blouse and squeezed her throat while they slapped her breasts and jammed their calloused fingers under her skirt. She'd said nothing, not even a curse.

After that, Hyo had returned with a woolen hood, and the world went black. They tipped her, in the chair, onto her back, and their knees crushed down into her collarbone as they sluiced ice water over her hood until she thought her lungs would explode. When her toes uncurled and stopped twitching, they tipped her back up, tore the hood off, and slapped her chest until she spewed up bile and water.

Still, she said nothing, and Hyo had stormed out trailing a wave of Asian epithets she didn't recognize but could well understand.

An hour or so had passed since then. A single guard was left in the room, standing beside the arched stone entrance which led out into a darkened corridor through which they'd dragged her the previous dawn. It was night again and now the guard, a young Korean sergeant, stood with his back to her—a small-caliber pistol on his hip. He smoked pungent cigarettes, and only occasionally turned to make sure she was breathing.

For that hour, she'd done nothing more than try to keep her fluttering heart beating. Nothing else...except slowly, methodically, twist her left wrist. Hyo had made one mistake, removing her cuffs so she could climb down from the Gulfstream jet. And then, in the back of the PLA truck, an officer had cuffed only her right wrist to the bench slat.

The cargo bed was dark, the ride to the temple more than an hour, and during the entire time she'd gripped the arteries of her left elbow with her cuffed right hand, a tourniquet effect that swelled her left wrist. When the cuffs were replaced at the temple, the cinches were no longer the same.

In addition to that, Lily had a congenital imperfection. Her thumbs were double-jointed, with no bone spurs on her primary knuckles. She could bend them straight back to her wrists, or make them nearly disappear into her palms. She'd never had much use for that...until tonight.

So, she welcomed the jaw-clenching cold, which by now had shrunken her left wrist. And still, as she twisted it slowly to the right and left, she felt her flesh ripping and the Freon-cold cuff going slick with her blood. She gritted her teeth from the pain but kept on. It felt like her thumb was breaking. In her swooning head, she silently cursed an adage: *Mind over matter, bitch. It only matters if you mind!*

With one last grinding wrench, her left hand popped from the cuff. She curled one finger just in time to keep it from clanging. Then she took a long, ragged breath, slowly exhaled, dropped her head to her chest, and moaned. She twitched her trussed body as if she was having a convulsion.

The Korean sergeant turned to look at her. His eyes narrowed, but still he just smoked and watched. Her chair bucked as she quaked, and drool dripped from her slack lips. After what seemed like minutes, he tossed his cigarette to the stone floor, crushed it with his boot, and ambled over. If she died on his watch, he might well find himself in that chair.

Lily's bruised eyes were half slitted, and she stared at the floor as she jerked in her chair and forced mewling sounds from her throat. Then she saw just the boot tips, stopping a few feet in front of her.

Closer, you bastard. Closer.

She bucked up hard one more time, then collapsed, and went still. The boots came closer. The Korean hissed something. Fingers crawled into her hair and gripped her mane hard, stinging her scalp, as he wrenched her head back.

Her green eyes snapped open, seemingly boring into his surprised brown ones. Her right arm swung up in a wicked arc, whipping the cuffs across the left side of his face with a strength that surprised them both. The cold steel sliced deeply into his cheekbone. To her delight, blood spurted out as he grunted and gripped his gushing wound, inspiring her to whip the metal up again from the left side—twisting in the chair to put all her strength and rage into it.

The cuffs rang off his skull like a prayer gong. He folded backward and slammed down on the cold stone floor as if he were a gavel being hammered by an angry judge.

Lily jolted upright from the chair, reached down under the seat, and yanked it straight up as the legs popped out from her ankle ropes. Then she spun to the left, gripped the chair back, and swung it up over her head as she twisted around to the writhing form of the guard on his back. She smashed him with it as if it were a sledgehammer. The legs splintered, and so did his bones. Just as she was taught, she pounded him again and again until he lay still.

Her body screamed at her to collapse or run. She told her body to shut the hell up as she fell to her knees and rifled the guard's pockets until she found the handcuff key. She freed her right wrist and dropped the cuffs on his chest at the same moment she pulled his blood-spattered pistol from its holster.

She gripped the side of the table and hauled herself up at the same second she swiped up her cell, passport, and ear comm. She wanted to make a beeline for the doorway but had to be satisfied with staggering. She gripped the sill as a wave of bile stung her throat.

I told you to shut the hell up! she internally shrieked, forcing the puke back as she stuffed the cell and passport into the front of her skirt, jammed the comm in her ear, worked the pistol's action to chamber a round, and sprang out into the corridor—barefoot and gasping for breath.

To the left, at the end of the corridor, moonlight gleamed through a leaden glass window. Her feet felt like concrete, and her legs were on fire, but she ran—seeing that the window was split down the middle with an iron turn-handle in the middle.

She was almost there when one of Hyo's young officers popped into the corridor from the right. He was carrying some sort of ration box, probably for the guard she'd just killed. His eyes flew wide as he saw her. He froze but not for long. He dropped the box and scrambled for his pistol. But she launched herself at him like a rabid raccoon, hugged him in a death grip, shoved her pistol deep in his belly, and fired.

His head snapped up, and he tumbled back into the wall just below the window. Lily jammed the pistol into her skirt, stomped on his chest, and launched herself up, grabbing the turn handle and twisting. The window flew open, and she scrambled onto the still and looked down.

Blackness. Goddamn blackness. She had no idea how high up she was. Enormous pines whipped in the wind out front. But below her, nothing. She heard shouts from behind her.

Her body started begging again, pleading, screaming.

What did I tell you? she screeched back at it as she jumped.

Chapter Thirty

Zeta headquarters had a coded alert system that was similar to a hospital's. It sounded like submarine sonar.

A single ping, ringing from the recessed intercom speakers at five-second intervals, meant that all personnel should return to their workstations. Two pings, at closer intervals, initiated an urgent communication to analysts and operators, wherever they were in the world—instructing them to scuttle their current tasks and prepare for action. Three steady pings, with only a second between trios, essentially meant "Get the crash cart."

It sealed all the access doors, sent tactical operators to the team room to don their gear and weapons, and ordered both drivers and pilots to the motor pool bay.

So far this morning, it had only been two pings. But now Lincoln Shepard raced down the hallway as if his hair was on fire, clutching his laptop—a pair of Bluetooth earphones with a boom mike bouncing askew on his head—as his sneakers flapped against the floor. He'd been the one to call the alarm, choosing the middle of three toggles under his desk, and he had a damn good reason.

He burst through the board room door. Paul Kirby was already there, at the head of the conference table, and Karen was just taking a chair. Bishop, Diesel, and Spartan stood off to the left in a corner, arms folded, all wearing similar leather jackets and the bored expressions of combat vets always being told to "hurry up and wait." Peter Conley rocked back in a leather chair, his flight boots resting on the arm of another. He was reading a copy of *Mad Magazine* and chuckling.

Linc slapped the laptop down on the table and covered his boom mike with a trembling fist.

"I got her!" he gushed breathlessly. "She's out, and I have no idea how, but I got her!"

Kirby leaned forward in his chair. "You've got *who*, Mr. Shepard?"

"Lily, for God's sake!" Linc slammed himself down in a chair, flipped open the laptop, and hammered away at the keyboard.

Conley put the magazine down, and the Tac team unfolded their arms. Karen covered her mouth with a hand, much like the image of Hillary Clinton when SEAL Team Six killed Osama bin Laden. Kirby was out of his chair, listing forward like a battleship in a rogue wave.

"Sloww. . . dowwn, Shepard," he ordered. "Facts, not emotions."

Shepard ignored him and pressed the mike to his mouth. "You still with me, Lily?"

No one could hear her feeble voice through Shepard's earphones, but he listened and nodded furiously.

"Just hang in. We're all here. Whatever you do, just keep going and don't let those bastards get you."

"Damn it, Shepard!" Kirby snapped. "Put her on hold and report!"

Shepard looked at Kirby and said, "Wait one," into the mike, then pushed it away from his lips, and muted it again with his hand.

"The aircraft made a hard landing in Dalian, China," he said. "The Koreans took her to some temple in Dalian Jinlon Forest and worked her over. I don't know how she escaped, but she did, and she's friggin' running through the jungle somewhere, and they're hot on her trail." He looked around, his eyes glassy and crazed. "Where's Diana?"

"Out of the office," Kirby answered. "I'm in charge here now." He snapped his fingers to get Shepard's focus again. "Look at me, Shepard. Does she have her cell?"

"Yes, yes." Shepard bobbed his chin.

"Do you have her on nav?"

"Yes!" Shepard jabbed a finger at his laptop screen. Bishop, Diesel, and Spartan rushed to the spot behind Shepard and loomed over his shoulders, looking at the screen. Karen jumped up and hurried around the table to join them. Peter Conley had his cell to his ear and was calling his aircraft mechanic at Logan.

"Jake, it's Cougar. Spin up the APU, top up the bird and get clearance for takeoff in half an hour."

Kirby shot a finger at Conley. "Belay that, Cougar."

Conley pulled the cell from his ear. "You got a better alternative, sir?"

"It's a fifteen-hour flight," said Kirby. "You *might* get there in time to recover her remains."

"Jesus," Spartan muttered. She had a special affinity for Lily: two female peas in a testosterone pod.

"We can't just leave her there," Diesel protested.

"Right," Bishop grunted. "If it was Cobra, I'd leave him, but not her." He still had a bandage around his huge bicep where Neika has punctured his flesh, and his mood hadn't improved since the incident. Conley glare at him.

"Settle down!" Kirby snapped. "All of you." He moved away from the head of the table and paced back and forth in front of the huge videoconference screen, his arms folded and a finger tapping the nose bridge of his glasses. Then he marched around the table to Shepard and snapped his fingers again.

"Give me the comm."

Shepard pulled off the headset and handed it up to Kirby, who wiped the sweaty headphones with his tie and put it on.

"Lily, this is Kirby. Do you copy?" He squinted behind his glasses as he tried to hear her; then he pushed the mike close to his flabby lips and squeezed the headphones more tightly to his ears. "Listen to me, Lily. How far are they behind you, and how many?" He closed his eyes, listened some more, and pulled in a breath through his nose." All right. Understood. Now hear me. We didn't put you through all that SERE training for nothing. You've escaped, and now it's time to evade. Do you copy?" Another long pause. "Good. And yes, I appreciate the urgency. We are addressing this now, but you must *not* be recaptured. Am I clear?" Another pause. "Excellent. Now focus on the task at hand, nothing else."

Kirby pulled off the headset and spoke to everyone in the room. "You may all stand down." Six pairs of Zeta eyes bugged at him. He turned to Karen. "Open two secure phone lines."

"Two?" she asked incredulously. "Where?"

"Just do it," Kirby said. "And leave me alone."

* * * *

The soles of Lily's bare feet were shredded, but there was nothing she could do about that except endure each rending slice as she ran onward.

She was pounding through a large field of elephant grass, the five-foot-high emerald blades glistening in the moonlight. With every stride she stamped them down, and with every stride, they avenged each crush with long, ragged cuts.

In her pumping left fist she gripped her cell phone, and in her right she clutched the dead Korean's pistol. Her passport had already fallen once from her skirt, and she'd had to scramble on the ground to find it. Now she gripped it in her teeth like a pirate's knife, nearly biting through the cover with each new shock of pain.

Her right knee was swollen from the jump, but she'd rolled into a parachute landing fall and hadn't broken anything. So many points of her body were screaming in neural shock that it was like a single, hellish chorus. She no longer bothered telling it to shut up.

Two hundred feet behind her, she had burst from the first swath of thick, sloping jungle. After her leap of faith, it had taken Hyo some minutes to marshal his forces, and for a good ten minutes she'd heard no one pursuing. But then the shouts had risen, and the flashlight beams sliced through the trees like searchlights during the London Blitz. Then finally, the gunshots.

They were wild for the most part, aimed through the blackness at the sounds she made. But that first patch of jungle had slowed her. She'd bounced off tree trunks and tripped over vines. She'd smashed into a thicket of thorns, then dove underneath, and crawled through. She'd splashed through a slim, shallow stream, which brought aching relief to her feet... but only for a minute.

Across the river and back into the trees, the first aimed shot had come too close—whacking into a bamboo trunk near her head and making a sound like a gong.

"Bloody communist buggers," she'd spat as she spun on her pursuers, took a knee, aimed her pistol, listened, and fired three quick rounds in succession. Someone had screamed.

She threw herself flat as a flurry of gunshots whipped through the palms and sent slivers of bark spinning. And then she was up again, running, and she'd burst out into the elephant grass.

For a few precious minutes after that, Hyo and his gunmen had grown cautious and slowed their pursuit. But then they must have realized that all she had was a single pistol, and now she could hear them pounding down the jungle slope—stomping like horses through the stream.

Altogether, she'd fired four shots, but she had no idea how much the magazine held. Five? Eight? She didn't dare stop to check, but she remembered the title of a book she'd read by a mercenary soldier: *Save the Last Bullet for Yourself.*

Yes. She would do it. She wasn't going to be captured again. Colonel Hyo was an evil bastard, and he'd only just begun to torture her. She couldn't last much longer. They had boots; she had none. They were well fed; she was starving and dehydrated. They were in China, a staunch ally, their playground. She was on another planet. No one was coming for her. It was impossible, and she knew it.

She should do it now, right now, just deprive them of their prize and die knowing that Zeta would wreak hell and havoc on their heads.

And then, for some reason as she sprinted through the tall knife-blade grass and gasped steam from her aching lungs, she'd yanked the saliva-soaked passport from her mouth and whispered, "Linc, Lord in heaven, where are you?" There was no way her ear comm could still be working, but...

"Holy shit, Lily! I'm here!"

It was like hearing the voice of God. Tears burst from her eyes and streamed down her face, the salt stinging her split, swollen lips. He asked her questions, and she babbled back whispers and heard his feet pounding through Zeta's hallways in concert with hers. Then Kirby was on the comm telling her that, no matter what, she had to keep going and that he would fix it.

How the hell would he fix it? Did he think he was some sort of magician? Could he could call down a spaceship from the sky and just beam her aboard? He sure as hell had the ego of a spaceship captain, so maybe he had some beatific trick up his sleeve.

All right, she'd keep going. She was no longer alone, and that knowledge surged the last vestiges of hope, and adrenaline, through her veins.

But if some miraculous intervention was going to happen, she had to give it time to develop. She couldn't outrun these men for much longer. She had to hide somehow. But where?

Two hundred feet in front of her, another line of trees bounced in her blurred vision. The pale, smooth poles of towering bamboo clacked against each other in the wind, and beyond that a higher forest of palms. Height and cover were her only options.

She ran faster, with each step slapping liquid that she knew was her own blood. The line of bamboo loomed closer. Of all her possessions, her cell was the most precious, because without it she'd be untraceable by Shepard.

She jammed it sideways deep into her teeth, bit down hard on the rubber casing, and stuffed the passport through her torn blouse, into her left bra cup. Then she twisted sideways and slammed into the line of bamboo—squeezing between trunk after trunk as they whipped back and cracked her in the skull. But she made it through the grove.

Then there were endless palms. Tall, powerful, and thick—arching high up to the star-clustered sky with thick canopies of feathered black fronds. She squinted in the dark and slalomed between them, searching madly for one she could manage. And there it was—fat and gnarled at the base yet quickly thinning and leaning over about twenty degrees.

She jammed the pistol deeply into the back of her skirt, squeezed the cold barrel with her clenching buttocks, and launched herself up as high as she possibly could—wrapping her bare arms and legs around the trunk like a monkey as the impact smashed the breath from her lungs.

She hung on, gripping the slimy bark with her trembling knees as she pumped her upper body up. She hugged it with her arms and dug her broken fingernails in. She pulled her legs up and took a breath. Then again, and again, and again.

She never looked down and saw nothing but the knots and ridges of plant skin before her eyes as she gripped and pulled and scrambled again. Then the top of her head hit something. She looked up to see a circle of thick frond branches.

She thrust her hands up into the mess, gripped two frond roots, and hauled herself up. Her knees slipped onto something sturdy and hard. It held, but she did it once more. And then she was up inside a nest of dark fronds, and she was able to swing one leg over a root. She sat there, panting, hugging the tree, and shuddering.

Something clanged below her. She snapped her eyes down. It was the pistol, spinning slowly through the air, as it bounced off the trunk and disappeared.

Well, that's bloody lovely. She cursed in her head as she heard the Koreans smashing through the line of bamboo.

She stopped breathing. She turned her eyes away from the ground, squeezed them shut, and became nothing but a lifeless slug of human flesh against the palm.

She heard Hyo's furious voice below hissing orders, and the tromping of many boots and curses as the butts of weapons smashed jungle aside. They rushed closer and swarmed around the base of her tree. A vibration shivered up the trunk, and she knew they'd seen her. It was all but over.

But then they moved on.

How long should she wait? Five minutes, no more. They'd soon stop to listen and, hearing nothing in the brush out front of them, turn back. She counted the seconds off in her head and then slid back down.

By the time she hit bottom she was coated in sweat, and her bare thighs and arms were rent raw and stinging. She spat the drool-coated cell into her hand and looked around for the pistol in the brush. It was like searching for a carpenter's nail in a pile of steel wool.

Forget it.

She could still hear them searching through the jungle out front, maybe half a kilometer on. Making as little noise as possible, she turned around and worked her way back toward the line of bamboo and the elephant grass field.

Just as she squeezed through the last pair of hollow shafts, she stopped to listen again. She heard nothing from behind anymore. The Koreans had frozen in place, listening.

Shit.

She carefully took a step in the dark, tumbled down a muddy slope, and crashed face-first into a pool of freezing, stagnant water.

"*Cheoi-joge!*"—Over there!—someone shouted.

"*Christ,*" Lily moaned as she scrambled up out of the pond, soaked from her scalp to her shredded feet but still clutching the cell phone. She charged over a berm, fell, got up again, and burst back into the field.

A gunshot echoed behind her, then another, but she ran flat out before realizing that she was heading right back for the temple.

"Linc!" she grunted. "For God's sake!" But she heard nothing in her ear except a short-circuit crackle.

She took a hard right turn, and dove through the slicing green blades— unable to see anything but more and more of them. The shouts behind, and now to her right, were growing—the Koreans already smashing their way back through the bamboo into the grass.

Flashlight beams flicked through the blades. She heard Hyo yelling and felt the boots of his men pounding closer—like the hooves of frothing steeds hunting a fox.

The elephant grass ended, and Lily stumbled out into a wide-open space. Her heart fell into her guts. It was an enormous, circular meadow of ankle-high lichen. She kept running with everything she had left, but she was totally exposed. She wept hopelessly, turned her head, and glanced back.

Hyo and his men had entered the meadow. There were at least ten of them. They had stopped moving—arrayed in a line, their rifles raised like a firing squad. She turned back around and kept on, but her sprint had turned into a ragged jog, and she heard his voice.

"Miss Stone, you are finished," he called out. "You will stop right now, or I will order my men to fire."

"Then bloody well do it, you filthy scum!" she screamed over her shoulder. She could almost hear the pleasure in his voice. "As you wish."

Something thundered in front of her from the far side of the meadow. A powerful wind rippled through the lichen, and a pair of bright beams stabbed down from the black heavens.

Lily stopped running in wide-eyed shock and stared at a huge, bulbous shadow looming behind the lights. The cell phone fell from her hand as she stood there, gasping and drooling, as a Chinese Army Changhe Z-8 helicopter thundered into the meadow.

The engine sounds spooled down to a whine, and the blades stopped turning. A side door opened, a short stairway flipped down, and a man in uniform appeared. As if it were just a holiday jaunt, he started strolling toward her.

Lily stood there staring like a cornered rat, and as the man emerged into the aircraft lights, she saw that it was General Deng Tao Kung.

"*Taeryeong Hyo,*" he called to her captor and torturer. His tone was an admonishing, condescending rumble, and she couldn't understand what he said next in Chinese. "You have taken undue advantage of my country's hospitality and treated our guest poorly." He looked at her with pity, put his fists to his hips, and switched to English.

"My apologies, Miss Stone," he said. "Korean dogs have no manners." He motioned toward the open door of the helicopter. "If you please."

Lily fainted.

Chapter Thirty-One

Jenny Morgan didn't know exactly what a female spy was supposed to look like, but she was doing her best.

She'd seen plenty of pictures of Valery Plame, the CIA's modern Mata Hari, whose cover had been blown during the Bush years, so those exotic images served as a model. She didn't own a trench coat, so she'd picked one up at Filene's in Chestnut Hill—a light tan number with big buttons, a wide belt she could tie off instead of using the buckle, and a short, sexy hem.

She'd also bought a light purple scarf, tortoise-shell sunglasses, and a lizard brooch with a nice long pin. She didn't have a weapon, but that long silver pike clutched in her fist would do, at least for a getaway.

She'd chosen the rendezvous point herself: the Boston National Historical Park down by the harbor. It was one of Dan's favorite places to chill, take in the salt air, enjoy a fat "gutter puppy," his slang for a vendor hotdog, and watch the seagulls wheeling in the sun.

But most of all he loved "Old Ironsides"—the USS *Constitution*, that beautiful four-masted frigate that seemed to always remind him of why his country came first before anything else. One of their very first dates had been a tour of the ship. Maybe she should have known right there and then.

Now she sat on a wooden slat bench just in front of the museum, with the fading sun behind her, the evening breeze rustling the water, and the last of the day's tourists heading for homes and hotels. She looked at the enormous old vessel tipping languidly in the wash—her slick black flanks and cannon ports, polished elm fittings, and towering white masts— and she felt a pang of jealousy. Where did she fit on Dan's totem pole of admiration? Had she ever been at the top? Or just somewhere farther down, beneath fast cars, sailing vessels, the army, and the CIA? Was she no more than an afterthought? Or the tip of his spear that he'd never confess?

Well, maybe she was about to find out.

After breaking into his storage locker, she'd mulled over the whole thing for a couple of days, feeling a mixture of guilt, resentment, and excitement. It wasn't her business to stick her nose into his, but it was way past unfair for him to keep her in the dark for so long. She'd looked at that message, and the telephone number she'd copied into her cell phone from his diary over and over again, wondering what would happen if she made the next move.

"Need to find me? Call the Civil War President."

That morning, she'd made her decision.

Yes, I need to find you, and you need to find me. Otherwise, we're both going to be finding a lawyer.

For some reason, she'd chosen to make the call outside of the house. Maybe she was getting paranoid, but that would be Dan's fault too. She'd gone out into the backyard, where the rain had washed away her finger scars from the stone garden, and tapped out the numbers with a trembling finger.

"Hello?" A youngish–sounding man answered.

"Hello, Sir. I'm looking for Mr. Lincoln."

"Yes, this is Lincoln. May I ask who this is?"

"This is Jennifer Morgan. My husband told me to call this number if I needed him."

There was a silence, and then the man said, "I see....Is this an emergency?"

"It might be," Jenny said. "For him."

"One minute, please."

Then there was a much longer silence, some footsteps and rustling, and the man named Lincoln came back on the line. "Mrs. Morgan, I'll call you back in ten minutes at this same number you called from. Is that all right?"

"Yes."

Jenny hadn't moved from the garden. She just paced, feeling her heart rate up a tick, and was somehow thrilled to be tasting even a small portion of Dan's game. Maybe, for the first time ever, she had an inkling of why he was addicted. She jumped when her cell buzzed again.

"Mrs. Morgan?" It was Mr. Lincoln again.

"Yes, I'm here."

"Would you be willing to meet privately?"

Now Jenny's heart really started to hammer. "What do mean by privately?"

"I mean one-on-one, but it'll be in a public place of your choosing."

She thought for a moment as her palms went slick and she touched her chest. "All right. How about Boston Harbor? Down by the *Constitution*?"

"That'll be fine. Can we say four o'clock this afternoon?"

"Yes." Jenny found herself nodding at the phone. "How will I find you?"

"I'll find you. What's your favorite book?"

"Excuse me?"

"A favorite book, Mrs. Morgan. Something you still have in your house."

"Umm...*Sophie's Choice*."

"Please carry it with you, in your right hand."

"Okay, but if for some reason you can't find me, can I—" She stopped when she realized he'd hung up.

She felt a bit silly now, in her femme fatale getup, sitting there clutching the book in her lap, and looking at her wristwatch every ten seconds. People were still walking by—parents with kids licking ice cream cones and some tourists chattering in some Scandinavian language—but the flow was definitely thinning.

A young man approached from the left, wearing a leather jacket and a baseball cap. She stiffened and tried not to stare, but he passed her right by.

What's this Lincoln guy going to look like? A frock coat and a stovepipe hat?

A couple of young navy sailors walked by, probably from the Charlestown Navy Yard off to the left. They were wearing those new, blue digital camouflage uniforms that Dan always made fun of.

"The whole point of navy whites was so they could spot you if you went overboard. With those getups on, you're nothing but shark bait. Nobody'll see you, for Christ's sake. Somebody in the Pentagon must have an uncle in the rag trade."

She smiled as she remembered his disdain and looked at her watch again—four on the button. It was starting to get chilly, and almost everyone was gone, except for one woman who had just come out of the museum gift shop carrying a small shopping bag. Jenny glanced at her briefly— lightweight tan coat over a gray business suit, glossy, short brunette cut, and photo-gray glasses gone dark from the sun. She looked away again, hoping the woman would just pass by. But she strode up to Jenny's bench and took a seat at the other end.

Oh no, The last thing I need now is company.

"Nice day today," the woman said as she placed her bag on the bench.

Jenny just grunted and kept her gaze fixed on the *Constitution*. If she was *really* impolite, maybe the woman would take a hint. But she didn't.

"I like that novel," she said. "William Styron's one of my favorites."

Again, Jenny said nothing. *For pity's sake, please go away!* she pleaded in her mind, but the darn woman kept on talking.

"You have much better literary tastes than your husband, Mrs. Morgan. He seems to only read about fast cars and firearms."

Jenny snapped her head around and stared. The woman smiled slightly and pushed her sunglasses up onto her head. She had large hazel eyes and manicured eyebrows, but no other makeup except for a hint of lip gloss. Something about that face looked very familiar, but...

"You're not Mr. Lincoln," Jenny whispered.

"No, I'm his boss, which, in effect, makes me your husband's as well."

A current of panic jolted through Jenny, and she gripped the paperback with both hands. Why would Dan's boss be here, unless...She felt a painful hitch in her chest.

"Is Dan all right?"

"Oh, of course, he's fine." The woman smirked "I mean he's out of contact, but he's always fine."

Jenny realized her knees were shaking, but she had to ask. "Alex too?"

"Alex too." The woman nodded. "Healthy as a thoroughbred colt." She got up, moved a couple of feet, and sat closer to Jenny. "I'm Diana." She didn't offer her hand.

"Nice to meet you...I think," she said. "I'm Jenny."

"Yes, I know." Diana Bloch leaned back, hiked her elbows onto the bench back, crossed her stockinged legs, and bounced a heel in the air. It was a very "male" posture. She turned her face away and looked out at Old Ironsides. "It's such a beautiful ship. We've actually met before."

"We have?" Jenny stared at her profile. She was pretty in a strong-jawed, angular, way.

"Yes. Starbucks"

"Oh my God," Jenny gasped.

"I apologize for that." Diana turned her face back again and looked at her fully. "I didn't enjoy having to manipulate you, but I had little choice I'm afraid."

"Well, you're certainly good at it," Jenny said in a tone that wasn't a compliment. "But why?"

Diana recrossed her legs the other way, turned to Jenny, and dropped her voice to a cooler murmur. "I will tell you. Actually, I *need* to tell you. But understand that this is a national security issue."

Jenny's pulse started beating in her neck. Did she really want to hear any of this? "Well, I can certainly keep a secret. But what do you want me to do? Cross my heart?"

Diana sniffed, then glanced at her lap. "I don't happen to have a bible on me. You can swear on *Sophie's Choice*."

Jenny looked down at the book where her fingers were trembling on the cover. "Okay, consider it done."

"That's meaningless, of course." Diana removed her sunglasses from her head and chewed on the stem. "But I'm a reader of souls, and I think I can trust yours. There are very few people I can talk to about this. The reason I did what I did is that we have a problem in our organization."

You're coming to me with a problem? Do I look like an espionage therapist? "What sort of problem?" she asked.

"Someone on the inside of the firm is apparently working for someone on the outside. A person or persons without our best interests at heart."

Jenny swallowed, looked around, edged a bit closer to Diana, tipped her face down, and looked at her over the top of her sunglasses. "Do you mean, like, a traitor?"

Diana just smiled, mirthlessly.

"Don't tell me you thought it was Dan."

"Jenny, a person in my position can never trust anyone fully. We're not like the civilian court system. In our game, you're always guilty until proved innocent, and that has to be tested on a regular basis. I've been going through this process with everyone, so I used you to help me with Dan."

"How?" Jenny wondered. "I don't get it."

"Your husband adores you." Diana smiled, reached out, and touched the back of Jenny's hand. "Frankly, I'm a bit envious."

Jenny felt the tears well up in her eyes. A stranger telling her this meant more than Dan's assurances ever could.

"You see, every intelligence professional has an emergency plan." Diana withdrew her hand and went on. "If he has been turned, as we say in the business, that plan would be some sort of escape route involving his true masters. But because of how Dan feels about you, I knew he'd never leave you behind. So, I used you to discover his last-ditch intentions."

"His locker, you mean?"

"Yes. And the emergency contact information he left for you. You see, Dan had you reach out to *us*. If he were dirty— and I'm sorry to use that term—he would have had you contact someone else instead."

"But, he didn't know," Jenny sputtered. "I mean he didn't know I was doing *any* of this. You *made* me do it, or you got me to, anyway, and he wasn't actually doing anything wrong at all."

"That's right." Diana smiled and placed her sunglasses back on. "When he left you that message, he was anticipating something in the future. And, he was leaving you in the hands of the only other people he trusts. I hope, Jenny, that you view that as a priceless gift. I know I do."

Jenny wiped the tears from her cheeks. Diana rose up from the bench, picked up her museum bag, and motioned for Jenny to join her. Still feeling shaky, Jenny got up. Diana took the crook of her elbow, and they started strolling in the direction of the park's exit gate. A flock of pecking seagulls fled from their feet and winged away through Old Ironsides' masts.

Jenny was overcome with what she'd just heard—frightened and thrilled and ecstatic all at once—but beyond being a loving wife, she was also a dedicated mother.

"What about Alex?" she blurted. "Don't tell me you're suspicious of her too."

"Oh, no worries there." Diana grinned as she led Jenny out into the big, bad city. "She's too smart for her age, an Olympic marksman, terribly rebellious, and a royal pain in the ass, just like your husband." She squeezed Jenny's elbow. "I adore her."

Jenny Morgan found her footing, realizing that her relief was not making her weak but was actually making her strong. Although she had been figuratively and literally leaning on the spymaster, she now found they were walking side by side in harmony and balance.

"So, is that it?" Jenny wondered. "Now I just go back to my life, without my husband and daughter, and you go back to yours with them?"

"Not quite," Diana said with understanding of Jenny's situation. "No, Mrs. Morgan. If you would be so kind, and brave, there's just one more thing I'd like to ask you to do..."

Chapter Thirty-Two

Morgan slept from Boise to Denver.

There were no trains running that route, so he'd dumped the Jeep in a long-term lot in Idaho, scribbled a note that said "Sorry about that, charge my card," and hoofed it over to the Greyhound station. The bus to Colorado was a day-long trip, so he'd passed right out and wallowed in dreamless slumber—the first good rest he'd had in a week.

At Denver International Airport, he gambled on the TSA's habit of glossing over men with military IDs in favor of frisking old ladies and boarded a Nashville flight, where he picked up the Shelby, and then Neika. She wasn't too pleased with her stay in the kennel and gave him the furry cold shoulder at first—but one that quickly thawed as they drove all the way back up to Andover.

It was late at night when they walked in the door. At that point he didn't care whether Zeta was watching the joint or not. He'd found the ordnance, he had the proof, and all was right with the world—except Jenny wasn't home. The house felt cold and empty, which didn't improve his mood.

But he left her an adoring note, put Neika to bed, and folded his aching carcass back into the Shelby for one more midnight ride. He figured if Paul Revere could do it, he could too. At least he wasn't on horseback, and the Cobra had a heater. He chuckled mirthlessly as he drove away. No, Zeta would be looking everywhere but his home for him. He bet they wouldn't have anybody watching Collins's place, either.

Sure enough, he saw no one waiting and watching on the block behind the general's house in Brookline. He was there, alone, clutching a mini-can of pepper spray. The last time, that Doberman had come out of nowhere. This time the beast would get a stinging surprise. He took a breath, lunged like a high school hurdler, and took off across the neighbor's mushy lawn.

He hit the brick wall at full tilt, slammed his palms to the top, and vaulted over into Collins's backyard.

No dog. Things were looking up.

He crouched in the shadow of the wall, scanning the old colonial. The house was dark, except for one soft light in the downstairs den that seeped out to the right and onto an empty side porch. Collins was expecting him, so he wouldn't be facing the general's nasty . 38 Python. He trotted softly across the back lawn and tiptoed up the back stairs. The door was supposed to be unlocked. It was.

Morgan slipped inside, closed the door quietly and stood in the darkened hallway, just listening. The low strains of something classical, maybe Beethoven, wafted in from the den beyond, but he heard nothing else. He opened his jacket and walked.

Collins was sitting on the sofa just below the front bay window, the blinds drawn tight. Next to him on a side table his . 38 gleamed in the dim light of a bronze lamp, along with a tumbler of Scotch, no ice. The general was dressed in laced leather boots, twill trousers. And one of those L.L. Bean oil jackets with a corduroy collar. He was freshly shaven and looked a lot healthier than during their last tête-à-tête.

Morgan nodded. "General."

Collins nodded back. "Dan."

Morgan walked past him to the side of the window, tipped the edge of one blind down, and peered out with one eye. "I don't see your tail."

"They're out there," Collins said. He picked up his tumbler and sipped. "Probably making a pizza run."

Morgan walked back and took a seat across from Collins in a puffy, flowered old chair. "You going duck hunting, Jim?"

"Nah." Collins smiled, but it didn't touch his eyes. "Was thinking about going outside for some air."

Morgan glanced to his right. The sliding glass doors to the porch were partially open, and a cold breeze drifted inside. He leaned to the right, dug into his left-hand coat pocket, and pulled out the three plastic file cards with the chips inside. He stretched his hand out. Collins leaned forward and took them.

"Well done." Collins slipped the chips into his hunting jacket. "You were always a good soldier." He took another swig of Scotch and put it down.

"Well, you always had my back." Morgan sat back and twirled the pepper spray tube in his fingers.

Collins looked at it. "Whatcha got there?"

"Lipstick. With a kick." Morgan smiled, but a tiny alarm was going off in his gut. It was something about Collins's stiff demeanor. "Figured I might run into that dog again."

Collins smiled back, raised his voice, and called out, "Otto."

Morgan heard something clicking on the floor of the kitchen. Then the huge muscled Doberman walked into the den. It was the same canine that had nearly torn his foot off, if not his ass. It turned toward Morgan, stared at him, and growled.

"*Platz*," Collins said to the dog. It sat. The general looked at Morgan again. "Otto only speaks German."

"He's *your* dog?"

"Affirmative."

"You didn't mention that last time." Morgan looked at the dog. "*Guten Abend.*" The dog bared his teeth—they were long, white, and sharp. When he turned back to Collins, the general was pointing the .38 at his chest. Morgan's pulse quickened. "Looks like you forgot to mention more than just that."

"Sorry about that, Morgan. Fortunes of war."

It wasn't a good sign. People tend to get fatalistic when they're about to kill you. He understood immediately that he'd been betrayed and used, and it was like a mule kick in the balls, but he wasn't going to show it.

"So what's in those chips, Jim?" Morgan asked. His action options were flipping through his mind, but they were few. That .38 barrel looked like a tank cannon, and it was rock steady in Collins's right fist. "They're not property logs, are they?"

"Nope," Collins said. "They're launch codes."

"Nice." Morgan hissed. "You sent an old friend into a dragon's mouth to commit a federal crime."

"Friend?" Collins made a noise that sounded like a tire going flat. "I don't have any friends. I sent a subordinate who took pride in never questioning his own judgment. And it was a federal crime even if I had told you the truth, Einstein." Collins's expression went granite cold. With his thumb, he pulled the revolver's hammer back. He was ready.

"What about General Margolis?" Morgan returned, grasping at straws.

"That bastard's next."

"And then *you*, Jim." Morgan raised his chin in defiance. "Whatever the hell's gotten into you, think it over. You pull that trigger and the people I work for'll strip your skin from your bones."

"I'm scared," Collins sneered. "They couldn't even find you, and you might as well have been covered in neon." Then he tipped his gun barrel down and up. "And don't bother going for your piece. What did I always teach you? Trigger pull's always faster than draw."

"What'd I ever do to you?" Morgan said. "Is this some beef I missed?"

"Nope. You're a good troop. Honorable, brave, loyal to the point of stupid. I just needed a dupe who could execute the task, which you always did. But now you're a loose end."

"You're bruising my ego. What are you gonna do with those missiles?"

"That's need-to-know," Collins said, "which you don't. And if you've got a last prayer, now's the time to say it."

Morgan took a deep breath and nodded, as if resigned to his fate. Collins wasn't going to issue one of those long, exculpatory speeches like the villains always did in the movies. He lowered his head, his calf muscles bunching as he envisioned his only option. He'd start the prayer, then launch himself to the left, and try slapping the revolver off-center. He didn't expect to make it, but it was his only chance.

He was just on the verge of exploding from the chair when a female voice from behind echoed Collins's last words.

"If you've got a last prayer, General, it's time for *you* to say it."

Morgan lifted his face and twisted around. standing in the gloom of the hallway was Commander Alicia Schmitt, and she looked like hell. Her Navy peacoat had ragged holes punched in the front, her blonde hair was a greasy mess, and her left sleeve was gone—replaced by her arm, which was encased in a green plaster cast.

But the Smith & Wesson automatic clutched in her right fist was gorgeous, and it was aimed directly at Collins's head.

"Well, well," Collins said. "Look what the cat dragged in."

Morgan turned back around and looked at the general. The Doberman rose to his feet and growled at Schmitt.

"Better tell your dog to stand down, General," Schmitt said. "Trigger pull's faster than fur."

Collins ignored the comment. "I thought my people took care of you." He kept his revolver trained on Morgan.

"The miracle of Kevlar," Schmitt said. "They left me for dead. I won't make the same mistake with you."

"Somebody throw me a bone," Morgan said.

"He put you onto me Morgan," Schmitt said, without taking her eyes or her gun off Collins, "because he knew I wasn't sure if he was dirty or clean. He was hoping I'd panic and try to kill you, and you'd kill me instead. He'd already given you Virginia, and he figured you'd work that out and do whatever he needed." She narrowed her eyes at Collins. "Now put the piece down, General. Slowly."

Collins's gray eyes narrowed back. "You pull that trigger, I'll pull mine, and Morgan here's gone."

"So?" Schmitt said. "I barely know him."

"That's harsh," Morgan said.

Collins laughed.

Morgan pressed his thumb on the pepper spray button and fired a thick stream at the Doberman's face as he launched himself out of the chair to the right. Collins's brain made a primary-threat decision, so he fired a shot at Schmitt, but she was already ducking. The bullet splintered the hallway jamb as she went down.

The dog was yelping and spinning in circles as Morgan dropped the tube, spun left, and slammed into Collins's chest at the same time he jetted his right hand out to grip Collins's gun wrist. But Collins reached over his head with his left, grabbed the bronze lamp from the table, and clanged it off Morgan's skull.

Half-blinded, drooling, and snarling like a demon, the Doberman went for Schmitt—slamming her into a wall. Collins banged Morgan's head again with the lamp, but Morgan wouldn't let go of his wrist. So he dropped the gun, kicked Morgan off him, and charged for the porch door. The Doberman was on top of Schmitt, trying to tear her throat out. She cracked him on the skull with her pistol butt until he went limp, then squeezed out from under him and scrambled up.

"Don't lose him!" Morgan yelled as he gripped his ringing head with both hands. They saw Collins outside, vaulting over the porch rail. That "retired old general" crap was just an act.

"I'll cut him off from the rear!" Schmitt charged through the den, out through the glass doors, and went after Collins.

Morgan pulled the front door open and staggered down the stairs into the front yard. He felt hot blood crawling through his hair and running off his jaw, but he ignored it as he starting loping off to the right. He heard the sound of a gunning engine, and then the double gate at Collins's front brick wall splintered off its hinges as a black van burst through the opening and swerved to a stop on the lawn.

It was one of Zeta's tac vehicles. Morgan stopped running as the doors flew open, and Bishop, Spartan, and Diesel jumped out.

"Perfect timing!" Morgan gasped as he shot his finger off to the right in the direction of Collins's flight. "Collins just took off that way." He started running toward them and the van. "Back in the truck. Let's get him."

Then he froze. Bishop was pointing a Taser pistol at him.

"We're not here for him," he said to Morgan. "We're here for *you*."

"What the ever-loving fu—"

Then Bishop fired. The darts plunged into Morgan's chest, and the high voltage twitched him like a marionette.

He went down hard. And this time, he didn't get up.

Chapter Thirty-Three

Lily woke up, naked, in what appeared to be Austria.

She lay there just breathing, staring at a pink stucco ceiling, fully convinced she was dreaming. Then she steeled herself for the awful truth, lifted her head from a thick down pillow, and looked around. She blinked, hiked herself up on her elbows, and the thick flowered quilt nestling her fell away from her nude breasts.

"I've bloody well died," she whispered. "And hell is a brothel."

She was lying on a king-sized bed, with curled brass bars at the head and foot, in the middle of a very large room. The walls were of textured pink stucco, the moldings and doors were made of chunky chestnut, and the tall windows were obscured by long lace curtains. To her left was a cushy, purple divan, and at the far wall beyond was a dressing table that looked like an antique from Salzburg.

Above that on the wall was an oval mirror ringed in brass cherubs, with a framed sign that said "Wilkommen."

She looked to her right, where a small bedside table held a lamp, a crystal water pitcher and glass, her false passport, and her cell phone. Just beyond that was an ornate wooden chair with a high curved back, carefully arranged with some clothes: a sleeveless red dress, long-sleeved white blouse, modest pink bra and bikini-cut panties, and a pair of high black leather boots.

She looked at the bottom of the quilt, where her turned-up feet were making a small tent, and carefully curled her toes. The bottoms of her wounded soles felt stiff, encased in something. She threw off the quilt and stared at a pair of medical pressure stockings running all the way up to her knees.

Well now, that's very attractive.

She swung her legs to the right and sat up, feeling a little woozy. So she took a long pull from the water glass. Tasty, refreshing, as if from a mountain stream. Then she stood, using the high mattress as a brace. She found her footing, walked around the bed, and made her way to the left-hand window. She fingered one edge of the curtain aside and looked down.

"Good Christ," she gasped.

She was in one of those quaint little towns on the shore of some Alpine lake. There were two long rows of pastel flats, capped with red and black tile roofs, embracing a long, curving lane of rain-washed cobblestone. Multicolored umbrellas hung above outdoor café tables, and at the end of the lane was a beautiful white church with a tall black spire and a Roman numeral clock.

Only one problem. The surrounding countryside looked nothing like any geographical spot she knew of in Europe. Her head swimming, she turned away from the window and pressed her naked cheeks against the wall to steady herself. Then she saw her image in the dressing table mirror, and carefully made her way over there to stare.

Her hair had been washed and braided. Her lips were healed and glossed, and makeup hid the bruises around her eyes. She could still see some welts on her inner arms and thighs, but they'd also been salved and soothed. Her broken fingernails had been preened down and manicured. Even her mound had been trimmed.

"Not bad for a cornered rat," she murmured. "I wonder who the customer is."

She had no idea how long she'd been there, but she'd obviously been drugged and treated while under. There was only one way to find out. She got dressed, not really surprised that everything fit. The boots were a trial, but even those had been selected one size too large to accommodate her swollen, socked feet.

She picked up her passport and cell, and smoothed her red dress in the mirror. She smirked at herself—a cross between a beer garden waitress and a Viennese escort. She flipped the brass door handle down and went out.

She took a few shaky steps in her boots and stopped. She was looking down the length of a long, straight stairway of glossy white wood, with a plush red runner and a thick chestnut balustrade on the left. She gripped the rail with her left hand and moved down slowly, clutching her passport and cell to her chest. At the bottom was a lead-framed stained-glass door. Her stomach murmured in hunger. She pushed the door open and saw flowers.

Hundreds of them. Roses and tulips of all colors—some arranged in half-cut wine barrels, some jutting from small fenced gardens, and many more popping from balcony boxes. The scent was almost too much.

Just below her was another short staircase of blue slate, and at the bottom of that, facing away from her, stood a woman in a throwback white nurse's uniform, including the nun-like hat. The nurse heard Lily's boots on the stones and turned. The front of her hat had a red cross on it, but her features were Asian. She smiled, walked up to Lily, and took her elbow to help her down.

"*Wo sind wir?*"—Where are we?—Lily asked in German as she realized there was no one else around. Not another soul, and the air was weirdly devoid of sound—no cars, footsteps, laughter, or music. But at least she heard some birds outside, or else she'd be sure she was dead.

"Hallstatt," the nurse said.

Lily nodded as they negotiated the last stair, wobbling a bit on the polished cobblestones. Hallstatt, she recalled, was that famous quaint village somewhere in upper Austria on the shores of the Hallstätter See. She'd seen it in travel brochures.

"Not the original," said a basso male voice. "But close enough."

Lily turned to her right. He was tall, in his sixties, and wearing a gray pin-striped suit with a cobalt tie and matching pocket leaf that was so expensive it didn't look expensive. But she knew it was costly because it looked like it had been tailored directly on to him. He had thick, swept-back, steel-gray hair, an angular face, and, incongruously, tortoiseshell sunglasses.

Lily looked him over and blinked. "Where'd you leave your DeLorean?" she asked because he looked exactly like John DeLorean, a famous playboy car designer, although he'd died in 2005. He also seemed to have appeared out of nowhere as if by magic.

The tall man smiled. "The comparison's often mentioned," he said. "But I don't drive."

Lily resisted for a second but had to ask. The situation was just too bizarre. "Are you God? Or the other guy?"

He laughed and nodded at the nurse, who stepped aside. He took Lily's elbow and began guiding her slowly along the lovely main avenue of the beautiful, empty town.

"It's Smith, actually," he said.

She looked up at him and her eyes went wide. "Not *the* Smith."

He nodded with a small oh-well shrug.

"But you're not..." Lily sputtered. "I mean I've seen you twice on the boardroom monitor. You're always in silhouette, but you were a bit tubby and bald."

"That's a stand-in," he admitted. "Always liked the *Wizard of Oz*."

Lily felt dizzy again, only this time from relief. "Well, at least that makes sense." She unhooked her elbow from his hand and switched, gripping the crook of his arm instead. "Since I'm dressed rather like a slutty Dorothy."

Smith laughed again and pointed down the lane, where a young woman dressed exactly like Lily was walking into a shop. "I'm afraid the only couture they had was the standard employee uniform."

Lily's brow furrowed at the sight of her doppelganger. "I have no idea what you mean."

"And look there," Smith said. "That's not right." He was pointing at a chunky red phone booth with glass windows and the word *TELEPHONE* stamped on its cap. "If they're going to pirate everyone's architecture, then dropping a London phone booth in Hallstatt is an additional crime."

"If who's going to. . ." Lily stopped walking and looked up at him. "Mr. Smith, I'm totally lost."

He smiled down at her. "You're not lost, Lily. You're in China."

She swallowed. "Excuse me?"

"Yes. In Guangdong Province, to be precise. There are actually nine such copycat cities in China, essentially Disneyworld versions of Paris, Milan, and so forth. The intent was to attract the wealthy strata of Chinese society, sell them all highbrow real estate and residences, and then lure in the tourists as well. Alas, so far they've all been failures and remain mostly empty. Therefore, perfect for clandestine, private meetings that could be considered socially sensitive."

Lily gaped as she gazed at their surroundings. That's why no one sat at the outdoor cafés and why the only people she saw in the distance were all dressed like her—the employees.

"This one was financed by Minmetal Holdings to the tune of nine hundred sixty million dollars," Smith went on. "It's an exact copy of Austria's well-known village of Hallstatt." He pointed off between a row of flats, past which a wide, empty square led down to a waterside quay and a wide body of rippling gray water. "That's not the quaint lake in the mountains of upper Austria. It's the South China Sea."

Lily felt dizzy. She was still in China; her dream was a nightmare. She hadn't escaped or been rescued at all. But Smith himself was here, which made absolutely no sense. She curled her fingernails into her palm and dug in.

Wake up, damn you!

Then she felt Smith's long strong arm enveloping her waist as he pulled her closer to steady her.

"I realize it's a bit much to take in," he said. "But you must be starving. So let's eat."

It took them awhile to descend to the quay. Lily's body still ached from her neck to her ankles, and she'd had no real nourishment for days. As she walked arm in arm with Smith, she noticed the bruise of an infusion needle on the back of her wrist. She'd been given something while she slept, perhaps simply sucrose or something else, so she still wasn't convinced that what she was seeing was real. At any rate, she felt unsteady on her feet but not faint.

At the bottom of a half-circle of marble stairs was a wide portico of cobblestones, which led to the right, and a winding road that circled "Hallsatt's" beautiful, empty, private town homes. Lily squinted past that to a strange vision across the flat oval bay—modern skyscrapers looming in the mist.

Smith guided her gently to the left, where a portico entrance of a typical Gasthaus awaited, complete with heavy wood-framed windows, inner sills lined with beer steins from the Middle Ages, and, just beside the thick double doors, a menu in German held by a smiling, plaster mountain elf. They walked inside, and Lily swallowed another gasp.

The restaurant's only customer was General Deng Tao Kung. He sat at a large, round wooden table, with two of his young adjutants standing behind him. The table was arranged with a typical Austrian repast—juices and mélange coffee, fresh eggs, strudels, and cheese of all kinds.

Kung rose from his chair, a white napkin tucked in his uniform collar, smiled his kindly uncle expression, and opened his hands in silent offering. If Smith hadn't been there, Lily might have run screaming.

But Smith was there, and he walked Lily over, pulled out a chair for her, and bookended her between him and Kung.

"How are you feeling, Miss Stone?" the general asked.

Lily glanced at Smith, who smiled and nodded. "Stone" it would remain then.

"Intact, General," she said. "Thanks to you, I expect."

A waitress hurried over to pour their coffees. She was dressed, of course, exactly like Lily, but she had "strudel" braids cupping her comely Asian face.

"I confess that your condition alarmed me," Kung sang as he spooned some steaming scrambled eggs onto Lily's white plate. "But, sadly, didn't surprise me. I must apologize for that once more..."

"There's no need, General," Smith said. "Lily's chosen profession engenders such risks."

"No, sir." Kung waved his hand, and Lily was surprised by his deferential tone. "I feel that I must." He dropped his fingers on Lily's arm as a father might do with his daughter. "You see, Miss Stone, I had no idea who you were, and I made a poor judgment. Once Mr. Smith explained to me your true target and intentions, I was very embarrassed."

"Please, Deng," Smith said before sipping his mélange. "It's all in the past."

Lily looked from one man to the other as she forked up some eggs while gulping some juice. Considering what she had been through, she was sure her slight bending of decorum would be forgiven.

General Kung was calling Smith *sir*, and Smith was calling the general by his first name. The latter smiled and leaned into Lily. "The general is a consummate gentleman," he said. "I only had to elucidate Colonel Hyo's ill manners, and he was aghast."

"Yes." Kung nodded. "*Chaoxian* have an unfortunate tendency for dissembling and flattery that masks their base intent. They do not yet seem to truly understand how this world of our works."

As the general spoke, Lily saw that he seemed to start suffering a bout of growing discomfort, perhaps indigestion. Smith, who apparently sensed it as well, interjected. "But where are my manners? The breakfast table is no place for such talk. Please eat, drink, enjoy."

So they did. It wasn't until afterward, when the general made his gracious good-bye and Smith began to chaperone Lily away from the restaurant, that any sort of recognizable reality resumed.

"What the hell just happened?" Lily all but blurted.

The Smith who replied was not exactly the same Smith who had met her at the bedroom, led her here, and joined her for breakfast. This Smith was calm but free of any artifice.

"My friendship with the general," he told her, "and your freedom, rests with the nature of our modern world. It supersedes all politics. Certain considerations, mostly financial, but also existential, outweigh political winds, which the pragmatic always expect to change. And the Chinese are nothing if not pragmatic." He nearly chortled. "Poor Kung. He was becoming ill from all our blunt talk. Pragmatic they are. Candid and direct they are not."

Although well fed, with her body regaining its strength, Lily found her mind still reeling. "Well," she managed. "They say that politics is the cake that's fed to the masses, while the real powers rule the world." She was trying to be clever, but then she saw the look in Smith's eyes. He seemed to be studying the way he would a prize pupil...or a pinned butterfly. "Oh," she realized. "Is that you? The real power?"

Smith lowered his head. Whether it was with false or real modesty, Lily couldn't decide.

"Oh, I'm not sure about power," he said. "But, yes, if I, and others like me and the general, left the world's matters to politico egos, we'd all wind up as singed ashes in a wasteland." He looked up with calm, sad eyes. "Even with us, we may still."

"So," Lily continued, emboldened by her rescue and the food. "You're actually Aegis?"

Smith's placid demeanor remained unchanged, but he did look up to survey the incongruous city. "What do you know of Aegis?"

"I actually haven't heard much," Lily said. "I'm merely a pawn."

"No, no." Smith smiled. "A knight, at the very least. Certainly no damsel in distress."

"Thank you," Lily said. "But at the moment I'm feeling as deadly effective as a rag doll."

"You'll be fine," Smith assured. "Your efforts unearthed a rat from his hole. This Colonel Hyo has evil intentions, but we're onto him and his friends now, thanks to you." Smith became serious. "However, his top operative and agents are still in play. You'll have to go back and help out."

Lily stopped and looked at Smith. "Enver Lukacs," she whispered.

Smith stopped beside her, but his manner returned to one of diffidence "Yes, and others of his ilk. Some we might call traitors. However, their betrayal of the peoples' trust is not of my concern." He removed his sunglasses and looked fully at her with a pair of ice-blue eyes. "I am not a government man, Lily. I am not a politician of any stripe or a spy or warrior like you."

"Then what are you?"

"A man of means who associates with other such men and women and patriots such as General Kung. We all love our countries, and wish for the world to remain inhabitable, nothing more. This is the task of Zeta and our most talented and trusted operators, such as yourself."

"I understand, I think," Lily said. "Sort of a power consortium."

"Correct," Smith said. "And given the trial you've been through, I thought you deserving of an explanation, which might also provide you further incentive to stay in our game." He raised a finger. "However, I do expect your discretion."

"Cross my heart," Lily said without the slightest bit of humor, and she did.

"Very good," Smith said. "You are a strong and admirable young woman."

Lily smiled her thanks in return. Suddenly she found herself standing by a gleaming black Hongqi limousine. Smith turned and looked at it too.

"And speaking of my associates, I believe this is your ride."

The limousine's uniformed driver got out and opened the rear passenger door. A tall man dressed in casual clothes emerged from the back and pushed his sunglasses up into his messy blond hair.

Lily's mouth fell open.

It was Scott Renard.

Her mouth remained open until she was seated beside her boyfriend in the back seat. But before she could leap into his arms, or inundate him with endless questions, Smith pinioned her green eyes with his icy blues a final time.

"Good luck, Ms. Randall. Do me proud." That should have been it, but Lily heard one more thing before Smith closed the door. "By the way, of your organization, only Ms. Bloch has my confidence. *Only* Ms. Bloch. Remember that."

Chapter Thirty-Four

Zeta headquarters had its own medical clinic.

It was a small affair, just an infirmary really—designed with the thought that wounded operatives might have to avoid a bona fide hospital and all the ensuing questions. A Boston-based surgeon and a registered nurse, both veterans of Special Forces, were contracted to be on call twenty-four-seven. But Zeta also had its own in-house medic, so, to date, their services hadn't been used.

The clinic was square in shape, and white from ceiling to walls—with a morgue-style, smooth, tiled floor, complete with drains for spilled fluids. To the left and right were two Stryker hospital beds with standing EKG, blood pressure equipment, and pulse rate monitors, along with defibrillators and other lifesaving accouterments, plus a pair of low steel cabinets on casters, containing every imaginable scalpel, syringe, and surgical probe.

And, last, in the open space between the two beds, sat a Steelcase table stretched left to right, and a matching chair on the far side—convenient for any doctor's administrative tasks. However, both were bolted to the floor because the clinic also doubled as Zeta's interrogation room.

"No sense in wasting good real estate" as Paul Kirby often said.

Morgan sat in the chair, his wrists behind him at the base of his spine, cuffed to the thick metal uprights. All of his professional possessions—pistol, cell, ear comm, and boot knife—had been removed and locked up somewhere. He wore only his T-shirt, black jeans, and gym shoes, and the tattoo serpent slithering over his bicep seemed to recoil from the fury of his expression.

The door to the clinic was positioned to the left, but Morgan faced forward, across the table toward the clinic's fourth wall, which was a top-to-bottom two-way mirror. Behind that was an anteroom, half again the infirmary's size, with two rows of chairs, and a single, slim, table mounted with recording devices and two-way audio.

Zeta personnel had dubbed the clinic "the Cage," but they called the anteroom "the Zoo."

It was crowded tonight. Lincoln Shepard manned the controls, wearing a pair of large earphones. He was perched before a microphone, like a World War II radio operator from Rangoon or a disc jockey in Vietnam. Behind him, in the back row, sat Bishop, Spartan, and Diesel—all looking vaguely uncomfortable. Karen O'Neal held the end of that row, alone, taking notes on her laptop, while Peter Conley stood off in one dark corner, arms folded, and more than mildly pissed.

Diana Bloch and Paul Kirby occupied the command row just behind Shepard. But they sat with two empty chairs between them, and the whole thing resembled divorce proceedings that weren't going to go well.

"I am absolutely against this, Paul." Diana Bloch slapped her knees and got up, leaned her palms on the control table, and stared through the glass at the image of Morgan.

"I'd expect you to be, Diana," Kirby replied, fully aware of his audience. "But this isn't a personal matter."

"Are you sure?" she posed, then turned her head and looked at the rest of them. "Were all of you driven to this by nothing more than professional convictions?"

"Yes ma'am," Spartan said from her chair.

"Ditto," Diesel said.

"Frickin' A," Bishop said as he smoothed his gleaming bald skull.

"Bullshit," Peter Conley said, and the rest of the Tac team turned to eye him.

Karen kept her head down and said nothing. She was merely a scribe tonight and hadn't had anything to do with Morgan's taking.

"Look, Diana," Kirby said as he leaned back in his chair. "I realize this is an anomalous event." He took off his glasses and angled one stem at the glass. "But Cobra's actions are beyond unsupportable."

"Like when are they ever?" Bishop murmured from behind. Spartan elbowed him to be quiet.

"After specific orders to stand down," Kirby went on, "he broke into a top-secret federal facility, stole government property, which was also classified, then assaulted a military service member, and stole an air force vehicle. There's a warrant out for him from the FBI. Would you have preferred that we let them take him first, Diana? Without preamble or a chance to debrief him ourselves?"

She turned away from Kirby and looked at Morgan again. "That is not the..."

"We're gonna hafta give him up to the feds," Bishop interrupted. "He's a loose cannon anyway."

"Bishop," Conley said from his corner. "You're muscle, not brains. Remember?"

Bishop turned to glare at Conley, who simply cocked his head and raised an eyebrow. It was Conley's bring-it-on invitation, which no wise man ever accepted.

"Hey, all you geniuses in the Zoo." It was Morgan's voice booming from the recessed speakers. From his manacled perch all Morgan could see was an enormous mirror, and he couldn't hear anything that was being said. But they could hear him, and he knew it. "While you're all talking shit in there, Collins is probably hauling ass to Central America."

Diana leaned over and touched the button at the base of the control table's mike. "Just sit tight, Cobra."

Morgan rolled his eyes. "Do I look like I'm going somewhere?"

Diana released the button, straightened, and folded her arms. She rolled her pearls in her fingers and squinted through the heavy glass at Morgan's rippling arms and hunched posture. Even cuffed to a steel chair that was bolted to the floor, she wouldn't be shocked if he burst free like some rampaging beast.

She had intentionally goaded Morgan into, well, being himself, consequences be damned. She'd also set Alex up in a similar way with a mirror task—after all, the kid was just like her father. Alex had gone after Sheldon Margolis, but she was now out of contact, and who knew where? Lily was safely en route back to Zeta HQ, hopefully soon to deliver a back-brief that would connect all the dots on this rogue missile thing. However, Diana had been forced to engage Mr. Smith himself to sort all that out, which could mean that she'd soon be out of a job.

And still, here she was, surrounded by her best analysts, operatives, and agents, one of whom was playing for some other team. She'd used Jenny to clear Morgan, and she had no doubts about Alex, so at least those pieces were off the board. Peter Conley? He was Morgan's best friend and had been for years, although that might mean nothing if someone had turned him. If someone had turned Collins, all bets were off.

Her Tactical team? They were all special operators—men and women of action who thrived on missions, were very well compensated, and rarely had dreams of greater ambitions. Lincoln Shepard? She shivered at the thought. If Shepard was dirty, then everything that happened at Zeta was in the hands of bad actors, and as explosive as a Washington hooker's black book. Karen O'Neal? She was in love with Shepard, but that could be a ploy. The quiet ones were often most dangerous.

Paul Kirby. He thrived on his position with Zeta and seemed to have no other life. But he was vain, ambitious, borderline insubordinate. Little he did had anything other than his own promotion in mind. And during Diana's recent, necessary, absences, he'd relished taking command. Now, emboldened, he was becoming overtly subversive.

She sighed inwardly. She trusted all of them. She trusted none of them. But that was the curse of a spy mistress.

Kirby cleared his throat. "Diana?"

She snapped from her mental calculations and turned her head. He was looking down at his cell.

"I've just had a text from the special agent in charge, Boston field office. He says, 'Either you're coming here, or we're coming over there. What's it going to be?'"

"Jesus," Diesel mumbled from behind. "Just what we need here, the feds."

"Tell him we're running an internal debrief," Diana said. "One hour."

Kirby raised his palms to the sides. "Diana...really."

"Tell him," she snapped. "Or just give me his number."

"All right, all right," Kirby said with exasperation and tapped.

"Ms. Bloch," Spartan said from the back row. Everyone turned and looked at her. Spartan rarely said anything in meetings or briefings. It was as if she considered all words weak, and only fists and feet had meaning. "Why don't we just take a vote?"

Karen O'Neal looked up from her laptop. Peter Conley came away from the corner wall and leaned on the back of a chair.

"Spartan," he said, "you're taking your code name too seriously. This isn't the Greek Senate."

"It's not such a bad idea." Bishop shot a muscled arm out and jabbed an accusing finger toward Morgan's cuffed-up form. "That dude's been off the reservation for months. He does more damage than good. We don't need him."

"That *dude*," Conley growled at Bishop, "has saved your sorry ass more than once. But his doggy took a piece of it, so now you're all high and mighty."

"I get it, Cougar," Bishop snapped back at Conley. "He's your battle buddy. But this is a team, and we have to work together. He's a loose cannon, and everyone knows it."

Diana slapped the control table hard. Shepard flinched as it rang in the room like a gunshot. "Stand down," she barked. "All of you. The minute this organization becomes a hippy commune, I'll be sure to let you know."

They all fell silent and stared at her. And at that very moment, an idea blazed in her mind.

"All of you will remain right here," she ordered. "I'm going to discuss this with Morgan."

She picked up her cell phone and marched to the exit door on the left and went out. The door to the clinic yawned open and she appeared on the other side of the glass.

"Lady Diana in the lion's den," Bishop muttered.

"Shut up and listen," Spartan said, and he did.

Inside the clinic, Morgan sat back in his chair and watched Diana approach. She had her head down and was thumb-tapping a message into her cell phone. But she finished that quickly and hiked herself up on the end of the doctor's table. Facing him and glaring down, her back to the glass, she started in.

"Cobra," she said. "You are riding very close to the edge."

"The edge of what?" Morgan looked up. "Retirement? Good. Maybe it's time."

Diana edged her cell phone onto her stockinged thigh, positioning the screen so that only Morgan could see it. She tapped the glass with a fingernail.

"You can be a smart-ass with me all you want," she said. "But the feds won't be impressed by your charms."

Morgan glanced down and quickly back up, but he'd seen Diana's message: PLAY ALONG. WE'RE MOLE HUNTING.

"Go ahead, turn me over," he sneered. "But before I tell the FBI anything, you'll have to rescind every nondisclosure document you made me sign. In the meantime, Collins is on the lam, he's got access and launch codes to some serious fireworks, and nobody knows what he's got planned next. Yeah, go ahead. Let's waste time."

Diana got up, dropped the cell phone into her suit jacket, and folded her arms. Then she paced, slowly, between the table and mirrored fourth wall.

"We received a call from your wife," she said.

"Yeah? What'd she want?" Morgan followed her pacing form with his eyes. "Did I leave the dishwasher on?"

"She claims to have urgent information."

"Right," Morgan scoffed. "Like she'd even know how to make contact."

Diana stopped pacing and looked fully at him. "You told her how. Does 'the civil war president' ring a bell?"

Morgan blinked. He was stunned by the revelation, but he had no other choice than to trust Diana. *Play along. We're mole hunting.*

"Bullshit," he snarled. "She doesn't know anything."

"I believe she does," said Diana. "She claims to know something about this organization, something she feels I must know. She hinted about a bad apple. My guess is she's referring to you."

"Jenny knows as much about Zeta as I do about knitting."

"She knows where your secret storage facility is."

Morgan blinked again. This shit was getting serious. *Play along.* Did he have a choice? The mole-hunting part of it meant...Diana was trying to flush someone out.

"Hey, if you've got a problem inside, it's not me," he said.

"Why did you break into Coldcastle Mountain?"

"I was trying to save Collins's ass. Turned out he was setting me up to burn mine. And with all your heads up your asses, looks like it worked pretty well."

Abruptly, a speaker inside the clinic crackled with the sound of Kirby's voice. "Diana, I couldn't stop them. They're here."

Still facing Morgan, she raised a hand in compliance, but she looked down at him, winked hard, and said, "You will cooperate *fully* with the FBI."

Morgan watched her face and remembered something she'd once said to him on the cusp of an iffy mission: "You will *never* cooperate with any governmental agency, unless Smith himself is standing in the room and telling you to do so."

"I'll cooperate with my lawyer," he said. "The feds'll get dick from me."

"As you wish," Diana said, and she turned toward the mirror and snapped her fingers. "Take him."

The door to the clinic swung open and the Tac team shouldered their way inside. Diesel and Spartan led the way, their expressions anything but enthusiastic, while Bishop brought up the rear. Diana stepped aside as Spartan walked behind Morgan, gripped the back of his neck, and leaned him forward in his chair. Diesel, taking no chances, was carrying another pair of handcuffs. He wasn't going to release Morgan's wrists from the chair before making certain he was still trussed up.

"Sorry about this, brother," Diesel murmured as he cinched a new pair above the first.

"No problem," Morgan said. "Screw you all very much. And I mean that deeply, no lube."

"It's not personal, Cobra," Spartan said as she unlocked him from the chair.

"Yeah, I heard that in a mob movie once."

Bishop looped his ham-hock forearm under Morgan's armpit and hauled him up. His face was twisted but he wasn't saying much.

"How's your arm?" Morgan turned toward him and smirked. "My dog liked the taste, and she's been asking for more."

Bishop pulled a stun gun from his belt and showed it to Morgan. "*You* want some more?"

"Sure, gimme a quirt," Morgan snarled. "But make sure you're still holding me so we both get the rush."

They frog-marched him over to the door. Morgan considered his fighting options. He could do an awful lot of damage with his feet alone, and maybe even get ahold of Spartan's handcuff key. But then what? and whose side was Conley on? Would he help, or was there a line even Cougar wouldn't cross? Then they passed the open door to the Zoo, where Conley was standing there, watching and brooding.

"*Et tu*, Cougar?" Morgan accused as he passed.

"I'm a cog in the wheel, brother," Conley said. "Just like you."

Morgan ignored his partner as the Tac team dragged him out into Zeta's main hallway. He vaguely noticed the faces of others: Shepard and Karen looking pouty and ashamed while Kirby stood there with folded arms and a disgusting victorious smirk.

But all he really saw was the coterie of strangers bunched at the end of the hall—four FBI agents in suits and three more in SWAT gear backing them up. Diana cruised up beside him. He lifted his chin in defiance.

"That's a lot of cop muscle for one tired old spook."

"Don't make this hard," she muttered. "You won't be there long."

But Morgan wasn't sure about anything now, not even that melodrama back in the cage. Those doors at the end of the hallway led out to the underground garage, where the FBI dudes probably had an armored Bearcat vehicle waiting. For all he knew, they'd be taking a long ride down to D.C., and by the time he got out he'd be wizened and gray.

Then the doors at the end of the lobby burst open, and a very tall man wearing an army full-dress uniform came stomping his way through the feds. He had stars on his epaulets and lots of ribbon bars, and he was trailing two younger officers who looked like guys on temporary duty from Delta.

But the most stunning thing about the vision was that Alex was right there along with the general, and she was dressed like that first day she'd interviewed for school. Diesel and Spartan stopped dead in their tracks, and Morgan squinted at the general's black nameplate.

Margolis.

The general marched straight up to Diana. "That's enough of this nonsense, Ms. Bloch. This man is not the enemy." Then he looked Morgan over, up, and down. "Come on, you poor, sorry son of a bitch. Let's go get the *real* lowlife traitor."

Chapter Thirty-Five

Six thousand feet above the Golden Gate Bridge, Scott Renard's private jet burst from a cloud.

It was a Bombardier Challenger 605, with an ice-blue skin, fire-red winglets, and the italicized letters *SR* on the sides. Inside the spacious nine-passenger cabin, the décor was all black leather and chrome, as if a Rolls-Royce Silver Ghost had been turned inside out. And much like everything else Renard owned, you could talk to the aircraft and it would do your bidding or, if elucidation were required, talk back.

"Feet dry," said the voice inside the large, lush cabin. It had the same female lilt as Scott's house.

"Give me the cockpit," Scott said. He was half-reclined in a puff leather chair, facing aft, where Lily was ensconced in the bathroom. Between him and there, Chilly and Hot Shot faced one another across a round chrome table, happily devouring freshly grilled steaks.

"Flight deck here," reported Scott's chief pilot.

"Morning, Bobby," said Scott. "Plane says we're over land."

"Roger that—welcome home. Want us to set her down in Frisco?"

"Not yet. Just cruise around for a while. What's your bingo?" Scott asked, a reference to fuel consumption.

"Got about a thousand nautical left, enough for a Sunday drive."

"Okay, just stand by."

"Yes, sir," said the pilot, and the Challenger winged over into an easy elliptical glide.

The door to the aft bathroom opened, and as Lily emerged, Scott sat up and smiled his gap-tooth smile. He'd brought her some clothes that fit her style, but they looked much different on her than the rack. Her lithe legs were snuggled in tight black jeans, with a roll-neck crimson sweater on top, and black running shoes on her feet. Her red hair was freshly washed and combed, so her mane fell loose to her shoulders. Whatever she'd been through, she looked like she'd left it behind—along with that Hallstatt outfit, which was now bunched up in a bag like a souvenir.

"Wow," Scott said as Lily walked up the aisle.

Chilly, whose back was to Scott, looked up from his steak, and Hot Shot twisted his head around.

"Can I second that?" Chilly asked.

"You may, as long as that's all."

Chilly dipped his gelled red head. "Then wow, dude."

"I'll just say you clean up real nice, ma'am," Hot Shot said. Some military habits die hard, such as addressing all men as sir and all women as ma'am.

"Thank you, lads." Lily dipped her head as she passed them.

"Yes," Scott said. "From Dorothy to Emma Peel in a flash."

"Who's that?" Chilly asked.

"Never mind. You're too young."

Lily flopped down into a chair across the aisle from Scott's.

"How'd you sleep?" he asked.

"Like the dead," she said, "though with a few fitful dreams. One of them was about a girl who's infatuated with a nerd in wolf's clothing. But then it turns out it's the other way around. He's a wolf, posing as a nerd."

Scott grinned. "Sounds like a fairy tale."

"Or a nightmare," said Lily, but then her smile widened. "With a happy ending."

A young woman emerged from the forward cabin, carrying a tray with two glasses of orange juice. Her outfit was "flight attendant casual"—just jeans and a blazer with an "SR" lapel pin. She had freckles, brown hair in a ponytail, and large, heavy glasses. Renard never hired to impress his clients—only based on resumes, nothing else. She set the juice down on their respective tables.

"Thank you, Susan."

"You bet. Anything else?"

"Not for now."

She went back to the galley. Lily sipped her juice and regarded Scott as if seeing him for the first time.

"We're going to have to have a long talk, young man," she said.

"Later. At the moment, we're going to war." He looked over at Chilly and Hot Shot, who were now plunging their steak-stained forks into steaming eggs and arguing the merits of the book version and TV adaptation of *Game of Thrones*.

"You there," he snapped. They both dropped their forks and sat up like obedient dogs. "You've got three minutes to snarf that up."

"Okay." Chilly wagged his head. "Then what?"

"Battle stations."

"Cool!"

They did it in two. Five minutes later, Chilly and Hot Shot were in the aft section of the cabin, hunkered side by side on a black leather sofa. They both wore Bose headsets with boom mikes, and faced a chrome worktable arrayed with identical Alienware laptops, Logitech ball mice, digital stylus pads, Bluetooth toggles, a single-side-band high-power transceiver, and, last but not least, quart-size silver thermos mugs filled with coffee. Clearly they weren't going anywhere, and if Scott had arranged for diapers, he would have had them wear those too.

Lily had taken a seat across from the boys, with her juice and coffee perched on a pop-up table, where Susan had arrayed a white ceramic bowl of fresh fruit, napkins, and silverware. She'd lost her ear comm in China, but a blinking Bluetooth perched in her auricle, and her cell sat next to her spoon. Scott slowly paced between his paramour and his hyped-up wizards.

"Okay, boys," he said as he walked. "Priority one is a manhunt. Lily?"

"Russian-affiliated arms merchant and all around bad-boy slime," Lily said. "Name is Enver Lukacs." She spelled it out as Chilly and Hot Shot pecked it into their keyboards like a piano duo. "Now on American soil."

"But we don't know when, where, or how," Scott said as he raised a finger. "And most likely not under that name."

Chilly and Hot Shot both looked up and said, "Oh."

Scott turned to Lily. "Lily, get Shepard on the line and tell him you need the very best, recent still image he can produce of Lukacs. Probably from your surveillance vids at that club in Seoul."

She looked up at him and blinked. "How do know about that?"

Scott smiled. "Shepard and I have become close."

"Good Lord," she whispered, and she made the call.

"Is that you, Mata Hari?" Shepard said in her ear. He was clearly pleased and relieved.

"The very she," she said.

"My day's already made," said Shepard. "What's your twenty?"

"Airborne, and let's just say I'm being thoroughly spoiled."

"Then you must be with Scott."

"Jeez." She rolled her eyes and told him what she wanted. After a minute her cell phone dinged, and Shepard said, "It's up."

Without polite preamble, Scott took her cell and handed it to Chilly. She watched his body language, a commanding demeanor she'd never seen before, and she somehow felt both thrilled and terribly off-balance.

"All right," Scott said to Chilly. "Take that image, enhance it, three-D it, invert it, then go deep net, and get me matches. And we're not talking Google Images."

"Hoppin' on it!" Chilly said with glee.

"He means 'roger,' sir," Hot Shot said to Scott.

"Yeah, that too!" Chilly said as he hammered away.

After a minute Chilly squinted at his Alienware. "Okeydokey, I got five good ones, and he's a gnarly-lookin' dude."

Scott didn't bother to look at the monitor. Instead, he spoke to his jet. "Aircraft, get me Homeland Security, Washington D.C., Deputy Director Operations."

The Bombardier's female voice filled the cabin. "Ringing." And shortly after that, a woman answered.

"Homeland Security, Deputy DOPS."

"May I please have Deputy Director Grogan? Tell him it's Scott Renard."

"One moment, sir," she said, and then a deep, gravelly voice came over.

"Scott! I was going to call you today. That software of yours is a great piece of ass."

Scott laughed. "Careful there, Charlie. You're on speaker."

"Oh, oh. Sorry, ma'am, whoever you are."

Lily looked at the aircraft's ceiling. "That's all right. I'm not the software, so I take no offense."

"Wow," Chilly whispered. "Boss got some juice!"

"That surprises you?" Hot Shot hissed. "Shut up."

"Charlie," Scott said. "I need you to use that software to run someone through your data. Let's call it a national security issue."

"Well, you've got TS clearance, so no worries there."

Lily stared at Scott. *Top secret clearance?* If she'd been standing up she would have put her fists on her hips.

"Okay," Scott said. "This guy's a foreign national, probably hit passport control somewhere during the last seventy-two hours. But you might want to bracket that further back."

"Coastal points of entry? Or central too?"

"No idea," said Scott.

"Well, that's about two million crossings or so." If Lily expected Scott to look crestfallen at that, she was disappointed, especially after Charlie

Grogan continued. "Take about five minutes. Send it to the secure portal, and I'll call you back."

"Much appreciated," Scott said and disconnected the call.

Hot Shot raised a finger. "Boss, can I hit the head?"

"Knew I should have ordered diapers for you guys," Scott said. "Pee fast." Hot Shot slid out from his seat and hustled to the rear.

"Me too!" Chilly said.

"Take turns," Scott said. He scrolled through his cell and showed Chilly an IP address with an access code. Chilly made quick work of sending Lukacs over to D.C. Then Hot Shot came back, and Chilly raced to the lav.

Scott took the opportunity to sit down in the seat across from Lily. The way she was looking at him, he almost laughed, but reached out and took her hand instead.

"I'm not sure I should let you touch me," she pouted disingenuously.

"Well, think it over," he suggested. "Then we can discuss it in side-by-side hammocks somewhere in the Virgin Islands, sipping tropical drinks."

"With those little umbrellas in them?" Lily asked.

"With those little umbrellas in them."

"Touch me." She grinned and rubbed his fingers.

The wizards were back in their seats when Charles Grogan's voice popped up in the cabin again.

"Okay, Scott. Day before yesterday at fourteen hundred, your guy hit LAX from Seoul, under the name Werner Siebolt, German national. After that, no record of any domestic flight."

"Outstanding!" Scott said. "Charlie, you're best."

"Always a pleasure," said Grogan. "Need anything else?"

"Nope, I think we can hack it."

Grogan laughed. "Pun intended?"

"Plead the fifth."

"Call me if you need me." Grogan hung up.

Scott released Lily's hand and got up again. He paced in front of Chilly and Hot Shot, then stopped, and faced them with his eyes shut.

"All right, boys," he said as he opened his eyes and shot a finger down at his wizards. "My guess is Lukacs, as Siebolt, rented a car. Chilly, starting with Alamo, crack all the rental car agencies at LAX and look for a match. If you find it, get us the plate number. Hot Shot, just in case he cabbed it somewhere instead, access the LAX Port Authority cams outside arrivals and run Chilly's FR software for a match. Got that so far?"

They both nodded furiously.

"All right, whoever pings first with a plate number, set up for a track. Chilly, you're going to hack the toll systems for all major highways out of L.A. And Hot Shot, while he's doing that, you'll script a search algorithm that scans for a plate or that vehicle-type image match. Then, wherever he terminates, pull the top ten hotels or motels in the area and find him. You can do that part by phone. Just call the desks." Then he stopped and changed his mind. "Scratch that, don't call. He might have told the desk to alert him if anyone calls. Hack the hotel systems. Clear?"

Chilly raised a finger and grinned. "I got some speeding tickets in L.A. Can I take care of that while I'm at it?"

"You're a moron," Hot Shot moaned.

"Do this right, Chilly," Scott said, "and I'll let you hack into the lottery system."

"Awesome!"

"He's joking, you idiot," Hot Shot said.

"Get on it," Scott said. "You've got thirty minutes, no more."

The boys dug into their tasks as if they hadn't eaten for a week, and what lay before them was an Easter feast.

Scott cocked his head at Lily. "Let's leave them alone." She got up, he took her elbow, and they moved forward and sat together again, close, on a black leather divan.

"You're good." She looked up at him and marveled. "MI5 would have loved you."

"They do." He grinned, and they both laughed, sitting back to listen as Chilly and Hot Shot bickered.

"You can't do it that way! It'll take forever. Just nab all the IPs and run the name through the servers."

"Dude, mind your own business and code! It's not my first rodeo, ya know."

With the jet crew forward and the hackers working furiously in the back, Scott took the moment to kiss Lily slowly, as if for the first time. She let it linger and then pulled back.

"Just a few days ago," she whispered, "I was trying to decide if our relationship would even work."

"Three days ago," he answered, "I was wondering if I would ever see you again...and not because our relationship might not work."

"Hold that thought," she whispered back and kissed him back, like she had never kissed him, or anyone, before.

Thirty minutes went by fast, but just in time.

"Boss!" Chilly called from his techno perch.

Scott and Lily surprised themselves by snapping out of their romantic torpor instantly. They took a second to realize that their professional side was as sharp as their emotional one, then got up, and hurried to the back.

"We got him," Hot Shot said through his Tom Cruise grin. "Tell 'em, Chill."

"You tell him, bro. Hate to admit it, but you did it."

"Someone tell me," Scott snapped, "or I'm dropping you off without landing the plane!"

"He's in Vegas," Hot Shot quickly explained. "Chilly got the plate from Hertz."

"Way overpriced, if you ask me," Chilly said.

"What does he care?" Lily interjected. "The North Koreans are footing the bill."

"I picked him up on the Ten out of L.A., then all the way up on the Fifteen. Then I did what you said and ran a back-door hotel canvas. He's at the MGM grand." Hot Shot's satisfied smile could have set the leathers on fire. Chilly punched Hot Shot's shoulder and ruffled his hair.

"My hotel hacker dude!"

Scott shook both of their hands, long and hard. "That bonus is starting to look serious." Then he spoke to his Bombardier. "Aircraft, cockpit."

"Here I am," the chief pilot said.

"Bobby," Scott said. "Flight plan for Vegas, and step on it."

"Roger that. A little five-card stud?"

"Blackjack," Scott said. "And we're bringing down the house."

Chapter Thirty-Six

There were twelve desk clerks at the MGM grand: six men, five women, and someone whose gender was up for grabs. The lobby was a vast field of polished marble, with islands of retro scooped chairs, a three-story ceiling, beaded glass chandeliers, and digital posters of Cirque de Soleil and magician David Copperfield.

Lily walked in the front entrance, wearing a quickly assembled "disguise." At the airport she'd picked up a half-length, brown leather car coat, large framed sunglasses, a plain purse, and a floppy gray fedora, beneath which she'd tucked up her hair. The chances of running right into Lukacs were slim, but Vegas had always been a place of shattered odds.

The six check-in counters to the right spanned the length of two Amtrak cars, each manned by a pair of uniformed employees. Lily scanned them quickly, looking for the one Chilly had picked out after hacking the casino hotel's employment records. She was a single mom who had seen better days but was doing her best to hold on to whatever looks and youth she had left. Lily took out a handkerchief, rubbed her nose a few times, walked over, and tugged at her arm.

"Ek-skoos me," she sniffed in a slight German accent. "May I speak viz you for a moment, please?"

The woman, whose name tag read "Dotty Singer" nodded at the distraught tourist, touched her coworker's arm, and said, "Back in a jiff." Then she followed Lily to the lobby floor. Lily stifled a sob, plopped into a chair, and fanned herself with the handkerchief. Singer perched on the arm of the chair.

"Are you all right, hon?" she said. "Did you lose at the tables?"

"No, no." Lily dabbed the corner of one eye. "I mean yes, but it is not money. I have lost my husband." She clutched at her chest and sobbed. "To another woman."

"Oh, dear." Singer touched Lily's shoulder and squeezed.

"Yes." Lily nodded. "I think he is here." She looked up and gripped the clerk's arm. "I must know! Our children are so young..... ." She trailed off.

"Hon, I've been there, done that, got the T-shirt," said Singer, as Lily well knew, thanks to Chilly's hacking. "And I'd love to help you, but it's against the rules."

"Please." Lily looked at her pitifully. "I only wish to know if he is here, and *with* someone." Then she took the woman's hand, turned it over, and pressed something into her palm.

The woman looked down, seeing a pair of hundred dollar bills and a torn scrap of paper with a cell phone number. "Oh," she whispered, and the quick mental image of her telephone bill past-due letter popped into her mind.

"*Please.*" Lily held up her cell phone in her trembling hand. "This is his photo. His name is Werner Siebolt." She dabbed at both eyes this time. "I do not understand. I have tried to be such a good wife."

Singer pocketed the cash and the number, looked at the image of Lukacs and patted Lily's hand. "Tell you what, Mrs. Siebolt," she said. "I'll see what I can do."

Lily forced a smile through her tears, despite recognizing the look on the woman's face. It was the look of a woman who would get revenge on her own cheating, abandoning husband through helping another. "You are a *vonderful* person," she whispered.

"Well, us girls gotta stick together." Dotty Singer smiled, got up, and went back to her desk.

"Bloody right," Lily murmured. "Good call, Chilly," she told her team through the advanced, invisible "SR" comm in her ear and left the hotel.

Outside, in the dazzling sunlight, she crossed over Tropicana Boulevard and turned around to face the MGM. She felt vigorous and sharp, back in the game again, and mentally flipped through all of her contingencies. With no way to anticipate Lukacs's next moves, she had to take rapid action and couldn't afford to wait for backup from Zeta. Scott, to his credit and Lily's burgeoning surprise, insisted that they could handle Lukacs. Letting him escape again wasn't an option.

A white Mercedes RV pulled up, the side door slid open, and Lily climbed in. It was an eight-passenger deal, with two split-bench rows behind the driving compartment and plenty of leg room.

"Drive on, Jeeves," she said with a highbrow flare.

"Yes, ma'am." Hot Shot put the van in gear and started east along Tropicana.

She looked down to see two rolls of duct tape on the floor—next to a small pile of handcuffs, leg shackles, and even ball gags. "Where did you find those?" she asked, eyebrows raised.

"This is Vegas, baby," Chilly replied from the passenger seat. "Just be glad I resisted the temptation of getting the full leather catsuit with zippered hood."

"Where's Scott?" she asked.

"We dropped the boss man off at a cash machine." Chilly grinned. "Dude said we needed more muscle."

"What's he bloody well thinking?" Lily wondered.

"No visual on that," Hot Shot said as he took a left on Koval Lane. "He jumped in an Uber, then shot me an address, and told us to pick him up at thirteen hundred."

"The man's a mystery, wrapped in an enigma," Lily remarked.

"Funny." Chilly giggled. "That's what he says about you."

Hot Shot drove north on Koval for a while, following the nav on his phone. The sidewalks seemed crowded with youngish, geeky-looking, tourists, rather than the usual middle-aged slot-machine addicts. Lily gawked at what looked like the wizards' kindred souls.

"What's the deal with these blokes? Is it spring break for science schools?"

"There's a large hacker conference at the convention center," Chilly informed her. "Talk about timing."

"Now, now, Chilly," Lily admonished, hoping that Dotty would check in sooner rather than later. "You can't go."

"Awww," Chilly exaggeratingly whined.

Hot Shot took a right on South Las Vegas, cruised past Circus Circus, hung a hard left on West Charleston, and pulled to the curb. Across the street was a sloppy jumble of red and blue buildings that looked like a strip mall, with a sign on top that said Johnny Tacco's and Home of the World Champions.

"What's this now?" Hot Shot said.

"Hey, eyeball the gloves in the windows, dude," Chilly snickered. "It's a boxing gym."

"That devious man," Lily said about Scott.

The front door opened, and Scott walked out, sporting a satisfied smile, and was followed by two very large men. One was white with oiled dark hair; the other was black and bald. Both had rippling arms bursting from cutoff sweatshirts above shiny blue workout sweats and high-ankle boxing shoes.

"Boss man's cray-cray," Chilly singsonged.

"Like a fox-fox," Lily added.

"When he said muscle, he wasn't shittin'," said Hot Shot.

The trio trotted across the road as Lily popped the side door open and slid to the right as the two hulking pugilists squeezed into the back. Scott climbed in last, settled next to Lily, and closed the door.

"Crew," he said, "meet Tony and Slam."

"A pleasure, gentlemen," said Lily.

Hot Shot and Chilly raised fingers. The boxers grunted greetings as Scott pulled a bank envelope from his trouser pocket, slipped out a packet of hundreds, and turned around.

"As we agreed," he said as he counted off bills. "Five Franklins apiece up front, and five more if you act as tough as you look."

"Hey, you just saw us spar," Tony said with a Brooklyn twang.

"Yeah, y'all can chill," Slam added. "Do we look like we lose?"

"Nope," Scott said. He winked at Lily. She gave him an approving nod.

"Hot Shot," she said. "Cruise back downtown and orbit the MGM. This may take awhile."

"Yes, ma'am," Hot Shot said as he made U-turn on West Charleston and eased back onto South Las Vegas. Then Lily snapped her eyes down at her cell. It was buzzing.

"Everyone hush!" she ordered, and the van fell silent. "Allo?"

"Mrs. Sielbolt?" Dotty Singer said, her voice a conspiratorial whisper. "We talked at the hotel."

"Yes, yes," Lily said. "Sank you *so* much for calling."

"I just saw him leaving," Dotty said. "Got a heads-up from the maid on his floor."

"Yes?" Lily said. "Did he...was he with someone?"

"Not a woman. Two men. Don't know if that makes you feel better or worse. Cheaters travel in packs. At least mine did."

"It's horrible." Lily sniffed.

"I followed them a bit," said Dotty. "Just out front, but they didn't get in a cab. They turned left like they were going out for a walk on the strip."

"Bless you. I am so grateful," said Lily. "I shall come back later. Perhaps we shall make more business together?"

"Whatever you need. Guys like him get my goat, but it's kinda, well, fun. Gotta scoot." She hung up.

"All right, Hot Shot," Lily snapped as she stripped off her coat. "Let's see how fast you can fly."

* * * *

Enver Lukacs could not have felt better. He had been to many of the world's gaudiest playgrounds, but Las Vegas was second only to Macau as the height of imperial, self-indulgent, capitalist-pig lust. The casinos were absurdly ornate and enormous, hunched one after the other like bloated tics. The nighttime shows were ridiculous, the meals disgustingly wasteful, the show girls caricatures of cartoon harlots. The weather was hot, the bikinis tiny, and the liquor flowed like the Volga.

Such a shame it was only a stopover.

He strode east along Tropicana Boulevard, wearing a white cashmere turtleneck and brown linen slacks—his silver-blond hair freshly combed back from his high forehead, and his Ray-Bans making him think he looked like a star. He'd been up till three, but he'd left the tables with ten thousand more than his nut, and he'd stayed up till dawn making a Colombian prostitute beg for more. Then it was breakfast at noon, a steaming bath, and now nothing more than a stroll. He was hoping the signal would come tomorrow so he'd have one more night to play.

"I do not understand these Americans," Lukacs remarked in Czech to the man on his left. "They gorge themselves on fast food and drink like Russian sailors, but the scent of tobacco sends them into a frenzy."

"It is a sign of a collapsing empire," the other man said. He was bald, with a face like a pale rat, and he was wearing a plaid beret. "When everything is a criminal enterprise, you focus on the one harmless vice."

"You are quite the philosopher, Stanislaw," said Lukacs as he tapped a fresh pack of Marlboros into his palm. "Considering that your only real talent is killing."

Stanislaw laughed. His gold front tooth gleamed in the Nevada sunlight. The man on Lukacs's right said nothing. He was North Korean and didn't understand Czech, but his job was only to keep Lukacs alive, so the social repartee didn't matter.

The three men continued along the sidewalk, where it passed the MGM's four-story parking structure off to the left. Straight ahead, it widened into a parklike area with a manicured grass oval resembling a golf course green with a canopy of desert cedars. It seemed a good place to steal a smoke in the shade.

"And so, if I may ask," Stanislaw said. "What now?"

"We shall soon be in the final phase," Lukacs said as he plucked up a cigarette with his thin lips. "Collins has duped their best agent, and now he has the codes."

"And after that?"

Lukacs stopped beneath a large tree and lit up with a silver Zippo. "After that, we collect our fees and go home." He glanced at his surroundings, seeing no one but waddling tourists. "In the meantime, Stanislaw, do your job."

Stanislaw nodded, cocked his head at the Korean, and the two moved away from Lukacs to take up positions higher up on the green, facing out. Lukacs squinted off toward the corner of Tropicana and Koval, where a pair of large men in gym clothes were rounding the bend in an easy jog, laughing at some joke.

Lukacs turned back toward the boulevard, dragging on his smoke and squinting across the street at the old Tropicana Hotel. It was there, he recalled from his tour book, that Frank Sinatra and the Rat Pack had spent many a night indulging their fame, wealth, and lust. Apparently, you could even book Sinatra's old suite.

I think I shall do that tonight, he thought. *And I shall have sex with an American blonde on his couch.*

That pleasant thought was interrupted when a white Mercedes van pulled up very close, blocking his view. And then, from behind, he heard a muffled shout. He spun around to see a man who looked like a young Sylvester Stallone pummeling Stanislaw's face. To the right, the North Korean, whose name he still could not pronounce, was spinning in a blurring Tae Kwon Do roundhouse kick. But his leg was instantly trapped by a huge bald black man who slammed his chin with an uppercut. Lukacs heard the crack of knuckles on bone.

His cigarette fell from his gaping mouth as he spun around to run. But the white van's door had slid open and a woman was striding toward him. She looked just like...

Oh no.

Lily kicked him, her foot whipping up into his balls. And she was wearing boots. Rockets of lightning shot into his eyes as he howled and dropped to his knees.

She bent down until her blazing green eyes were boring into his now-bloodshot ones. "That's for Seoul," she said. Then she brought her right hand up to her left collarbone and sliced her bladed palm into his temple. "And that's for China," she said as he keeled over.

She bent over his writhing form, dragged him up by his hair and said. "And this one's for Prague and that C-4 strap-on I didn't fancy very much." She kneed him straight in the nose, and his nostrils gushed blood.

At that point, Chilly was leaning out of the van, arms outstretched, and yelling, "Let's go! Let's go!"

Lily stepped back from Lukacs as Tony and Slam came hurdling toward her like linebackers. They hauled Lukacs up like an errant toddler, ran for the van, and threw him facedown on the floor.

Like champion rodeo riders, Scott straddled Lukacs's spine while Chilly grabbed his ankles and folded them up. Tony and Slam leapt inside to the back as Lily hopped in and slammed the door. Hot Shot burned rubber.

Lily crashed back in her seat. She picked up her hat and used it to wipe the sweat from her brow. Lukacs was moaning from the floor.

"You *bastards*." He was shaking and drooling blood. "You cannot do this! I am a foreign national. You have no authority!"

"Authority?" Lily laughed and jammed a heel in his buttocks as Scott and Chilly cuffed him hand and foot. "We don't need no stinking authority."

Hot Shot gunned it straight out of town.

Chapter Thirty-Seven

It was a cold, misty midnight in Boston. The ceiling in Zeta's War Room glowed with a languid blue sky, winging black geese, and wispy white clouds, but it wasn't fooling a soul. The long boardroom table was strewn with Chinese food cartons, ravaged microwave dinners, Styrofoam coffee cups, and crushed Red Bull cans, and there wasn't an empty seat to be had.

Diana Bloch had the helm, with Paul Kirby hunched at her right elbow, and General Margolis at her left. Kirby's thin hair was finger-comb crazy while Margolis still looked like he'd just arrived from a ball. The general's adjutants, both captains, sat quietly plucking at tablets while Shepard and Karen hunched over pairs of humming laptops.

Across from them, Morgan and Conley sat side by side, perhaps no longer the pictures of youth they'd been way back when but intensely focused nonetheless. And the rest of the chairs were occupied by Diana's young analysts and interns, who all knew better than to utter a word.

"Bring her up," Diana said to Shepard. He nodded and tapped.

The wall-length monitor behind Morgan and Conley came to life, so they both swung around in their chairs. The screen filled with the image of Lily, waist up, with nothing behind her but a shabby curtain. A series of zeros popped up in the right-hand corner and started ticking off numbers. This was Zeta's version of Skype—secure and always recorded.

"Welcome to the witching hour," Lily said. For an operative who'd recently been through hell, she looked very relaxed.

"What's your location?" Diana asked.

"Safe house," Lily said.

"Where?" Kirby asked.

"If I tell you," Lily said with a smirk, "it's no longer safe."

"Brief it," Diana ordered as she bridled a bit at Lily's tone. The girl was obviously feeling smug.

"Hold on to your proverbial hats," said Lily. "It appears that Mr. Enver Lukacs is the linchpin. He put General Collins together with Colonel Hyo and those lovely North Koreans."

General Margolis leaned over to his nearest captain and murmured, "Make sure you're getting all this. That's a UCMJ life sentence right there." He meant Uniform Code of Military Justice.

"Lukacs is the middle man," Lily went on. "Taking a cut from the DPRK payments to Collins. Apparently, Collins plans to execute his mission and then bugger off and retire to a little place in the Alps. Seems the general was miffed about something, and Lukacs found out."

"We passed him over for his second star," Margolis growled. "Bastard didn't deserve it with all the crap he pulled in Iraq."

"Lily," Diana said. "This is General Margolis."

"A pleasure, sir." She could see everyone in the War Room.

"Get to Collins's objective," Diana said.

"It's a nightmare," said Lily. "Collins set up the Tomahawk heist for Hyo's men, eighteen of whom are here. Sleepers, and they've been in the States for a year."

Morgan was counting on his fingers all the Koreans he'd already killed, and he needed both hands. "Should be only eleven by now," he said. Conley looked at him as if he was bragging. Morgan just shrugged.

"Go on, Lily," Diana snapped impatiently.

She did. "Six missiles were hijacked. I believe Morgan found three."

"Correct," Kirby said. "Those have been recovered by the FBI's HRT and secured by the army."

"Well, that leaves them with three," Lily said. "Their plan is to take over a nuclear storage facility, probably somewhere on the eastern seaboard. But that might be a feint. Lukacs doesn't know where."

"Are you sure about that?" Kirby asked.

"*Believe* me, he doesn't know," Lily affirmed. Shepard and Karen glanced at each other. "Furthermore, they're going to bring the Tomahawks in there."

"What's the point of that?" Margolis wondered as he loosened his tie. "If they intend to destroy the facility, you can't just detonate a Tomahawk warhead. It has to be in flight, with the gyros already spun up for it to be armed."

"General." Lily turned her gaze on him. "How does one target a Tomahawk?"

"You have to have the launch codes," he growled impatiently. "And then you feed it the target's coordinates."

"Utilizing GPS?"

"That is correct."

"So, then, can one target oneself?" Lily asked.

Margolis blinked. "What the hell do you mean?"

"I mean, General, that they bring the missiles into the facility, launch them, and leave in all good haste. The code name of Collins's hellish little gambit is 'Boomerang. ' Are we all on the same page now?"

Margolis's mouth dropped open. "Oh my Lord."

"If only he were available," Lily said. "But I believe he's on sabbatical. At any rate, that's all I have." Then she raised a finger. "Wait, one thing more. The point of all this is to false flag the whole thing as a North Korean attack. Apparently, Colonel Hyo has also gone rogue."

"Jesus," Conley hissed. "Those goons are bad enough when they're straight."

"Lily, you've done superbly well," said Diana. She was touching her chest, where her heart rate was up and thumping. "How did you ever get all this from Lukacs?"

"Ms. Bloch," Lily said sardonically. "Don't ask."

Diana nodded. She didn't really want to ask Lily how many fingers Lukacs had left. "All right," she said. "Hold your position and stand by."

Lily issued a two-fingered Boy Scout salute, and the monitor went black. Diana turned to Margolis. "General, your assessment?"

Margolis rubbed his jaw. "Well, operational nukes are stored on WS Three—that's Weapons Storage and Security System. It's a structure of electronic controls and vaults, built into protective aircraft shelters for strategic bombers or ICBMs. Similar arrangement for nuclear subs."

"How many such locations are there?" Kirby asked.

"Scores of them, all over the States. Mostly at big air force bases like Nellis or naval facilities like Kings Bay, Georgia." Then Margolis waved a dismissive finger in the air. "But I'm not buying this boomerang thing."

"Why not, General?" Diana asked.

"Because Collins can launch those birds from anywhere. He doesn't have to be on-site. He can set up in a field in Ohio and just target a nuke dump in Nevada."

"No he can't," Morgan said. Everyone in the room turned to Morgan. Margolis glowered at him. "State your case."

"If it's a false-flag op," said Morgan, "his Koreans have to engage the base security guards, hand to hand, face-to-face. And they've got to leave at least one witness alive to finger them later. If they just stand off and fire, no one'll know who did it. It's a useless blind hit."

Margolis leaned back in his chair and stared at Morgan's unblinking expression. "Morgan," he said, "you're a whole lot smarter than you look."

"That's what everyone says," Conley said.

Morgan dipped a thank-you nod at the general, thinking, *this teamwork thing might have some merits after all.*

Diana pushed away from the table and got up to pace. "Speaking of blind, that's us," she said. "We don't have a clue where he's going." She turned to Margolis again. "We'll have to flash the Pentagon, General, have them alert every facility in the States."

Margolis turned to his nearest captain. "Wells?"

"Already composing that, Sir," the captain said as he typed. "Skipping condition Bravo and going right to FPCON Charlie."

"This is absurd," Paul Kirby moaned. He took off his glasses, dropped his face in both hands, and massaged his furrowed forehead. "It's like telling all the national banks that Bonnie and Clyde are out there, somewhere. We're completely impotent."

"Speak for yourself, *Paul*," Conley sneered.

"People!" Diana snapped. "I'll thank all you to..." Then she stopped as she noticed Shepard waving his hand in the air.

"Morgan," Shepard said breathlessly. "I've got an intercept here: call coming into your cell."

Morgan pulled his head back. "You're ambushing my calls now?"

But Shepard tore off his headset, arched across the table and nodded furiously. "Take it, take it!"

Morgan grabbed the headset and pulled it on. "Morgan here. Speak." Then his eyes went wide, he covered the boom mike, looked right at Margolis, and whispered, "It's Schmitt."

Margolis shot both hands in the air, trigger fingers up, demanding silence. No one moved.

"Commander," Morgan said into his mike. "Slow down." He closed his eyes and listened intently for a while before saying, "How the hell did you do that?" He listened some more as he nodded over and over, and a small smile curled his lips. "Roger, copy. Now listen. I know you're toast, but you're all we've got at the moment. Stay on him, but don't try to take him." He covered the mike again and whispered to Shepard, "Lock on her cell." Shepard shot him a thumbs-up and pointed down at his laptop. He'd already done it. "All right," Morgan said to Schmitt again. "Hang tight. There's no way to thank you for this, but we'll try."

He tore off the headset. "That woman's frickin' Joan of Arc."

"Spill it," Margolis snapped.

"I was sure she lost Collins in Brookline," said Morgan. "But she didn't. Instead of trying to take him, she tailed him, almost all the way down to Washington on I-95."

Margolis slapped the table. "He's going for Kings Bay in Georgia. The nuclear sub pens."

"Negative." Morgan replied. "He made a U-turn at a rest stop in Maryland and headed back up north. She doesn't think he made her. He was just trying to shake any tails."

"Is she still on him?" Kirby fumbled his glasses back onto his face.

"Yes. She's just outside New Haven, Connecticut, heading east on I-95."

Margolis jumped up from his chair, planted himself between his two captains, and slammed their shoulders. "Give it to me, boys. Now!"

His captains hammered on their tablets; then the one to the left looked up. "Groton, Connecticut, Sir. It's the nuclear sub base, New London."

"Damn," Conley said. "Right in our own backyard!"

"General," Diana said. "Can you task Delta?" Her fingers were laced together in prayer.

"Negative," Margolis said. "Posse Comitatus."

"What the hell's that?" Kirby asked as one of the young analysts at the end of the table whispered to another, "Did he say pussy and tatas?" But no one heard him.

"It's the law," Margolis said. "Can't task the army for domestic ops without Congressional approval. But Delta's down at Fort Bragg anyway—no time." He stood up fully and looked at Diana. "We can't do it. But you can."

She looked over at Shepard. "Condition Three. Get the Tac teams spun up." Shepard jumped up, grabbed his laptop, and rushed out. The rest of the analysts froze in their chairs. "All of you," Diana snapped. "Move!" They hustled out the door after Shepard.

Margolis looked at his watch. "New Haven to Groton. Midnight, no traffic. Maybe an hour and a half, tops." He turned his gaze on Diana. "Who's your point man on this?"

She looked over at Morgan, and they locked eyes. "Him."

"Ms. Bloch," Margolis said, but he was also looking at Morgan. "You're the boss here. But if I were in your shoes, I'd make the same call."

* * * *

Morgan and Diana stood just outside the War Room, side by side, watching Zeta personnel sprinting through the hallways, calling out orders to one another, and shouldering loads of support gear. Morgan thought it looked like a hornet's nest that had just been stomped by a boot. General Margolis had remained inside the room with his captains, and they could hear his voice booming as he spoke on the phone to an unfortunate naval duty officer somewhere south.

"Well, tell him it's General Sheldon Margolis and to get me the chief of ONI! You've got sixty seconds, Sailor, and then you'll both be posted as mess men in goddamn Djibouti!"

Diana touched Morgan's arm, but she didn't look at him. "I would apologize to you properly, but there isn't time."

Morgan nodded slightly as he watched the frenetic activities. "Well, give it a shot. The short version."

"I used you," she said. "I knew you'd disobey orders and follow your own instincts, based on that stubborn sense of honor you've got. I couldn't task you formally because as you saw from my message, there's a leak in the plumbing."

"I got that much," said Morgan. "But you didn't really trust me either."

"Like you trusted Collins? Trust is a liability in this business," Diana said. "But I also owe you for using Jenny to clear you."

"That's three." He glanced sideways at her and grinned. "Must be a record for you."

"And you. Don't push it."

"It's all good," Morgan said. "Can't wait to hear Jenny's side."

"She did well."

"Yup. I didn't marry her for her looks." He grinned harder. "Well, maybe a little."

The door of the Team Room banged open, and Alex walked out to grab a range finder from a runner. Morgan saw her, stuck two fingers in his mouth, and whistled. She turned and jogged over. She was already geared up, all in black tactical, with fingerless gloves and a headset rig. Morgan took her face in both of his hands and looked in her eyes.

"It's times like these when a father should say something meaningful," Morgan said. "Something poetic, maybe about faith and family and love." Alex said nothing. Her eyes gleamed. Morgan smiled. "Go zero your rifle in the sim. And get yourself a balaclava but no scarf. You're gonna be on the skids, and it'll be cold up there tonight. Five minutes. Hustle up."

Alex grinned, pulled away, and ran.

"That was very touching," Diana said. "For you."

Morgan dropped his voice to a murmur. "You think it's Kirby, right?"

"No, you hope it's Kirby. But if you find yourself flying into an ambush, we'll know."

The Team Room door burst open again. Spartan and Diesel, both fully geared up and bristling with weapons, marched straight up to Diana and Morgan. Their expressions were tight, dark and brooding.

"What's up?" Morgan said. "We're heading for the strip in five."

"It's Bishop," Spartan said. "He's MIA."

"What do you mean, missing?" Diana said.

"I mean missing. As in AWOL. As in...gone."

Chapter Thirty-Eight

Jenny Morgan was trying to stifle her sobs.

She lay in utter darkness, all curled up in a ball, her hand clamping her mouth as the tears streamed from her eyes and waves of nausea stung her gullet. She was on her right side, knees pinned to her chest, her hip grinding and bumping on the carpeted floor. It was freezing cold, the noises deafening. She'd never in her life felt so helpless, or scared, or alone.

She was locked in the trunk of her own car.

"Help me, Dan," she moaned into her drool-soaked palm. "God in heaven, please help me."

But Dan wasn't there, or anyone else who could help her. The closest human being was the madman driving her car.

How could I have been so stupid? She admonished herself as the car hit a rut on the highway. Her head bounced up and smacked the metal trunk. She gasped and gripped her stinging skull with both hands. *I'm no spy! That's him, not me. What the hell was I thinking?*

She rubbed the aching spot on the left side of her head until the throbbing calmed down. Then she took a deep breath and smeared the tears from her face.

Think, she demanded of herself. *Think! What would Dan say?*

That's all it took. She asked something of her brain, and it delivered. Dan had said, "If you're ever in trouble, just talk to yourself."

She had asked him where he had gotten such a silly idea, and he had answered, "Because whenever I'm in trouble, the one person I always want to talk to is the wisest, smartest person I've ever met. You."

Then they'd made love. She prayed that they would again someday. But, for now, she was in the deepest shit she had ever been in, so what did she have to lose?

"You'd better start thinking fast now, or you're going to die," she said softly.

How long had that bastard been driving? She tried to look at her watch, but it didn't have a luminous dial. Maybe an hour, she guessed. Maybe more.

She'd been cruising over to Home Depot, just to drop off an old cell phone for recycling, and pick up some paint for the mud room when it happened. Her cell phone had buzzed, with no caller ID, but ever since meeting Diana Bloch she'd been answering everything, just in case.

"Hello?"

"Mrs. Morgan?"

"Yes?"

"I'm calling on behalf of Mr. Lincoln." It was a different voice, dark and authoritative, and right away her heart had started thumping. "Ms. Bloch would like to meet with you."

"Now?"

"Yes, now. What is your current location?" the man asked.

"Well, I'm in Andover, heading over to Home Depot."

"Wait one, please," he said and then, after half a minute of silence, "Please drive to the West Parish Garden Cemetery. Do you know where that is?"

"It's in West Andover."

"Very good. Half an hour, the main entrance."

"Okay," Jenny said as the line went silent. And she'd actually grinned with the thrill.

Idiot. She belittled herself now.

So she'd turned around again, picked up Broadway, crossed over the Merrimack River, and headed south for the cemetery. It was, of course, all dark and spooky, and no other cars were in the parking lot. She got out of the Camry, walked to the high stone archway, and was happy that at least there was moonlight.

I'm not really dressed for this. She was wearing jeans, sneakers, a college sweatshirt, and her black leather car coat. She laughed at herself as she leaned back on the thick stone buttress—wishing she had a cigarette so she'd at least look the part. But then her mirth ended.

A black, two-door Audi rolled into the lot and parked next to her Camry. A man got out. He was huge, black, and bald, with gleaming eyes and wide nostrils. He wore black cargo trousers and a thick motorcycle jacket with a turned-up collar. Her heart started pounding like crazy as she came away from the wall.

He strode right up to her and looked down. "Mrs. Morgan," he said. It wasn't really a question, but her shoulders sagged with relief. He knew who she was, so he wasn't just some mugger, even though he had a voice like a hoarse panther.

"That's me," she said. "Where's Ms. Bloch?"

"She's not coming," Bishop said. Then he reached inside his jacket, pulled out a huge handgun, and pressed the barrel right into her chest. "But you are."

"Oh my God," she gasped and jerked back against the stone as her knees started shaking.

"First things first," he said. "Give me your cell phone."

She had no idea why she did it, but instead of giving him her iPhone from her left-hand pocket, she pulled out the old dead one from the right. He snatched it from her trembling fingers, stuck it in his pocket and gripped her elbow, hard. Then they walked toward her car.

"Give me your keys."

"What do you want?" she sputtered. "Who are you?"

"I'm a man on a mission, and you're my insurance policy. The keys, now."

She handed them over, and he popped the Camry's trunk. Then he stood back and waved the black automatic. "Get in."

"No!" She shook her head madly as the tears sprang to her eyes.

"I'll drop you right here," he snarled. "Then your husband and Alex won't have to haul your corpse so far."

She was shaking like a leaf as she looked at the black maw of the trunk. But she somehow managed to hike one foot over the bumper and folded herself inside. He looked down at her once more, smiled slightly, and slammed it shut. She had sobbed like a child.

And now she was here, on her way to only God knew where.

They were moving fast; she could tell that much. At the beginning, that man who called himself Bishop had stopped a few times at some lights. But after that there were no more stops, and the car zoomed faster. She heard the deep bellows of truck horns twice, like ships out there in the night.

They were on some highway, maybe 495? But was it south toward Rhode Island or north to New Hampshire? She couldn't tell. Who was he? Did he really know Dan and Alex? Or was he some vengeful villain from Dan's past? There were plenty of those, she was sure.

It doesn't matter! You're a hostage. He can pull off the road at any minute, take you out into a field, and kill you! Or worse...

"You're my insurance policy," he'd said. Did that mean some sort of exchange? and with whom? Was this some sort of a ransom thing? and who'd want her back except Dan?

Call him!

She suddenly remembered her cell phone, and she squeezed her left arm between the ceiling and her up-thrust left hip—fumbling in her jacket pocket. She got it out and cradled it to her chest like a precious, blessed amulet. She managed to squeeze her trembling right fingers to the screen and swipe it, and the soft yellow glow on her face nearly made her cry again.

Then she froze. She'd heard nothing from up front through the trunk until now—no radio, talking, or even a cough. But now she heard that man called Bishop talking to someone on his own phone.

"Roger, General. I'm thirty minutes out. And I've got a package you'll like."

General? General who? She couldn't hear the other person talking, so her kidnapper was using an earpiece. Was he some sort of army guy? But why would a soldier do something so horrible like this? and then...

"That's right," he said. "Morgan's wife." And he laughed but said nothing else.

Sweet Jesus! Call Dan! She started to tap out his cell number, but her mind was a swirling fog. She flubbed it, cursed, and started again. Then she stopped. *What's Dan going to do? You can't even tell him where you are, and you've only got less than half an hour now!*

Oh God...

She froze as she remembered. She switched hands, clutching the phone in her right as she snaked her left arm back over her hip and butt cheek. Her fingers scrambled into the trunk's rear shelf until they gripped something. The shotgun!

She'd completely forgotten that she'd stuffed it in there. But so what? She had no idea how to use it, except as some sort of club. Even if he opened the trunk and she swung it, he'd just shoot her or beat her to death with it.

You'd damn well better figure it out!

She twisted as much as she could onto her back and dragged out the case, inch by inch. Then she squirmed back around onto her right side until it was stuffed lengthwise, between her knees and her face. By the dim glow of her phone, she unzipped it.

There it was—long, black, gleaming, and totally incomprehensible. She fumbled for the box of shells, tore it open, and they spilled all over the trunk floor. They were green and plastic, with a shiny copper base on one end.

I don't even know which end goes in where!

She started to sob again, feeling hopeless and helpless. Then she whispered hoarsely, "Shut the hell up!" She stared at her phone. What did Alex say every time she had a question? "Google it, Mom." No matter what the question was—from archeology to zoology. "Google it, Mom."

So she did. She tapped on the multicolored "G" app icon, which she hardly ever used. Her thumbs twitched on the digital screen keys until she managed to type out "How to shoot a shotgun."

A whole bunch of videos popped up. She tapped on the first one, but then the trunk filled with sound. She clutched the phone to her chest and hissed at it, "Hush!" Her fingers pressed madly at all the side keys until the thing got quiet again.

Shit! Did he hear that? Then the car went over some kind of rut, and her head banged the ceiling again. It hurt like hell, but she ignored it. *Focus!*

She brought the phone back up to her face, nearly touching the screen to her nose, and squinted at the video that was already running. She carefully keyed the volume up just barely enough. A man in some sort of hunting garb was holding a gun like the one right there in front of her. He smiled and pointed at all its strange parts.

"The standard twelve-gauge shotgun is one of the simplest, and most effective, home defense firearms. Even a child or a housewife can use it..."

Jenny's eyes were like saucers as she watched. She swallowed hard and prayed as the car seemed to pick up even more speed—racing faster to the end of something horrific.

"Hurry up!" she commanded the phone. But unlike her, the man in the video had all the time in the world.

Oh God....

Chapter Thirty-Nine

At the naval submarine base in Groton, Connecticut, a six-ton dump truck packed with wet sand smashed right through the main gate.

It didn't matter that the rolling iron fences had been closed and locked or that the bright orange, water-loaded car-bomb barriers had been dragged into place. The gate itself, constructed of concrete, with three wide lanes and a twenty-foot-high green-tile roof, had been designed for its guards to check credentials rather than weather a full-on armored assault.

By the time it happened, the base had gone into its highest alert. But it was well after midnight, and the sailors, who moaned and rolled from their bunks, dragged their fatigues on and picked up their rifles, assuming it was just one more tiresome active-shooter drill. After all, this was Connecticut, not Kabul.

One mile northwest of the gate, where the nuclear subs rolled in the wash of the Thames River, snug in their pens like whales in repose, things were a bit different. Just off the pens to the east were the hardened bunkers of nuclear warheads and Polaris missiles, and their round-the-clock guards had received a call directly from Naval Special Warfare in Quantico.

This was no drill, they were told. Enemy action of some kind was imminent. However, the naval armorers and Marine Corps FAST leathernecks were ordered to remain in place. They were to stay on station at all costs, to stand and fight. Only a single navy lieutenant from Security Forces had scrambled his stand-by team of eight men and two women and rushed to the main gate.

From exit 86 off I-95, the ride was just over two miles. The dump truck, driven and manned by two North Koreans who, up to that minute, were sure they were doing Kim Jong Un's bidding, picked up steam again as it hit Route 12 and was soon doing a mile a minute. A hundred yards behind it, General James Collins was driving a black Chevy passenger van, which he'd switched to at a highway rendezvous rest stop.

Seven more Koreans filled the seats, but they were no longer carrying their 9mm MP5s. Now they gripped fully automatic AK-47s and wore combat vests loaded with topped-up magazines of 7.62-mm ammunition, three hundred rounds per man. Collins had ordered them to not wear their caps. He wanted everyone to see their faces, and eyes. And just behind the van trundled a single eighteen-wheeler, its roof removed and replaced with tear-away camouflage netting—its interior walls lined with blankets of Kevlar.

Inside the cargo space a massive, pneumatic, steel-gray Tomahawk launcher hulked. Only three of its four tubes were loaded, but that would do, and its firing system controls had been rewired to an MBITR radio module clipped to Collins's belt. He'd wanted the Koreans to make it work from his cell phone, but apparently there was no app for that.

When the dump truck turned left onto Crystal Lake Road, its driver had the pedal to the metal. Half a mile later, it swerved hard to the right, then left again, and was bearing straight down at the gate when the young sailors in their blue digital cammies saw it.

The lieutenant yelled, "Scatter!" and his team threw themselves to the left and right, but he stood his ground and opened up with his rifle. A couple of bullets punched high through the truck's windshield, and then he disappeared as the beast flattened the fence, exploded the water barriers in bursts of spray, and took out the central booth and its columns. A pylon shot up and split the green tile roof, which yawned open at the sky like a roaring dragon.

Collins's van came next, bouncing over the fallen gate like it was nothing more than chicken wire. The fallen lieutenant's sailors, enraged by just having seen him crushed into pulp, took knees on both flanks and opened fire. But Collins had prepared for all that and had had the Chevy up-armored at a chop shop.

Bullets scarred the heavy Plexiglas windshield and punched through the skin, but didn't get any farther. The side windows were already open, the Koreans' bristling AK barrels exploding white light from both flanks, and they mowed down the sailors as if the van were a rocketing frigate. However, as instructed, they left one alive.

Collins drove on, feeling nothing. Five million dollars was a shit ton of money. He knew from his youth that once you picked up the gun, you took your chances and, one way or another, would get paid until you eventually paid it back with your life.

He glanced in the rearview mirror. The big rig was roaring through the shattered gate, hard on his heels. He'd never been to Groton before, but he knew where to go from a DoD classified map, and he curved to the right and took a left on Tang Avenue. The dump truck had pulled off the road and stopped. Two Koreans were out there waving him down. He roared right past them.

Let 'em run.

He didn't need to get to the bunkers themselves. That would have just meant drama. The Tomahawks were already targeted to those coordinates, and a thousand feet up on the left was a big soccer field and a red clay running track—no power lines above to mess with the birds. Five more minutes, then fire and exfil. Too easy. Then they'd race south to the mouth of the Thames, where Bishop had anchored the boat they had secretly bought. Maybe he'd use him as his bodyguard in the Alps. Or maybe he'd just kill him.

Sirens were going off all over the base—blue lights spinning and flashing off buildings. They were almost at the field, and he glanced over at the Korean in the seat next to him. The kid was grinning, pumping his fist. Collins grinned too—until a high-caliber bullet punched through the windshield and exploded the kid's head.

Alex Morgan, lying flat in the open back of an MD500 "Little Bird" helicopter, worked the bolt on her Accuracy International L115A3 sniper rifle, resighted it, and fired again. But the freezing wind and rotor wash were screaming through the helo and making it buck, and she saw her second 8.59mm bullet smack through the passenger van's windshield just above the driver's head.

"Damn it, Cougar, hold it steady!" she yelled through her throat mike.

Peter Conley, who was flying the bird left-seat with no copilot, grunted back. "I'm holding this bitch as hard as I can!"

He had just swung the bird into a broadside hover, twenty feet high and two hundred feet from the front of the van. He looked down to the right, where the van was taking evasive action as it bounded over a red clay track and slewed right into a soccer field. Then he saw gun barrels thrusting from the side windows, straight up. He pulled power, banked the bird ninety degrees to the left, and then forward as a web of red tracers just missed the rotor.

"Jesus!" Alex howled as the floor tilted up and she slid backward. If she hadn't been wearing a harness clipped to a D ring on the floor, she would have zipped straight out. Behind her, standing on the skids, Tac team operators Dizzy and Rip were jerked to the ends of their safety harnesses, wide-eyed and staring at the spinning ground.

Morgan's bird, another black MD500, showed up next. It came screaming down from the north along Tang Avenue at fifteen feet and a hundred knots, with Morgan and Spartan perched on the right skid while Diesel and an antitank gunner named Pipe were on the left. All of them had switched out their M-4 rifles for Springfield Armory .308 SOCOMs, because Morgan had a hunch they'd be facing AKs. They were all wearing wind goggles and MICH helmets, but no night vision, because he knew the base would be well lit.

"Diesel," he said through his throat mike as the wind whipped his cheeks. "You and me on that van."

They both opened up from each side of the Little Bird, raking the van below stem to stern, but it just kept going as if they'd pinged it with BBs.

"Damn thing's armored," Morgan said. "Pipe, can you take it?"

"Negative," said the antitank gunner. "I ain't got a shot."

"Zipper." Morgan spoke to the pilot, a young Peter Conley protégé. "Take it hard around and set her down."

"Roger." Zipper heeled the bird over to the right, careening around the field's perimeter.

Spartan, facedown with her boots on the skid and her head hanging down, twisted around and looked past the tail boom, where the eighteen-wheeler was just thundering onto the soccer pitch. "Cobra," she said. "I got eyes on the launch vehicle."

"Shit," Diesel said. "Light her up?"

"Don't bother," Morgan said. "That's armored too. Zipper, hustle up and set her down."

"Hang on for a hard one!" Zipper grunted as he straightened it out on the far side of the field. He raced at ten feet over the whipping grass, pulled the pitch nose up, and slammed it down on the skids.

Morgan, Spartan, Diesel, and Pipe had already unclipped their carabiners. They jumped from the skids, spread out in a flying wedge, and charged straight across the field toward the van—their gun barrels spouting flame as their spent shells spun through the air.

Behind them, the helo lifted off again and disappeared while, over to the left, Conley's bird touched the grass. Dizzy and Rip jumped off and hard-charged it straight at two Koreans who were sprinting up Tang Avenue from the abandoned dump truck.

Collins slammed on the van brakes, grabbed his .45-caliber handgun, popped the door, and rolled out onto the wet grass as the eighteen-wheeler roared close by on his left, then slid to a stop fifty feet on. It was facing south, but that didn't matter. The Tomahawks had minds of their own. Bullets were punching into the van, but all the doors flew open and the North Koreans rushed into the field, firing and screaming. Collins rolled onto his stomach and crawled toward the launch truck as he fumbled for his MBITR—yanking it off his belt.

"These bastards are all kamikazes!" Morgan yelled in his mike above the gunfire. "Go flat!"

In the middle of the field, all the Zetas went prone, taking long breaths and squinting into their red dot sights as the Koreans came on. They looked wild and crazy, fully erect, marching forwards, yelling war cries and spraying their AKs at the black-clad Zetas spread out in the grass.

Spartan took one in the legs. He smashed down on his face but kept firing, and she hit him again. Diesel shot one in the throat, and that was that. Morgan dropped one center mass, but the dude got up, and he had to hit him again.

Then his bolt locked back, and just as he was switching magazines, the Korean on the far-right flank spotted him and came charging, his AK barrel spitting yellow flame, the bullets whip-cracking just over his head.

I ain't gonna make it, he thought as he slammed the fresh magazine home. And then the Korean's head snapped back, he dropped his AK, sank to his knees, and folded flat back. Morgan twisted his head around and looked up as Conley's Little Bird floated by, with a long sniper barrel poking from its cargo bay. Alex. He grinned. He couldn't help himself.

"Damn, I'm hit." It was Rip's voice in his ear, and he looked left, where the kid was rolling back and forth in the grass. The Korean who'd shot him was coming on fast to finish him off, but Spartan whipped around and shot him sideways in the head.

"Cobra!" Alex's voice startled Morgan in his ear. "You better do something. That truck's getting a hard-on!"

Morgan twisted around and looked at the truck. Something was rising from the cargo bay, a canopy of camouflage netting sliding slowly off toward the back. *Launch tubes...Shit!*

"Alex," he said. "You got eyes on Collins?"

"Negative. He might be in the van."

Morgan spun left again. But either he was out of ammo or his AK had jammed. He was coming straight for Diesel and pulling a knife from his chest rig. Diesel got up and looked at him. Morgan heard him say, "Nah, don't feel like dancing tonight." And he shot him.

"Pipe!" Morgan said over the comms. "Take that van!"

Pipe got up on his knees, pulled a LAW tube from the rig on his back, popped it open, dropped it on his shoulder and fired. A long gout of flame spat from the back and the rocket hissed across the field and blew the van into a roofless mess of flaming seats and hissing tires.

Morgan was already up, pounding across the field. His knee was screaming, and the heavy SOCOM was slowing him down, so he dropped it on the run and pulled a Browning Hi-Power from his thigh holster.

The eighteen-wheeler loomed in front of him. One last Korean burst from the left side of the cab and came running around the front. Morgan dropped him with a doubletap on the run. Then he saw Collins.

The general was hunkered down near the truck's rear bumper, his back toward Morgan, gripping an MBITR module in his left hand and punching its keys. But as Morgan came on, Collins sensed his presence. He spun around with a .45 at the end of his arm, and both men stopped at ten paces, muzzle to muzzle.

"You're getting to be a pain in my ass, Dan." Collins was breathing hard, his flushed cheeks streaked with sweat.

"Feeling's mutual, Jim. But it's over. So put it down."

"For what?" Collins scoffed. "A noose at Leavenworth?"

Morgan glanced to left and up. Conley's bird was sliding broadside into position, hovering a hundred meters out. He could see Alex's sniper barrel glinting, and the rotor wash was fluttering the grass. Then his eye caught something else. It was a red car, racing along Tang Avenue toward him. But he focused back on Collins as it crossed over the clay track and eased to a stop, facing him and Collins at twenty feet. The flames from the burning van flickered in its windshield.

The door opened, and Bishop got out. He was gripping a black .357 Desert Eagle. But he didn't point it at Morgan. He was training the barrel on the car.

"Well, lookie here." Collins grinned. "It's the flip side of fate."

"That's me," Bishop said as he walked slowly backward and aligned the handgun barrel with the trunk. "The grim stinking reaper. Now Morgan, drop the piece and send the general over to me."

"Right, asshole." Morgan snarled. "For what?"

"For your wife," Bishop said. His smile was now triumphant.

Morgan glanced down at the license plate and a wave of nausea rushed up to his throat.

"Dad, that's our car!" Alex's desperation moaned in his ear.

"Bullshit," Morgan to Bishop said. "So you jacked her car. Think I'm gonna fall for that?"

"Tell you what," Bishop said. His barrel was now angled straight down at the trunk. "I'll fire one round, and then you can decide if I'm bullshitting."

Spartan, Diesel, and Pipe had appeared around the rear of the burning van. They all had their weapons trained on Bishop.

"You slimy traitor," Spartan called out.

Bishop laughed. "That's all you got, Spartan? I'll be far away and filthy rich while you're still trying to figure out if you're a girl."

"You're bluffing," Morgan called out to Bishop. "Show her to me."

"Dad!" Alex pleaded in his ear. "I can take him!"

"*No*," Morgan snapped to Alex as his gun still pointed at Collins. "His finger might twitch."

"Fair enough," said Bishop. "But first, guns on the ground."

Morgan looked over at his team. He nodded. They reluctantly bent and put their SOCOMs on the ground. Bishop raised his chin at Morgan. "You too."

Morgan had no choice. He cursed and leaned over, letting the Hi Power fall. Bishop grinned wider and walked around to the Camry's rear bumper. With Collins still pointing his .45 at Morgan's head, and everyone else with their hands empty, he was top dog now. Alex wouldn't try for a shot with him hovering over her mother. He tipped the barrel of his Desert Eagle up and thumbed the trunk button on the key fob.

It opened, and the last thing he saw was gaping maw of a twelve-gauge shotgun. It exploded two feet from his face. He snapped back and went airborne in a spray of lead pellets and gore.

Morgan ducked as Collins fired the .45. The round singed his hair, but he dove under the gun and hit Collins with everything he had. The general went down on his back. Morgan gripped the barrel and wrenched it out of his hand, but it slipped from his fingers and went spinning off as Collins snapped his shin up and connected with Morgan's groin.

Morgan grunted hard and collapsed as Collins scrambled out from under him, clutched the MBITR, and started sprinting away, across the clay track. Morgan struggled up and chased after him. To his right, he heard the launch tubes lock, and their nose doors clang open.

Collins was running, gripping the MBITR module in his left hand, punching his right fingers at the keys. And then, out of nowhere, headlights blazed from the left, and a beat-up blue Saturn sedan came roaring off of Tang Avenue and hit him dead-on.

Collins's arms flew up as the bumper cracked him in half. Then his broken body went under, and Morgan saw the MBITR spinning up into the air. He jinked to the right, then left, then stretched out his palms, and caught it.

The Saturn had stopped. Morgan stood there, gasping for breath, clutching the module and staring at the car. One of Collin's bloody legs was sticking out from under a rear wheel. The driver's door opened, and Commander Alicia Schmitt got out.

She glanced under the car, then leaned on the roof with her green arm cast, and looked at Morgan. "Better late than never."

Chapter Forty

Morgan held Jenny for a long time. She couldn't stop shaking.

There were ambulances and navy security trucks all over the field—lights flashing everywhere and shouting people moving quickly.

He stroked her matted hair and glanced around. Sailors were zipping up body bags, and the two Little Birds had settled at the far end of the field. He saw Alex sprinting toward them with her rifle slung over her back. He caressed Jenny's head, moved her wet face from the crook of his neck and looked at her.

"Where'd you get the shotgun?" He smiled.

"From your stash," she sobbed.

"Finders keepers," he said. "It's yours."

Then he held her face and kissed her. Her lips were swollen and salty.

"You'll just have to forget what you saw," he said, knowing that the vision of blowing Bishop away would be in her mind forever.

"I didn't see anything," she confessed. "I had my eyes closed."

Morgan laughed. Alex smashed into them both and hugged them so hard he thought she might crack their ribs.

"Mom!" She murmured. "What the hell?"

Jenny both laughed and cried. "Guess you're a chip off both blocks, huh?"

Bloch's voice popped in Morgan's ear. "Morgan, you copy? I need you here for a back-brief. Kudos come later."

Morgan ignored her and looked at Jenny. "Where's Neika?"

"At home. Probably eating your slippers."

"Let's go get her."

"Morgan?" Bloch snapped. "Do you copy?"

"Five by five, Diana," Morgan finally answered. "But that briefing's gonna have to wait."

"What? Why? Where the hell do you think you're going?"

"Disneyworld." He lied.

He put his arms around Jenny's and Alex's shoulders, and they walked off together toward the family car.

Dark Territory

Don't miss the next exciting thriller starring Zeta operative Dan Morgan

Coming soon from Lyrical Underground,
an imprint of Kensington Publishing Corp.

Keep reading to enjoy an excerpt . . .

Chapter One

Alex Morgan was lying face down on a hillock of freezing Russian snow.

She had been there for more than two hours, barely moving, and now her body was starting to rebel. It didn't matter that she was stuffed in a cocoon of polypropylene thermals, Icelandic socks, Sorel mountain boots, a bone-white Gore-Tex suit and a polar bear Inuit hat. The temperature had dropped to minus three degrees Celsius. She felt like one of those wooden sticks wrapped in an ice cream bar.

Suck it up, Morgan, she told herself as she tried to stop her teeth from chattering. *Just make the shot.*

To her left and right were lines of enormous pines, the edge of the forest from which she'd crawled. Their branches speared upwards into an inky sky, needles barely fluttering in the windless night. Below her, out front, the hillock dropped off into waves of avalanche snow before smoothing out at the bottom across a vast plain of unmarred white—maybe three kilometers across and surrounded by more pine-crested hills. A couple of trees in the snow bowl were bent under coats of gleaming ice.

It looked like a scene from *Dr. Zhivago*, an old movie her father, Dan Morgan, liked—except she wasn't watching it next to dad on a couch. She was in it, up to her neck.

The first sound that reached her frozen ears was a thin, distant squeal, like someone turning a rusty pump handle. Then came the rumble of a piston engine. She squinted as a track-equipped Snowcat vehicle emerged from between two faraway hills on the right and started inching to the center of the snow bowl. Then, from the left, a Russian Zil military truck appeared, crawling cautiously forward as well.

Game on, Alex thought as she reached to her left with one Gore-Tex glove and carefully slipped the white tarp from her rifle. She glanced up at the sky, where a frothy filigree of clouds was splitting at the center—revealing a huge, glowing perfect orb. Her teeth stopped chattering, and she smiled.

Alex loved a sniper's moon.

A day earlier, she'd arrived in Vladivostok aboard a Zim Lines tramp steamer—a 650-foot container vessel that had six berths for adventurous passengers. Zeta Division analysts knew that Russian border controls at the ports were tight, so she'd come off the boat with nothing but her US passport, visa, winter clothes, and a backpack containing her photographic gear. No weapons but a ceramic, undetectable Benchmade boot knife.

From there she'd found her way to a prearranged safe house, where she picked up her sniper-hide clothing, rifle, ammunition, and range finder. Then she'd moved to a second garage location, scooped up her motorcycle, and headed north for Rozdolnoe—a nothing little town on the road to Ussuriysk.

She'd had Lincoln Shepard talking in her ear comm—using GPS back in Boston and satellite overheads—to get her off the main road at Rozdolnoe, twenty klicks west, and then here to this snow-cone hill. She'd hauled all her gear, plus a pair of short skis, up through the forest as the night fell, hard and cold. Then she'd said good-bye to Linc, pulled the comm out, and stripped the battery. Her dad had taught her that. If Linc sneezed at the wrong time, he could screw up her shot, and she wasn't going to get a second chance.

The Snowcat and the Zil were approaching each other toward the middle of the snow bowl. Alex rolled to her right, popped the top of her snow suit open and pulled a Sig Sauer KILO rangefinder monocular from the relative warmth of her chest. She rolled back onto her stomach, pushed her snow goggles up on her white fur hat, and peered through the scope.

The Russian Zil's windows were all frosted up. She couldn't tell how many men were in the cab, but that didn't matter. It was an old Soviet vehicle, which she knew was manned by rebel Ukrainians. In the back, under the canvas cover, was Satan's pitchfork, a high-yield tactical nuke lifted from Ukrainian military inventory.

The Snowcat's windows were heated and clear, and she could plainly see four figures inside. One of them was Colonel Shin Kwan Hyo of the Democratic People's Republic of Korea. Pyongyang had just tested its latest long-range ballistic missile, the Unha-3. It couldn't carry a heavy payload, such as the bulky North Korean atomic warheads, but it had a range of ten thousand kilometers. Pop a compact tactical nuke in the nose cone, and the DPRK could take out Los Angeles. Alex thought the Hollywood whackos could use some pruning, but not this way.

In a couple of minutes those two vehicles were going to meet, and the world's power balance would irrevocably change for the worse.

She figured Colonel Hyo would be easy to spot. He'd be the one carrying a briefcase, or satchel, of cold, hard cash. Plus, she had a very clear image of his face in her mind. Lily Randall had described exactly what he looked like—thick arching eyebrows, black eyes, a flat nose, and a white scar to the left of his thin lips. It was the face that had sneered down at Lily for hours while Hyo tortured the hell out of her in China. Lily was Alex's friend—a very close friend. Alex only wished she could send Hyo a good-bye note along with her bullet.

The vehicles slowed to a stop, facing each other at twenty meters—engines idling, exhausts blowing steam in the air. Their occupants started to get out, forming a small cluster in the glow of the headlights. Alex pressed the range finder trigger—730 meters, or 2,395 feet, with a downward angle of five degrees. It would be a long shot, just at the end of her rifle's effective range. Could she do it? Damn straight she could, but now she had to move fast.

She slithered to her left through the snow and got behind her Accuracy International Arctic Warfare. It was a beautiful weapon in lime green furniture, with a free-floating stainless steel barrel, and a Schmidt & Bender 6x24 PMII variable magnification scope. And hers was the special-ops version, with a folding stock and suppressor. She pulled the glove covers off her fingers, adjusted the bipod, popped up the scope covers, and nestled the beast to her cheek. It felt like being kissed by an ice cube.

Alex didn't need a range card. She'd memorized every possible variable, which was sort of amusing since she'd been so lousy at math in college. Maybe it was a matter of motivation. She started running calculations in her head as she peered through the scope, worked the bolt quietly, and seated a round in the breech. Linc had told her the rifle would already be zeroed; he'd better be right. And she'd warned him to tell the armorers not to clean the barrel afterward—a pristine barrel could give you an off-the-mark, cold bore shot.

Okay, M118 Special Ball ammo, 7. 62×51mm, range at 730 meters...That'll mean a bullet drop of minus seventy-nine inches. Zero wind, so no lateral adjustment. Got to compensate for the suppressor, which slightly increases muzzle velocity, so kick the bullet drop back up to seventy-eight inches.

She reached for the scope's elevation knob and turned it, counting off minute-of-angle clicks, which tilted the front of the scope downward. This meant that when she set the crosshairs on Hyo's face, her barrel would actually be tilted up, shooting at a spot six-and-a-half feet above his head.

Gravity would pull the bullet down precisely that much and, hopefully, ruin his life.

She pulled the scarf up over her nose so her lung steam wouldn't fog up the scope and pressed her eye socket to the rubber ring. Her heart rate picked up, thumping through her suit against the hard pack snow. The shapes of five men filled her reticle, huddled close and talking. The two on the left were Ukrainians, easy to spot by their leopard camouflage, fur hats, and AK-47s. On the right were two North Koreans in full-body, black, ski suits—also slinging weapons—but she couldn't tell what kind. In the middle, facing her, was a broad-shouldered man wearing a long winter coat—collar turned up— and a fur hat with the ear flaps snapped skyward. Next to his right boot a dark briefcase sat in the snow. But was that Hyo?

Then he lifted a gloved hand to his lips, one of the Ukrainians extended a fist, and a cigarette lighter flamed up. His face glowed yellow as he dragged on the cigarette, blew out the smoke, and smiled. Nice white scar, right next to his snarling lips.

Wait! She suddenly remembered she'd have to compensate for the five-degree downward angle. *Okay, Colonel John Plaster's drop table...I'll have to hold low...Five degrees means multiply seventy-eight drop inches by point zero zero four...uhh...hold low on the target by a third of an inch. Aim for the throat.*

Her hands were trembling. By pure force of will, she sent what was left of her body heat into her fingers, balled them into tight fists, and slowly released. Better. She turned the scope's magnification ring and filled the reticle with Hyo's ugly face, sitting it right above the vertical crosshair post. She slipped her right thumb into the rifle's thumb hole, curled her fingers around the icy grip, and barely touched the trigger—easing it past the first stage until she felt the secondary pressure.

Hyo was laughing at something, his black eyes open to the sky as his lung steam poured from his mouth. *Laugh it up, mofo,* Alex thought as she inhaled a breath, released it halfway, and held it. Her entire body stilled except for one thing: her trigger finger.

She heard her dad's voice in her head: *"Don't squeeze the trigger with your finger. Squeeze it with your mind. And always let the shot surprise you."* Squeeeeze...

The crosshairs jumped as the bullet left the barrel and the butt pad bucked her shoulder. Because of the suppressor, the only sound the rifle made was like a closed-mouth sneeze, and there was barely a flash. Alex stared through the scope. A second went by, then two. Hyo pulled the cigarette from his mouth. Then his head exploded.

Alex didn't wait. She knew the rest of those men were in shock, slimed with Hyo's blood and brain matter, and scrambling to bury themselves in the snow or to haul ass back into their vehicles. She shifted her shoulders to the right, cranking the barrel left, and took a bead on the Zil's cargo bed as she worked the bolt. She fired again. While that round was still in the air, she put one more down range. If she was lucky, a round might hit the nuke warhead. It wouldn't go off, but it would make it useless.

She quickly shifted left, swinging the barrel to the right toward the Snowcat. Now she could hear thin, panicky shouts echoing from the surrounding hills, and the Snowcat was roaring backward. She laid her crosshairs two feet behind the moving cab, squeezed off another shot, and then raised her head up, both eyes open. The Snowcat's side window shattered, and it sluiced across the snow like a drunken ice skater.

Enough. Time to get the hell out of Dodge.

She snapped her scope covers down, her bipod up, jammed her range finder into her Gore-Tex suit, and slithered backward into the tree line—leaving a gouge in the snow like a sea turtle's tail. She rolled over, sat up, swung the rifle behind her, shoved her arms in the double slings, and staggered upright. She was breathing hard now, almost panting with the adrenaline surge, and then she heard the first gunshots. They sounded wild, un-aimed; which made sense since her suppressor had masked her location. Then a short AK-47 burst sliced off some branches just above her head.

Okay...wrong!

She took off, tramping downhill through the maze of black pine trunks. The forest was about a hundred feet deep, but then it ended at the head of a five-hundred-foot slope—the snow gleaming in the moonlight, marred only by her own footprints from her climb uphill. Her short skis were right where she'd left them, sticking up like a pair of rabbit ears. She yanked them out, slipped her boots into the old-fashioned cable bindings, pushed off hard, and squatted low as she heard more gunshots whip-cracking through the trees above and behind her.

She made a dead-straight run down the hill, no turns, picking up so much speed she wasn't sure she'd be able to stop. Then she spotted the low mound of hand-shoveled snow with her signal twig jutting up. She sat hard on her left buttock and skidded in, showering a plume of snow.

She kicked off her skis, got up, and hurled them away as far as she could. Then she shoved her gloves in the snow mound up to her elbows and grunted hard as she hauled herself backward. Up popped a Ural 750cc Russian motorcycle—the Sahara model, sand tan with a black engine. She'd already named it.

"Come on, Natasha," Alex whispered as she jumped on, cranked the ignition, and stamped on the starter. "Growl for me, baby!"

The engine did as she asked, and Alex hunkered low, twisted the throttle, fishtailed onto the icy road, and sped off like a demon back toward Rozdolnoe.

* * * *

By the time she got close to the bridge over the western vein of the Rasdolnaya River, she had her ear comm fired back up, and Linc was talking to her.

"You should see it coming up in about one klick," he said. "Looks like an old British Bailey bridge."

"I see it," said Alex as she took a swipe at her snow goggles. "You picking up any radio chatter, Linc?"

"Negative. I don't think the Yukes and the NKs will be complaining to the Russians. Did you pass any traffic?"

"One truck," Alex said as she slowed the bike on the bridge. The heavy steel structure was perched about fifty feet above the river, its roaring black water peppered with swirling ice floes. "If the driver saw my rifle, he probably thought I was out for some biathlon practice."

Linc laughed. "Diana's very pleased, by the way."

"Good."

Linc hesitated, but he just had to ask. "What'd you feel when you hit him?"

"Recoil," Alex said. She got off the bike, looked around, and stamped the kickstand down. "I hate this part, Linc," she complained.

"Just do it," he said. "It's only a tool. We'll buy you a new one."

"Yeah, but not *this* one."

She unslung her rifle, sighed, kissed it, and leaned through the girders. Then she let it go and watched it slowly spinning down through the darkness. She waited until it made a tiny splash and disappeared. Then she pulled out her range finder and got rid of that too.

"Done," she said.

"Outstanding," Linc said. "Get crankin'."

An hour later, she pulled into the outskirts of Ussuriysk. She was exhausted, shivering, and hungry. Her last two PowerBars hadn't done much, and she'd finished all the water in her pocket flask. Thankfully, Linc was with her, so she didn't have to navigate or think much. He guided her along the snow-shouldered streets of the small Russian town, past one pretty church with gleaming red onion-spire caps, and then into the mouth of a dark, slimy alleyway that had frozen bedsheets crackling from clotheslines strung across the apartments above. Two blocks down at the end of the alley, she could see the back of a tavern that must have been a hundred years old.

Alex stopped the bike, dismounted, and sighed. "Guess it's time to dump Natasha too."

"Don't worry about her," Linc said. "She'll get recycled."

"Is that a pun?"

"Sort of."

She stripped out of her sniper cocoon, fur cap, and goggles, leaving her dressed in a blue-black Mountain Hardwear jacket, jeans, and boots. She found a garbage can that reeked of rotten fish and stuffed everything deep inside, including her sniper gloves—they'd be covered with gunfire residue. The she pulled a back pack from the Ural's saddlebag, rummaged past her photography gear, slipped into a pair of girlie-pink woolen gloves and matching ski cap, whispered "Thanks" to Natasha, and walked.

"How's my train timing?" she asked Linc as she clipped along the alleyway.

"Perfect. It's just pulling in from Vladivostok. But those things can sit in the station for two hours or be gone in five minutes. Better hustle."

Alex walked faster as the rear service door of the tavern loomed. She yanked it open and strode right through the steam-fogged kitchen, where a couple of Mongolian cooks stared at her. Then she pushed through the doors and into the tavern. It was long and dark, filled with roughhewn tables and benches, with a heavy wooden bar on the right. The place was packed with nothing but men, and in one corner, a balalaika musician strummed Russian folk songs. His half-in-the-bag audience sang along while their beers slopped over their tankards.

Alex walked up to the bar, where a huge man with a Santa Claus beard was just bringing a large shot of vodka to his lips. She snatched it out of his hand, threw her head back, and swigged the entire thing down. Then she grabbed his beard, kissed him wetly on his merry red cheek, and said, "*Spaseebah*!"

"*Pajalstah*!" The big man laughed. His belly jiggled as Alex marched right past his approving comrades and out the front door.

The train station was nothing—just one small stop on the Trans-Siberian's 9,289-kilometer trip from Vladivostok to Moscow. There was only one small ticket building, closed for the night, but she already had her ticket. Her dad had told her long ago that you never went near an airport after a hit. Trains were much easier, and the conductors could be bought if you had to.

The Trans-Siberian was just pulling in to the platform. The locomotive was a hulking steel box with a blazing light up top, two glass windshields for eyes, three red stripes across its face, and a big red Soviet star for a nose. The follow-on cars were long and silver and lined with curtained windows. The first passenger car stopped in front of her, and its door slid open. Nobody got off, and there were no other passengers on the platform. A conductor leaned out, wearing a long green woolen coat and a fur hat. He looked like a Stalin relic.

"Passport," he said in heavily accented English.

Alex smiled her college girl smile and handed it up, along with her ticket. He looked at them both, glanced at her backpack, and handed them back.

"Where you come from, young woman?" he asked.

"Vladivostok."

"Um-hmm. And your profession?"

"I'm a funeral photographer."

His thick eyebrows furrowed. "What is that?"

"It's like a wedding photographer, except the groom doesn't move."

He cocked his head and smiled. "Welcome to Russia."

She got on.

More from Leo J. Maloney

Don't miss these thrilling novels from Leo J. Maloney!

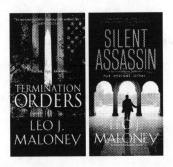

Acknowledgments

I must thank my immensely talented team at Kensington Publishing Corp., who work tirelessly to help make my novels the best they can be and are there whenever I have questions or concerns. Thank you to Steve Zacharius, owner of Kensington Publishing Corp., who has made me part of the Kensington "family." There are just not enough words to convey how fortunate I am to have Michaela Hamilton as my editor. Her patience and guidance have been invaluable—she is a very special person.

I want to express my appreciation to my literary agent, Doug Grad, as well as to Mayur Gudka, my webmaster and social media consultant. I also want to thank my partners in writing and creating my novels, Caio Camargo, Steven Hartov, and Richard Meyers. I am so fortunate that you are members of my creative team.

Last, I want to thank all of my very loyal fans whose support has helped grow the Dan Morgan series from one novel to seven and still writing...

Meet the Author

Leo J. Maloney is the author of the acclaimed Dan Morgan thriller series, which includes *Termination Orders, Silent Assassin, Black Skies, Twelve Hours, Arch Enemy*, and *For Duty and Honor*. He was born in Massachusetts, where he spent his childhood, and graduated from Northeastern University. He spent over thirty years in black ops, accepting highly secretive missions that would put him in the most dangerous hot spots in the world. Since leaving that career, he has had the opportunity to try his hand at acting in independent films and television commercials. He has seven movies to his credit, both as an actor and behind the camera as a producer, technical advisor, and assistant director. He lives in the Boston area and in Sarasota, Florida.

Visit him at www.leojmaloney.com or on Facebook or Twitter.

Photo by Kippy Goldfarb, Carolle Photography

Printed in the United States
by Baker & Taylor Publisher Services